Croissants for Breakfast

~

~

All characters in this book are fictional,
and Coulaize is a fictional village.

BOOKS BY THE SAME AUTHOR

Escargot Days - novel
Thorny Acres - novel
They Called Her Miranda - novel
On Wet Foundations - humorous memoir
Barging On - sequel

CHAPTER ONE

'So you see,' said Miss Pinkerton, peering at Mike over the top of her glasses. 'You will need to contact the other lawyer who is dealing with this matter.'

'Er, yes, I see.' Mike nodded. Not that he knew why he was nodding when he didn't see at all. In fact, he hadn't got a clue why this woman was telling him all this stuff that didn't seem to have anything to do with him.

When he'd received a letter from a Miss Pinkerton of Lawson and Thomas, all the letter had told him was that she wanted him to make an appointment to see her regarding the estate of the late Monique Lanteine. Who the devil Monique Lanteine was he had no idea, but, as you do when you get a letter like that from a solicitor, he'd phoned and made the requested appointment.

And he was trying to concentrate, really he was, but he kept being distracted by Miss Pinkerton's long string of pearls. Well, it wasn't the pearls as such that were a problem. They looked like your bog-standard pearls, and if they'd hung down the front of her chest in a normal manner, he probably wouldn't have even noticed them. As it was, he was struggling to control the urge to reach across and unhook them from her left boob.

'I'll leave you to do that, Mr Flint.'

'Sorry?' Mike swung his eyes from Miss Pinkerton's pearls and tried to focus on her face.

'I'll leave you to contact Miss Lanteine's lawyer.'

'Yes. Right.'

Removing her half glasses from the end of her nose, Miss Pinkerton said, 'You look somewhat bemused, Mr Flint. Have I not made everything clear to you?'

'Not exactly,' said Mike. 'To be honest, I'm finding this all a bit sort of difficult.'

'I see.' A sniff accompanied the replacement of her glasses. 'Which part do you find difficult to comprehend?'

'I think – well, most of it really.'

'Right, Mr Flint. Shall we perhaps run through it again?'

'Yes please,' said Mike. 'I'll pay attention this time, promise.'

Was that a slight twitch of a smile he saw? No, probably not, but as if she were talking to a child, Miss Pinkerton spoke slowly and began to repeat what she'd already told him.

'Okay, right.' Mike held up a hand. 'Sorry about that, but I think I did hear you first time. It's just that I did wonder if you'd got the right Michael Flint.'

'I can assure you, Mr Flint, that we are not in the habit of mistaking identity.' She collected a sheaf of papers together and put them in a yellow cardboard folder. 'As long as you are now fully conversant with the situation?'

'Well, sort of,' he said. 'Except...I mean...who exactly is this Monique Lanteine?'

'As I believe I've already told you, Mr Flint, all I know is that she was the sister of the late Mrs Flint.'

'Okay, yes...' Mike ran a hand over his head, trying to form the question that was bothering him. 'And you think that late Mrs Flint was my mother, Delphine Flint?'

'So I've been informed, Mr Flint. You'll find the details in here.' She patted the folder. 'Now, if you could just sign and date this receipt.'

'Right, I think I can do that.' He scrawled his signature then said, 'Um...what exactly is the date today?'

'The sixteenth of March,' she said. 'I assume you know the year is 2006?'

'Thanks, Miss Pinkerton, I probably did know that. There you go, one signed and dated receipt.'

Sliding the folder across the desk, she said, 'Peruse this at your leisure, and don't hesitate to call if there's anything still not clear.'

What was clear to Mike when he left clutching a yellow cardboard folder was that Miss Pinkerton was under the impression he was short of the requisite number of brain cells. Meanwhile, he was anxious to get home and try to explain it all to Annie.

Yes, well, that was easier said than done. As usual, Annie was engrossed in work, and if her lack of reaction was anything to go by, she wasn't grasping what was being said either. On the other hand, was she even hearing what he was saying?

'Would you believe she was wearing jodhpurs?' he said to

2

Annie's bowed head. 'Fluorescent pink ones, with silver sequins on the side.'

'Hmmm?'

'Yep, I knew you wouldn't believe it,' said Mike, sitting on the edge of the kitchen table.

'What?' Without looking up, Annie pulled an exercise book from beneath his left buttock. 'What wouldn't I believe?'

'Ah. At least you heard that bit, then. Catch anything else, did you?'

'Mike, what are you on about?'

'Oh, nothing much.' He shrugged. 'Just that the solicitor was wearing pink jodhpurs.'

'Solicitor? What solicitor?'

'The one who I got that letter from yesterday. Remember?'

'Oh, right.' Annie glanced up at him. 'What did she want to see you about?'

'Annie, have you heard anything I've been saying?'

'Um...sorry, I...'

'You weren't listening.'

'Sorry, love.' She closed the book she'd been marking and leaned back in her chair. 'Did you say something about jodhpurs?'

'Ah, I lied about that bit.' He grinned. 'Got your attention, though, didn't it?

'Okay, okay.' She held up her hands. 'You've got my attention, so shoot.'

'Well, it's like this, see...'

Ten minutes later, Annie was shaking her head and saying, 'I don't get it.'

'What's not to get?' said Mike. 'My aunt has left me her house. It's all quite straight forward, according to the Pinkerton woman.'

'Well, I wouldn't say it's that straight forward,' she said. 'I mean, what the hell are we supposed to do with a flipping house you're not allowed to sell?'

'It's just for five years I can't sell it,' he reminded her. 'That was the only stipulation in the will.'

'But you could rent it out, couldn't you?'

'Well, maybe.' He pulled his earlobe. 'Might be a bit difficult, though. On account of where it is.'

'Come on, Mike. It shouldn't be hard to rent out a house in Leeds.'

'True.' He nodded. 'Except it's not in Leeds.'

'But that's where your aunt lived.'

'That's not the one who died.'

'Yes she did, Mike. I distinctly remember going to her funeral.'

'Well, yes, that one did die. But not this time.'

'Okay,' said Annie. 'Do you want to tell me about the aunt who did die this time?'

'I would if I could, Annie. But this is the first I've heard of her.' Shaking his head, Mike stood up and asked if there was any wine left in the bottle they'd opened the night before.

'Probably still in the lounge,' said Annie, going to the sink. She took two wine glasses off the draining board, rinsed the residue of red wine from the bottom and put them on the table. 'So,' she said, resisting the urge to moan at him for not washing up when Mike came back with the half empty bottle. 'Exactly who is this woman who's given you a house?'

'That's just what I said to that solicitor woman.'

'And?'

'Well, after she'd adjusted her jodhpurs…'

'Mike!'

'Okay already.' He rubbed his thumped arm. 'The thing is, Annie, I never knew my mum had a sister. So it's all come as a bit of a shock you could say.'

'Your mum? You mean she had a sister who was your aunt?'

'Well she would be, wouldn't she? That's sort of how it works, isn't it?'

'Yes, all right. I know that, idiot,' said Annie. 'But what I don't get is how come you didn't know about her. And it's not like the name rings a bell, is it?'

'It doesn't, no.' He poured wine into both glasses before saying, 'But it does make sense that, being French, Mum could easily have had a sister living in France.'

'Yes, but if this sister was living in…hang on a minute.' Annie grabbed his arm. 'You're not telling me you've inherited a house in France!'

'That's what I said, Annie.'

'When? When did you say that?'

4

'When I got back from the solicitors and tried to talk to you. But then, you weren't listening at the time.'

'Oh come on, Mike, I was busy.'

'Annie, you're always busy as soon as you get home from school.'

'Yes,' she said. 'And you know why. You know I like to get the marking done straight off so we can settle down to eat by seven.'

'Yeah, well, there's something I'd like you to know. Actually, two things.'

'Which are?'

'I hate it when you shut off from me as soon as you get home.'

'And?'

'And I forgot to put the casserole in the oven before I went out.'

Reaching for the vinegar bottle, Mike said, 'We should do this more often.'

'Mhmm,' Annie mumbled through a mouthful of battered cod. 'Sho whach…shorry.' She swallowed and tried again. 'So what are we going to do about your Tante Monique's house, then?'

'Good question. Are you going to leave those two chips?'

'Gerroff.' She slapped his hand away from her plate. 'Are you going to leave that wine in your glass?'

'Swapsie?'

'Okay.' She pushed her plate across and grabbed Mike's glass. 'Done deal.'

'We could go at Easter,' he said.

'What, to France you mean?'

'No, I was thinking Butlins at Skegness.'

'Very ho ho. Whereabouts is this flipping house anyway?'

'Dunno.' He shrugged. 'Somewhere between Brittany and Bordeaux.'

'Uh huh. That sort of covers most of France. Any chance you could narrow it down a bit?'

'Probably, if I could remember where I put that yellow folder thing the solicitor gave me.'

After they'd searched the kitchen, lounge and hall, and Mike had again tipped out the contents of Annie's briefcase – just in case he'd missed a yellow folder the first two times – things were becoming what you might call fraught.

He was searching the fridge when Annie suggested there was only one logical thing to do.

'Nope,' he said. 'I've already looked in the washing machine.'

'Mike, I did say logical. You need to go outside, come in through the front door and retrace your steps and movements.'

'How the hell is that going to…'

'Mike! Just do it!'

'Right, I'll do that then.' And he obediently went outside, came back in, walked into the kitchen and asked if Annie wanted a cup of tea.

'What?' she said. 'You really think this is a good time to stop and drink tea?'

'Well no, not really. It's just that you said I had to retrace all my movements, and what I did when I got home was put the kettle on.'

'Mike – for heaven's sake!'

'This isn't working, is it?' he said. 'And I wish you'd stop pulling at your hair like that, I don't think I'll fancy you bald.'

'Think, man, think. What did you do after you left the solicitor's office?'

'Now let me think about that.' He clasped his forehead. 'Ah yes, I walked to the car park, got in the car, started the engine and drove home. What else would I have done?'

'What I think you may have done is drop the bloody folder in the car park.'

'Well, I suppose…' He paused to smooth down Annie's hair. 'Do you reckon I should…'

'Yes. I think you should drive back to the car park and look around. Just in case.'

'Yeah, right, in case it just happens to be still there several hours later?'

'And your better idea is?'

'Okay, okay, I'm going. Put the kettle on for when I get back, will you?'

'Mike, just go and get in that bloody car.'

Less than a minute later he walked back into the kitchen and said, 'Yep, that did it.'

'Huh? You haven't been gone long enough too…'

'Tarrah!' He waved a yellow cardboard folder. 'You see, Annie. If only you'd told me to get back in the car and retrace my movements from there.'

But obviously she wasn't listening again. He could tell that because, having grabbed the folder, she'd taken it into the lounge, emptied it onto the coffee table and was asking where the devil Coulaize was.

'In France?' he suggested.

'Yes, but where in France? Ah, it says here it's in Burgundy.'

'That'll be where it is then,' he said. 'Do you know where Burgundy is exactly?'

'Not sure.' She shook her head. 'Somewhere around the middle bit below Paris, I think. We could try Google Earth.'

'Tell you what,' said Mike, clicking on the computer. 'Let's try Google Earth.'

'Flipping heck,' said Annie, staring at the laptop screen. 'It's in the middle of nowhere!'

'Looks like a nice sort of nowhere.' Mike clicked on the map to enlarge the satellite view.

'Yeah, great, if you happen to be big on hills and trees.'

'What, all of a sudden you don't like trees?'

'Of course I like trees, Mike. In parks and places.'

'How do you feel about lakes?' he said, scrolling with the hand icon.

'Lakes are fine. How do you feel about decent-sized roads leading to decent-sized towns?'

'Well that looks like a sensible road.' He pointed at the screen after scrolling back to Coulaize.

'Um, Mike, I think that's a canal.'

'Wow, Annie. There's a canal going right through the village.'

'Oh brilliant,' she said with a snort. 'If we did consider renting out the house, we could probably do so with the added attraction of tenants being able to row to the nearest town to go shopping.'

'We're not doing positive here, are we?' said Mike.

'If by that you mean I'm not being particularly enthusiastic, let me ask you something. What the hell is there to be positive about when we've got a house we can't sell? It seems unlikely we'd be able to rent it out and – No, let me finish…' She flapped a hand in front of his face. 'What we've got here is a liability that's going to cost money we can't afford to fork out.'

'What money?'

'Oh, just odd things like French inheritance tax, insurance and probably some sort of community tax just for owning a property whether it's occupied or not.'

'Is that how it works in France?'

'I don't know, do I?' she said. 'I've never needed to look into it, but I reckon you should do some internet searches tomorrow and find out.'

'I reckon we should do it now. This could be bad news, Annie.'

'Mike, my bad news is that I've still got four more essays to mark before the morning.' Stifling a yawn, she said, 'I'll do it in the kitchen, away from that damn telly next-door. Then I'm off to bed.'

Getting on for a couple of hours later, Mike climbed into bed, shook Annie's shoulder and said, 'You're not asleep, are you?' Not satisfied with her "Herumph" as she burrowed deeper beneath the duvet, he shook her harder and told her they had to talk.

'Talk away,' she mumbled. 'I'll just sleep while you do it.'

'Aw, come on, Annie Pannie.' He wrapped his arm round her and whispered in her ear, 'I've brought you a cup of tea.'

She peered at him through one open eye and said, 'That serious, eh?'

'Deadly serious.'

'Too deadly serious to wait till morning?'

'Absolutely. The tea will be cold by morning.'

Sighing heavily, she struggled into a sitting position and asked what he'd found out about French taxes and stuff on the Net.

'Not a lot,' he said. 'Didn't get as far as doing that bit, I thought I'd look through that yellow folder to see what info I could find in there.'

'And?'

'That's what I want to tell you about.'

Looking at the bedside clock, she said, 'Shit, Mike – this had better be good.'

'Sorry, babe.' He pulled her to him so she was snuggled against his chest, kissed the top of her head and said, 'It's just that it's all got a bit heavy, and there's something I need to share with you.'

CHAPTER TWO

'What I can't understand,' said Annie, 'is why your mother never told you.'

'What I can't understand,' said Mike, 'is why you're sitting there in your dressing gown at...' Glancing at the kitchen clock, he said, 'Good grief, woman, don't you know it's after eight?'

'So?' She shrugged, picked up her coffee mug from the kitchen table and wrapped both hands round it. 'Surely you don't think I'm going to calmly swan off to work and leave you with this?'

'Yes, but...' He reached across the table and squeezed her hand.

'Bugger!' She looked at coffee dripping off the table onto her lap. 'Mike, in case you hadn't noticed, I was using that hand.'

'Sorry,' he said, getting up to grab a cloth. 'No worries, there's still some coffee in the pot.'

'Cold coffee,' she muttered. 'I made it when you were in the shower, which is why I'm not leaping around with scalded legs.'

'Oh well, you weren't really enjoying it then.'

'Only slightly more than I enjoyed being doused in the stuff. Anyway, what were you saying?'

'Saying?'

'Yes. I think you got as far as saying "but".'

'Did I?' He scratched his head. 'What was I butting about?'

She stared at him blankly, shook her head and said, 'I've got no idea.'

'Sleep deprivation,' he said.

'No, we weren't talking about that.'

'What I mean is...' He sat back at the still dripping table. 'We *were* awake most of the night, so I think we must be suffering from sleep deprivation.'

'Oh. A bit like jet lag, you mean?'

'Exactly like jet lag.'

'How would you know?' she said. 'I mean, it's not like you've ever had jet lag, is it?'

'I did fly to Amsterdam and back in one day, didn't I?'

'Yeah, like that would mean you know all about jet lag.'

'Okay, but that client of mine from Australia did tell me – Annie, why are we talking about jet lag?'

'Because we seem to have lost the plot.'

'That's it!' He snapped his fingers. 'You were plotting not going to work.'

'So I was. Mike, would you like…'

'Yes, I'd like you to stay with me this morning.' Reaching across, he asked if it was safe to hold her hand.

'Sure,' she said, taking his outstretched hand and squeezing it. 'But you'll have to give it back so I can phone Hilary and let her know I won't be in.'

'What will you tell her? You've got swamp fever?'

'Like she'll believe that? Nah, I'll just say I've caught a serious dose of jet lag.'

'All okay?' asked Mike when Annie came back from using the hall phone. 'What did you tell Hilary?'

'The truth. Oh good, you've made fresh coffee.'

'What truth?'

'That I've been up most of the night dealing with a family crisis.'

'And she just accepted that?'

'Why wouldn't she? Families do have crises. Hilary knows that, and being discretion personified, she didn't ask for details.'

'Just as well,' said Mike. 'I mean, this isn't exactly what you'd call a family crisis, is it?'

'You what!' Annie stared at him. 'I'd say what you've just discovered at thirty-five-years-old is a bit of a hard thing to take on board.'

'For me, yes…'

'And for me, Mike. I can only imagine how you must feel.'

'You know what, Annie? I don't really know how I feel. Well, except frustrated, that is. How long is it now before I can phone my dad?'

'Um…' Annie looked at the kitchen clock. 'It's after nine here, and I think Chicago is something like six, maybe seven hours behind.'

'Well sod it,' said Mike, getting to his feet. 'As far as I'm concerned, we're talking a lot of *years* behind. As in thirty-five years behind. I'd say my dad owes me some sort of explanation.'

'Which you want him to give you in the middle of his night?'

'Annie, how did we spend the middle of our night?'

'In a fit of angst,' she said. 'And not just the middle bit. I seem to remember angsting for several hours.'

'Exactly so.'

'Meaning?'

'Meaning I'm going to phone my dad now. Who gives a shit that he's fast asleep the other side of the bloody Atlantic?'

'Him, maybe?'

'Tough, is what I say.' And with that, Mike strode into the hall and dialled an American number.

'Well?' asked Annie when he came back into the kitchen less than a minute later.

'No, Annie. Not well. The bugger has left an answer phone to deal with his calls because – would you believe? – he's gone fishing.'

'In the middle of the night?'

'No, in the middle of the month. And – wait for it – he'll be back home sometime next month.'

'What? As in May?'

'Unless Chicago has a different calendar as well as a different time.'

'That's it then,' said Annie. 'Not a lot we can find out until he gets back.'

'What I think,' said Mike, 'is that we should go over there.'

'To Chicago!'

'To France, Annie. We need to go to this Coulaize place and take a look at this liability I've been landed with.'

'Oh, right.' She stretched her arms above her head and yawned. 'What I think we should do is go back to bed.'

'What we still have to do,' said Annie, pushing a piece of bacon round her plate at two in the afternoon, 'is do that internet search and see what's what with French house taxes and stuff.'

'Am I allowed to finish your breakfast first?'

'Help yourself.' She passed her plate to him. 'Take it with you and go and boot up the computer.'

'Ouch,' said Mike, staring at his laptop screen a few minutes later.

'What's ouch?' Annie peered over his shoulder. 'Oh. But a percentage of what?'

'The current value of the house.'

'Which is?'

'Search me,' he said. 'Who knows what this Monique Lanteine's house is worth, but whatever it is, I have to pay inheritance tax whether I want the damn house or not.'

'Okay,' said Annie, sitting on the settee beside him. 'Let's see what else we're lumbered with.'

After hitting Google search a few more times, they looked at each other almost speechless. Annie had been right about house insurance, which was apparently an obligation, and about community tax. Except it was called taxe d'habitation.

Leaning back, Annie said, 'Well thanks a bunch, Auntie...I mean...'

'What you mean, Annie, is thanks a bunch, Mére.'

'Shit, Mike!' She laid a hand on his arm. 'All this time you thought Delphine was...'

'I know.' He passed a shaky hand over his head. 'All my life I thought she and Norman Flint were my parents. Now I find out I didn't even know who my mother was.'

CHAPTER THREE

It wasn't as if many people in Coulaize actually knew who Monique Lanteine was. In fact, when they heard she'd died, some of them said, "qui était-elle?". Even so, when a memorial service was held several weeks after her death, presumably enough villagers did know who she was, and the little village church was far from empty. As to be expected, Janinne and Jean-Claude Lucott from the farm by Monique's place were there. As was Carol from Escargot Cottage, the only other dwelling in the lane which ran upwards from the village towards the Lanteine house and the Lucott's farm.

Not that Carol understood the Latin bits of the service, or some of the French for that matter. Maybe it was the smell of incense and burning candles making her feel strange, or possibly the heavy atmosphere and an overdose of a foreign language. Whatever it was, thinking that Liz with her cheery Cockney chatter was what she needed, Carol declined the Lucott's offer of a lift home and walked the few steps to the village café.

'Hiya, Carol.' Liz looked up from the beer mats she was unpacking. 'Go alright, did it? I seen a lot a people comin from the church.'

'Yes, the church was more than half full. I think I was the only Brit, though. I did wonder if you'd attend.'

'Nah, don't do funerals or memorials, me. Mostly local people then, was it?'

'I think so.' Carol hoiked her bum onto a bar stool. 'Although there was one old man I didn't recognise. Mind you, I probably wouldn't have noticed him if he hadn't kept taking his glasses off and polishing them.'

'Probably someone what went ter school wiv her or somefin. You okay, ducks? Only you look a bit peaky like.'

'Nothing a glass of red won't put right,' said Carol. 'Just a bit of a restless night, you could say.'

'You ain't still frettin about that Monique woman, are yer?'

'Well, sort of, Liz. She is – was – our nearest neighbour, after all.'

'Yeah, but it weren't your fault you dint know anyfin about her, was it?' said Liz. 'I mean, it's not like anyone in Coulaize knew much about her really, cept the Lucotts, that is.'

'A bit weird, don't you think?' said Carol.

Handing her a large glass of house red, Liz shrugged and said, 'Yeah, weird, but thas the way she was, weren't she? Now get that down yer neck and stop lettin it bovver yer.'

Left to her own thoughts as Liz served beer to a group of French farm workers who came in regularly for a lunchtime darts session, Carol sipped her wine and told herself Liz was right. It was silly to dwell on something she'd had no control over. Monique Lanteine *had* been an oddball, and no mistake. She'd shunned any friendly advances, so the easy thing to do had been to leave her to herself. Even so…

'Maybe I could have tried harder,' she said, when Liz came back and leaned her elbows on the bar. 'If I'd…'

'Carol! What did I tell yer?'

'Okay, okay.' Carol grinned and emptied her glass. 'Am I allowed to worry about the cat, though?'

'You sure there's one still missin, are yer?'

'Well, according to Lucie Lucott, Monique had seven. But when the animal rescue bods came to take them away, they could only find six.'

'Lucie'd know, I spose. That kid bein the only one the old girl would let get near her like. You up fer anovver?' She held up the wine bottle.

'Better not,' said Carol, pushing her empty glass aside. 'The thing is, Lucie says it's not much more than a kitten.'

'Oh well, animals come an go, an little Lucie knows that, innit. What wiv her livin on a farm an all.'

'Sure.' Carol shrugged. 'She's seen enough of her dad's cows and sheep carted off to the slaughter house.'

'Yeah, an I'll get slaughtered an all if I don't see ter that arrer slingin lot,' said Liz, moving away to serve more beer to the darts players.

Enjoying the early spring sunshine as she left the Café Carillion and strolled across the bridge, Carol paused to lean on the bridge's ancient stone wall and breathe in the tangy aroma of canal water and damp earth. A smell that always reminded her of the first night she'd spent in Coulaize nearly two years ago.

Shaking her head at the memory, Carol winced at the thought of that pathetic, wrecked woman she'd been then. Bruised and bewildered by divorce, not to mention shit scared, she had looked out of the window of a bedroom above the café and sniffed what had then been an unfamiliar smell of fresh country air. But then, everything about this move she'd made to France had been strange. Well, let's face it, she'd been strange herself. Or, as her daughter had put it, she'd totally lost her marbles.

Yes, well, she thought, watching some ducks float beneath the bridge. Plenty of water had flowed under her personal bridge since she'd flipped her lid and bought her derelict cottage. But she'd definitely found her marbles here in this friendly little French village, hadn't she?

The driver of the car that stopped beside her wasn't looking for marbles, he was looking for a house. Yes, okay, Monique Lanteine's house wasn't easy to find, tucked away as it was down a track beyond Carol's cottage. Pointing to the lane that ran uphill from the main road, she directed the man and wondered if he was a relative of Monique's. But he informed her that he was a surveyor who had come to value the house.

So that must mean the house was to be sold, then. Obviously whoever now owned it wasn't wasting any time, and Carol wondered what sort of neighbours she and Lars would eventually have. And thinking that Lars was probably wondering what sort of lunch he would eventually have, she went to the village shop to get the fresh baguette and pâté she was supposed to be picking up.

The school bus was discharging its little passengers when she left the shop, and Carol was pleased to see she'd have the company of one of her favourite people on her walk home.

Calling, 'Bonjour, Carol,' Lucie Lucott ran and threw her skinny arms round Carol's waist. 'We are walking together, yes?'

'Certainement,' said Carol, bending down to kiss Lucie and gently tug the silky black ponytail which sprouted lopsidedly from the child's head.

'Certain*ly*,' said Lucie, wagging an admonishing finger. 'Today we are speaking English.'

'Really? So why did you say bonjour?'

'I am forget,' said Lucie with a giggle.

'No, you had forgotten,' Carol corrected her. 'And *you* made the rule that we must speak French or English alternate days, so you're not allowed to forget.'

15

'Allowed is permitted, yes?'

'Yes, and you are permitted to walk me home, young lady.'

'Thank you, old lady, and I am allowed to carry your bread?'

'Think yourself lucky I don't hit you over the head with it,' said Carol, handing her the baguette. 'Come on, you cheeky brat. Your mum will be wondering where you are.'

'I am wondering where is the small cat,' said Lucie as they made their way up the lane.

'Oh, Lucie, don't worry about it. I'm sure it will be okay.'

'I search all the days after Madame is die, Carol.'

'I know. But maybe it will arrive at your farm one day, then you could look after it, couldn't you?'

'Yes, I could.' Her solemn expression transforming into one of delight, Lucie pointed and said, 'Here is your cat arrive.'

'She was probably wondering why I've been so long,' said Carol, smiling as Sue Ellen sashayed towards them, her long tail high in the air with the tip curled in the customary question mark. Squatting, Carol said, 'Hello, baby. Have you missed me then?'

'Mrrrup,' said Sue Ellen, leaping on to Carol's lap to rub noses before transferring her attention to Lucie kneeling beside them.

'Right,' said Carol after Lucie had stroked Sue Ellen for a while. 'Get home, young lady, before your mum sends out a search party.'

'What is search party?' Lucie's brow furrowed.

'I'll explain another time.'

'Okay,' said Lucie with a mini-Gallic shrug. Getting to her feet, she said, 'What is brat?'

'You are. Now git outer here, and I'll explain all that another time as well.'

What wasn't explained was how the devil the village postie found out that Madame Lanteine's house was not for sale. With an air of importance, Pascal la Poste delivered this news to Escargot Cottage, along with a letter he informed Carol was from her daughter. Fair enough, she had long ago accepted that the postman, who was as wide as he was tall, took pride in identifying the Essex postmark. And she had so far resisted the urge to ask him which of her daughters had written to her. But she did ask how he knew about Madame's house, and the only response she received was the postie's finger tapping the side of his nose.

CHAPTER FOUR

'Well, you're right about one thing,' said Annie, putting Chinese take-away on the coffee table. 'We'll have to go to this Coulaize place. We could do it in the Easter holidays.'

'Two days, I reckon,' said Mike, digging into a foil carton with a fork.

'Come on, Mike. I think we should go for longer than that.'

'No, I mean it'll take two days to get there because we'll have to make an overnight stop somewhere.'

'Really?'

'Well, put it this way,' he said. 'We're talking at least four hours drive to Dover, a couple of hours on a ferry, followed by probably another six or seven hours drive to Coulaize.'

'By which time, we'll be totally knacked,' she said.

'Exactly. And I sure as hell don't fancy driving through Paris totally knacked. Actually, I don't fancy driving anywhere near Paris on the wrong side of the bloody road, knacked or otherwise.'

'Eurolines,' said Annie, grabbing the carton of egg noodles out of his hand. 'Pig, you've had more than your share of that.'

Sneakily reaching for what was left of the chop suey whilst she was occupied scraping egg noodles out of the foil carton, he asked what Eurolines was.

'They run coaches,' she said. 'All over Europe.'

'How do you know that?'

'Because Clive went on one to Frankfurt.'

'Did he really? Who's Clive when he's not in Frankfurt?'

'Our school music teacher. He got on a bus in London, at Victoria station, I think he said. There's bound to be one from London to Dijon.'

'Then what?' he asked. 'We get as far as Dijon, but I think we worked out Coulaize is about twenty miles from Dijon.'

'What we do, Mike, is pick up a hire car.'

'Do we? Where, exactly, do we pick up this hire car?'

'Well, Clive said the drop-off and pick-up points were at railway stations. And there's always car hire places at stations, aren't there?'

'True.' He nodded. 'I suppose that's the way to go, then.'

'I think so. And you needn't think I didn't notice you pinch that chop suey when you thought I wasn't looking.'

'You ate most of the prawn crackers.'

'Okay, I'll swap you,' she said. 'What have you got left?'

'Well now...' He grinned. 'I'll see your prawn crackers and raise you this fried rice box.'

'That's what we'll do then,' she said.

'If you insist.' He passed the rice carton over and took what was left of the prawn crackers.

'We'll take a train to London and...Oi, you sod – you've bloody eaten all the rice!'

Having to wait until Annie's school closed for the Easter break had been making Mike twitchy. He'd wanted to go to France to see this flipping house of his, and he'd wanted to go now. Except that, when Annie pointed out that his work didn't prevent him from going whenever he liked, the thought of tackling it without her had made him even more twitchy.

Sighing, he switched off Google Earth and the tantalising view of a Burgundian village, and went back to the design he was supposed to be working on for his current assignment. Another one was waiting for his attention, so it was probably just as well he hadn't sodded off to France when work was piling up.

Yep, that was looking good, he thought an hour later. A bit of tweaking and this one would be done and dusted and ready to send off to his client. Glancing at the kitchen clock, he wondered if it was worth starting on his next commission. But, no, probably not. What with them leaving for France tomorrow, best to leave it until they got back when he could give the project his full attention. Anyway, Annie would be home soon and claiming the table so she could get on with marking whatever was in those books she brought home every day.

Besides which, bugger it, he hadn't washed the breakfast dishes yet.

'Yes, Mike,' said Annie for the third time. 'I have got all the tickets and, yes, they have got today's date on them.'

'And both passports?' he asked again.

'Yes, Mike. Both passports, all the tickets and the hire car paperwork. You've got the yellow fever and cholera vaccination certificates, haven't you?'

'So not funny, Annie.'

'Neither is you doing my head in. For heaven's sake, man, the way you're fussing, anyone would think we're going to the bloody moon.'

'Right,' he said, picking up the travel bags when a taxi hooted outside. 'All is calm, yes?'

'Mike, all we have to do is get in that taxi, get on a train at the station, get off at Victoria and get on a flipping coach which will take us to Dijon. What's not to be calm about?'

Annie freaking out as soon as it became apparent the Eurolines coach was going through the Channel tunnel was bad enough. But at least that was fairly short-lived, and Mike was able to reclaim and massage his mangled wrist when they emerged some twenty minutes or so after entering the tunnel.

It was about an hour later when the real nightmare began. Starting with Mike trying to get his long legs into some sort of comfortable position so he could join Annie in her zonked out state.

Ah, that was better. By turning slightly sideways in his seat, he was able to tuck his legs to one side. Hoping his knees wouldn't go into cramp seizure, he settled down for some much needed sleep for what was left of the night.

Which was when the elderly woman in the seat behind them started to snore.

What felt like a week later, Mike shook Annie's shoulder and told her they'd arrived.

'Wha...' She rubbed her eyes and looked out of the window. 'We're here already? I thought we were supposed to have a couple of rest stops on the way.'

'You slept through those,' he told her.

'Really? To think I'd been worrying about travelling overnight, but it really wasn't too bad, was it?'

'Speak for yourself,' he muttered, reaching up to retrieve their bags from the overhead rack.

'Oh dear,' she said. 'Do I take that to mean you didn't have a good night?'

'You could say that. If trying to sleep through the 1812 Overture counts.'

'I'm not even going to ask,' said Annie.

'Well I am,' he addressed her upturned bum. 'What the hell are you doing?'

'Looking for my shoes,' came a muffled reply.

'Um, Annie...' said Mike, looking down at his socks. 'Could you fish mine out while you're under the seat?'

Calling out to the bus driver that, yes, they were getting off here, Mike grabbed his shoes from Annie and told her not to sit down again unless she wanted to be taken on to Lyon.

'Do I have time to put my shoes on now?' she asked when they were in the bus park.

'Take as long as you like,' he said. 'We've got quite a wait until the hire car office opens.'

Tucking her arm through his as they walked across to the station building where they hoped to be able to get some coffee, she glanced at him and asked if he'd remembered to pack his razor.

A couple of vending machine coffees and a trip to the station loo later, they collected the keys and located their hire car. Looking at Mike across the Renault Twingo roof, Annie said, 'Jeez, you do look rough. Do you want me to drive?'

'No thanks, I think I'm traumatised enough as it is.'

Within half an hour of leaving Dijon station, the Twingo's sat nav had got them to the town where the notaire's office was. Even to the right street, where all they had to do was look for the number. That had been easy enough because, amazingly, they'd been able to park in front of the office. Well, it was amazing to them, being more accustomed to having to find a multi-storey car park in Sheffield then leg it to wherever.

'At least we'll have no problem finding the notaire tomorrow,' said Annie. 'Shall we go and find the house?'

'Breakfast first,' said Mike, opening the car door and sniffing. 'Get a whiff of this air, Annie.'

'What air? All I can smell is...flipping heck, can you smell it?'

'If you're talking freshly baked bread here.'

'Some baker is busy on a Sunday morning,' she said. 'Where's that smell coming from?'

'Follow my nose,' he said, striding into the wind.

In a matter of minutes, they'd found a café down a cobbled side road and were sitting at a pavement table trying not to salivate too obviously while they waited for croissants and coffee to be brought out to them.

Neither of them could think if they'd ever had croissants straight from the oven before. But, agreeing that this was a treat that called for an encore, they munched their way through a second batch. And who could resist those crusty baguettes? Or that array of cheeses in the shop they passed as they walked back up the hill to the car.

That was lunch sorted, and although they wouldn't be able to get into the house without keys, they reckoned the warm spring weather was conducive to a picnic in the garden.

'What did I say about trees?' said Annie, after they had taken the turning the sat nav told them was what to do next.

'You said you liked them.'

'I said, I like them in parks and things. You know, when you can see something other than the damn things. I just hope we get out of this lot soon.'

"You have reached your destination," announced the sat nav voice.

'Huh?' said Annie, gripping her seat belt. 'This can't be the village, we're in the middle of a flipping forest!'

Pulling onto a grass verge to let an approaching tractor pass, Mike said, 'Are you sure you spelled Coulaize right when I fed it into the sat nav?'

'Mike, whether either of us spelled it right isn't the point. This isn't anywhere called anything. Where are you going?' She grabbed his arm as he opened the car door.

'To ask that bloke on the tractor if he can tell us where we are.'

After some nodding and pointing, Mike got back in the car and said, 'Round the bend.'

'Oh great!' Annie clutched her head. 'All we need is barmy locals to add to the joy of this tree-infested place.'

'Coulaize,' said Mike, easing the car from the verge. 'Apparently it's just round the next bend.'

Sure enough, as soon as they'd rounded the bend, they were driving out of the dank, dark forest into brilliant sunshine. And there before them was a pretty little village with a bridge over a canal.

21

Clustered either side of the canal were stone houses, and a church was nestled amongst the ones beyond the bridge.

'Oh,' said Annie. 'It…it looks…'

'Yes?' Mike grinned at her. 'You're allowed to say it, you know.'

'Yes, all right, I admit it looks a lot nicer than I expected.'

'Nicer!' said Mike. 'It's bloody gorgeous.'

'Okay, Mike, let's just find this house of yours, shall we?'

After driving slowly round the village twice, they hadn't seen anything that looked like the photo the notaire had sent them.

'It would help,' said Annie, 'if there was an actual address as such.'

'Well it does say Rue de la Ferme,' he pointed out.

'It may say that, Mike. But have you seen a road name anywhere?'

'Well, no.' He scratched his chin. Shit, he really needed a shave. 'I reckon what we need to do is look for a farm of some sort.'

'Yep, that would give us a clue,' she agreed. 'But have you seen one of those either?'

'Can't say I have. I saw a café, though. We could ask there if anyone knows where this flipping house is.' Scratching his chin again, he said, 'If I can remember where I saw the café.'

'Beside the canal,' said Annie. 'Can you remember where that is?'

At least the canal was easy enough to find, and the Café Carillon was open. Telling Mike she could murder a beer, Annie sat at an outside table under a red and white umbrella. When Mike came out and joined her, he was shaking his head.

'What's wrong?' asked Annie. 'Don't they know the house?'

'I haven't asked yet,' he said. 'To be honest, I was a bit distracted. I'll ask Barbara Windsor when she brings the beers.'

'Who?'

'That woman in there.' He nodded his head towards the café door. 'She's the spitting image of a young Barbara Windsor and – would you believe – she speaks French with a Cockney accent.'

'Yeah, very funny, Mike.'

'No, really, you wait till she…ouch, what was that for?'

Leaving Mike to rub his shin, Annie smiled at a petite woman with bubbly blonde hair as she approached with a tray.

'Here y'are, ducks,' said the woman, placing two glasses of beer on the table. Grinning at Mike, she said, 'Sorry, I din't realise you was English. On account of you comin in a French car, an you do

22

look sorta French. Anyfin else I can get yer?'

Casting an *I told you so* look at Annie's startled face, Mike said, 'There is something, actually. I don't suppose you know where we can find a house?'

'What, ter buy, yer mean?'

'No, no.' Annie fished the photo out of her bag. 'We're looking for this house. Do you know where it is?'

'Oh, right.' The woman looked at the photo and said, 'That'll be Monique's house, that will. You haven't come ter visit her have you? Only she's dead, innit.'

'Yes, it…she is,' said Mike. 'But I take it you knew her?'

'Not really.' She shook her head. 'Don't fink anyone could say they knew her, like. Cept maybe the Lucotts. They did sorta look out for her in case she got in any bovver. Anyway…' She pointed across the canal. 'You'll find her place up there.'

Lifting her sunglasses, Annie said, 'That house halfway up the hill?'

'Nah, not that one,' said the woman. 'You'll have ter go past that, then, just before you get to a farm, hang a left down a narrer lane. Monique's place is the only house down there, so you can't miss it.'

'I thought she said we couldn't miss the narrow lane,' said Annie, after Mike had turned the car in front of a farm.

'What she said, Annie, was that we couldn't miss the house. What we missed was the lane we were supposed to hang a left down.'

'Well I hope you're going to miss that cat! – Oh, it's okay it's shot into that garden.'

Mike stopped the car anyway, slapped Annie's hand away from the handbrake and said, 'We've missed the damn lane again.'

'She'll know where it is,' said Annie, as a woman came from the garden and walked towards them with a little black cat trotting at her heels.

'Vous êtes perdu?' called the woman.

'Yep, you could say we're bloody lost,' Mike muttered before getting out of the car and calling, 'Oui, madame.'

Yes, she was able to tell him where to find the house. Mike thanked her, walked back to the car, got in and said, 'I don't know what it is about the people round here, but that one seemed to be speaking French with an Essex accent.'

'Yeah, very ho ho, Mike. Does that mean we're still lost?'

'No,' he said, executing a five point turn in the narrow lane. 'It means we have to find a big walnut tree.'

'Uh huh. Do you want to tell me what that means?'

'What it means is that we couldn't see the flipping lane because it's hidden by that damn great tree.'

'I'd hardly call it a lane,' she said, as Mike turned under the tree's huge branches and they bumped their way along a rutted track. 'More of a…Oh heck! Is that it?'

Stopping the car, Mike stared at the house in front of them and said, 'Would you like to define "Oh heck" for me?'

'Um…well…it's…'

'Yes?'

'It's a lot bigger than I expected. And I thought there'd be more trees.'

'Annie, there are trees. We've just passed under a big bugger, and I can see some beside the house.'

'Yes, but it's not like the house is in the middle of a tall forest or anything, is it?'

'True. Shall we go and have a poke around?'

Frustratingly, all they could see of the house was its ancient ivy-clad stone walls and a slate roof. Any chance of peering through windows to get a glimpse of the interior was thwarted by wooden shutters, which looked as if they hadn't seen a paint brush for some time.

'Not too shabby, though,' said Mike.

'Neither is that,' said Annie, standing in the back garden and staring at a panoramic view of distant hills and undulating meadows dotted with sheep. From where she stood, she caught a glimpse of sunlight reflecting on water, and a few steps further revealed that the canal lay at the base of the valley.

'Yep, very pretty,' he said. 'How about those flowering trees, then?'

'Where?'

'At the side of the garden. Do you suppose that's an orchard?'

'Looks like it. I think that's cherry blossom. And those sort of gnarled trees might be apple or something.'

'I wonder how many bedrooms,' said Mike, turning to look up at the back of the house. 'I can see two upstairs windows.'

'That would be two bedrooms, then, I should think. Or maybe one is the bathroom. Unless one of the two upper windows at the front is the bathroom.'

'Oh well, we'll see once we've picked up the keys from the notaire. Annie, when can I go to bed? I can't get my head round anything more today.'

Once they'd found and checked into the chambres d'hote Annie had booked online, her first suggestion was that Mike have a shave. But top of his agenda was to get some sleep. He did, however, attack the growth on his chin before they ate a delicious evening meal, at a very acceptable price, in the restaurant beyond the bridge which spanned the canal in the little village called Oisey.

Pausing in the moonlight to look up at a star-filled sky on the way back over the bridge, Annie asked why they had never been to France before.

'Probably because you fancied Portugal or Spain for holidays,' said Mike.

'Only because they were cheap package jobs,' she said. 'But, Mike, didn't you ever have the urge to visit your mum's country?'

'Occasionally, I suppose.' He shrugged. 'But I had a stronger urge to do what you fancied.'

'Aw, bless.' She squeezed his hand. 'But I think we have to accept that even cheap package holidays are out for the next few years anyway.'

Wrapping his arms round her, he said, 'I'm sorry, love. This flipping house is going to cost money we can't actually afford.'

'Not your fault, is it?' she said. 'I suppose we could look on it as our French holiday home. In fact...'

'In fact what?' He leaned back to look at her face.

'Well, I did only confirm the B & B for tonight. We could save money by camping out at the house the rest of the week, couldn't we?'

'Camping probably being the word, Annie. I mean, what if the electricity and stuff has been turned off?'

'So? Tents don't have electricity, do they? And plenty of people go on holiday in tents.'

'Yeah, roughie-toughie types. As in guys who stride across moors and yell ultra-hearty greetings to fellow outdoorsy maniacs wading through cow shit in wellies.'

'You do have some weird ideas,' she said, as they carried on walking. 'All I suggested was that we could sleep in the flipping house.'

'And you expect me to believe you're serious, woman?'

'Come on, Mike. It might be fun.'

'It might be hell.'

'Sure,' she said. 'Waking up to that view has to be anyone's idea of hell.'

'Now I know you're not serious. You don't like acres of open fields any more than you like trees.'

'Mike, I couldn't live with them, but I'm okay with fields and stuff on a temporary basis.'

'Bloody townie,' he said, as they walked down a towpath towards the chambres d'hote.

'Oh yeah? Like you think you could live without a Sainsburys supermarket round the corner?'

'Shhh.' Putting a finger to his lips as he opened the chambers d'hote door, Mike whispered, 'Seems like we might be the only ones not in bed.'

'How do you know that?'

'I can't hear a telly.'

Waiting until they'd crept upstairs and closed their bedroom door, Annie said, 'Maybe they don't have television round here.'

'That would be a bit serious,' he said.

'Absolutely. Heaven forbid that anyone should live without Coronation Street!'

'No, not having Sainsburys round the corner, I mean.'

CHAPTER FIVE

Silently thanking the woman he'd called Mum for ensuring he was conversant with the written as well as spoken French language, Mike followed what the notaire was saying rather better than he'd followed the English solicitor. But then, this French guy had the advantage of knowing the full situation. Well, regarding the property and rightful ownership of it, that is. Whereas Miss Pinkerton of the hooked pearls had only been in possession of the bare facts.

When it came to the question of why Mike had become the rightful owner of Monique Lanteine's estate, the notaire simply said that, under French law, a person's property was automatically inherited by a child or children of the deceased. On the issue of the five-year no-sale clause, the notaire said that he had merely been instructed to include the codicil when he was asked to draw up the will.

Armed with a heavy bunch of keys and a green cardboard folder, which Annie insisted on holding on to, they left the office and walked across the street to the car. When Annie asked Mike why he was lifting up the windscreen wipers, he admitted he was looking for a parking ticket. 'I mean,' he said, 'we left the car here, just where we stopped on the side of the road, for nearly an hour.'

'Well maybe they don't have traffic wardens here,' she said when he got into the driving seat.

Mike fastened his seat belt, turned on the engine and said, 'Annie, I wish you wouldn't do that.'

'Sorry, but I've never been a passenger in a left hand drive car, and it's instinctive.'

'Yes, I can see that. It's instinctive to be in control from where you're sitting, but you really have to stop yourself operating the handbrake.'

'Okay, okay.' She raised her hands.

Pulling onto the road, Mike added, 'And don't think I haven't noticed the way you put your foot down when you think I should be braking.'

'I get the message, Mike. You're in control of the car. Right?'

'Yes, Annie.'

As the lilting voice emanating from the sat nav told them to proceed ahead, Annie slammed her foot onto the floor and yelled, 'Am I allowed to ask why that van is coming straight for us?'

'Shit!' said Mike, wrenching the steering wheel to the right. 'I'm on the wrong side of the bloody road.'

'Annie, you're going to have to stop doing that.'

'What? I haven't touched the flipping handbrake.'

'That's not what I'm talking about,' said Mike.

'So what am I doing wrong now?'

'Every time we drive under that walnut tree, you duck.'

'Do I?'

'Yes, and it's doing my head in.'

'Well, I don't like those thumping great branches above my head.'

'Annie, in case you haven't noticed, there's a car roof between you and them.'

'I know that,' she muttered. 'It's just...'

Stopping in front of the house and engaging the handbrake without her help, Mike turned to Annie and said, 'Look, it's your idea to spend the rest of the week here, but I'm not sure I can handle that if you don't stop freaking out about frigging trees.'

'Okay. Right.' Getting out of the car, she said, 'It was you freaking out at *my* idea to sleep in the house, so let's just go inside and suss out if it's even possible for *you* to handle the next five nights here.'

'Sure,' he said, sorting through the bunch of keys to find the right one to open the heavy oak front door. 'Let's just take a look inside and see what we're talking about here.'

Once inside the house, Annie suggested it would help if Mike switched some lights on. The problem with that idea being that he'd already groped the walls but hadn't been able to locate any light switches. Deciding the answer was to open some shutters to let daylight in, that's what he did.

Which was when he said, 'Ah!' And pointed to the oil lamps.

'You don't want that last bit, do you?' Mike looked at the lump of cheese on the garden bench.

Picking up the piece of Beaufort and breaking it in half, Annie said, 'At least there's an outside tap. I suppose that's something to be thankful for.'

'True.' Mike nodded. 'Well, it would be if water came out of it.'

'I suppose…' She paused to pop her half of the Beaufort in her mouth. 'I shpose shomeone turned it off.'

'Shame they didn't have to turn any electricity off while they were at it,' he said. 'Annie, what the hell are we going to do with this place for the next five years until I can sell it?'

'Sell the furniture? I mean, it's not like anyone could live with that stuff.'

'Well, Monique whasaface obviously did.'

'Yeah,' said Annie, pointing at a wooden shack. 'Like she lived with that instead of a bloody indoor loo. Mike, was that a car?'

'No, I'm sure that's always been what passes as a toilet.'

'Seriously, I could swear I heard something. Do you think you should go and see?'

'Maybe I should. Or maybe we should hide in the loo shed in case it's the local law bods wanting to find out why we're here.'

'He doesn't look like the law,' said Annie.

'Who doesn't?'

'That man in dungarees coming round the side of the house.'

'Bonjour,' called the man, coming towards them with an outstretched hand. 'Je suis Jean-Claude.'

With mutual introductions over, he said, 'You are the Eenglish, non?'

'Oui, yes, we are English,' said Annie.

'Okay.' He paused then said, 'I am come parce que Leez.'

'What's a leez?' said Annie, looking at Mike.

'I have no idea. But he's come because of it.'

'Mike, why don't you try speaking to him in French?'

'Er, right. That could work.' Turning back to the man, he said, 'Pardon, Monsieur, je ne comprends pas.'

With what could only be described as a look of total relief, the man said, 'Vous parlez Français?' Without waiting for a reply, he launched into a voluble spate of French.

'Well?' said Annie, when Mike returned from escorting the man back to his tractor. 'What was that all about? I didn't understand half of what he said.'

'You wouldn't have. On account of his Geordie accent.'

'Mike, could you do serious for once?'

'Okay, I admit he doesn't have a Geordie accent. More of a Suffolk or Norfolk one, I'd say.'

'Mike, if you don't want me to hit you…'

'No, really, Annie.' He caught hold of her raised arm. 'It was a bit like trying to understand an East Anglian agricultural worker.'

'If you say so. But did you understand enough to tell me what a leez is?'

'Oh, that's Liz. She's the woman we met in the Café Carillion. Apparently she phoned the farm up there to tell them some Brits had been asking about Monique Lanteine's house.'

'So? What has that got to do with this Jean-Claude bloke?'

'You remember she said the only people who knew Monique were the Lucotts?'

'Yes, the people who looked out fer her in case she had any bovver, like.'

'Well, that was Jean-Claude Lucott. He'd seen our car and came to check out why we were here.'

'And what did you tell him?'

'I had to assure him we weren't trespassing because we own the place. And he said to let him know if there's anything we need.'

'Really? At least the natives are friendly, then,' she said. 'We might even be safe if we do decide to sleep here overnight.'

'If those oil lamps don't explode. But, Annie, I don't suppose there's any basic stuff like clean bed linen or anything.'

Yes, there was a stack of neatly folded bed linen in an ornately carved wooden chest. And pillows, blankets and a quilt piled up on an otherwise stripped bed. Which, if they put them outside in the fresh air for a few hours, would probably be acceptable to use. And neither of them doubted that the air was anything less than what anyone would call fresh.

They were draping the quilt over the garden bench when a pretty little dark-haired girl, maybe nine or ten-years-old, appeared. She solemnly shook their hands, told them her name was Lucie Lucott, and her Mama would be happy if they would please to arrive at the farm to have lunch tomorrow.

Yes, they would be happy to accept. 'Please thank your mama and tell her she is very kind,' said Mike.

'C'est normale.' Lucie shrugged. 'Are you see a small cat?'

'No,' said Annie. 'Have you lost one?'

'She is the cat of Madame Lanteine, but we do not know where is she.'

'Well, if we see it, we'll let you know.'

Looking at the quilt, Lucie said, 'You are sleep in Madame's house?'

'We think we will,' said Annie. 'Maybe just tonight, but we'll see after that.'

After Lucie had left, Annie turned to Mike and said, 'Are we up for this sleeping here plan, or what?'

'I reckon it's worth giving it a whirl.' Putting an arm round her shoulders, he turned her to face the vista of meadows and hills beyond the house. 'Like you said, it would be anyone's idea of hell to wake up to that view.'

'Absolutely.' She grinned. 'And you do realise the back bedroom windows open out onto that god-awful view?'

'Sod it. Oh well, maybe we can put up with it on a temporary basis.'

'Um, talking of temporary, Mike. Could you, sort of temporarily, put up with a bucket in the house?'

'Bucket?'

'You know, one of those plastic things with a handle.'

'Annie, I know what a bucket is, but why do you want one?'

'Come on, Mike. Do you really expect me to wander out in the middle of the night to pee in a wooden hut?'

'Fair comment,' he said. Executing an exaggerated bow, he pledged to buy his fair lady a bucket for her personal convenience that very afternoon. 'And...' He waggled his eyebrows. 'I might even produce some running water if you're very good.'

'Oh yeah? How are you going to pull that one off?'

'I'm not going to pull it, I'm going to twist a stopcock thingy that Lucott bloke showed me under that outside tap affair.'

'Are you kidding me?'

'Nope. Anymore than I'd kid you about the gas.'

'Gas?'

'Yep. It's in these metal cylinder things, which he also showed me how to turn on.'

'Uh huh.' She sat on the quilt and stared up at him. 'Then what happens?'

'Well, you see, Annie, it works like this. Gas runs along a rubber pipe to that peculiar cooker affair in the kitchen.'

'Okay, I think I'd worked that out,' she said. 'But d'you think it would be safe to light that thing?'

'I should think so.' He shrugged. 'I mean, we have to assume that's what this Monique woman did.'

'Well, yes. But, Mike, we don't actually know how she died, do we?'

As it turned out, the ceramic chamber pot Mike found in a cupboard obviated the need to go bucket shopping. After christening the poo pottie, as Mike called it, Annie utilized water spurting from the outside tap to rinse it out before they went to the Café Carillion in search of an evening meal.

'Damn,' said Mike, seeing the closed sign on the café door.

'That's us blown,' said Annie. 'Hang on, maybe that bloke can tell us where there's an open restaurant.'

'Puis-je vous aider?' called out the man, as he ducked beneath the café doorway and walked towards them.

'I hope he *can* help us,' said Mike, getting out of the car. Tilting his head to look up at a face a few inches above his own, he asked if there was somewhere nearby where they could get a meal. In rapid French, the man apologised about the Carillion being closed, and directed him to a restaurant called La Chouette in a village a few kilometres away.

He then asked if they were English. 'Fought yer might be,' he said, when Mike told him they were. 'You must be them ones what's come ter look at the Lanteine house, innit.'

'Yep, that's us.'

'Yeah, my Liz said about you bein here. We're always closed on a Monday night, like, but we can do grub fer yer any uvver night.'

'We're here for the rest of the week,' said Mike. 'So no doubt we'll take you up on that.'

'You stayin at the house, are yer?'

'Tonight, anyway.' Mike nodded. 'We'll decide after that about roughing it again.'

'Yeah, right.' The man scratched his head then said, 'Hang on a minnit, I'll get yer somefin.' And, ducking as he went through the open door, he disappeared into the café.

'Well, at least it'll be nice an clean at the house if Janinne's had anyfin ter do wiv it,' he said when he came back out of the café.

'Janinne?'

'Yeah, her up at the farm. I'll phone an tell the Chouette yer comin, shall I? Only they shut up the kitchen after eight if there's no one in.'

'Thanks,' said Mike. 'We'll see you again before we leave.'

'Okay, don't say it,' said Annie, when Mike got back in the car.

'What?'

'He speaks French with a Cockney accent. Right?'

'No he doesn't,' said Mike, as he turned the car. 'Actually, I was going to ask you if he reminded you of anyone.'

'Like who?'

'Bernard Breslaw.'

'Who's Bernard Breslaw?'

'Annie, have you ever watched a Carry On film?'

'Not if I could avoid it. Why, what's that got to do with anything?'

'Never mind,' he said. 'Jeez, I'm starving. I hope that bloody restaurant *is* still serving meals.'

'And let's hope we can see to read the menu.'

'What's that supposed to mean?'

'Oh, nothing.' She shrugged. 'I was just wondering why that Bernard Breslaw bloke gave you a torch.'

'Shit, Mike, this is scary!' Annie clutched the parcel shelf as, after driving back through a dimly-lit Coulaize an hour later, they turned into the dark lane. Increasing her white-knuckled grip on the shelf when they turned onto the track leading to the house, she wailed, 'I don't think I can do this.'

Passing her the torch as he stopped the car in front of the house, Mike said, 'Well at least we now know why that Café Carillion guy gave me this.'

'Huh,' said Annie, switching on the torch. 'I don't know who the hell he is, but I bloody love him.'

Aided by the torch's powerful beam, finding an oil lamp and some matches was the easy bit. Lighting the lamp turned out to be rather more difficult. After watching Mike's several failed attempts, Annie said, 'What's that little knob thing for?'

'Good question,' said Mike. 'I have no idea, but maybe we should

33

try winding it or something?'

'Wick,' said Annie.

'Charming! Annie, there's no need to be…'

'Mike, that cloth thingy I've just wound up – it's called a wick.'

'Is it? How do you know that?'

'What the hell does it matter how I know? Just put a match to the bugger, will you!'

'Yay!' he said as a flame spurted into life. 'Mission accomplished.'

'God, it stinks,' said Annie, flapping a hand in front of her nose.

'It does, doesn't it? Maybe we should take it outside.'

'Won't it blow out if we do?'

'Not if I put the glass tube back on. There you go. How's that?'

'Wow, it gives out quite a lot of light now. It still stinks in here, though.'

'True.' He nodded. 'Is there any wine left in that bottle we opened at lunchtime?'

'Some,' she said. 'Why, what are you going to do with it?'

'Drink it, woman. Out there on the garden bench under the stars, would you believe?'

Accustomed as they were to street lights, it took a few minutes to adjust to the fact that the night wasn't as inky-black as they'd thought. What with being mellow after star gazing while emptying the wine bottle and drinking in the sight of the meadows and distant hills bathed in moonlight, they slept like babies with the bedroom window open to the fresh night air.

CHAPTER SIX

Waking up to see Annie wrapped in a blanket standing at the bedroom window, Mike asked her what she was doing awake at…

'Bloody hell,' he said, looking at his watch. 'It's after nine!'

With a smug expression on her face, she turned from the window and said, 'Well I was right about one thing.'

'Which is?'

'Waking up to that bloody awful view. Get your arse out of bed, Mike, you've got to see this.'

Snuggled inside the blanket with her, his naked bum juxtaposed with hers, Mike agreed that maybe – just maybe, mind you – she had been right about them spending the rest of the week in the house. 'It does have one advantage,' he said. 'Your mum would never find us here.'

'Wicked!' Annie grinned. 'Not even a phone for her to hassle me with her constant moans.'

Meanwhile, he reminded her, he had a half ten appointment with Monique Lanteine's bank manager. So shouldn't they get their arses into gear so they could find out if the woman was in the red or the black column when she died and left her affairs for him to deal with?

'Right,' said Annie. 'If we get our act together now, we'll have time to have breakfast at that place where we had those brilliant croissants.'

A plan that, as it happened, turned out to be a bit ambitious. Which was partly due to the fact that they'd both wasted time being hesitant about swabbing their faces and armpits with cold water from the outside tap, and partly due to Annie being at the wheel of the car while Mike attempted to use his battery shaver throughout the jerky drive.

A situation that wasn't helped by Mike yelling at Annie about swerving to the right and mounting the grass verge whenever another vehicle came towards them. So it was that, when they arrived in front of the bank, Mike got out of the car with a feeling of relief, albeit with a rumbling stomach. In answer to her plaintive cry about where he expected her to park, with an air of a man accustomed to having to do so, he told her to drive around until she found an unoccupied parking meter.

'Well?' said Annie, when Mike re-emerged from the bank and climbed into the car which she'd simply parked by the side of the road a few metres away. 'Are we just hard up, or are we very, very hard up?'

'Ish,' he said, taking the car keys from her.

'Meaning?'

'Meaning we're hard up-ish. Although it might not be quite as bad as we thought.' He handed her some papers. 'If you look at the habitation tax one, you'll see it's a fraction of what we pay in council tax for our piddling little house in England.'

'Is that a monthly standing order, or what?'

'No, Annie, that's what it costs for a year.' Pulling out from the kerb, he told her to look at the account balance sheets.

'Um, if I've got the right bit,' she said, 'it looks like there's a current balance of just under seventy Euros. And...oh, hang on, this looks better. It seems there's a few grand in a savings account.'

'Which I'm told will cover the inheritance tax and any outstanding bills with maybe a bit to spare.'

'I see. Mike, could you define a bit to spare for me?'

'Not off the top of my head. But we'll go through it all when we get back to the house.'

Looking at her watch, Annie said, 'It'll have to be after we've done the lunch thing at the farm. We're supposed to be there at twelve, and it's twenty past eleven now.'

First to greet them when they walked up to the farm was little Lucie. She then announced in slightly quaint English that her parents were happy to welcome them to their home.

'Cute kid,' said Annie as, apparently having done her reception duty bit, Lucie skipped ahead of them calling, 'Mama, il sont arrivés.'

'Cute mum, too,' said Mike, when a petite woman looking for all the world like an adult version of her daughter appeared in the open doorway.

With a warmth they wouldn't have expected from total strangers, Annie and Mike were indeed welcomed into the Lucotts' home. With introductions dealt with, they were led through a huge farm kitchen to another room, where a spread of food to die for had Mike's face looking as if he thought he *had* died and arrived in Heaven.

'This is very kind of you,' said Annie. 'And, Janinne, is it you we should thank for the house being so clean?'

'Poof, is nothing,' said Janinne. 'Now I must tell Lucie to give to you the clé…the key?'

'No hurry,' said Annie. 'It might be best if you hang on to it.'

Although quick to pour glasses of wine, the burly farmer seemed hesitant when it came to conversation. In fact, his stumbling attempt to speak English led Mike to suggest they use his own language instead. Which the man seemed to welcome with the same relief he had displayed the previous day, and he informed them in French that they would eat when two other guests arrived.

'Non, Papa.' Lucie wagged a finger at her dad. 'Today is English, yes?' Her face lighting up at the sound of voices from the kitchen, she said, 'Ah, Carol and Lars are arrive.'

Carol they recognised as the woman from down the lane who had helped them find the track to the house. And when she greeted them in English with a hint of an Essex accent, Mike shot Annie an *I told you so* look. The stocky man with the unruly straw-coloured hair and beard shook hands with a warm, strong grip and introduced himself as Lars. There was a hint of an accent there, too, but difficult to define. One thing was for sure, he wasn't French.

During the course of what turned out to be a surprisingly enjoyable couple of hours, Annie and Mike learned that Lars had arrived in Coulaize in a canal barge.

'I was intending to explore the complete France,' he said. 'But this lady…' He laid a hand on Carol's shoulder. 'She captured my heart and put a stop to my travels. But I don't know,' he added with a grin, 'if it was I or my barge that captured *her* heart.'

'Definitely the barge,' said Carol, winking at Annie. 'But I haven't let on about that yet.'

'And do you live here all the time?' asked Annie, as Mike and Lars went to replenish their plates.

'Of course,' said Carol, as if that was a strange question. 'Either in my cottage, or on Lars's barge when we go cruising. What about you two?'

'Sorry?'

'I mean, are you planning to live here?'

With a slight shudder, Annie said, 'No way!'

'Oh, it's just that we assumed you were interested in Monique Lanteine's house,' said Carol. 'Except there's some doubt about it being for sale, so...'

'It's not.'

'Sorry, I shouldn't go poking my nose in.'

'No, no, it's okay. Sorry if I sounded a bit sharp there. The thing is...' Annie hesitated because, well, you don't go around broadcasting your business to strangers, do you? But these people were so friendly, and the Carol woman did seem genuinely interested, in a non-nosey sort of way.

'Look, don't mind me,' said Carol. 'Let's just say I've got used to the way of things round here which, let's face it, isn't quite the way of things in England, is it? Mind you,' she added with a grin, 'I wasn't that good at doing or saying the right thing there, either.'

'No, Carol, it's no problem, really. It's just that it's...well, it's just a bit of a sensitive issue for Mike.'

'Nuff said.' Carol held up her hands. 'Is it okay to ask what you think of Coulaize?'

'It's okay, in a rustic sort of way,' said Annie. And then – what the heck – she looked at the older woman's friendly face and proceeded to explain their situation.

'Bugger,' was Carol's response. 'And I thought my life was complicated when my husband dumped me!'

'Oh, so Lars isn't...sorry, I didn't mean to...' Annie tailed off, feeling herself blush.

'And you didn't.' Carol grinned at her. 'Lars and I met when I'd been here a few months, and he played a big part in sorting my stupid head out.'

'Well, I have to say you look pretty sorted to me.'

'I am now,' said Carol, looking across to where Lars and Mike were chatting. 'Thanks to quite a few people, actually. Like the Lucotts, for example. And the people at the Carry On Caff, of course.'

'The what?'

'Ah, maybe you haven't been to the café by the canal?'

'We did call in yesterday,' said Annie. 'There was this little woman who looked and sounded like Barbara Windsor. Then last

38

night we met a big bloke who – oh, is that why you called it the Carry On Caff?'

'That's what the Brits round here call it,' said Carol.

'Are there lots of Brits round here, then?'

'Not lots, no.' Carol shook her head. 'And we're a bit of an odd mixture, really.'

'But you get on, though, do you?'

'Surprisingly, yes.'

'Oh.' Annie looked at Carol and wondered how anyone would not get on with her. But then, you couldn't always tell from a first meeting, could you? So she asked why Carol thought it was surprising.

'I suppose because...' Carol's brow puckered as if she was only now querying that. 'I suppose it's because no one around here seems to give a shit who you are or where you came from.'

'I enjoyed that,' said Mike, as they walked back to the house.

'Me too,' said Annie. 'You talked to Jean-Claude quite a long time, did you find out anything about the mysterious Monique?'

'Well, she didn't blow herself up or gas herself, you'll be pleased to hear.'

'Thanks, I heard about her death, but I'm more interested in when she was alive. As in did Jean-Claude tell you anything about her?'

'No. As far as he knows, she'd always lived in the house. He does remember her parents dying when he was a kid, and there was another daughter who married and went to England, but that's about it.'

'Bummer,' she said. 'I was hoping he'd know something about her supposedly being your mother.'

'I did ask if he knew about her having a baby, but he just seemed surprised at the – Watch it!' He grabbed Annie's arm as she tripped over a rut. 'Anyway, you seemed to be getting on well with that woman.'

'Carol? Yes, I really liked her, only...'

'Only what?'

'Mike, I'm sorry. I don't even know why I did that, but I told her about you inheriting the house and how it was going to leave us strapped for cash.'

'Good,' he said, guiding her round a cow pat. 'Makes it easier for me to fess up about telling that Lars bloke.'

'What did he say?'

'What he said was that it may have possibilities as a gite.'

'Good one.' Annie snorted. 'A holiday let without water or electricity should be well popular.'

'Well, he was a bit surprised about that. But then he wondered if we could sort that and live in the house.'

'Yeah, right. Very ho ho,' she said. 'Janine and Jean-Claude are lovely, don't you think? And their Lucie is adorable.'

'True on all counts. Annie, are you up for sleeping here again tonight?'

'Are you up for finding a B & B for tonight?'

'Nope. What I'm up for is a siesta. That wine Jean-Claude kept pouring was high octane stuff.'

'He's Dutch, by the way,' she said.

'Is he? I would have staked my life on him being French.'

'Lars, I mean. He's Dutch.'

'Okay, got that.'

'And I found out why Bernard Breslaw speaks English like a Cockney.'

'Let me guess. Liz taught him English?'

'She didn't teach him French, though, and he's Croatian.'

'And you, my love,' he said, as she stumbled over another rut in the track, 'are ever so slightly pissed.'

'I'm bloody well not. All I am is a bit mellow.'

'Is that the same as being as relaxed as a newt?'

'Yeah, like you've ever seen a flipping newt?'

'I have seen a newt,' he said, grabbing her arm as she stumbled again. 'On telly.'

'Sure you have. And I suppose you're going to tell me it was as relaxed as a piss-head.'

'I didn't call you a…Annie, why are we talking about newts?'

'Search me,' she said, fumbling with the door key. 'Mike, can you do this? I can't seem to locate the sodding keyhole.'

It's true to say they did take a short nap. But when they were woken by bleating sheep that sounded as if they were below the bedroom window, things became somewhat more active than a siesta is supposed to be.

Stretching like a cat replete with the proverbial cream, Annie said, 'I reckon you were right.'

'About what?' Mike mumbled.

'About that being relaxed thing.'

'Was I?' Mike propped himself up on an elbow and looked down at her smug face. 'I thought I was…well, you know.'

'You were,' she said, grinning up at him. 'We should do this again.'

'What! Already? Are you insatiable, woman?'

'What I mean is…' She hoisted herself into a sitting position and leaned against the brass-knobbed bed head. 'I mean, we should come here instead of a package holiday to Spain in August.'

'Which I think we've agreed we can't afford now anyway,' he said. 'You haven't booked anything yet, have you?'

'No.' She shook her head. 'I wanted to wait and see if there would be a late booking deal, but that's the trouble with being restricted to school holiday times. It's bang in the middle of peak prices.'

'Talking of money, where's that stuff I was given at the bank this morning?'

'Downstairs, on that big dresser thing in the kitchen. And there's a calculator in my handbag.'

'Okay,' he said, getting off the bed. 'Let's go and find out just how deep we are in the proverbial brown stuff.'

'Mike, don't you think you should put some clothes on?'

'If you insist.' He picked up his shirt from the floor. 'Although I don't know who you think's going to see me. It's not as if anyone's likely to stroll down the street and peer in the window, is it.'

'Good point. Chuck me a tee-shirt out of that bag, will you? I quite like the idea of not having to cover my bum for the sake of the neighbours.'

'And we'll do it outside on the garden bench, shall we?' he said. 'Now what are you grinning at?'

'Oh, just thinking how our next-door neighbours would react to that. Not that we've got what would class as a garden, let alone a garden bench at home.'

'What I meant was, Annie, we could take the bank stuff outside and sit in the sun while we check out what the situation is, fiscally speaking.'

'Okay, ready when you are.'

'Um, Annie, haven't you got a longer tee-shirt?'

'You don't like?' she asked, doing a twirl.

'I'm not about to complain.'

'So come into the garden, Mike, and I'll check out your fiscals in the sunshine.'

'You think?' said Mike, when Annie put her calculator and notepad on the bench. 'You really think we can hack this?'

'Well, I'm not saying it won't be tight. But with what's in Monique's savings account, I think we'll survive.'

'Yes, but…'

'But what?'

'We've only just started building up some savings so we can buy something a bit bigger than our one bedroom rabbit hutch.'

'Yes, well.' She shrugged. 'That'll have to go on hold for five years until we can sell this place.'

'Unless…' he said.

'Unless what?'

'Well…' Mike took a deep breath and said, 'I've been thinking about going back to work for Harlington Graphics.'

'No, Mike!' She grabbed his hand.

'But, Annie…'

'Mike, remind me again why you left Harlingtons to start up on your own from home.'

'Okay, so I wasn't happy doing the rubbish designs they wanted when I thought my ideas would work better.'

'Not happy! Mike, you were downright bloody miserable.'

'True, but…'

'Oh, for heaven's sake stop saying but,' she said, getting up from the bench. 'I don't want to hear any more crap about you throwing in the sponge after you've spent the last year making an impression in your own right.'

'Um, Annie…'

'What now?'

'Did you know the bench slats have left an impression on your bum?'

Turning the dial on the bottled gas was as straightforward as Jean-Claude had said it would be. It was when it came to Mike striking a match and telling Annie to turn a knob on the ancient cooker that they hit a problem because that was when she bottled it. After the third match had burned down and scorched Mike's fingers, he gave in and conceded that maybe Annie was right about the range thing in the kitchen fireplace possibly being a safer bet. As she said, it wasn't as if the logs they'd found in the garden were likely to explode, was it?

Which turned out to be an accurate assumption, given that the only thing to respond to a whole box of matches was a lot of crumpled paper that would have kept an avid news reader going for a week. Declaring that she needed to breathe, Annie opened the front door and, peering through the smoke that belched out, spied someone coming along the track.

Carol hadn't actually come to light their cooker for them, but she did it anyway, after assuring them there was nothing to freak out over. What she *had* come for was to say that, as the weather had cleared up again after yesterday's rain, she wondered if they fancied a barbecue lunch.

Resisting the urge to ask if Paddington Bear fancied marmalade, Mike handed her a pack of raw Merguez sausages and asked if that would do as their contribution.

'So, this seems to be a problem for you,' said Lars, putting a juicy slab of meat on Mike's plate.

'Problem?' said Mike, his mouth going into drool overdrive at the tantalising smell of the barbequed steak. 'I don't think so.'

'What I mean is,' said Lars, 'I got the impression you are not quite delighted about inheriting Monique Lanteine's house.'

'Oh, that. Yes,' said Annie. 'It's to do with having to pay bills for the house here as well as our house in England.'

'And the bills for your England house, are they high?'

'You could say that,' she said. 'Well, certainly compared to the ones here, they are.'

'So you have a very grand house in England?' he said, topping up Annie's wine glass.'

Passing Annie a dish of salad, Carol grinned and said, 'Don't mind him. He's lived on a boat for years, and he wouldn't have a clue about what it costs to own a house anywhere, let alone in Britain.'

'Yeah, well,' said Mike, mopping his plate with a lump of crusty baguette. 'Could you explain tiny terraced house in a grotty street to him?'

'Ah,' said Lars. 'I think that sounds like the one Danny and Tina had.'

'On a par, probably.' Carol nodded. 'Any more wine in that bottle, Lars?'

'Who's Danny and Tina?' asked Annie.

'A young couple from Kent who now live not far from here,' said Carol. 'Come on, dig in, you two. We've got Lars's lemon meringue pie to come as yet.'

'You what!' Mike's mouth fell open before a forkful of steak even reached it. 'We're really expected to eat more than this lot? What on earth is this meat, anyway? It's truly epic.'

'Charolais entrecote,' said Carol. 'Sorry, Annie, what were you saying?'

'I was asking how come this Danny and Tina live here. I mean, you said they were young.'

'Not like us wrinklies, you mean?' Carol grinned.

'I'd hardly call you that,' said Annie.

'Thanks, but I did hit the big five O last year.'

'Really? It doesn't show. I suppose what I meant was, I just associate moving abroad with older people. You know, like people who don't have to worry about jobs anymore.'

'Which you do have to worry about,' said Lars. 'But didn't you tell me you work from home, Mike?'

'He does,' said Annie. 'But I teach at the local comprehensive school. No thanks.' She shook her head at the plate of meat Lars passed her way. 'I'm saving space for that lemon pie thing.'

'Good move,' said Carol. 'Trust me, you won't regret it.'

And she wasn't wrong about that. Declaring she absolutely couldn't manage even a morsel of cheese, Annie leaned back and announced that she was going to find it hard to go back to school canteen lunches next week.

'What sort of teacher are you?' asked Carol.

'A good one, I hope,' said Annie. 'But if you mean what do I teach, English mostly. Except...'

'Except?' Carol prompted.

'Well, a lot of my pupils struggle to even speak English, let alone write it. Would you believe I had to do a TEFL course?'

'I might,' said Carol, 'if I had any idea what one of those is.'

'It's to qualify to teach English as a foreign language.'

'Ah, yes. I seem to remember Tina doing something like that so she could teach English here.'

'Oh? Is that what she does?'

'Some of the time, yes. Apparently it augments what she earns from writing magazine articles and a weekly column for a Kent newspaper.'

At which point, things went on to a different subject which was triggered off by Mike asking if there was such a thing as telly here.

'Sure there is' said Lars. 'This is Burgundy, not another planet.'

'But what about internet?'

With a shrug, Lars asked if that was important.

'You could say that,' said Mike. 'I only rely on it to do my job.'

'Okay,' said Carol. 'I don't pretend to know much about internet, and Lars probably even less. But there's a guy further up the canal who uses it. He's got what he calls wideband or something.'

'Broadband,' said Mike. 'I don't suppose you know how fast it is?'

'Mike, I don't even know *what* it is,' said Carol. 'Right, anyone up for coffee?'

'Think I'll pass, thanks,' said Annie. Turning to Lars she asked if his barge was one of the ones moored near the café. On being told that it was the one called Reiziger, she asked if they ever went anywhere with it.

'Not so much now,' he said. 'But Carol and I will make some trips in the summer months.'

'Oh. So maybe you won't be here next time we come.'

'Next time?' said Mike, throwing a surprised look in her direction. 'Are we planning one of those?'

'Well, it's just that I don't really fancy spending six weeks of summer school holiday in Sheffield, so I thought...'

'Annie, you know I can't take six weeks off work.'

'And you know I can't take six weeks without a break from my mother thinking that, because I just happen to be at home during the day, she can phone at anytime.'

'Okay, I'll vote for that,' said Mike.

'Anyway.' She shrugged. 'I'm not talking about six weeks. I just thought maybe a short…Mike, shall we discuss this another time?'

'Don't worry about us,' said Carol. 'To be honest, I'm interested to hear what Mike has got against the idea of spending time here. I mean, it's not that much of a hell-hole, is it?'

'Compared to August in Sheffield with only a tiny backyard squashed in between other people's backyards, no, it's not,' said Mike. 'I was thinking more on the lines of things like not having electricity and stuff.'

'At least your house up there has got a complete roof,' said Carol. 'Which was more than could be said for this place when I moved in.'

'You're joking, right?' said Annie.

'I kid you not. D'you want to hear about glass missing from windows, no front door and no kitchen sink? Well, no kitchen, actually.'

Looking at Lars, Annie said, 'She is joking, isn't she?'

'I think she is not,' he said. 'But I wasn't here at the beginning, so I can only take her word for it.'

'Which reminds me,' said Carol. 'Lars, did I ever mention the galvanised iron bath I used to ablute in before Lucie and I built the shower room?'

'Yes…but…' Annie still didn't know whether or not to take any of this seriously. 'You did have a loo, didn't you?'

'Sure I did.' Carol grinned. 'There was this sentry box thing in the garden.'

'What did you take away from that?' asked Mike, as they walked back to the house.

'What, apart from about four inches on my waistline and a recipe for homemade lemon meringue pie?'

'What I mean is…'

'Yes, I know what you mean, Mike. What I took away from that is that we're being wimps about the house not having all mod cons.'

'Okay, but Carol did say one of the first things she did was get electricity installed.'

'And you heard what she paid for that?'

'I did.' Putting his arm round her shoulders, he said, 'Annie, if we sold the Peugeot and bought an old banger…'

'Are you serious?'

'Were you serious about spending time here this summer?'

46

'Actually, Mike…' Stopping in front of the house, she said, 'You know what I said about looking on this as our holiday home?'

'Yes, I remember you saying that. So?'

'So, I was joking at the time. But now…'

'Now what?'

'Mike, I wish we didn't have to go home tomorrow.'

'Is that it, then?' said Mike, with his hand on the zip of the bag Annie had packed. 'You sure you haven't forgotten anything?'

'Just that rubbish bag in the kitchen.'

'Right,' he said, closing the zip. 'You're ready, are you? Only we should get going if we want to grab a meal at the café before we drive to Dijon.'

He was loading their bags in the car when Annie said, 'Listen!'

'What?' Clunking his head on the boot lid as he looked up at her, he asked what he was supposed to listen to.

'Shhh.' She flapped a hand at him. 'There, did you hear it?'

'What am I supposed to be hearing, Annie?'

'That,' she said, as a faint meow could be heard coming from the orchard beside the house.

'Okay, so it sounds like a cat,' said Mike. 'Carol and Lars have got three of them, so it's probably one of theirs.'

'Yes, but they did say they don't wander much beyond their garden.'

The plaintive meowing becoming louder as it seemed to be getting closer was too much for Annie. Grabbing the torch from the front seat where Mike had left it so they didn't forget to give it back at the café, Annie shone it towards where the sound was coming from.

'Oh heck,' she said, as a tiny bundle of white fur launched itself at her and wound its skinny body round her legs.

'Oh shit,' said Mike, when she picked it up and cuddled it. 'We haven't got time to do this.'

'But, Mike, it's purring at me.'

'Put it down, Annie. We've got just over an hour to grab something to eat then drive to…what the hell are you doing? I've just put that in.'

'It won't take a minute,' she said, taking the rubbish bag out of the car. 'I'm sure there's a bit of milk left in that carton you chucked out.' Sorting through the bag, she fished out a half empty pâté tin,

47

then scraped the meat onto the doorstep with her finger and emptied the leftover milk into the tin.

'Can we go now?' asked Mike. 'It would be good if we get to Dijon before that bloody bus leaves without us.'

'But, Mike,' she said, prising pâté out of a finger nail with a tissue. 'I promised to tell Lucie if we saw it.'

'Annie, do you want to get back in time for school on Monday?'

'Doncha worry, ducks,' said Liz. 'We'll get Carol ter tell Lucie an she'll sort it, won't she, Gus?'

'Yeah,' said Gus, bending down to put big fluffy omelettes and a dish of salad in front of them. 'That'll do yer, won't it? You don't want ter go eatin anyfin too heavy before bein cramped up on that bus all night, innit.'

Two hours hour later, still trying to get his legs into something that might come close to a comfortable position, Mike said, 'Annie, about that selling the Peugeot and buying an old banger...'

'Yeah, well.' She opened one eye. 'Forget it, Mike. We'll sell the grand piano instead.'

'Huh? What grand piano?'

'The one I bought on ebay last week. Didn't I tell you about that?'

'Annie, get serious, will you?'

'Mike.' She opened the other eye and sat up in her seat. 'I am seriously saying we can't get rid of the car because we'll need it to drive to France in August, won't we? Unless you fancy the journey in an old banger, that is.'

'Well, I sure as hell don't fancy it on a bloody coach again.'

'Precisely. Now would you shut up? Those of us who can would like to get some sleep here.'

'Annie.'

'What?'

'You didn't really buy a piano, did you?'

'Get real, Mike. Where the hell would we have space to put a bloody piano?'

CHAPTER SEVEN

They'd been home a week, and Annie was still trying to adjust to how small their house really was. And had the street always been so noisy and busy with constant traffic? On the other hand, she'd adjusted well enough to hot showers, light switches and a washing machine, hadn't she?

The grey, drizzly weather was another story. Fair enough, they'd had a couple of days during the week in Burgundy when the April weather hadn't been great, but it hadn't been as dismal as this. And living with damp laundry hanging in the bathroom wasn't helping. Sure, she'd said to Mike when he'd pointed out that they had a functional electric tumble drier, but did he realise how much it cost to run that thing?

Gazing out of the kitchen window at rainwater dripping off the clothes line in the tiny back yard, she asked Mike how he felt about half term. Getting nothing more than a grunt, she turned to where Mike's head was bent over some papers and said, 'Are you listening?'

'I am,' he said. 'But I didn't understand the question. What am I supposed to think about half term?'

'About us going to Coulaize.'

'Oh?' He looked up. 'I must have missed that bit.'

'That would be because I didn't say it out loud.'

'So what am I, a mind reader now?'

'Forget it,' she said. 'It was just a thought going round my head.'

'Okay.' He passed a sheet of paper to her. 'What are your thoughts on this?'

She peered at a photocopy picture and said, 'Um...yes...it's a campervan.'

'A small one,' he said.

'Okay, so it's a small campervan with a large hedgehog painted on the side. What about it?'

'Forget the hedgehog and think about this, Annie. It's got a cooker, a chemical loo and – you're going to love this – a mini shower.'

'So? Mike, what's to love about any of that?'

'Depends,' he said, 'on what's to love about driving one of those

49

to France at half term and being able to sleep overnight en route. And...' He paused for effect. 'It's even got a TomTom.'

'A what?'

'A TomTom. You know, one of those sat nav things that hired car had.'

'So what you're saying is, we wouldn't have to rely on me me with a map map.'

'Which, let's face it, Annie, you gotter admit would be good news.'

'True,' she said. 'If it means you not yelling at me every time you take a wrong turning.' Trying not to let her mind go into overdrive about things like having a semi-decent loo and a shower parked in the garden at Coulaize, Annie sat down and said, 'But don't those camper van things cost an arm and a leg?'

'Not twelve-year-old ones like this, Annie. Well, not compared to what a three-year-old Peugeot will fetch.'

'How do you know that?'

'Because some guy told me.'

'What guy?'

'That car dealer in Faulton Road who offered me a generous exchange job yesterday.'

'You mean...like...this camper van you're on about is a few minutes drive away?'

'Yep.' Mike stood up and said, 'Do you want to go and look at it now, or do you want to go and look at it now?'

'Yes, Mike, I want to...Oh, sod it!' she said when the phone rang. 'Now what does she want?'

'It might not be Lillian,' he said. 'I'll answer it, and if it is your mum, I'll tell her you've gone to Tescos.'

'Forget it,' she said, stomping out of the kitchen. 'If I don't deal with it now, she'll only put a stopwatch on how long it takes to do a supermarket shop and call back when she's decided I should be back home.' Grabbing the phone, she said, 'Yes, Mother, what can I do for you?'

Annie listened to the bleat about how her mother had woken up in the night with a panic attack because the kitchen tap was dripping, and how Annie's dad could at least have been expected to come round to fix it because, well, he'd left her to cope on her own when he took off to Norwich with his fancy piece, hadn't he?

Stomping back into the kitchen, Annie said to a startled Mike, 'I don't give a shit what this camper van is like. Just put me in it and drive me away, I so do not need my bloody mother phoning me daily to tell me what a bastard my dad is.'

'Ah,' said Mike. 'Does that mean I'm not the number one villain today?'

'Oh, don't get complacent, Mike. Today's crisis seems to have something to do with Dad, a dripping tap and me living in a poxy terraced house. When – given my background and educational advantages, of course – I shouldn't have ended up with an impoverished artist who isn't in a position to provide anything that even remotely approaches a suitable life for her precious Annestine.'

'Have you done?' he asked. 'If so, Annestine, my precious, allow me to take your arm and escort you to a vehicle with all mod cons which could afford you the life of luxury to which I would like you to become accustomed.'

'I *so* do not need this!' said Annie, slamming her briefcase onto the kitchen table.

'Whoa!' said Mike, moving his laptop to safety. 'What don't you need, Annie?'

'That cow from next door. Not satisfied with doing our heads in with the volume of her bloody telly blasting through the wall, she's now having a go at me about parking the camper van in the street.'

'What? Does she suddenly own parking rights in the street, or what?'

'No, Mike. According to her, what she has the right to do is complain that I parked a couple of feet of the campervan in front of her house.'

'Annie, did you point out that her son often parks his whole car in front of our house?'

'No, I didn't.'

'Why not?'

'Because, Mike, I walked away before the police got involved.'

'Come on,' he said. 'Like the police would be interested in a dispute about who parks whose car where?'

'Let's just say they would have followed up a report of a woman strangling her next-door neighbour.'

'Annie, if she threatened you…'

51

'She didn't. And before you ask, I was the one who left the scene before *she* got strangled.'

'Look, Annie,' said Mike, putting a cup of tea on the table, which he had decided she so did need. 'We've got something a bit wrong here, haven't we?'

'What?' She raised a tear-streaked face and looked at him.

'Well, I've been thinking…'

'Go on.'

'Annie, I'm not sure how to put this,' he said, sitting at the table and grasping her hand. 'But could we just take stock of what we're trying to do here?'

'Which is?'

'Struggle to get by while we hope to someday be able to upgrade to something a bit better than this house.'

'True,' she said, getting up and tearing off a piece of kitchen roll to blow her nose. 'But what choice do we have?'

Instead of immediately answering that question, Mike went into the lounge and returned with a yellow cardboard folder.

'Maybe this is our choice,' he said, placing the folder on the kitchen table.

It can't be denied that, before the decision was eventually reached, it took a lot of discussion over a period of days. Discussion which involved the fact that, while they couldn't sell or rent the house in France, there was nothing to stop them doing either of those things when it came to the Foundry Street house.

If they rented, was Annie's theory, that would cover the mortgage and someone else would pay the council tax. Maybe even give them a few quid income until such time as she might be able to pick up some teaching work.

If they sold, was Mike's argument, they could afford to do whatever was needed to make the French house habitable. Which, obviously, included getting internet broadband connected so he could continue his business.

In the end, a compromise was reached. They would put any final decision on hold until they'd made another trip to Coulaize at half term in Mrs Tiggy Winkle, as Annie had named the campervan. After all, they had swapped a decent car for a slightly tatty campervan with a painted hedgehog on it so they could do that, hadn't they? And, yes, of course Annie was right. It did make sense to go back and check out if they were even seriously considering moving to France.

Except that, as far as Mike was concerned, he'd already ticked that particular box. What he still seriously needed to do, though, was talk to his father about why they'd been given that option at all.

CHAPTER EIGHT

'Ah,' said Norman Flint's voice in Mike's ear. 'So you know about Monique, then.'

'Yes, Dad. I've only inherited her house, haven't I?'

'Oh, so she's died, has she?'

'What do you think? Yes, she's dead, but what I want to know is exactly who she was when she was alive.'

'Look, Son, I don't know what you want me to tell you, but…'

'Dad, I've waited three weeks for you to get back from a bloody fishing trip. Now I've managed to get hold of you, I want you to tell me what I think I probably should have been told years ago.'

'Yeah. Look, Mike, I did think you should be told, but your mother…'

'Who apparently wasn't actually my mother.'

'To all intents and purposes, she was, Mike.'

'Yes, okay.' Mike twisted the phone cable and said, 'Don't get me wrong, Dad. I loved her to bits, and in my heart she'll always be my mum, but that's not what this is about, is it?'

'If it's about Monique's house…'

'Dad…' Trying to keep a grip on his patience, Mike said, 'Sod the house. What I want here is the truth about who I am.'

'Yes, I realise that, Son, but it's complicated.'

'Er, yes, you could say that – Dad…Dad, are you still there?'

'Yes, Mike, I'm still here.'

'Good, because I need you to be there for me on this one.'

His voice sounding a bit unsteady, Norman Flint said, 'I always was there for you, Son. Just like your mum and me were when you were born. And…well…'

'And well what?'

'Michael, if we hadn't been there, you wouldn't be alive now.'

'Sorry I'm late,' said Annie, putting her briefcase on the coffee table. 'There was a staff meeting, and you know how those things…Mike, are you okay?'

'I will be now you're here.' He looked up from the settee where

54

he'd been sitting for the last hour. 'Annie, I spoke to my dad this afternoon.'

'I see.' She sat beside him, placed her hand on his knee and said, 'Okay, Mike, I'm listening.'

'To be honest,' he said, 'I don't quite know where to start with this story.'

'Why not at...sorry, I was going to say at the beginning. But it's your story, so tell it as it comes, hey?'

After taking a deep breath, he said, 'Remember when I said Jean-Claude didn't seem to know anything about Monique Lanteine having a baby?'

'Yes.'

'Well that was because apparently she didn't.'

'So what you're saying, Mike, is that she wasn't your mother after all?'

'No, what I'm saying is she *apparently* didn't have a baby. Except, technically speaking, she did.'

'Um, Mike, I'm not sure I'm following this. Are you saying that, technically speaking, there might have been a baby, and it could have been you she either did or didn't have?'

He looked at her blankly and said, 'Was I supposed to follow that?'

'Sorry. How about I shut up and let you tell me what you want to say?'

Scratching his head, he said, 'I seem to have lost track. How far did we get?'

'Not very, and we still haven't got to the crucial point. Was Monique Lanteine actually your mother or not?'

'Yes, she was. But it was hushed up because she wasn't married and, according to my dad, she threw a total wobbly.'

'What sort of total wobbly?'

After running a hand over his face, he said, 'When I was born, she had this neat idea that the most convenient thing to do would be to kill me and bury the evidence.'

'Mike!' Annie's hand flew to her mouth. 'How – Who – Christ!'

With a weak grin, he said, 'I doubt he had anything to do with it. He probably wasn't there at the time.'

'What! For heaven's sake, man, how can you make stupid jokes at a time like this?'

'I suppose...' He shrugged. 'I suppose because I've had some time to digest it all, and I sort of feel lighter now I've said the worst bit out loud.'

'So that killing you thing *was* the worst bit, then?'

'Well, yes. It does get better after that.'

'Thank Christ for that,' she said. 'And I am talking to that other feller. Um, Mike, I was busting for a pee when I got home. Could we put a hold on the bit that gets better till – Damn!'

'What? You haven't...'

'No, I haven't wet myself, but if that's my mother on the phone, tell her I'll call back.'

Shaking his head at Annie as she came down the stairs a few minutes later, he said, 'Yes, I see, Lillian...Ah, she's here now. Hold on.' Handing the phone to Annie, he winked at her and said, 'A crisis that can't wait.'

Rolling her eyes skywards, Annie took the phone. 'Yes, Mum?...Uhuh...Well, I can see that, but...Look, Mum, I've got stuff going on here, so...No, Mike and I are not having a row, it's to do with his mother...No, I said his mother, not his father...He did what!...For heaven's sake, Mum, Delphine had been dead three years when that happened!'

'Well?' said Mike, dropping tea bags into two mugs when Annie joined him in the kitchen. 'How serious was this one?'

'Deadly,' she said, pulling out a chair and sitting at the table. 'I mean, how can any woman possibly be expected to cope with a broken tumble drier? After all, it is raining in Norfolk.'

Shaking his head, he said, 'Probably just as well we haven't had any kids.'

'Yeah, well, not for want of hoping, was it?'

'Oh god, Annie.' He sat on the other chair and stared at her across the table. 'I'm so sorry. I can't believe I said that.'

'It's okay,' she said. 'I know you didn't say it to be hurtful.'

'All I meant was, two ga-ga grandmothers could pass hereditary stuff on.'

'Oh well.' She gave him a weak grin. 'Let's just hope we both got our fathers' genes. Except...Mike, did you find out anything about your actual father?'

Shrugging, he said he hadn't found out much about anything beyond the fact that his parents had whisked him away and brought him to England. 'To be honest, Annie, I think my brain went sort of numb at that point. Like it wasn't up to taking anything else on board until I'd got my head round what I'd just heard.'

Grabbing his hand to stop it stirring a tea bag round and round in a dry cup, she said, 'I'll put the kettle on, shall I?'

'Sorry.' He turned his hand and squeezed hers. 'I don't think I'm firing on all cylinders right now.'

'Hardly surprising,' she said. 'And we could do without that bloody phone busting a gasket. If you let go of my hand, I'll go and shut it up.'

'No, you do the kettle, I'll get the phone. Dad said he'd probably call back later.'

'Was it him?' she asked when Mike came back shaking his head.

'No, it was your mother wanting to know if you were having your period.'

'Huh?'

'Well, apparently you put the phone down on her rather abruptly.'

'Guilty as charged,' said Annie, waving her hands in the air. 'It was when she got to the bit about your father going off with some American floozie before your mother was hardly cold in her grave.'

'But, Annie…'

'I know, I know,' she said. 'And I did remind her he met Mary-Lou three years later.'

'No, what I was going to say was that my mother was cremated.'

'If that's her,' Annie muttered, getting out of bed, 'I'm going to drive to Norfolk and wrap the effing phone cable round her effing neck!'

'No, you go back to sleep,' said Mike. 'It'll be my Dad calling from Chicago.'

'How do you know?'

'Because, Annie, it's two o'clock in the effing morning.'

Realising that going back to sleep wasn't going to happen, Annie was debating whether or not to go down and put the kettle on when Mike came back and got into bed.

'That was quick,' she said. 'Was it him?'

'Yes, and he wasn't making a lot of sense. He muttered something about being stirred up what with all this coming back at him, and he sounded as if he'd been hitting a bottle.'

'Well, did he say anything that made any sense at all?'

'Some slightly garbled stuff.' Mike ran a hand through his hair. 'About signed agreements and a diary.'

'What diary?'

'My mum's. Apparently she kept a record of everything so I'd know the full story one day.'

'So he's going to send you this diary, is he?'

'No,' said Mike. 'He hasn't got it because he didn't think he should take it to America.'

'So where is it, then?'

'He says he left it with those solicitors who told me about the house and, the thing is...' Putting his arm round her, he said, 'Annie, I'm going to need your help here.'

'Okay,' she said, snuggling into his armpit. 'What do you want me to do?'

'I want you to come with me when I go back and ask that Pinkerton woman why she didn't give me the diary like she was supposed to.'

'Sure, I'll do that. But, Mike, why do you need me to go with you?'

'Because I can't face dealing with her and her damn pearls on my own.'

Mike put the phone down, went into the kitchen and told Annie that Mr Thomas Senior plays golf at Gleneagles for three weeks in May.

'Well bully for him,' said Annie. 'But what's that got do with anything?'

'Basically, it means we're stuffed till he gets back, because he was the one who dealt with my mother's affairs.'

'Which mother?'

'The Delphine one.'

'Okay, but couldn't the Pinkerton woman help?'

'Ah, well there's the rub, see,' said Mike. 'She only dealt with stuff from the Monique one's notaire, and she doesn't know anything about a diary.' Assuming a falsetto voice, he said, 'You see, Mr flint, I only came to Lawson and Thomas in February of this year. And I must ask you to understand that anything in respect of the late Mrs Flint occurred prior to my time.'

'That's it, then.' Annie bent down and unplugged the iron. 'You won't need this shirt to look respectable for Miss Pinkerton.'

Plugging the iron back in, he said, 'You may as well finish it so it's ready for the appointment I've got booked for when we get back from France.'

'Fair enough.' Attacking the second sleeve of Mike's second best shirt, she said, 'Do you need me to hold your hand for that?'

'If it's safe to assume Mr Thomas Senior doesn't have pearls wrapped round his left mammary gland,' said Mike, 'I can probably manage him on my own.'

CHAPTER NINE

It was all systems go for the half term week in Coulaize. The main issue being if Tiggy's systems were up to the trip. But then, as the dealer who'd persuaded Mike to take the campervan and some cash in exchange for the Peugeot had said, the VW had run sweetly for twelve years for the previous owners, hadn't it?

Mike would probably have felt more confident if the info on offer hadn't included the fact that said previous owners had hammered it through Africa. But there you go – if the vehicle could make it from Egypt to Cape Town, not to mention its previous trek through India, what was to say it couldn't manage Northern England to Burgundy?

Eschewing the idea of even a short break in a lay-by beside the M25, they decided to get to France before taking a rest stop. Albeit that, out of deference for Annie's nerves, the Channel Tunnel was also decided against in favour of a two hour ferry crossing. So it was that, by one o'clock in the morning, they were happily snuggled in to what the French call an aire de repos. Which, basically speaking, means they pulled off an auto-route, tucked the van behind some trees and slept for a few hours before travelling on to Coulaize.

'It's purring,' said Alfie, kneeling beside Lucie in the long damp grass and stroking the little white cat in the late Monique Lanteine's garden. 'Don't that mean it's happy?'

'You must say doesn't that mean it is happy,' said Lucie, wagging a finger at the eight-year-old English boy. 'We must all the time speak good English, Alfie.'

'Yeah.' He shrugged. 'Me mum's always on about that an all. But I still reckon that cat's happy.'

'That is because we are here.' Lucie picked up the purring bundle and cuddled it. 'I think when she is by her own, she is sad.'

'Then why don't…why doesn't she stay with you at your farm?'

'This I do not know,' said Lucie. 'I know only that she likes for me to come with food.'

'You been doing that all along, have you?'

'On all days from since Carol is say the English people have seen her.'

'Few weeks, then.' He nodded. 'Lucie, how do you know it's a her?'

'Poof, is easy. She does not have the little balls.'

Saying his mum would have his for garters if he didn't get going, Alfie gave the cat's head a quick stroke and went off round the side of the house. He then came running back and hissed, 'There's a van come. If it's those English people, they might tell us off for being in their garden.'

'Merde,' said Lucie, getting to her feet and pointing to a way out through the orchard. 'Vite, vite.'

But before they had a chance to escape, Annie came round the side of the house and called out, 'Hi there, Lucie. Oh, you've got the cat!'

'That's likely saved us getting bawled out,' muttered Alfie. As if to guarantee it would exonerate him from trespassing, he plucked the cat from Lucie's arms and held it up.

Annie was exclaiming about how pleased she was it was okay, and how much it had grown, when Mike appeared and asked what was going on.

'We've got a lovely welcome committee,' said Annie. A cat, a Lucie and a young man who hasn't told me his name yet.'

'He is Alfie,' said Lucie.

'Bonjour, Alfie. Je suis Annie.'

'He can speak English,' said Lucie. 'He is coming from Kent.'

'I see.' Annie smiled at the boy and said, 'So maybe he can speak for himself?'

'Yeah, well, she's bossy like that,' said Alfie. Passing the cat to Annie, he said, 'Pleased to meet you, but I got to go now.'

'Oh,' said Mike, looking at Alfie legging it across the garden. 'I hope I didn't scare him away.'

With a giggle, Lucie said, 'He is anxious he is late to home, and his mama will have his balls for graters.'

'Um, Lucie,' said Annie, 'I think you mean she'll have his guts for garters.'

A frown marring her cute little face, Lucie stared up at Annie and said, 'What is guts?'

After listening to Annie's explanation about both guts and garters, Lucie said that this she had not learned at school. Before sprinting off home, presumably to avoid the fate that awaited Alfie, she gave strict instructions that, as the cat had had food today, it must not have anymore until tomorrow. But, oui, a little milk with water was permitted because that would not make the problem for its guts.

As the little cat clawed its way up her chest and patted her chin, Annie turned to gaze across the meadows to the distant hills bathed in afternoon sunshine and said, 'That's it, then, Mike. We seem to have got ourselves a horrible cat as well as an awful view.'

'Yep.' Draping an arm round her shoulders, Mike poked the cat's head with a tentative finger and said, 'I'd say we're stuffed, wouldn't you?'

When they'd been at home discussing the possibility of moving to France, it had been quite easy for Annie to be objective. To be sensible, even. After all, there were things to be considered. Like her job, for example. And you didn't give up a regular salary lightly, did you? Then there was...

What was it now? Annie was buggered if she could remember.

After lifting the cat off his lap and putting it on the ground yet again, Mike brushed grass off his notebook and said, 'Seems like this electrician guy is the way to go. According to Liz, he's handy wiv the amps, is Victor.'

'And according to Gus, he does a good job for not a lot of dosh,' said Annie. 'So that leaves the Danny bloke's estimate for the plumbing. What d'you reckon, then?'

Putting the calculator and notebook on the garden bench, Mike said, 'What I reckon is, we should put the rabbit hutch on the market as soon as we get back.'

'So we're sure about that, are we?'

'Annie, was there ever any doubt?'

'Well, just a smidgen. Which is why I asked Hilary to hold on till we got back.'

'Hold on to what?'

'That envelope I – Oi, you!' She bent down and scooped up the cat to stop it nibbling her bare toes.

'Um, Annie, what envelope?'

'The one with my resignation in it.'

'You what!' Mike stared at her. 'Are you saying you've already done it?'

'Well, if I want to be free before the next school year begins in

September, I have to give notice by the end of May, don't I?'

'That's blown it then,' he said, slumping back against the bench. 'We don't get back till the beginning of June.'

'Precisely.'

'What the hell does that mean? Have you resigned, or have you resigned?'

'In theory. Pass me the bottle, will you?'

'Wait,' he said, grabbing the wine bottle and putting it between his legs. 'Not till you've explained "in theory" to me.'

'Mike, didn't you hear what I said about a letter I've given Hilary?'

'Yes, Annie, I did hear you say you gave one to her last week, but – Ah!'

'Great,' she said. 'I do believe you've just had what is called a *duh* moment. Can I have that wine now?'

'In a minute,' he said, removing a bundle of white fur from her arms. 'There's something I need to do first.'

It was actually rather more than a minute before they surfaced, and Annie got her lips back so she could suggest that Mike go and fetch another bottle to replace the one that was dripping its contents down his legs.

Still not confident that he could get an adequate Internet setup in this remote situation, Mike asked at the Carryon Café if they used it.

'The DDTs is the ones you want ter talk wiv about that,' said Liz.

'Oh,' said Mike. 'Is that the company who supplies Internet here?'

'Nah, that'd be France Telecom, I reckon. But I do know Don and Dora Turner have got it, so best ter talk to them, innit.'

With assurance that the Turners wouldn't mind a bit if they just turned up, Liz directed them to Maison Lavande. 'It's furver up the canal and round a bend,' she said. 'But yer can't miss it.'

Sniffing the air through the open van window as they rounded a bend, Annie said, 'She was right about that can't miss it thing. I can smell lavender from here.'

Even without that as a clue, they would have recognized Maison Lavande by the colour of the door and shutters. And the woman who looked to be in her sixties who was weeding the front garden raised a head of blue-rinsed hair that blended beautifully with the immaculate paintwork of her chocolate box cottage.

'Crikey,' muttered Mike, as he stopped the van. 'She looks like one of those woman from that Lavender and Old Lace film.'

'Mike, I'm not sure about dropping in without an appointment,' said Annie. 'This all looks a bit posh and formal.'

But before they had a chance to bottle it, Dora Turner came towards them calling, 'Hello there. I do hope you're coming in to join us in a drink.'

'Well that sounds friendly enough,' said Mike, getting out of the van. Leaving Annie to follow, he walked towards the woman and took her outstretched hand. 'Hello, I'm Mike.'

'And you must be Annie,' said Dora, clasping Annie's hand with both of her own. 'We've heard about you, of course, and we were hoping to get to meet you this time.'

'Well, actually,' said Annie. 'I hope you don't mind, but Liz at the Café Carillion suggested you might be able to help about Internet.'

'Mind? Good gracious no.' She smiled at Mike and said, 'Mind you, I know nothing about Internet, but you'll find Don in his study.' Taking Annie's arm and leading the way onto the terrace, she said, 'You and I shall leave them to it while we get to know each other.'

With a crystal glass of white wine in her hand – at eleven in the morning, for heaven's sake! – Annie commented on how friendly people were around here.

'They are,' agreed Dora. 'We're particularly fond of Carol and Lars, of course.'

'Yes,' said Annie. 'I have to admit we were disappointed to find they're away at the moment.'

'Cruising, lucky things. Down the Rhone, I believe.'

'Oh? They'll be gone all summer, will they?'

'No, no.' Dora took the bottle of Chardonnay out of the ice bucket. 'Too hot for the cats in the South, so they'll be back in August. Top up, dear?'

'Thanks, no.' Annie put a protective hand over her glass. 'I'm not good at drinking in the morning.'

'It takes time to get used to it,' said Dora with a grin. 'Ah, sounds like the boys are about to join us.'

'Well?' said Annie, when the two men came out of the house. 'Are we in business?'

'I should say so,' said Mike. 'Not only has Don told me it took less than a week to have his telephone and Internet connected, he demonstrated how fast his own broadband system is. Annie, you won't believe how fast my website came up on Don's computer.'

'A very professional website,' said Don, moving a pale mauve cushion before lowering his large frame into a wicker chair. 'I must say, I was most impressed.'

'And I must say you've got a beautiful home,' said Annie, gazing at the immaculate garden where a lavender-lined path led to the canal beyond the neatly-trimmed hedge.

'They met here, you know,' said Dora.

'Sorry?' Annie looked at her.

'Carol and Lars. He moored his barge at the bottom of the garden, Carol was having lunch with us and – poof!'

'Poof?'

'Absolutely. Coup de foudre, you could say.'

'What!' said Annie. 'You're not telling me they were struck by lightening?'

'As good as.' Dora smiled. 'If that's what you call a flash of instant attraction. Now tell me, are you two young people planning to come and live permanently in our lovely part of Burgundy?'

'Just as soon as we can,' said Mike. 'There's stuff to attend to back home, but we'll be back at least for a visit in a few weeks.'

Lucie promised that, until they returned, she would continue looking after Perdue. Well, what else could she have called a cat that was lost? And how could Annie and Mike change the name the flipping cat had come running to the weeks when Lucie had come to feed it?

In fact, as Annie pointed out, the name was a bit sort of symbolic of how she and Mike would have stayed lost in the Sheffield jungle if it hadn't been for the enigmatic Monique Lanteine.

And, as Mike said, the enigma might well turn out to be less of one once he'd collected his mother's diary from the golf-playing Mr Thomas Senior of Lawson and Thomas.

Of course, they still had to break the news to Annie's mother that her constant phone calls were going to involve the cost of reaching a French number. But what the heck – were they going to lose any sleep over that?

CHAPTER TEN

After sliding a kitchen knife under a wax seal on a large brown envelope, Mike tipped the contents onto the coffee table.

The awaited diary turned out to be a leather-bound book covering five years, and Mike skim-read the early entries about his parents' wedding, Delphine's first home in England and her nursing training at Leeds Infirmary. He then skipped to the following year when he was born. Which was when he learned that Monique had had an affaire d'amour with a married man she had refused to name. Entries in Delphine's hand spoke of her sister suffering from dépression nerveuse, and how Delphine had travelled to France to help her parents deal with the situation in the latter stages of Monique's pregnancy.

Entries dating from a few days before Mike's birth told of everyone's increasing concern over Monique's mental health. And how, in answer to his wife's panic-stricken phone call, Norman had driven from Leeds to France overnight, arriving in time to hold Monique down while Delphine cut the cord Monique was frantically trying to use to strangle her new born baby. Several subsequent pages were blank, and no further entry appeared until ten days later, when it was recorded that Delphine and Norman were back home, and had registered Michael's birth in Leeds.

Thanks, Mum. Mike ran a shaking hand through his hair. *Dad wasn't kidding when he said you and he had always been there for me.*

Putting the partially-read diary aside, Mike turned to the other papers on the table. *Right, Dad, let's see what these agreements you mentioned are about…*

'Okay, so it's making some sort of sense,' said Annie, looking up from the signed agreement Mike had handed her when she got home. 'I get the thing about your parents insisting that Monique was never able to make any claim on you.'

'And this one?' He handed her another paper, signed by both Monique and Delphine. This one being an agreement that, although the Lanteine's house was left to both daughters, Delphine had

66

relinquished any claim to it on condition that Michael would eventually inherit the property.

'That seems fair enough,' said Annie. 'But it doesn't say anything about you not being allowed to sell it for five years, does it?'

'Well, I don't suppose my mum would have agreed to that, so…'

'So,' said Annie. 'This crafty Lanteine dame slipped it into her will without your mum knowing. But why would she do that?'

'Search me.' Mike shrugged. 'And there's something else this lot hasn't explained,' he said, gathering up all the paperwork and pushing it back into the large brown envelope. 'I still don't know why, if my birth mother was my mum's sister, it says Delphine Flint née Labois on my birth certificate.

'Well, your dad will know the answer to that one, won't he?'

'True, but I didn't think of it last time I spoke to him. And would you believe he's gone incommunicado again? Visiting Mary-Lou's sister in Texas this time.'

'Oh well, you'll find out in time. Is it very important to you?'

'Not crucially. Except…'

'Now what?' said Annie, when he stood up and went to stare out of the window.

'Annie, I'm still not convinced those solicitors got the right Michael Flint.'

'Yeah, right,' she said. 'Could be one of those cases you read about, when some nurse gets name tags mixed up in a maternity hospital and two mothers leave with the wrong babies.'

'What's that supposed to mean?'

'Come on, Mike. Like your mum was there when you were born, stopped you being murdered, then left with the wrong you?'

Turning from the bleak outlook of the backs of houses their kitchen window afforded, he said, 'It is ours, Annie, isn't it?'

'What is?'

'That house in Coulaize.'

'Yes.' Going to him and putting her hand on his shoulder, she said, 'Trust those solicitors, Mike, the house is absolutely legally yours.'

Shaking his head as he pulled her to him, he said, 'It's just that, sometimes, I lie awake at night and wonder if it's just a dream.'

'Well…' Snuggling against his chest, she said, 'It could turn out to be a nightmare, but we've got to give it a whirl, haven't we?'

'Does that include the cat?'

67

'What? Are you talking nightmare or whirling it?'

'Annie, I've never had a cat before.'

'So? You don't even like cats.'

'I know, but I just bloody well hope the little sod is still there when we get back.'

The offer for number 77 Foundry Street was close to the asking price, and the even better news was that the newlywed couple were in a hurry to take possession before the baby was born. Well, they would be, given that, as Kylie told them when they came back to measure for curtains and stuff, 'No one woun't believe what bloody purgatry it is livin with his mother.'

When Gaz and Kylie had left after saying they'd deffo take on whatever furniture was left behind, and they was ever so grateful about the curtains bein left, Mike looked at Annie and said, 'Talking of mothers from hell, have you told Lillian yet?'

'No.'

'Um, don't you think it's time?'

'What, to boldly go where no daughter has gone before, you mean?'

'Annie, stop putting it off. Do it, and do it now.'

'Tell you what, Mike,' she said, grabbing the hall phone. 'Why don't I do it now?'

'I'll be in the kitchen ready to pick up the pieces when you've done.'

'Coward – Oh, hi, Mum, it's Annie.'

'Annestine? Good gracious, you hardly ever phone me.'

'Well, that's because…'

'Of course, I should have realized your father would get his version in first.'

'Mum, I'm not calling about him. And thanks for asking, yes, I'm fine.'

'That's rather more than can be said for me. Would you believe what he's done now?'

'Probably not. But, Mum, I've got something to tell you.'

'Of course, I blame that woman of his because she…'

'Mum. Shut up for a minute, would you?'

'Well, really, Annestine. There's no need to jump down my throat.'

'Mum, we've sold the house.'

'So it's come to that, then. I always knew it would, but make sure you get your rightful share, is all I can say.'

'Mum, it's not about rightful shares, it's…'

'As you know, Annestine, when your father left me, he…'

'MOTHER!'

'There's no need to shout, Annestine.'

'Okay. Sorry. But are you listening, Mum?'

Sniff.

'We've sold the house because we're moving to France.'

'What! Have you gone mad?'

'No, Mother, I think what we've done is opt for a route with a flipping sanity sign on it.'

With all credit for Annie's self control, she didn't slam down the phone at that point. It was, in fact, at least twenty seconds later when she walked into her kitchen, sat at the table and banged her head on it.

Not daring to put the glass he was holding on the table, Mike said, 'How did she take it?'

'Don't even ask.'

'That bad, hey?'

'To be honest, Mike, I didn't hear most of it.'

'Really? Even from here I could almost hear what she was saying.'

'Yes, well…' Annie raised her head, grabbed the glass from his hand and took a large gulp of the French red they'd brought back in the campervan. 'That would be because I was holding the phone in the air so it didn't do my head in.'

The trip to Norfolk to say goodbye to Annie's parents was something they had to do. But, as Mike said, the look on Lillian's face when they turned up in the campervan was worth the 150 mile drive. When Lillian suggested they park the van round the corner, Annie said Mrs Tiggy would be fine where she was because it would only be parked in front of Lillian's house a couple of hours while they had lunch, wouldn't it?

Actually, they managed an hour and twenty minutes before, thanking Lillian for the bowl of soup, Mike said they had to get on if they were going to have a bit of time with Annie's dad. And, yes, of course they weren't going to leave the country without saying goodbye to him and Maureen as well.

'Well at least *she* won't be there,' said Lillian. 'Tesco cashiers work on Saturdays, don't they?'

Refraining from reminding her that Maureen was actually a manager at Waitrose, Annie kissed her mother briefly on each rouged and powdered cheek before leaving. She even managed to keep her mouth shut about the comment that she'd already picked up fancy French ways with this stupid kissing both sides of the face affectation.

It was with warm hugs all round that they were greeted at Maureen and Graham's flat. And their exclamations over how idyllic the house in France looked far outweighed Lillian's refusal to even look at photos of some ridiculous French house. Several hours later, after an enjoyable dinner Maureen had taken the afternoon off to prepare, Mike and Annie decided they should get going if they wanted to get back to Sheffield before midnight.

'We'll be thinking of you,' said Graham, releasing his daughter from a bear hug. 'Be happy in your new life.'

'As happy as you and Maureen are in yours, I hope,' said Annie.

'Yes, well, you know how things were with your mother and me.'

'Yes, Dad, I do know.' Turning to kiss Maureen's plump shiny face, she said, 'Don't let her take advantage, hey?'

'She's not so bad really,' said Maureen.

'Liar.' Annie grinned and hugged her. 'Why do you think I left home as soon as I could?'

As he negotiated his way through Norwich, Mike said, 'What I don't get is why they're living in that little flat while your mother has that flipping great house to herself.'

'Trust me. You don't want to know,' said Annie.

'But isn't a divorce settlement supposed to be a fifty-fifty split of all marital assets?'

'Look, Mike, my dad opted to escape the marital horror scene and grab a life of happiness. Compared to what he and Maureen have got, it's hardly surprising they were content to leave the assets grabbing to Lillian.'

'Fair enough.' He changed gear and looked for a gap in order to join the stream of Saturday evening traffic thundering up the motorway. 'If we're talking quality of life here, I'm up for grabbing a chance to live without so much bloody traffic.'

Raising a reverse victory sign to the driver who hooted as Mike slipped into the gap in front of a lorry, Annie sighed and said, 'Just think. This time next week, all this and next-door's telly will be history.'

Annie's last day at the school where she'd worked for four years turned out to be a bit emotional. The staff room leaving gift came as no surprise. After all, she'd contributed to plenty of whip-rounds for numerous teachers who hadn't been able to hack the difficulties involved in a large, inner-city, multi-cultural comprehensive school.

It was the handmade presents and cards from the kids in her class that had made it hard to focus through the moisture Annie somehow couldn't stop forming in her eyes. Okay, she hadn't got a clue what Damien's lump of painted papier-mâché was supposed to represent. But the fact that Damien, the most belligerent class thug, had made it for her, seemed to suggest she'd somehow got through to him. Respect wasn't something the fourteen-year-old lad knew much about, but it didn't stop him giving her a high-five and saying that she'd "bin a bit of a ace teacher".

The messages in most of the cards were written in English, albeit sometimes misspelled English. Others contained sentences consisting of some English words mixed in with words from other languages. Maybe Jameela from Algeria was being a lazy sod by not attempting to write in English at all, or maybe, given the circumstances, she'd deliberately chosen to use her native French language. Whatever – when you were about to nervously go and live in that language, wasn't getting a card saying "Bonne chance et bon courage" the sort of message you'd need at a time like this?

Kylie and Gaz had not been joking about gasping to move out of his mum's place. But then, as Gaz had said when he'd knocked on the door of number 77 Foundry Street the day before they were due to move in, they didn't want to miss the chance of a mate offering to deliver their bits and bobs, did they? So, if they didn't mind, like, would it be okay to dump their stuff now?

'No problem,' said Mike, looking at a garishly painted Transit van parked fully in front of next-door's front window. 'Take your time, I'll put the kettle on.'

And it wasn't as if Annie and Mike minded being restricted to the kitchen with an interior wall between them and next-door's telly belting out the East Enders theme tune. Although, judging by what was cluttering up the lounge, Kylie and Gaz didn't seem to own a lot of stuff. It would have been no big deal to move the ghetto blaster Gaz had dumped on the settee that he and Kylie "was thrilled to bits about bein left". It was more a case of there not being a lot of room to move in the lounge on account of the set of drums.

Standing in the lounge doorway after a last fish'n'chips supper, Annie raised a glass to the dividing wall between her and her neighbour's television and said, 'Bonne chance et bon courage.'

CHAPTER ELEVEN

'Underneath the spreading walnut tree,' sang Annie, raising her arms as if to embrace the over-hanging branches when they turned on to the track.

'You've changed your tune.' Mike grinned at her.

'No I haven't,' she said. 'That's the tune my dad taught me when I was a kid. Except it was a chestnut tree we used to sing about.'

'So, we like trees now, do we?' he asked, as he brought Tiggy to a stop in front of their new home.

'What's not to like. Oh, look, Mike, some of the orchard trees are full of flowers.' Getting out of the van, she flexed her stiff knees and breathed in the scent of apple blossom and freshly cut grass.

Freshly cut grass! How did that happen? It had been nearly knee-high the last time they'd seen it. And the fluffy white bundle that crept cautiously towards them between heaps of grass had been half the size it now was.

Sitting cross-legged in the grass, Annie stretched out a hand. A hand that the cat first sniffed then licked before climbing into Annie's lap. Mike of the *I don't even like cats* squatted down and said, 'Hi there, Perdue. We're pleased to see you too, and this time we're here to stay.'

'We've done it, Mike,' said Annie, clutching his arm. 'We've bloody done it.'

'Not quite,' he said. 'We still have to get the van unloaded.'

'Sod that.' Getting to her feet with a purring Perdue clutched in her arms, she said. 'I just want to look around and take on board the fact that we're really here.'

'Sure.' Hugging her, he said, 'Garden or house first?'

'House, I think. Let's go and open all the shutters and windows and let this wonderful air in.'

By the time Mike had got the casement doors to the garden open, Annie had collected a bottle they'd left in the kitchen for just this occasion and had wiped a tea towel round a couple of dusty glass tumblers. What did it matter that it was only four in the afternoon? That garden bench out there in the August sunshine was beckoning, and they could empty the van later, couldn't they?

It wasn't as if it was much beyond some bags of clothes and boxes of books and personal items they had to bring in to the house. After all, there had seemed little point in shifting furniture from England when they'd got a fully furnished house waiting for them to move in to. Besides which, the look on Gaz and Kylie's faces had been a joy to behold when they'd been asked if it was okay with them if any of the furniture was left.

Although, in the anticipation of eventually having the electricity to run them, they had brought the fridge and washing machine. And Gaz and his heavily-tattooed mate had come in well handy when it came to loading those in to the campervan. Now all Annie and Mike had to do was work out how to unload them at this end, but the answer to that came a couple of hours later in the form of Lars turning up with an insulated cool box.

Handing the box to Annie, he told her the dish inside had only just come out of the oven, so would stay hot for a while until they were ready to eat. He then asked if there was anything he could do while he was here.

'Well, if your body is on offer…' said Mike, and went to open the back door of the van.

While sharing a welcome to their new home drink with them, Lars told them it was probably Jean-Claude who had been responsible for the grass being cut.

'Really?' said Annie. 'Why would he do that?'

'That's JC for you,' said Lars with a shrug. 'Apparently he used to send one of his men to do it for Monique.'

'Looks like we've got ourselves some good neighbours here,' said Mike, thanking him again for his help. 'Annie and I would have seriously struggled to get the fridge and washing machine unloaded.'

'And thanks for whatever is in that cool box,' said Annie. 'That's really kind of you.'

After he'd left, Annie opened the cool box, inhaled the heady aroma of bouef bourguignon and said, 'Oh my god! I hardly know the man, but I think I'm in love.'

It was Mike's turn to go jelly-kneed and gaze adoringly at an engineer who arrived soon after ten in the morning. Fair enough, Mellisa of France Telecom was an attractive young lady, but it was more to do with Mike not really believing his arrangements made online from England were going to pull off a connection to the world within forty-eight hours of them arriving.

Mind you, he was a bit taken aback to see a man attaching overhead cables to what looked like a new telegraph pole. Mellisa, whilst assuring him this was normal, did advise that it was a good idea to disconnect the Internet box when lightening was around. Sadly, though, she informed him, the box and actual connection to Internet would not arrive for maybe two days. Which was a sadness Mike felt he could probably take in his stride.

'Bugger, that was quick,' said Annie, when Mellisa packed her tool box and departed, leaving them with dangling wires.

'Yep,' said Mike, grinning like a loon and fingering the wires. 'What we need to do now is go and buy a telephone to go on the end of one of these. Just think, you'll be able to phone your mum and give her our number.'

'On your bike, Mike. I told her it would be weeks before we got a phone installed. Although it would be nice to let my dad know how to contact us.'

'Right, so we'll do it now,' he said. 'I gather we can pick up a phone at a hypermarket this side of Dijon.'

'Can we buy a microwave oven as well?' she asked. 'I still don't trust that gas affair.'

'Um, Annie,' said Mike. 'These are telephone wires, not electric cables.'

'I know that, idiot. But that handy with the amps Victor bloke did say he'd be here Thursday, didn't he?'

'And you believe that?'

'Why not? When I took the cool box and casserole dish back, Carol said he turned up the day he'd told her he would. And, by the way, she also said he was a bit tasty.'

'What the devil does that have to do with anything?'

'Oh, nothing.' She grinned. 'Just that you had your treat today with the tasty Mellisa, so it's only fair I get my turn on Thursday.'

Which turned out to be fair comment. Victor of the amps was not someone any normal woman would kick out of bed. In fact, the gap between his jeans and his tee-shirt as he crawled along with his bum in the air clipping wires in place was what you might call a tad too distracting.

Grinning at Annie, Mike reminded her that Carol had promised to show her how to get to the nearest supermarket.

'Shit, yes.' Annie looked at her watch. 'I said I'd be at her place at ten, and it's five past now.'

'You'd better move it then,' said Mike. 'You can probably trust me to be left alone with this young feller.'

Leaving Mike designing business cards with his new contact details, Annie got into Carol's ancient Vauxhaull estate and said, 'Oh, you drive a right-hander as well.'

'Yep,' said Carol. 'It's about all that's left of my former Essex life.'

'Do you miss it?'

'What's to miss about Essex? Why? Do you think you'll miss Sheffield?'

'Like I'd miss a verruca,' said Annie. 'Except I at least knew where to go shopping. Once the plumber and the water board have done their job, we'll need to buy bathroom stuff. And we're going to need shedloads of paint.'

'Castorama,' said Carol. 'My mate, Glynis, is addicted to the place.'

'Okay,' said Annie. 'I'll deal with that one stage at a time. What is Castorama, and who is Glynis?'

'Casto is where to go for your stuff. Glynis was my next-door neighbour in that former life I mentioned.'

'Oh. Do you miss her?'

'I did when I first came here, but she and her husband bought a holiday place a few miles away, so we see each other a few times a year. Actually, she's keen to meet you.'

'Yeah. Right.' Annie looked at a woman she already regarded as a mate in this strange new life and said, 'So what's this Glynis like?'

'They'll be coming next week, so you'll be able to judge for yourself,' said Carol. 'But I'll tell you one thing. Any mention of needing paint and bathroom equipment and she'll be on your case and whisking you off to Casto Rambo, as she calls it.'

'That sounds good,' said Annie. 'There's no rush because this Danny plumber guy can't start for a couple of weeks, but we'd really appreciate it if your friend is prepared to show us where this Casto place is.'

'You can bet on it.' Carol grinned as she turned into a supermarket car park. 'That treat is yet to come, but today you get to be introduced to our answer to Sainsburys or Tescos.'

Spoilt for choice with Atac's selection of unfamiliar food, Annie walked round the aisles like a fart in a trance for several minutes. Then, getting her act together, she started to load a basket with whatever looked tempting. So hard, though, to resist the meats and cheeses on display. But good sense kicked in, she remembered they didn't yet have electricity to run a fridge, so she settled for things like tins of duck cassoulet and escargots.

Not that she or Mike had ever eaten snails, but what the heck. Time to live dangerously, or what?

'Ah,' said Lars, when Carol got home after delivering Annie and her shopping and saying a quick *nice to see you again* hello to Victor of the delectable bum. 'You missed a phone call from Glynis.'

'Bugger. Was she calling about anything important?'

'Very important. To do with crumpets for you and Bovril for me.'

'Lovely,' said Carol, opening the fridge to put the perishable shopping items away.

'Shouldn't that be lovely, lovely, lovely?'

'Stop it, Lars. Glynis doesn't do that triplicate speech thing anymore.'

'You think?' he said, moving a cat away from the bag of meat it was sniffing. 'She did say she'd brought three jars of Bovril.'

'It's okay, Bovril,' said Carol, stroking the black cat. 'It's not you he's going to eat on toast. Anyway, Lars, don't you mean she's *going* to bring three jars?'

'Are you questioning my understanding of English?' he said.

'Yeah, right, like anyone would do that. But Glynis and Ken aren't coming till next week.'

'Okay.' He stroked his beard and said, 'So maybe I did misunderstand when she said they are here.'

'What! Did she say they are here, as in actually here in France?'

'No.' He grinned. 'She said, and I quote: "Tell Carol we're here, we're here, we're here".' As the phone started to ring, he said, 'That's probably her now, now...'

'Shut up, man, and deal with that bag of meat before Bovril does.'

Grabbing the phone, Carol said, 'Do I say hello or bonjour?'

'What you say,' said Glynis's voice, 'is welcome to France.'

'Well, yes, I'm always pleased to welcome you and Ken to my

world. But I've done that a few times already, haven't I?'

'Not like this time, Carol.'

'Okay, so what's different about this time?'

'The difference is, this time it's sort of permanent.'

'What the hell does that mean?'

'Carol, I'm talking about us being here to stay, stay, stay. We've moved everything we need from Billericay and we're now officially residents of our house in Maiseronne.'

'You sneaky sod!'

'Funny, that's more or less what Ken said you would say.'

'Well, he's not wrong there. Come on, Glynis, the last I heard you were due out here next week for a month.'

'Aren't you even a little bit pleased?'

'No, Glynis. What I am is over the moon.'

'Yes, Ken got that bit right as well. It's just that…'

'What?'

'He thinks I haven't brought enough crumpets for you.'

When Carol eventually put the phone down and went into the kitchen, Lars opened the fridge door and said, 'Oh good, you've stopped squealing at last. I was beginning to think about starting this without you.'

Looking at the condensation on the obviously well-chilled champagne bottle in his hand, she said, 'You knew, didn't you?'

'What, that you'd quite like cold champers before lunch?'

'Lars, we never have champagne in the house. When did you buy that?'

'Last week, when Glynis phoned and threatened to slit my throat if I breathed a word to you.'

Taking a glass from Lars before the content carried out its threat to bubble even more over his hand, Carol said, 'Are you okay about this?'

'What?' He licked his hand. 'Would you be okay about someone saying they'd slit your throat?'

'I'd be okay with a full glass of this,' she said, draining what little had remained below the bubbles eruption. 'No, let me pour this time.'

'Nice one,' said Lars, raising his properly replenished glass and clinking it with hers. 'Here's to our friends who have come to live nearby.'

'So you are okay about it, then?'

'Why wouldn't I be?'

'Well, you know what Glynis is like…'

'Yes,' he said. 'And I know I like her.'

'They are, aren't they?'

'They are what?'

'Our friends,' she said. 'Not just mine.'

'Is Bovril my cat, and Sue Ellen and Rupert are yours? Or are they *our* cats?'

'That little devil,' said Carol, pointing to where Bovril was dragging a steak across the floor, 'is definitely yours.'

'No, Carol, I think that is your steak. You left the bag of meat on the floor.'

'Which I asked you to put away. Never mind.' She held up her glass. 'Enjoy Lars's steak, Bovril. I'm drinking to the closest thing I ever had to a sister coming to live a few miles away in the same country as me.'

Annie was unpacking the shopping when Mike sauntered into the kitchen and said, 'Shame you were out when your mum called.'

'Yeah, like hell she did.' Holding up a tin, she said, 'You okay with snails on toast for lunch?'

'I might be if we had any way to make toast.'

'Good point,' she said. 'When we've got working amps we'll have to get a toaster.'

'Annie, we have got a working phone.'

'Oh yes, so we have. Lobster soup do you? We can heat that on Tiggy's gas ring.'

'It's spooky,' said Mike.

'What, Tiggy's gas ring?'

'Not having Lillian call at least once a day.'

'Well, enjoy it while it lasts, hey?'

'Annie, you have told her our number, haven't you?'

'Hmm. How do you fancy this with lobster soup?' She held up a crusty baguette.

'Fine,' he said. 'How do you fancy giving your mother a ring?'

'Now that's not a good idea, Mike. Seeing as I wrote and told her we wouldn't be likely to have a phone installed for a few weeks.'

'Come on, Annie. What if she has an emergency?'

'What, like a dripping tap, you mean?' Handing him a tin of soup and a tin opener, she said, 'Look, if anything goes wrong in my mother's life, my dad will be the first to hear. And before you ask, yes, he has got our phone number. So how was your morning?'

'Okay,' he said, tipping soup into a saucepan. 'I got the new business cards done, but I'm not happy with the address.'

'What's wrong with it?'

'Well.' He shrugged. 'All we've got is 21304 Coulaize, which sounds a bit like a PO Box or something. Just doesn't have a professional ring to it somehow.'

'Good point,' she said. 'How about you add a house name?'

Over lunch, they tossed around ideas, trying to come up with something that sounded fairly businesslike. Cherry Blossom was dismissed as being too twee. Orchard Lodge was maybe a bit pretentious. In the end, it was Annie who came up with the suggestion that the huge walnut tree at the entrance to the track could come into it.

So it was that what had always been known to the indigenous villagers as the Lanteine's house, and latterly, old Monique's place, became Walnut House.

CHAPTER TWELVE

'You got some real quality stuff here,' said Danny, running his hand over the heavy dresser in Annie and Mike's kitchen. 'Solid oak, that is.'

'Hmm,' said Annie. 'A bit dark and oppressive, though.'

'You reckon?' The burly, freckled-faced man ran a hand through his floppy hair and said, 'Teen would kill for stuff like this.'

'Yes, well, the house is full of stuff like that,' said Annie. 'Who's Teen?'

'Me wife. She's big on old furniture, is Tina.'

'Oh. Would that by any chance be the Tina who teaches English?'

'She does, yeah. Makes handy dosh out of it an all.'

'Is there much work round here?' said Annie. 'Teaching English, I mean.'

'Fair bit.' Danny shrugged. 'More than she wants sometimes, on account of her first thing being writing articles and such.'

'So…um…' Annie hardly dared to ask. 'You think there might be teaching work going spare, then?'

'I reckon,' said Danny. 'Why, you up for that, are you?'

'Not half.' Annie grinned. 'I only left a full-time teaching salary to come here, didn't I?'

'Yeah, well, best you have a chat with Tina, then. Now, where do you want this plumbing done?'

'Well, here in the kitchen, obviously. And we thought of turning one of the bedrooms into a bathroom.'

'Got a bedroom above here, have you?' he asked. 'Only the shorter the run, the cheaper the job, like.'

Leaning against the door frame of the bedroom Annie took him to, Danny surveyed the room and said, 'Teen would do her nut if she saw this lot. This is choice stuff.'

'Choice it may be,' said Annie. 'But it will all have to go if we're going to get a bath and loo in here.'

'I can see a vanity basin in that chest of drawers,' he said. 'Would only need the top drawer messed with, leaving the others for storing towels and such.'

'But the bed, wardrobe and everything else needs to be cleared, doesn't it?' she said.

'So what's your plans for that, then?'

'Well, Carol said something about an outfit called Emmaus, who she thinks would come and collect it.'

'They would, yes, but they wouldn't give you anything for it. Whereas…'

As it didn't seem as if he was going to finish the sentence, Annie prompted him with, 'Whereas what?'

After walking over to an ornately carved hardwood chest, Danny said, 'It's about my estimate for the job.'

'What about it?' said Annie. 'We've been told we can rely on a fair price.'

'Okay, so let's talk about fair.' He went to the heavy wardrobe Annie hated and stroked it. 'What say I take some of this stuff off your hands, and some of the price off the plumbing job?'

'Are you serious?'

'Yep.'

'But why would you do that?'

'I got my reasons,' he said. 'But you'd best run it by your bloke first.'

'Run what by me?' said Mike, poking his head round the doorway. After hearing the proposed plan, he said, 'We want rid, you want hands on. What's to discuss?'

'Well, your kitchen, for starters,' said Danny. 'I'll be done on my current job next week, and if you're happy with my quote, I'll get stuck into getting some taps over that sink of yours.'

'About the sink,' said Annie, when they were back in the kitchen. 'I was thinking about replacing it with a stainless steel one.'

'You what!' Danny looked at her with an expression that could only be described as aghast. 'That's a real Butler, that is.'

'Is it?'

'Yeah. Beaut at that. You could bath a baby in there.'

'If only,' muttered Annie.

'Sorry.' Danny's face flamed and clashed with his freckles. 'Did I…'

'No, it's okay. So you think it should stay, then? The sink.'

'Your call really,' he said. 'Only you'd be talking dosh to repair the wall if you took it out.'

'Oh, right. Guess I'll settle for taps and running water, then.'

On his way home, Danny took a slight detour and slowed down as he approached Harriet and Luc's place. Yep, the posh four-wheel-drive Landcruiser was in the drive, so worth popping in to put his plan into action. Hopefully it would be Luc who answered the door, so there'd be no danger of the over-the-top kissing stuff Harriet was prone to.

Not that Danny had anything against Harriet – well, except the kissing thing, that is – it's just that he'd never really taken to that. He was from Kent, wasn't he? And Kent people didn't go in for that kissing both cheeks malarkey. No, in all honesty, Harriet was what you'd call a diamond sort of woman. In spite of her plummy accent and all.

Generous, was Harriet. Danny was still convinced she'd paid him more than the going rate for the work he'd done on their two cottages, and then passed those sort of figures to her mates who'd wanted a holiday home sorted. All winter that job had kept him employed, and good money it was too. And weren't those the very mates who wanted to get their hands on old French stuff to furnish their posh house in France? And didn't he, Danny, know just where to lay his hands on the sort of quality gear they wanted?

Worth a try, anyway, he thought, pressing the doorbell and cringing at the sound of some female voice giving a full-on blast from Figaro. Not that Danny recognised it as Figaro, but he knew it was some fancy opera or other. But that was Harriet for you. Nothing as normal as a bog-standard ringing sound for her doorbell.

'Sweetie!' said Harriet, opening the door and planting a smacking kiss on both Danny's cheeks. 'Frightfully opportune time to call. I'm just about to pour drinkies by the pool.'

'Not for me, ta,' he said, following Harriet and surreptitiously wiping his cheeks. 'I just want to run something by you.'

'Abso brill,' said Harriet on hearing about the furniture Annie and Mike didn't want. 'Sounds just what the Fortescues are simply gasping for. And you're sure the owners want rid?'

'For a decent price, yes,' said Danny. 'Only thing is, y'see, I got no idea what it might be worth.'

'No prob, Danny Boy.' Harriet emitted a wicked-sounding chuckle. 'Let me negoush, okay?'

'Negoush?'

'Negotiate, as it were.'

'Oh, right. You'd do that, would you?'

'With pleash. Prob best when you're there. Which will be when?'

'Next week I'll be starting their job.'

'Give me the phone contact number. I'll give a buzz at the weekend and make a rendezvous to view and value said items.'

'You'll make it fair, won't you?' said Danny. 'Only I get the impression they're a bit strapped for cash like.'

'Danny, have you ever known not fair when dealing with me?'

'Um, no. Sorry, it's just that…well, I sometimes wonder if you sort of take it too far.'

'Trust me.' Harriet winked. 'I do so know the Fortescues have oodles. Fifteen per cent sound about right?'

'Sorry?'

'For your part of the deal.'

'Oh, that.' Danny felt his face heat in that embarrassing way he never seemed able to control. 'I was thinking along the lines of a bit of a cut. I'd sort of planned to take whatever it was off their plumbing bill.'

'No way to do biz,' said Harriet. 'Let's say twenty, shall we?'

'Per cent, you mean?'

'Split the prof. Ten for you, ten off your bill.'

'Harriet's right,' said Tina, spooning shepherds pie onto Alfie's plate. 'This Mike and Annie get cash for what you reckon is quality furniture, they get ten per cent knocked off your plumbing bill, and you get to make some profit as well.'

'You reckon?' said Danny.

'Well, it's not like you're ripping anyone off, is it?'

'Me dad in't going to do that,' said Alfie, plunging a fork into his shepherds pie.

'My dad isn't,' Tina automatically corrected her son. 'Christ, sometimes I wonder if you'll ever learn to speak English properly.'

'Don't matter,' said Alfie. 'I reckon it's French what's important now we live here. Anyways, I get enough grief from Lucie about speaking proper English.'

'Good,' said Tina. 'I spend several hours a week teaching French people how to do that.'

'Which reminds me,' said Danny. 'It seems Annie is a bit keen to get hold of some English teaching work if there's any up for grabs.'

'There often is,' said Tina, sitting down and picking up a fork. 'I can put some her way provided she's qualified.'

'Well, it seems she's got that teflon thing,' Danny mumbled through a mouthful of mashed potato.

'TEFL.' Tina nodded. 'Brilliant, I'll go and have a chat with her.'

'Is there any more of that shepherd stuff up for grabs?' asked Alfie, scraping his plate. 'That's real quality grub, that is.'

Handing Danny a mug of coffee to kick-start his working day, Annie said, 'So who is this Harriet who's coming this morning?'

'English woman, married to a Frenchman,' said Danny. 'What you might call a high-class dame, but a real diamond, is Harriet.'

'And you think she's interested in our old furniture?'

'Nah, not her style. All Habitat and modern in her cotts, as she calls them.'

'So why is she coming to look at our stuff?'

'Well, it's like this, see.' Danny drained his mug and opened his tool bag. 'She's got these wealthy mates who she reckons are hot for your sort of stuff.'

'Sounds like she's arrived,' said Annie, going to the kitchen window. 'Bugger, she looks as if she's stepped straight out of Vogue magazine. Um, are she and her husband what you might call wealthy as well?'

'Rolling in it,' he said. 'You should see their place.'

'To be honest,' said Annie, 'I'm a bit nervous about her seeing our place. I mean, it's a bit sort of sub-standard for her type, isn't it?'

'No worries there. That lady doesn't know what the word snob is supposed to mean.' Wriggling his way under the sink, he added, 'Just ignore the plumbs.'

'Plumbs? What plumbs?'

Getting no reply, Annie went to open the front door. Which was when she realised what Danny meant about the plumbs.

'Annie, sooo nice to meet you,' said a voice which wouldn't be out of place at a hunt ball.

'And you,' said Annie. 'Please come...' But Harriet had already stepped past Annie and was gazing up at a brass candelabra mounted to a wall in the hall.

'Super,' she said. 'Are there others?'

'There is another one. In the dining room.' Wondering if she had time to rinse a bone china cup and saucer, Annie said, 'Um, can I offer you some coffee?'

'Later.' Harriet flapped a diamond-encrusted hand. 'Biz first. Where shall we begin?'

'Er, here, I think.' Annie opened the nearest door.

'Fantas!' announced Harriet, waving arms in a gesture extravagant enough to encompass the entire contents of the dining room. 'Felicity has *such* a pash for anything positively ancient.'

'Well, yes, it's quite old,' agreed Annie. 'You think your friends would go for some of it, then?'

'Absolutely, sweetie. Talk price, shall we?'

'Um…to be honest, we have no idea what any of it's worth.'

'Trust me,' said Harriet. 'I just happen to know what Toby Fortescue is worth.' She snapped her fingers and said, 'Pen. Paper.'

Armed with Mike's sketch pad and a felt-tip pen, she went from one piece of furniture to another and compiled a list with a suggested price beside each item. She then tore the sheet of paper off the pad, passed it to Annie and told her to peruse and consider.

Gasping for breath, Annie looked at the figures and said, 'You're not serious! This lot can't be worth that sort of money.'

'Deffo is,' said Harriet. 'Help to finance your bathroom, d'you think?'

'Could do,' said Annie. 'Not that we were thinking in terms of Italian marble tiles or solid bronze taps.'

'No, no.' Harriet flapped a perfectly manicured hand. 'Far too extrav. But you'll need to refurnish this room, of course. Look at what's in this potential bathroom, shall we?'

Yes, the hideous wardrobe Annie hated was *so* Felicity, but maybe not the iron bedstead with the brass knobs. On the other hand, the marble-topped washstand, complete with its huge ceramic jug and basin was very much the thing.

'Piccies, I think,' said Harriet. 'Could you do some digital ones I can send by email?'

'No problem,' Annie assured her. 'Mike is well up to that.'

'Excellent. Can't be too optomiz, but I do believe the punts would positively grab at least half of what I've seen.'

'Punts?' said Annie. 'I thought their name was Fortescue.'

'Punters, sweetie. Punters.'

Leaving Harriet oohing and aahing over a walnut chiffonier in what she called the salon, Annie went to the kitchen and, addressing what she could see of Danny, she demanded to know if this Harriet woman was for real.

'Real as they come,' said Danny's muffled voice. 'Why? You got a problem with her?'

'Not as such. It's just...Danny, could you come out from under the sink? Only I've got a problem talking to your legs.'

Called away from his computer, Mike joined Danny and Annie at the kitchen table. Pausing with a coffee mug halfway to his mouth, he stared at the paper in his other hand and said, 'Good grief! That much for an armoire!'

'What's an armoire?' asked Danny.

'A couple of hundred quid bit of kit, according to this list,' said Mike. 'Grab the calculator, Annie, I'm having trouble getting my head round these figures.'

A few minutes later, all three of them looked at a sum total that was only a few digits short of a phone number.

'Frigging hell,' was Danny's comment.

'I'll be buggered,' said Mike, at the same time as Annie said, 'Jeez!'

First to recover, Danny whistled through his teeth and said, 'Told you she was a diamond dame, didn't I?'

'Well, I know,' said Annie. 'But...I mean...good god!'

'You called?' said a voice from the doorway. 'Oooh that coffee smells delish. Pour me some and I'll let you call me Harriet in private.'

CHAPTER THIRTEEN

Carol picked up the phone and heard Glyinis's voice announce, 'Game on.'

'What?'

'We've got the net and everything, and Ken is marking out the court as I speak.'

'Really? So, um, Glyinis, why are you calling to tell me that?'

'I'm not, Carol. I'm calling to ask you and Lars to come for lunch on Sunday.'

'Okay, I can grasp that. Thanks, we'd love to. But tell me something. What's that got to do with Ken's court?'

'What I mean is, Carol, that you should bring some shorts and suitable footwear.'

'Right.' Carol glanced down at her bare feet. 'Could you define suitable footwear for me?'

'Plimsolls or trainers, of course.'

'Of course. What else?'

'Nothing else. I told you, we've got everything. Shuttlecocks and whatever.'

After putting the phone down, Carol went out to the patio and asked Lars if he knew how to play badminton.

'Sure,' he said. 'Played a lot in Abu Dhabi. Why?'

'It's just that we're invited to Glynis and Ken's for lunch on Sunday.'

'And that is a problem for you?'

'To be honest,' she said, plucking Sue Ellen out of a geranium pot. 'I'm not totally sure I got what Glynis was on about. But either we're having grilled shuttlecocks to eat or I'm expected to make a right tit of myself trying to play a game I haven't got a clue how to play.'

'Right or left tit, who cares?' Lars grinned. 'But how come you didn't get the full story?'

'Because I lost concentration when she started twittering about paint colour charts she'd got for Annie, and...bugger!'

'Now what?'

'She said she'd give them to her on Sunday, so they must be

invited as well. I tell you, Lars, there's no way I'm prancing around with a racquet in front of an audience.

Chuckling, Lars said she'd be okay if she remembered to wear a cast-iron bra with a right and a left cup.

'I can't find one that feels comfortable,' Annie moaned, rummaging through the bras in her drawer. 'Jeez, Mike, I've definitely put on weight since we've been here.'

'Contented living,' he said.

'Yeah, and overdosing on croissants, goat's cheese and that pâté we keep buying by the ton. For heaven's sake, these flipping shorts fitted me perfectly a couple of weeks ago.'

Sliding his arms round her and caressing her bum, Mike said, 'They fit ultra perfectly now. And I like you a bit more curvy and cuddly.'

'A bit I can live with,' she said. 'But I really should at least cut down on croissants for breakfast. Meanwhile, can I borrow a pair of your shorts?'

'No worries, my love.' He let go of her to fish a pair out of the cupboard. 'But I'm fresh out of clean D cup bras.'

'Very ho ho – not. Oh well, this bra will have to do.'

'Yep, if you're planning to wear a tee-shirt, it'll disguise the bulgy overflow.'

'This one, I think,' she said, holding up a tee-shirt. 'At least it's long enough to hide the fact that I'm wearing your shorts.'

'And you reckon having Snoopy draped across your boobs is appropriate to go out for Sunday lunch?'

'We're not talking about lunch at an elite country club,' said Annie. 'Casual barbecue is how Glynis put it. Come on, Mike, we're supposed to be picking Carol and Lars up at twelve.'

'So much for casual,' said Mike, slowing down as they approached the house where Lars had told him to stop. 'Please tell me that's not mine host.'

'Fraid so,' said Lars, as Ken came out of his house dressed in immaculate white shorts – with a crease down the front, for heaven's sake! – and a sparkling white shirt complete with Lacoste logo and gold-edged collar.

Looking down at his faded khaki shorts with the frayed hems, Lars said he was glad he'd dressed for the occasion.

'Pretentious prat,' muttered Carol.

'Come on,' said Lars. 'You were the one to insist I wore my best pair.'

'And I really thought he'd changed.'

'I did, Carol. I got out of my sawn-off jeans and...'

'Lars, put a sock in it.'

'Ah, you didn't tell me I had to wear socks.'

Striding towards the van when Mike pulled Tiggy onto the grass verge by the house, Ken called, 'Excellent timing. We're just about to set fire to the charcoal.'

Which actually meant Glynis was just about to do that. Understandable, really, given Ken's white attire. Whereas his wife was at least suitably dressed for the job. And she did wipe her hands on her denim shorts before shaking hands with Mike and hugging the others.

'Right. Drinks,' said Ken. 'Red wine? White wine? Or a cocktail aperitif, anyone?'

'Wine for me, please,' said Annie. 'Whatever colour it comes.'

With everyone agreeing they'd have the same, Ken turned to Glynis and said maybe she'd like to get changed while he saw to the drinks.

'No, Ken. I'm fine as I am.'

'So, Mike – may I call you Mike?' said Ken, placing a tray of glasses on the patio table. 'What made you come to France?'

'Maybe something to do with the fact that I just happen to be French. Why, what brought you here?'

'Ah,' said Ken. 'Yes, you do have that French look about you. You'll appreciate this, then.' He held up a wine bottle with the Châteauneuf du Pape label facing Mike.

'No more than I appreciate cheaper stuff, like Cotes du Rhone,' said Mike.

'My favourite,' said Lars. 'Except we tend to drink mostly from a plastic bottle on an everyday basis.'

'We should get some of that, Ken,' said Glynis. Turning to Carol, she said, 'Remember when we used to get sloshed on that Villageoise wine when I came and stayed with you on my own?'

'I do.' Carol nodded. 'And I seem to remember you got a bit hooked on it, didn't you, Ken?'

'It was alright for a while,' he said. 'Fun on a temporary basis, but not quite what I'm used to.'

'How sad,' said Mike. 'Now Annie and me, we find cheapo stuff suits our pleb lifestyle.'

'Er, well…Glynis, shall we start cooking? The charcoal looks about ready.'

'Right, right, right,' said Glynis, leaping to her feet and sending her wine glass flying. 'Oops, sorry.' She grabbed a linen napkin and dabbed at Lars's legs.

'No worries, Glynis. I don't mind being bathed in Chateauneuf.'

'We've got real English sausages we brought out with us,' she said, twisting the napkin in her fingers. 'I hope that's okay with you all?'

'Fine with me,' said Mike. 'Although I don't have a problem with French food, myself.'

As soon as their hosts had gone into the house to fetch the food, Annie glared at Mike and asked what the hell was wrong with him.

'Sorry.' He looked sheepishly at Carol. 'It was nice of your friends to invite us, and I'll try to behave – promise.'

'Don't fret it,' Carol replied. 'He can be an arrogant prick at times, but he's okay when you get to know him.'

'Well, I like Glynis,' said Annie. 'So, if you don't mind, Mike, could you try to be a bit less churlish with her husband?'

It had to be assumed that Ken had also been ticked off because, when they came back, he left Glynis to the cooking while he sat and chatted with Mike about the fact that they were both bosses of their own business. 'Mine's a sports shop,' Ken said. 'Left my manager in charge so we could come and live here while he makes the money to support us.'

Suddenly humble, or what?

'Mind you,' Ken added. 'The shop is in a prime position. Extortionate rates, of course, but the business did enable us to buy this place outright, as well as owning our UK house.'

Oh well, maybe not so humble after all.

'Food's ready,' trilled Glynis. 'Ken, could you fetch the salad and stuff from the fridge please. Now, if you all grab a plate and help yourself. It's just that I thought we'd keep it casual.'

'Right,' said Ken, once lunch was over. 'Anyone up for a game?'

91

'Count me out,' was Carol's response. Followed by Annie saying she needed more time to digest lunch.

'How about you?' Ken turned to Mike. 'Badminton your sort of game, is it?'

Omitting to mention he'd played for the county in his teens, Mike said he'd give it a whirl. Although he admitted it had been a few years since he was on a badminton court.

Lars said he'd been quite good in his time, but hadn't played since he'd ploughed a helicopter into an Arabian sand dune.

'Right, looks like we're a mixed ability bunch,' said Ken. 'I suggest we toss a coin for partners.'

'Beats throwing keys into the middle of the floor, I suppose,' muttered Carol.

'Sorry, sorry, sorry,' said Glynis, when Mike called heads, the coin landed tails up and he landed her as a partner. 'I'm hopeless against Ken.'

It took two sets for Glynis and Mike to wipe out Ken and Lars, and it took a couple of minutes for Annie to nip indoors, remove her constricting bra and take Lars's place on court while he recovered with a cold beer.

Yes, well, Annie had always been a good match against Mike at the Sheffield club where they'd met. And it had to be admitted that Mike had the weaker partner. Happy with a win in his favour, Ken declared they should play regularly.

'Agreed,' said Annie, flopping into a patio recliner. 'I enjoyed that, and I need to get my recently acquired flab off.'

'And I need to get this sweat off me,' said Mike. 'Thanks, guys. For lunch and the games, but would anyone mind if Annie and I head for home?'

'Fine with me.' Lars got to his feet.

'Oh.' Glynis looked from him to Carol. 'You don't need to leave yet. Ken'll drive you home, won't you, Ken?'

'No, it's okay,' said Carol. 'I'm happy to go back in the Tiggy van.'

'I'm sorry,' said Mike, pulling off the grass verge and turning Tiggy. 'It was nice of them to invite us, and I behaved badly.'

'Actually,' said Carol. 'I thought you were quite restrained.'

'I don't agree,' said Annie. 'Mike, they're Lars and Carol's friends, and you were rude to them.'

'I was not rude to Glynis.'

'Yes you were.'

'When? When was I rude to her?'

'About the English sausages.'

'Oh come on! All I said was I don't have a problem with French food.'

'Mike, it wasn't so much what you said, but the way you said it.'

'Yeah, okay. Maybe you didn't notice the patronising way Ken said I had the look of a Frenchman about me.'

'Meaning?'

'Meaning I am a bloody full-on Frenchman, but I only recently found out about that, didn't I?'

'Um, if I may pitch in here,' said Carol. 'Is this an issue you need to discuss in private, or is it something we can help with?'

Sighing deeply, Annie said, 'To be honest, I didn't even know it was that big an issue. Except…'

'Except, Annie, I don't actually know who the hell I am, do I?'

Which was when Lars stepped in and said, 'If there's anything we can help you with…I mean, anything it might make it easier to share with someone not as closely involved with whatever the problem is.'

'Think I'll take you up on that offer of help,' said Mike, pulling into the side of the road and hitting the brake pedal. 'Right now I've got a problem being responsible for driving us all safely home.'

As the two men got out to change seats, Carol said to Annie, 'Look, if this is about the way Ken behaved.'

'I'm not really sure what it's about.' Annie's voice was a bit wobbly. 'Mike isn't usually like this, and Glynis and Ken are your friends.'

'Well, Glynis is,' said Carol. 'You know what? I lived next door to them for twenty years, but I never really knew Ken.'

With Lars at the wheel, they continued heading for home, and Carol continued her conversation with Annie. Telling her that, in fact, she didn't even get to know the real Glynis until she came over to France to visit on her own.

'I really like her,' said Annie. 'I just hope none of what went on today will affect us being friends.'

'It won't. Glynis likes you, and Glynis does her own thing now.'

'Now?'

'Yes. Let's just say Ken doesn't control her so much anymore.'

'That's funny,' said Annie. 'Seeing how she went mad in Castorama the other day, I can't imagine anyone controlling her.'

'That's our Glynis.' Carol chuckled. 'I did warn you. Are you coming in for a drink?' she asked as Lars stopped Tiggy at Escargot Cottage.

'We'll pass if you don't mind,' said Mike, getting out to go round to the driver's side. 'Thanks for rescuing us, Lars.'

'He's good at that,' said Carol. Squeezing Annie's hand as Lars got out of the van, she added, 'And if Mike does want to talk anything through, I'm personally qualified to recommend Lars.'

'He's a nice man,' said Annie, looking to where Lars was standing with a hand on Mike's shoulder, talking to him. 'But Mike's not that good when it comes to his private life. As you saw today, he can be a bit prickly.'

'Tell me about it,' said Carol. 'Was I prickly, or was I prickly a year ago.'

'What happened?'

'Lars is what happened. He got through some barriers without me even realising he was doing it, and...well, let's just say he got stuff out of my head that I was refusing to admit was in there.'

'Are we fit, then?' said Mike, taking his place at the wheel again.

'Yes, Mike, if we give Carol a chance to get out.'

'Right, I'm gone,' said Carol, climbing out through the back door. 'See you soon, okay?'

After driving the short distance to their house in silence, Annie waited until they were in the kitchen before saying, 'Okay, Mike. Do you want to tell me what that was all about?'

Without answering, he slumped onto a chair, put his elbows on the table and buried his face in his hands.

'Mike, what the...' Seeing his shoulders heave, Annie went to him and said, 'For heaven's sake, what is it?'

CHAPTER FOURTEEN

The only time Annie had seen a man cry was when her dad had sat on her bed and told her he was moving out. Although that in itself had hardly come as a shock. At sixteen, Annie was well aware things couldn't go on as they were, but seeing tears in her dad's eyes was more than disturbing.

'I'd planned to wait until you went away to college,' he'd said. 'But then I met Maureen, and…well, it got more difficult.'

Attempting bravado, Annie had said, 'Oh, right. You'd reckoned on subjecting me to living in this impossible atmosphere for the next two years, had you?'

She'd missed having her dad around, of course she had. But she sure as hell hadn't missed the constant rows. Fair enough, she and Mike sometimes had rows, but they got sorted, didn't they?

Right now, though, Annie had no idea how to sort what was happening with Mike. Let's face it, she didn't even know what *was* going on in his mind, so how could she even begin to help him? He'd stomped off, saying he was going to the van to have a shower, but that was over an hour ago. Should she go to him, or leave him to work things out on his own?

Standing at the kitchen window, staring at Tiggy in the hope that Mike would come out wasn't helping. After grabbing a kitchen roll, Annie went into the back garden, sat cross-legged on the warm grass and waited.

Calling a greeting as she ran across the lawn, Perdue came and jumped into Annie's lap. With a sound that was a cross between a meow and a purr, the little cat reached up a paw and patted Annie's face. 'At least you're talking to me,' said Annie, and buried her face in white fluffy fur that was soon wet and salty.

She didn't hear him walk across the grass. Didn't know he was there until she felt his hand on the back of her head. Not turning or looking up at him, she said, 'If you're ready to talk, I'm ready to listen.'

Sitting on the grass beside her, he said, 'Annie, I'm sorry.'

'Okay, that's a good start,' she said, still not looking at him. 'Do you want to tell me what I've done?'

'Nothing. You haven't done anything.'

'So why am I being punished?'

'Annie, I'm not punishing you.'

'Oh, right. Sorry if I got that wrong, but you stomping off and refusing to speak to me is what you call reasonable behaviour, is it?'

'Look, I know I shouldn't have taken it out on you,' he said. 'It's just...it's just...' His voice sounded wobbly and croaky. 'It sort of swamped me, and I didn't know how to handle it.'

Now she did turn her head and look at him, and was shocked by what looked like anguish etched on his face. Her voice softening, she said, 'Tell me, Mike. I want to help, but I can't if you don't let me in.'

As if sensing he needed comforting, Perdue climbed off Annie's lap and planted herself on Mike's outstretched legs. Staring at the cat, Mike said, 'You've been there, haven't you? Not a good place to be, is it?' Reaching for Annie's hand, he said, 'I feel so lost.'

'Lost? Mike, what on earth do you mean?'

'No, no, lost isn't the right word.' He shook his head. A few seconds of silence ensued while he stroked the cat before saying, 'The thing is, Annie, it's tearing me apart not knowing who I am.'

Ripping off a sheet of kitchen roll, Annie handed it to him and said, 'Mike, I had no idea you felt like that. Why didn't you tell me?'

'Because I'm not sure I fully knew myself until bloody Ken hit a nerve. Yes, okay, it was a shock to find out my parents weren't actually my parents. I mean, it's not the sort of thing you just take in your stride, something like that.'

'Well, yes, I can understand that. Of course I can, but a lot of people suddenly find out they're adopted and...well, I suppose they deal with it in their own way.'

'But that's just it, isn't it? It isn't like that for me.'

'How do you mean?'

'Annie, adopted kids have a birth certificate. There's a record of when and where they were born, and some adoption authority or other has paperwork on file.'

'So what you mean is...'

'What I mean, Annie, is that someone somewhere knows who those kids are.'

'Um, Mike, I'm still not quite getting where you're coming from here. I mean, it's not like you haven't got a birth certificate.'

'Sure I've got one,' he said. 'That's if a false one counts.'

'Oh,' said Annie. 'So what you're saying is...'

'You read my so-called mother's diary, Annie. What did it tell you?'

'Well, just that they took you to England and registered your birth in Liverpool or somewhere.'

'Leeds. But I wasn't born in England, and I wasn't born to the people who just sort of acquired a baby and registered it as their own.'

'They did what they thought best, Mike.'

'I know, I know.' He ran a hand through his already tousled hair. 'And don't get me wrong, I love them for that. It's just...'

'Just what?'

'It was illegal, what they did. Which means I'm illegal.'

'Oh come on, Mike. None of it makes *you* illegal!'

'You reckon? How about I've got a British passport, which I shouldn't have because it's based on a bloody fictitious birth certificate.'

'Oh.'

'Oh indeed. It was when Ken said I look like a Frenchman that it hit me. I am fully French. But no one knows who my father is or was, I can't find out anything because my mother died before I even knew she existed, and she would have preferred I didn't exist at all.' Clutching Annie's hand even harder, he said, 'She tried to fucking kill me!'

Trying to ignore the pain in her hand, Annie said, 'She was sick, Mike.'

'Yes, so I gather, but...' Letting go of her, he buried his face in both his hands and said, 'Annie, do you have any idea what it feels like to know your mother didn't want you?'

'No, I don't.' She kneeled beside him and gently eased his hands from his face. 'But Delphine and Norman *did* want you.'

'Did they?'

'Mike, they loved you and looked after you, didn't they?'

'I'm not denying that,' he said. 'But it's not exactly like they chose to have someone else's baby dumped on them.'

'You feel you were dumped on them?'

'How else would you put it? Jeez, Annie. It's screwing me up to think what a burden I must have been.'

97

'Oh Mike, Mike, Mike.' Annie wrapped her arms round him and said, 'I don't know what to say. I want to help you, but I don't know how.'

'You can start by passing me some more kitchen tissue,' he said. 'Then I need to know that you love me, whoever I am.'

'For Christ's sake, Mike. Who you are is the man I love to bits. I don't give a shit about anything else.'

'Ah, but...' He managed a weak grin. 'When you fell in love with me you didn't know I was a bastard.'

'Soon found out though, didn't I?' she said with a shaky laugh. 'I knew that the first time I came home from a hard day's work and you hadn't even washed the friggin breakfast dishes.'

'Someone's got a sweet tooth,' said Dora Turner as Annie piled several packets of liquorice ribbons onto the village shop counter.

'Oh, hi, Dora.' Annie grinned sheepishly. 'I don't usually eat much sweet stuff, but I can't seem to resist liquorice these days.'

'Newly acquired taste, is it?'

'Yes, a bit like my newly acquired weight, you could say. So no coincidence there.'

'Fresh air, country living, less stressful lifestyle,' said Dora. 'All plays a part, you know.'

'Yep, like this stuff is playing its part on my waistline.' Annie took three packets off the counter and said maybe she should put them back on the shelf.

'No, no, dear. If you have to crave something, liquorice is not bad for you. High in iron, you see.'

'Really? I didn't know that.'

'Ah, well, it seems your body does know it needs iron. Funny things like that, bodies. Have a mind of their own sometimes. And we don't want you to become anaemic, do we?'

'Er, no, I'd rather that didn't happen. So you reckon it's okay, then? Eating this much liquorice, I mean.'

'Depends, depends,' said Dora. 'Just not so good if your blood pressure becomes high later. But the doctor will keep a check on that, of course.'

'Well, actually, Dora, we haven't needed to register with a doctor yet.'

'Oh but you must, dear. Can't take chances at this time.'

'No worries,' Annie told her. 'We're both fit as fiddles. Never better, really.'

'Doctor Devreua's a good man,' said Dora. 'Keeps an eye on Don, and quick to spot anything amiss.'

'Oh? I hope there's nothing wrong with Don.'

'Nothing a good diet and sensible exercise can't control,' said Dora. 'And that goes for you too, dear. But do go and see a Doctor soon, won't you?'

Promising Dora she would do that, Annie paid for her items, left the shop and began walking home. So deep in thought was she that she wasn't immediately aware of the car coming down the lane towards her. She hurriedly stepped onto the grass verge to let it pass, but it stopped beside her and a young woman with short spiky red hair asked through the open car window if she was Annie, by any chance.

'Just come from your place,' said the woman, when Annie confirmed that was her name. 'Left a message with your feller about a job tomorrow if you want it. Only a couple of hours, mind, but it's a foot in the door for you.'

'Um, right...' Annie forced her mind from where it had been and stared at the face in front of her. A face that was flanked by ears carrying a cluster of studs and rings. 'You say you left a message with Mike?'

'Hope you don't mind,' said spiky head with a cheeky grin, 'but he took me upstairs.'

'Did he, indeed.' Not knowing quite how to handle what was a bit of a weird conversation, Annie said, 'And here was me thinking I'd stopped him doing that as soon as my back is turned.'

'Now she tells me!' The grin threatened to take over what was a small, pixie-like face. 'Had I known about that, I'd have taken advantage of him. Mind you,' she added. 'What with my Danny screwing in the same room, it could have been a bit tricky.'

'Ah!' said Annie. 'I'm guessing you must be Tina.'

'Yours truly. Sorry, I should have said.'

'Er, yeah, it would have helped.' Annie felt her grin probably matched the one in front of her. 'Pleased to meet you, Tina, but tell me something. Why did Mike take you upstairs?'

'Said he had a chest he wanted me to see.'

'Okay, let me get this straight. My bloke took you upstairs, where your bloke was screwing, and my bloke showed you his hairy chest. Have I got that right?'

'Almost,' said Tina. 'But if we're talking detail here, the chest was more sort of carved with knobbly wooden bits.'

'Gotcha. It's the one Danny thought you'd go nuts over.'

'And he wasn't wrong. If you're planning on selling it, I'd die for it. But to get back to why I'm here, are you up for a couple of hours of teaching tomorrow afternoon?'

'Definitely,' said Annie.

'Nice one! I've left some stuff for you.'

'Stuff?'

'Yeah, notes about lesson plan, what level of English and whatever.'

'Thanks, that's great,' said Annie. 'Whereabouts do I have to go?'

'Dijon, but no worries, I'll pick you up about half two.'

'Brilliant. I'll walk down and wait at the bottom of the lane. Um, Tina, before you go, could you tell me what Danny was screwing in my upstairs room?'

'Some sort of shower head thing to a wall, I think. Not that I took much notice, on account of I was more interested in your bloke's chest.' With the little car already on the move, she called out, 'Oh, and we'll talk about the other thing tomorrow. See ya.'

Finding Mike and Danny drinking coffee in the kitchen, Annie told Danny she'd just met his wife, then told Mike there was something they needed to talk about.

'Hope it's not something Teen did,' said Danny.

'No,' said Annie. 'More something Mike may have done.'

'That's okay, then. Just so's you know, she can be a bit pushy about getting stuff for her articles.'

'Articles?' said Annie. 'She didn't mention anything about articles.'

'She will. As for me,' he said, draining his mug and putting it on the table. 'I need to get that last connection to your toilet done, and you'll be in business by tonight.'

After closing the kitchen door behind Danny, Mike turned to Annie and said, 'Okay, what have I done now?'

'Actually, Mike, I think you probably did it several weeks ago. In fact, it could well have been the first night we moved into this house.'

'Okay, I give up.' He shook his head. 'You're going to have to give me some clues here.'

Holding up her fingers and ticking items off, she said, 'We ate Lars's fabulous boeuf bourguignon, we sat in the garden drinking wine by moonlight, we went to bed and...'

'And?'

'Are you telling me you don't remember what happened next?'

'Well of course I remember. It was...it was...'

'Go on.'

Scratching his head, he said, 'Well, it was a bit sort of special, wasn't it? Not that I'm suggesting it's not *always* special, it's just that...well, that night...um, Annie...'

'Yes, Mike?'

'In case I'm digging myself in the shit by not saying the right things, would you like to tell me where this conversation is supposed to be going?'

'Oh, you're doing fine so far. The thing is...' She tapped the side of her nose. 'I think it was possibly more special than we knew at the time.'

'Huh? Annie, are you saying what I think you're saying?'

'Hold on.' She held up her hands. 'I don't know. It's too soon to jump to conclusions, but it could explain how I've been feeling lately.'

'How have you been feeling lately?'

'Well, apart from being pissed off about my bras getting tight, I've been a bit nauseous in the mornings.'

A huge grin splitting his face in two, Mike said, 'And then there's that liquorice thing you've got going on.'

Annie clutched the table as she sank onto a chair and said, 'It's been so long, Mike. I'd given up even hoping, and I'm scared in case...'

Crouching down in front of her, Mike grabbed her hands and reminded her she hadn't had a period since they got here. Which she said she'd put down to the upheaval of leaving England and settling in here and everything. Sure, he understood that could have an affect, but he told her to think back to when she did last have a period.

'It was after the end of term, I think. In fact, yes, it was about a week before we left.'

'You're sure about that?'

101

'Yes. I can remember thinking I wouldn't have that to deal with while we were travelling. So we're talking…what…seven weeks ago! For heaven's sake, Mike, why the hell didn't we realise?'

'Because we're a couple of thick shits. Well, at least one of us, that is. What made you realise now?'

'I didn't. It was Dora Turner. When I met her in the village shop.'

'What? You're telling me you met Dora Turner in the village shop, and she just happened to say, *by the way, dear, did you know you're pregnant?*'

Annie started to giggle. Just a little giggle at first, but it led to two normally sane adults clutching each other and erupting into a near hysterical state.

'Is it safe to come in?' asked Danny, peering round the kitchen door. 'Only it's a done job up there, and I thought I'd let you do the honours of the first flush.'

That night, each time Annie moved nearer the edge of the bed, Mike tightened his arm round her. In the end, she lifted his arm so she could wriggle out of bed.

'Where you going?' he mumbled.

'To the loo,' she said. 'Unless you want me to wet the bed, you'll have to let go of me.'

'Thas a bugger.'

'What is?'

'Forgot to bring the poo pottie up.'

'Damn,' she said. 'I'll just have to use the real thing then, won't I?'

'Huh? Wassat?'

'Go back to sleep, Mike. I'll tell you about our proper toilet in the morning.' Grunting, he turned over, and Annie made her way to the new bathroom.

Bliss or what? She sat on the new toilet longer than was strictly necessary as she gazed around at the wonderful luxury Danny had created in what had once been a surplus front bedroom. By the time she'd visualised how smart it would be when they'd finished painting over the dingy walls, her buttocks were in danger of becoming welded in place.

Not wanting to wake Mike again, she put the light off before opening the bathroom door and heading back to their bedroom. Or, more precisely, to where she thought their bedroom was. After groping her way along the landing in the dark, she went through a doorway and walked into a piece of furniture that wasn't supposed to be there. Which was when she shouted at Mike to put a light on.

'Wh-what! Whas going on?' he yelled back. 'Where the hell are you?'

'Just put a bloody light on, Mike. I haven't got a clue where I am.'

'You scared the shit out of me, yelling like that,' he said, when he found her in the bedroom next to theirs. 'Why the devil didn't you put the landing light on?'

'Because I didn't want to disturb you,' she said.

CHAPTER FIFTEEN

The first thing Glynis saw when she rounded the bend was Annie standing on the corner of the lane. Oh heck – now what? Should she just wave and turn into the lane, or would that look a bit off? What Glynis didn't want to do was make a sensitive situation even worse. She liked Annie, was hoping they'd be on-going friends, but she was worried about the way she and Mike had hurriedly left on Sunday.

In fact, that was why she'd decided to go and talk to Carol. If Annie and Mike were pissed off, Carol would know, wouldn't she? And if they were, it would only make matters worse if Glynis seemed to be avoiding Annie. But Annie was smiling and waving, so maybe it was best to stop and speak to her as if everything was normal.

Stopping the car before turning into the lane, Glynis draped an arm out of the window and called, 'Hi. Are you okay?'

'Fine,' said Annie, walking towards the car. 'Just waiting for Tina to pick me up. Everything alright with you?'

'Fine, fine, fine. I just wondered…well…if maybe you and me…'

'We're good, Glynis.' Annie laid a hand on the other woman's arm. 'But I should probably apologise for the way Mike was on Sunday.'

'Yes, well,' said Glynis. 'I've been more concerned about Ken upsetting him. He did, didn't he?'

'Glynis, I admit Mike was in a bit of a state, but it wasn't really Ken's fault.'

'Hmm, it looked like it was from where I was sitting.'

'No,' said Annie. 'It was a combination of things and…and, in a way, I think it helped Mike to face some stuff he'd been avoiding. Ah, here's Tina. Sorry, I'll have to go.'

'Okay. As long as you and me…'

'Glynis, as far as I'm concerned, you and I are fine. We'll talk soon, okay?'

Feeling much happier than she had for a couple of days, Glynis carried on to Escargot Cottage, only to find Carol wasn't at home. Oh well, she should have phoned first, but she'd been too anxious to just get out of the house. But at least it hadn't been entirely a wasted journey. No, not wasted at all. It was a huge relief to find Annie was still willing to be friendly, but that didn't put aside the fact that Glynis still felt the need to talk with Carol. As friends, they'd seen a lot through together, and if it hadn't been for Carol, Glynis and Ken wouldn't even be here in France.

In fact, there was a good chance they wouldn't even still be married.

On their way to Dijon, Tina briefed Annie about what was in store for her. 'You'll have two, maybe three students for each hour's session.'

'Huh?' said Annie. 'I'm used to about thirty of the little buggers.'

'These aren't little buggers, though,' said Tina. 'They're big, fully mature buggers.'

'You mean they're adults?'

'Sorry, I thought you realised that. Did the notes help?'

'Yes, big time. At least I knew what sort of lesson prep to do. I just hope I can pull it off.'

'You'll be fine,' said Tina. 'You're used to teaching, aren't you? Me, I was nervous as hell my first time.'

'Oh, right. I gather your field was more journalism?'

'Was, still is. And I'll be on your case next.'

'Sorry?'

'What I write these days is mostly articles, some of them about Brits living in France. Relocation sort of stuff, like why they came here and how they coped.'

'So where do you get your material?'

'From people like you.' Tina grinned. 'So far, I've done Carol, of course. Well interesting, she was. In fact, her story was turned into a mini series and got syndicated.'

'What's syndicated mean?'

'It means my paper passed it on to other publications, and I get dosh for copyright whenever it's used. Good, hey?'

'Sounds great,' said Annie. 'Who else have you done?'

'Gus and Liz. Another neat story there. Gus coming to France from Croatia, how they met and her teaching him English and whatever.'

'Which I gather accounts for his Cockney accent when he speaks English.'

'Great, isn't it?' said Tina. 'I love that about him. There was other stuff that came out later, but I'd already written the article. Not that I'd have used it anyway.'

'Why not?'

'Too heavy and personal. Didn't want to go there, but I did Don and Dora Turner. Or the DDTs, as Liz calls them.'

'Er, Tina, is Dora a witch?'

'Not so's I've noticed,' said Tina, bringing the car to a stop at traffic lights. 'Why?'

'Well, it's just that…'

'What?'

'Um, she sort of sussed out that I'm probably preggers.'

'She would,' said Tina. 'Are we talking good news or bad news here?'

'Brilliant if it's true. We'd more or less given up hoping after five years.'

'Wow, Annie. That's good copy, that is. I'm writing it in my head now. Brit couple desperately want baby, but…'

'Tina, in case you haven't noticed, there's a green light in front of us.'

'Oh, right.' Putting the car in gear, Tina slowly moved it forward, but her mind was apparently racing ahead. 'I can just see it,' she said. 'They move to France and, wham! Jackpot!'

'Hang on a mo. How do you know it happened in France?'

'Don't need to, do I? I'm a journalist, honey, and my job is to write what people want to read.'

'Look, Tina, don't get carried away over this. It's not actually official yet.'

'Okay.' Tina swung into a car park. 'There's a pharmacy across the road from here. When we've done what we came here to do, we'll get one of those test jobs and make it official.'

'But what if it isn't? I mean, we could be jumping the gun here.'

'No way,' said Tina. 'Not only is she a nurse, she's a very switched on lady is Dora Turner.'

Disappointed at not finding Carol at home, Glynis had gone to sit on their patio and wait in the hope they'd come back soon. Half an hour later, she was driving through the forest away from Coulaize when it occurred to her Carol and Lars could be on the barge. Worth a try anyway, she thought, making a decision to turn and go to the canal. After all, the alternative was to go home, but she felt she needed some space between her and Ken for a while.

A bit like she'd felt when she'd come out on her own to visit after Carol had moved here. Her excuse to Ken at the time had been that Carol had been through a rough time, what with the divorce and everything, so could probably use some moral support.

Although, as it turned out, it had been more the other way round. Carol had been coping pretty well with her strange new life, whereas Glynis, on the other hand, had been struggling to maintain the façade of her supposedly perfect marriage. So it was Carol who had given Glynis the moral support she'd needed at the time and, right now, Glynis needed some more of that.

But, dammit, she couldn't see any sign of life on board Reiziger. Undecided whether or not to give in and go home, she was about to turn the car again when Gus came out of the Carry On and opened up the parasols over some tables. Right, that was the answer then. What she'd do is go and have a drink to while away some time. What the hell, she'd even have lunch there, and let Ken get his own.

Yes, good move. Liz's beaming smile and cheery, 'Hiya, ducks. Lovely ter see yer,' greeting was a tonic anyone could do with.

'On yer own, are yer?' asked Liz, pouring Glynis a glass of house red.

'Yes.' Glynis grabbed the wine glass and took a big swallow. 'I came over to find Carol, but she's not at home.'

'Gone ter Dijon, innit,' said Liz. 'They wanted ter pick up some paint on account of the barge needs touchin up after all them locks they done on their last trip.'

'Oh, right.' Glynis drained her glass and handed it to Liz for a refill. 'So they'll be back later, then?'

'Yeah. Said they'd call in an pick up a pizza fer lunch about twelve before gettin down ter work.'

'Is it okay if I wait here for them?'

'Course it is, ducks,' said Liz. 'Tell yer what, I'll get Gus ter make it a big pizza enough for three, will I?'

Which would have been fine if Carol and Lars hadn't stopped off at a garden centre on their way home. As it was, Gus was serving food at an outside table when they arrived, and there was no mistaking the look of relief on his face when he said, 'Effin glad you're here. Only it's gettin a bit hard like, what wiv us bein a bit busy wiv lunches an stuff.'

'Oh,' said Lars. 'Do you need some help in the kitchen?'

'Nah.' Gus shook his head. 'It's just…well, if you could take over wiv your mate, Glynis.'

Laughing, Carol said, 'Why, what's she doing? Thrashing your regulars at darts, or what?'

'That wouln't be a problem if she was,' said Gus. 'It's more like she int in any fit state ter be flingin arrers around.'

The first thing Carol said when she walked into the bar was, 'Oh shit!' Followed by, 'Sorry, Liz. If we can just get her on her feet…' Grabbing Glynis's arm, Carol asked her if she could stand.

'Coursh can,' said Glynis, wriggling her bum off the bar stool and leaning against Carol.

'Okay, let's get you home, shall we?'

'Don't wanna g'ome, Charroll.' And she slowly slid down the length of Carol's body.

'Best fing would be if someone was ter carry her,' said Liz. Looking up as Gus walked in with a tray of dirty plates, she said, 'You'll do that, woncha, darlin?'

In a seemingly effortless series of moves, Gus scooped Glynis up off the floor, carried her to Carol's car and fed her onto the back seat. Getting her out of the car and into Escargot Cottage wasn't quite so easy, and Carol was cursing like a trooper by the time they'd got Glynis safely onto the sofa.

Even Lars was puffing when he picked up the phone to let Ken know his wife was safe.

'Ah, so she's with you, is she?' said Ken.

'Yes, and we'll bring her home later.'

'Good. Given that she took the car, I can hardly come and fetch her.'

'No worries, we'll be happy to deliver her for you.'

'And when can I expect that to be?'

'When she's ready,' said Lars, and put the phone down.

Telling Tina she was happy to be dropped off at the end of the lane, Annie got out of the car as Lucie came running from the direction of the village shop.

'We are walking together to home?' said Lucie.

'I'd like that.' Annie smiled at the upturned face and wondered whether or not to correct the child's phraseology. But switching from full teacher mode to less obvious, she said, 'It will be nice if we walk home together.'

Trotting beside Annie, Lucie said, 'We walk home together. That is the way to say it?'

'That's better, yes.' Annie nodded. 'Tell me, Lucie, why do you always speak English with me, but you insist on alternate French and English speaking days with Carol?'

'That is…' She frowned. 'Parce que?'

'Because.'

'That is because you have the good French, but Carol, she is need to learn more.'

'I see,' said Annie. 'You think Carol needs to learn more French?'

'Carol needs to learn more French,' Lucie repeated. 'And I needs to learn more English.'

'You need to learn.' Wondering why she'd let herself in for this, Annie explained. 'When you talk about yourself, you say I need, I want, I like. But when you talk about one other person, you say she needs, he wants, my mother likes.'

Seeing the frown on Lucie's face, Annie could almost hear the little girl's brain ticking into overdrive, and was waiting for the next question about what to say when it's more than one other person.

But she was obviously let off that one for now because Lucie said, 'What is insist?'

Okay, at least that was easier to deal with. When they reached the walnut tree, Annie asked if Lucie had time to come to the house.

'Yes, I have the time. Is it now?'

'Now is good,' said Annie. 'I've got something I keep forgetting to give you.'

Leaving Lucie making a fuss of Perdue in the kitchen, Annie went to the lounge and picked up a pile of children's books, then hesitated. She'd brought them for Lucie, as a thank you for looking after the cat, but that was before. When she didn't think she'd ever have a child of her own to pass them on to.

'You're looking pensive,' said Mike, coming through the open casement doors. He gave Annie a hug and said, 'Things not go well?'

'What?'

'Your lessons.'

'Oh, that. No, I mean, yes, I really enjoyed them.'

'So what's your problem?'

'These books. I brought them for Lucie, but now...well, you know...'

'I see,' said Mike. 'But we could buy new ones.'

'True.' She started to sort through the book pile. 'But these were my favourites. My dad used to read them to me, and I kept them for...if...'

'So keep some, and give the others to Lucie.' Taking the books from her, he said, 'Which ones do you particularly want to keep?'

'The Beatrix Potters, I think. Except, she'd like that one, wouldn't she?'

'I'm sure she'd love it,' said Mike. 'But it's your call if you're prepared to part with it.'

'I don't know...' Annie clutched The Tale of Tom Kitten to her chest. 'It's a bit of a hard call, that one.'

In the end, seven books were left in the keep pile, and Annie carried the other five to the kitchen. 'These are for you,' she said, handing the books to Lucie. And the look on the little girl's face dispelled any reluctance Annie had felt about parting with them.

Running her hand almost reverently over each one, Lucie spread the books out on the kitchen table. With her eyes seemingly taking over her face, she looked up at Annie and Mike and said, 'They are the books of English children?'

'Yes.' Annie nodded. 'You might not be able to read them yet, but...'

'I can read them,' she said. Picking one up, she slowly read the title aloud then said, 'This word I do not know.'

'Beatrix,' Annie told her. 'That's the name of the lady who wrote the story.'

'And she is also make the pictures?'

'Yes. Do you like them?'

Running her finger over a picture of Tom Kitten and his sisters, Lucie said, 'Yes, I do like them.'

'Good call,' said Mike, putting his arm round Annie and kissing the top of her head. 'Now, I think we need to find a bag so Lucie can carry her books home.'

Carefully packing the books into an Atac supermarket bag, Lucie said, 'Are you like…non.' She giggled and started again. 'Do you like the pictures of Madame?'

'What?' Mike drew his breath in sharply then said, 'Lucie, I've never seen a picture of Madame.'

Looking at him as if he was half-baked, she said, 'They are here.'

'Where? Where are the pictures?' asked Mike.

'In all places.'

'What places? Can you show me?'

Giving him another *are you all there?* look, she went into the hall and pointed to an oil landscape painting on the wall. She then went to the lounge and pointed to other pictures. Some were oil, others were water colours. With a tingling feeling, which was only partly due to relief that they'd told Harriet not to include any of the pictures in her inventory of items for sale, Mike asked Lucie if she knew who had painted them.

'Oui.' She shrugged. 'They are the pictures of Madame Lanteine.'

After Lucie had left, cradling a bag of books in a manner appropriate to the times her dad had handed her a sickly new-born lamb, Annie said to Mike, 'Well, we learned something today. At least we now know where you got your artistic talent.'

'It would seem so,' he said. 'But for a minute there, I thought Lucie was going to show us photos of my real mother.'

'Mike, I hadn't thought about it, but I haven't seen any photos in this house. That's weird, isn't it?'

'Bizarre.' He shook his head. 'I mean, what sort of home doesn't have family photos in it?'

CHAPTER SIXTEEN

When Glynis started to emerge from her semi-comatose state, she vaguely wondered where she was. Not that it seemed to matter much because, wherever it was, she felt comfortable and at ease. For a few seconds, she kept her eyes closed and allowed her mind to absorb the peaceful atmosphere. And when she did open her eyes, it came as no surprise to find herself in Carol's cosy, slightly scruffy sitting room. How on earth she'd got there she had no idea, but, right now, that didn't seem to be important either.

Except...becoming aware of muted voices drifting in from the garden, her brain jolted into full-alert mode as she realised it would sure as hell have mattered to Carol and Lars. A quick glance at the clock on the mantelpiece told her it was after four, for heaven's sake! Hadn't Liz said something about them painting the barge this afternoon?

Yes, well, thought Glynis, persuading her legs to get off the sofa and support her. I've obviously messed up their day, haven't I?

'Ah, we have life,' said Lars, looking up from the veggie patch he was weeding.

'Walking dead, more like,' was Carol's comment. 'God, she looks awful.'

Shading her eyes with her hands, Glynis called, 'I heard that, and you're not wrong.'

'Strong coffee coming up,' said Lars, heading for the house. 'One lump or two?'

'I don't take sugar,' said Glynis.

'I was asking about paracetamol. And I'll make you a sandwich.'

'Thanks, Lars. Think I'll pass on the sandwich, but at least six lumps of the other please.'

'Right,' said Carol, sitting beside Glynis on the patio 'Where do you want to start?'

'I don't,' said Glynis. 'I want to go back.'

'Fine. Let's get some coffee down your throat and we'll drive you home.'

'That's not what I meant, Carol.'

'Uh-huh. Do you want to tell me what you did mean?'

'I…I…I want to…'

'Yes?' Carol reached for Glynis's hand as a big fat tear rolled down her friend's face and escaped off the end of her chin. 'Am I right in assuming this is to do with Ken?'

'Carol, you saw what he was like on Sunday.'

'Um, yeah. But, Glynis, that was a couple of days ago. Are you telling me you're still hacked off about that?'

'If hacked off means not wanting to speak to him, then, yes, you could say that.'

'You what!' said Carol. 'You two haven't been speaking to each other since Sunday?'

'Oh, we've spoken to each other. As in *would you please pass the salt* sort of speaking. But, like I said, I want to…'

'Go on.'

'Carol, what did you think on Sunday? About Ken, I mean.'

'Well, I…um…Oh good, here comes the coffee.'

'There you go, ladies,' said Lars, putting two steaming mugs and two tablets on the table. 'You'll excuse me not joining you? I think perhaps I should get started on the painting for Reiziger.' Looking enquiringly at Carol, he said, 'Unless…'

'No, Lars, that's a good idea,' she said.

Dropping a kiss onto her forehead, he murmured, 'I'll take my mobile phone with me.'

'Thanks.' She nodded and gave his hand a quick squeeze. Turning her attention back to Glynis when Lars had left, she said, 'Er, where were we?'

'You were about to say what you thought about my husband.'

'Oh – was I?'

'Yes. You saw what I saw on Sunday, didn't you?'

'Okay, Glynis, I'm not going to lie to you. What I saw was the old Ken. What I mean is…'

'I know what you mean, Carol. What you saw was the Billericay Ken.'

'Yes, but he changed when you came here together. He was different when you bought your place at Maiseronne.'

'Exactly!' Glynis stood up and looked towards the fields and hills beyond the garden. Carol sat back and waited to hear what was coming next. She didn't have to wait long, but she was a bit thrown by what Glynis said when she sat down again.

'It's white. With a little pleated skirt, would you believe that?'

'I might,' said Carol. 'If I knew what the hell you're talking about.'

'You heard him tell me to get changed.'

'Sorry?'

'When he said *maybe you should get changed* in that voice of his.'

'But you didn't, did you? Get changed, I mean.'

'No. I was blowed if I was going to put on that prissy dress.'

'What prissy dress?'

'I've just told you, haven't I? It's white with a stupid pleated skirt.'

'So? What's the big deal about that?' asked Carol.

'The big deal, Carol, is that Ken chose it. He brought it from his shop because he decided it was what he wanted me to wear to play badminton.'

'Oh. You mean like when he used to choose all your clothes?'

'Not used to,' said Glynis. 'He still does.'

'Look, correct me if I'm wrong here,' said Carol. 'But wasn't it Ken who talked me into taking you clothes shopping in Dijon?'

'Did he?'

'Yes, when you were staying with me that time you both came last year.'

'I think you did say that, but I didn't believe you,' said Glynis. 'Did he say why?' She picked up her coffee mug and stared into it as if she expected to find the answer there.

'He said…' Carol looked at her mug of rapidly cooling coffee and considered abandoning it in favour of a wine bottle. 'Um, what he said was that you were too dependent on him, and he thought you should be able to choose what to wear for yourself.'

'I did that, didn't I?' said Glynis. 'It was fun, wasn't it?'

'Yes.' Carol nodded. 'That green dress you bought was well smart.'

'Still is,' said Glynis. 'Well, it would be seeing as it's never been worn.'

'You what? Glynis, are you telling me…'

'It was subterfuge.'

'What was?'

'Ken making out he wanted me to be more independent.' With a shaking hand, she put her mug on the table and said, 'It was funny, wasn't it?'

'Funny?'

'Yes. That time you and me got sloshed on wine out of those square plastic bottles.'

'Yes, well, if you mean when you came to visit me on your own last year, I seem to remember that happened a few times.'

Producing something that came close to being a grin, Glynis said, 'I'm talking about that time when I said I didn't want to look like a Barbie doll dressed by Ken. Remember?'

'Oh, right.' Carol chuckled. 'And wasn't there something about you wanting a yellow Kangoo, even though you couldn't drive?'

'But I can now, can't I? Otherwise I wouldn't have been able to drive the Volvo here.'

'There you go, see,' said Carol. 'You said Ken didn't want you to learn to drive, but you told me you were taking lessons, so...'

'I did it when he was at work.'

'You mean you didn't tell him! Jeez, he must have been pissed off.'

'I know. You should have seen his face when I got in the Volvo and drove off this morning.'

'I'll tell you what's pissing me off,' said Carol. 'You didn't bother to let me know when you passed your driving test, did you?'

'I didn't.'

'No, you didn't. Come on, the least you could have done was phone to tell me so I could congratulate you.'

'Carol, I didn't do that because I never took a flipping driving test.'

'What!' Leaning forward in her chair, Carol stared at Glynis and said, 'You're telling me you drove the Volvo illegally!'

'So what?' Glynis shrugged. 'It's not like anyone can take my license away.'

At a loss to answer that, Carol's urge to go for a glass of wine was getting stronger. Which wasn't unreasonable, given that she and Lars had allowed themselves just one glass each at lunchtime, based on the fact that one of them was going to have to drive Glynis back to Maiseronne. Now, sod it, it would take both of them, one to take Ken's bloody car back.

'Your phone's ringing,' said Glynis.

'Good,' said Carol, getting to her feet. 'I can put off strangling you until after I've answered it.'

'Ken here,' said the voice in Carol's ear. 'How are things?'

'Well now, Ken. Do you want the truth, or something you can believe?'

'That bad, hey?'

'Let's just say it's not that good. So, what can I do for you, Ken?'

'Um, I'd like my wife back when it's convenient.'

'Fine. I'll check with her and find out when will be convenient for her.'

'Carol, I...'

'Yes, Ken, of course. I do understand you'd like your car back as well.'

'Sod the car.'

'What?'

'I said, sod the car. It's Glynis I'm worried about.'

'Ah.' Feeling her raised hackles abating, Carol said, 'I'm pleased to hear that, Ken.'

'So, how is she?'

'Better than she was a few hours ago. She's had a good sleep, and I'd say she's probably about ninety-percent sober now.'

'I see. Carol, if you could just tell her I'm sorry, and...and I want us to talk. When she's ready, that is.'

Going back outside, Carol told Glynis it was Ken on the phone.

'Oh. How did he sound?'

Shrugging, Carol said, 'I think contrite could cover it. And he thinks the two of you need to talk. When you're ready, that is.'

Getting unsteadily to her feet, Glynis flexed her legs and said, 'I'm as ready as I'll ever be.'

'And those?' said Carol, pointing at Glynis's legs. 'Are they up to walking to my car?'

'Carol, have you got one going spare here?'

'Sorry, I'm fresh out of spare limbs till Tuesday.'

'Don't be silly, Carol. I'll replace it, of course I will, but if you've got just one I could take home with me?'

'Glynis, if I've got it, it's yours.'

'Thanks.'

'You're welcome. Except, could you give me a clue as to what we're talking about here?'

'That wine you drink, Carol. If you could let me have a spare bottle?'

'Um, don't you think you've had enough today?'

'Him and his Chateauneuf du Pape,' muttered Glynis. 'What I want is some of that cheap plastic stuff so I can pour it down his stiff neck.'

'Good luck,' said Carol as Glynis got out of the car.

'Aren't you coming in?'

'Nope. Ah, here's Lars and your car.'

When Ken opened the house door and stepped outside, Glynis said, 'It's just that it might be easier if you...'

'Glynis, we've delivered you and your car back, so I'd call that mission accomplished. You know where we are if you need us. Okay?'

Taking the Volvo keys from Lars and thanking him, Glynis walked towards her husband, held up the keys and said, 'These are yours, I believe.'

Catching hold of her arm, Ken said, 'Actually, I believe they are ours.'

'Yes, well, this is definitely yours,' she said, handing him a square plastic wine bottle.

'Do you think they'll be all right?' asked Lars, when he got into Carol's car.

'I think so,' she said, looking in the rear view mirror and seeing Ken put an arm round Glynis and lead her into the house. 'So will we be when we've stopped off to buy some Villageoise. The thing is, I gave Glynis our last bottle.'

CHAPTER SEVENTEEN

'What's supposed to happen?' asked Mike, peering at a plastic stick Annie had just peed on.

'According to Tina,' said Annie, pulling up her knickers before going to the hand basin to wash her hands, 'it'll show pink or blue lines in a few minutes.'

'You mean this bit of kit can tell us if it's a girl or a boy?'

'No, it'll tell us if I'm really pregnant or not.'

Scratching his head, Mike said that he wasn't at all sure he'd got the hang of this test thing. 'What's the story if it turns blue as opposed to pink?' he asked.

'I don't know, Mike. You're the one who reads French around here, why don't you read the instruction leaflet in the packet?'

'Okay. Right. I'll do that. Where's the packet?'

'Er...I think I left it in the kitchen.'

'You hang on to this,' he said, passing the stick to her. 'I'll go and get the instructions.'

'What does it say?' she asked when he came back into the bathroom.

'Give me a chance, woman. I haven't had time to read it yet.' Frowning, he said, 'What it says here is, if the clear little window thing shows one line...'

'Skip that bit. Just tell me what two pink lines mean.'

'Why?'

'Because...' She passed him the stick.

After looking again at the leaflet, he screwed it into a ball and threw it in the air. Grabbing hold of Annie, he said, 'You're going to have to phone your mum.'

'Am I? Why?'

'She ought to be told.'

'Wh...what? What's going on, Mike?'

'What do you think, Annie? We're only definitely pregnant, aren't we?'

Half an hour and half a toilet roll's worth of face mopping and nose blowing later, Annie announced that she was hungry. 'I think we somehow missed out on lunch,' she said.

'Lasagne!' Mike snapped his fingers. 'It's only got to be heated through.'

'What! You made lasagne?'

'No, Gus made lasagne. I picked it up on my way back.'

'From where?'

'From the Carry On café,' he said. 'Where else do you think?'

'No, I mean where were you coming back from?'

'From the shop where I bought the microwave oven.'

'You went out and bought a microwave?'

'Yes, Annie. How else do you think I was going to heat up lasagne for my working woman?'

Practically drooling as the tantalising smell wafted from the dish Mike placed on the table, Annie grabbed a fork and dived in.

'Hang on.' Mike grabbed her wrist. 'Give it a chance to cool down a bit.'

'Oh god,' she moaned, clutching her stomach. 'How long will that take?'

'Not long if you give me a chance to put it on a plate.'

'Oi,' she said when he'd spooned it out of the dish. 'You've got more than me.'

'No I haven't, my love. This one's yours.' Passing her the larger portion, he asked her if she'd had a good day at the office. Between mouthfuls, she told him how brilliant it was teaching adults. How she'd only had two each session, and they were so attentive and keen.

'The thing is,' she said, pushing her scraped-clean plate aside. 'The thing is, they *wanted* to be there. They've paid money to learn and they really *want* to learn. Oh, Mike, it was so satisfying.'

'So you wouldn't want to go back to teaching kids, then?'

'Ah, well. Kids like Lucie, maybe. She's like a sponge the way she absorbs words. How they should be pronounced and in what order. Trust me, Mike, that kid will go far.'

'Talking of that particular little devil,' said Mike, nodding towards the kitchen window. 'I'd say that right now she's just going as far as our front door.'

'These are for you,' said Lucie, emulating the exact words Annie had used when giving her the books. Proffering a tray of eggs, she said, 'My mama is hope you like them.'

Annie was deciding whether or not to correct the last sentence when Lucie shook her head and corrected it herself with, 'My mama hopes you like them.'

'I do like them,' said Annie. 'And Mike likes them too.'

Turning to look up at Mike, Lucie asked him if he likes the pictures of Madame. On being told that, yes, he was very happy with them, she told him there were more, but they were hidden.

'Where?' he said. 'Can you show me?'

'Oui.' She pointed upwards and said, 'It is permitted to go on your steps?'

'Yes, of course.'

'Then I can show.' And she went into the hall and scampered up the stairs with Mike right behind her. When she went into the new bathroom, she stopped and looked around with a perplexed expression. 'There is much different,' she said. 'Où est la boîte en bois?'

When Mike told her they had given the wooden box to Alfie's mum, she put her hands on her hips and said, 'Merde. C'est un problème sérieux.'

Realising the little girl had become too agitated to deal in English with whatever was bothering her, Mike switched to French to ask about the serious problem.

Ah, okay. It didn't take long for him to find out that Monique had kept secret things in the wooden chest. Secret things that only Lucie had been allowed to see. When he asked if the things were important, Lucie gave a mini Gallic shrug and told him she didn't know why, but, to Madame, they had been très important. Lucie was sure about that because, when Madame showed her the pictures and things, Madame had been crying.

Feeling hairs standing to attention on the back of his neck, Mike yelled down to Annie, asking her where she'd put the stuff she'd cleared out of the chest before Danny took it away.

'What's the panic?' asked Annie, running upstairs.

'Annie, what did you do with what was in that chest?'

'There wasn't much. It was only a tatty old shoe box with old letters in it, and things that looked like junk.'

'Okay.' He ran his hands through his hair. 'But what I'm asking is, where is it?'

'In the bin bag, waiting for when the bin men come tomorrow.'

'And the bin bag is where?'

'Where we always put it, Mike. In the cupboard under the sink.'

When Annie and Lucie followed him downstairs, they found him in the kitchen with the content of the bin bag scattered across the floor. Totally ignoring Annie asking him what on earth was going on, he looked at Lucie and asked her if any of the things from the chest were here. After wading through ankle-deep debris, and seemingly oblivious of eggshells crunching beneath her knees, Lucie knelt on the floor and flicked potato peelings off an old shoe box. She then cast her eyes around the rubbish and pointed to a large brown envelope.

'Any more?' asked Mike, wiping tomato juice off the envelope with his shirt sleeve.

'Oui.' Grovelling beneath empty food cans and cartons, she pulled out a faded cloth bag and said, 'Voila. C'est tout. Here is all the secrets of Madame.'

'I don't know where to start,' said Mike, staring at a shoe box, a cloth bag and a large brown envelope on the kitchen table.

'How about starting with clearing this lot?' was Annie's response, pointing at the rubbish strewn across the floor.

But either he didn't hear her, or he chose to ignore that suggestion because he opened the bag and took out what looked like an old-fashioned cash box. She had scooped up nearly half the rubbish and put it back in the bin bag when he said, 'Christ, Annie. Take a look at this.'

Peering over his shoulder, she said, 'Um, it looks like a tooth.'

'Only my bloody tooth, would you believe!'

'How do you know it's yours?'

'The clue is on this,' he said, showing her an envelope yellowed with age with the words "la dent de Michael" written on it.

Picking up the tooth, Annie said, 'That was some clever tooth fairy, that. Not only did she nick your tooth from under your pillow and replace it with a twenty pence coin, she transported it to France.'

'Yeah, those fairies are obviously devious little buggers,' he said, taking a lock of hair out of another envelope. 'This got transported to France as well, but I don't remember being paid for it.'

'Mike, you realise what this means, don't you?'

'Do I?'

'Think about it.'

'I'm thinking, I'm thinking.'

'And?'

Scratching his head, Mike said, 'All I can come up with is that my mum must have sent them to...to my mother.'

Abandoning the bin bag, Annie perched on the edge of the table, caught hold of Mike's hand and said, 'She cared about you, Mike.'

'Who did? The mum who brought me up and looked after me, or the one who wanted to kill me?'

'Okay, Mike.' Annie got off the table, sat on a chair and turned it to face him. 'You've got to get over that wanting to kill you thing. No, let me finish.' She held up a hand when he looked about to interrupt. 'That was thirty-five years ago, and the woman was obviously mentally unstable at the time. But look at these things on the table and ask yourself if she'd have kept and treasured her child's tooth and a bit of his hair if she didn't care.'

It was a while before he spoke, and when he did it was to say, 'All she had was bits of me.'

'Yes.' Annie nodded. 'Can you imagine how hard it must have been for her?'

'I think...' He stopped and cleared his throat. 'A few days ago I probably couldn't have begun to relate to how that would have been. But now...what with us...'

'I know, love, I know.'

'Oh god, Annie. I've been feeling so bitter. So...so resentful.' Clutching his head with both hands, he said, 'I hate that. I don't want to feel like that, especially now.'

'Then don't,' she said. 'Just try and put it aside and move on.'

Taking his hands from his head, he placed them each side of her face and promised her he would do that. 'I think I can now.' He looked at the stuff on the table. 'Who would have thought a tooth and a lump of hair could make so much difference?'

'Thanks be to Lucie,' said Annie.

'Amen to that. Tell me something, Annie...'

'I know, I know.' She held up her hands. 'I should have properly checked what was in that bag before binning it.'

'Actually, what I was going to ask was, what made you think the fairy paid twenty pence for my tooth?'

'Because that's what I used to get, so I assumed it was the going rate.'

'Not for me, it wasn't. The stingy little beggars only gave me ten pence a go.'

'That,' she said, 'is because I lost teeth a few years later than you. I believe it's called inflation.'

Letting go of her face after kissing every inch of it, Mike looked at the floor and said, 'I believe that's what's called a bloody mess. Shall we do something about it?'

'Let me,' she said, getting up and grabbing the bin bag. 'You've got business to attend to in that bag, and you haven't even delved into a shoe box and that big brown envelope.'

'Later, I think. I'm not sure I'm ready yet for what else I'm going to find.'

'Fair enough,' she said. 'How about we sit in the garden and chill out for a bit?'

'I'm up for that. Um, Annie…'

'What?'

'About you phoning your mum…'

'What about it?'

'Do you think you should do it now?'

'Sod off, Mike. So far, I've had what you could call a brilliant sort of day.'

'I know,' he said. 'So I was wondering if maybe tomorrow would do. To phone Lillian, I mean.'

At about the time Annie and Mike were sitting outside enjoying a balmy warm evening and watching their cat romp around the garden, Ken was picking up a plastic bottle and pouring himself a fourth glass. Albeit that Glynis had only managed half a glass, it's true to say that, by then, they had become quite mellow.

But to back-track to about an hour earlier, it has to be said that the atmosphere between them had been somewhat thick and tense. Starting with Ken apologising because he was sometimes an arrogant so-and-so, and Glynis agreeing that, yes, he often is.

'Is?' he'd said. 'I know I haven't always been especially tolerant in the past, but…'

'Yes, well.' She'd shrugged. 'I do understand it can't be easy having an air-head as a wife.'

'Come on, Glynis. When did I ever suggest you were an air-head?'

123

'How about whenever you reloaded the dishwasher after I'd stacked it because, according to you, I didn't do it right?'

'But, Glynis...'

'And what else am I useless at? Ooh, let me think now.' She held up a finger and, as if marking a list in the air, reminded him that she had terrible dress sense, didn't know one end of a screwdriver from the other, had to be taken shopping because, heaven forbid that she could find her way round a supermarket on her own. As for being capable of driving a car – well, that couldn't possibly happen, could it?

He stared at her for several seconds before saying, 'Why didn't you tell me?'

'Tell you what?'

'That you wanted to do those things for yourself?'

'I did try, Ken.'

'When? When did you try to tell me?'

'It wasn't too bad at first,' she said. 'But then...well...'

'What?'

Cringing within herself, Glynis had known she was in danger of going too far. But she also realised there was no going back now. Taking a deep breath, she said, 'It was as much my fault as yours. I should have stood up for myself, but it just seemed easier to...to...'

'Yes? To what?'

Getting abruptly to her feet, she walked towards the open door and said, 'To give in and accept that I was married to a control freak.' And she walked out into the lovely messy garden. So vastly different from their one in England with its manicured lawn and neat flower beds. Focussing with difficulty through the moisture gathering in her eyes, Glynis looked around at the untidy hedge and overgrown areas they hadn't yet got under control.

Under control...control...control...

Ken's hand landing on her shoulder made her jump. What he said startled her even more.

'Take me for a drive.'

'Wh...what!'

He lifted her hand, placed the car keys in it and said, 'I'm asking you to take me for a drive.'

Brushing aside all her protests, he led her to the car and got into the passenger seat.

It hadn't been a long drive. Just long enough for Glynis to get over her initial nerves, brought on by having him beside her. There was a moment of panic when a tractor came towards them in a narrow road, but Ken had just sat back and told her she could do this. It was helped by the fact that the tractor driver pulled onto the grass verge to let her pass and, gaining confidence, Glynis drove her husband along a few deserted lanes, round a lake and back home. Where she slid competently into the driveway and parked exactly where Ken always parked. In response to him asking why she'd parked on that exact spot, she shrugged and said, 'Because you obviously think that's how it should be.'

'Fair enough. But what do you think?'

With a tremulous smile, she looked at him and said, 'What I think is, that old habits die hard.'

Putting his hand over hers that was still clutching the steering wheel, he said, 'Glynis, it's not going to be easy, but if we work on it together…'

As a few tears slid unchecked down her cheeks, she said, 'I'm tired, Ken. It was all supposed to be wonderful once we moved over to France, but I've run out of steam, and I think we both need help.'

'Okay.' He tightened his grip on her hand. 'We'll get help, and tomorrow we'll book you a driving test and I'll make…no, you can make yourself some of those A plates learner drivers have here instead of L plates.'

'Ken, I'm sorry about the wine.'

'What about the wine?'

'That bottle I brought you. I know you like nicer stuff, but I just…'

'Lead me to it,' he said. 'If it's that cheap plonk we got plastered on when we stayed with Carol last year, I reckon it's just what we need right now.'

Which brings us back to the bit where things had become quite mellow. For the time being, anyway. But even as she admitted to herself that she *was* a scatty air-head, Glynis wasn't stupid enough to believe everything was now going to be fine, fine, fine.

CHAPTER EIGHTEEN

Tapping Mike on the head with a spoon, Annie said, 'I'll take that as a no, shall I?'

'What?' He looked up and rubbed the back of his head.

'Mike, I've asked you three times if you'd please clear the table so we can have lunch.'

'Sorry.' He swiped an arm over a pile of envelopes he'd tipped out of a shoe box and pushed it to one end of the table. 'Will that do?'

'Sure.' She put plates and cutlery on the resulting space. 'Do you want Parmesan?' Getting no reply, she said, 'Hel-loo. Earth to Mike.'

'What?'

'I was asking if you want Parmesan on your spag bol.'

'Oh.' He looked up from the letter he was reading, then glanced at the plate she'd put in front of him. 'Yes, if you like.'

'Mike, it's not about what I like. I was asking if you...what is that you're so absorbed in anyway?'

'Letters from my mum to my mother. I think she did know about it.'

'Did she now,' said Annie, sprinkling grated cheese on her food. 'About what in particular?'

'That five year thing. It's beginning to look as if they flipping well agreed to that.'

'Really?' She paused in her attempt to wind spaghetti round a fork. 'You mean about you not being allowed to sell the house right away?'

'It's looking that way,' he said, reaching for the Parmesan. Peering into the packet, he asked if that was all she'd left for him.

'There's more in the fridge. How do you know? About the five year clause, I mean.'

'I don't for sure. And I won't until I've finished reading these letters.'

'Okay.' She stood up and picked up his plate. 'I'll put this in the microwave for later.'

'No.' He grabbed the plate. 'I can read and eat at the same time.'

'Mike, you don't do multi-tasking.'

'True.' He put a letter aside and picked up his fork.

'But, Mike. I want to know about…'

'Well here's something you need to know about,' he said.

'What?'

'When spaghetti is warmed up in a microwave it goes all rubbery.'

Don and Dora were just finishing one of Gus's delectable lunches when Carol and Lars arrived at the Carry On. Leaving Carol to stop and chat with the DDTs, Lars went to the bar and said, 'Liz, that pizza we ordered yesterday and didn't collect.'

'Not ter worry, ducks,' she said. 'Come in well handy, that did. What wiv a coupler people from the camp site droppin in fer a take-away in the evenin.'

'Ah, so it's okay for us to ask for a fresh one, then?'

Having been assured that Gus would get right on it, Lars went to Don and Dora's table and asked if it was okay to join them.

'Absolutely, dear,' said Dora, as Don said they had a carafe they needed some help with, so if Lars just collected a couple of glasses?

'I'll bring em,' Liz called. Putting two wine glasses on the table, she asked Carol if Glynis was okay.

'I think so,' said Carol.

'It's just me an Gus is a bit worried, like.'

'Are you?'

'Yeah. Carol, can we have a private word?'

'Of course,' said Carol, getting up and following Liz to a corner of the bar.

'What I want ter ask, Carol, is if Glynis is really okay? It's just she was in a bit of a state yesterday. Goin on, she was, about bein married ter two different men or somefin.'

Reluctant to discuss Glynis's marital problems with anyone, Carol simply shrugged and said, 'She was a bit out of her head, wasn't she? But she's safely at home with Ken now.'

'Yeah, well,' said Liz. 'What I'm hopin is, it's the one what she wants ter be wiv.'

Looking at Liz's concerned face, Carol said, 'Okay, they've got a few things to sort out, but I'm sure they'll be fine.'

'I bleedin well hope so, Carol. She's a diamond mate, she is. Done us a big favour gettin stuck in behind the bar when we was pushed that time we was run off our feet. You remember, doncha?'

Switching to French, Liz called to some people who had just come in, saying that she'd be right with them.

It was a few minutes after Carol sat down again before, turning from a conversation she was having with Lars and Don, Dora said, 'It's not our business, of course, Carol. But if there's anything we can do to help.'

Remembering what a rock Dora had been when Gus had cracked a few months ago. How she'd seemed to understand what was happening to him, and how to deal with him and Liz, Carol looked at the older woman's concerned face and thought, what the heck. If Glynis had already aired her problems to Liz…

Not that Liz would talk about it to anyone else, but then, neither would Dora. Anything Dora was told would, without a doubt, be treated in strict confidence. But even so…

As if he could read Carol's mind, which he had that uncanny knack of doing, Lars said, 'Shall we take our drinks outside, Don?'

'Right.' Don got to his feet. 'Leave the ladies to it, hey?'

With a feeling that it might be a relief to share something she herself didn't really understand, Carol gave Dora a very brief outline of how Ken insisted on being in control of everything. 'Well, that's how he'd always been,' she said. 'But when they came to France, he seemed to be a different person.'

'In what way?' Dora asked.

'I'm not sure I can explain it.' Carol shook her head. 'All I know is that, when I lived next door to them in Essex, their house and everything was perfect. But when they bought the house here, that all went out of the window, and it didn't seem to be a problem that they were living in a mess.'

'And now?'

'It's…it's like…well, actually, what Glynis said yesterday is that she'd brought the wrong Ken with her this time.'

'And do you have any idea what she meant by that?'

'Yes, I do.' Carol ran a finger round and round the top of her glass and wondered just how much she should take the liberty of telling what she knew. It was when Dora laid a hand on hers, stilling the constant movement, and said, 'I'm sorry, dear, I didn't mean to make you agitated,' that Carol realised she *was* agitated. Bloody agitated.

Taking a deep breath, she thought, sod it, and she told the kindly woman in front of her about how Ken was such a perfectionist at home in England. About how different he was when he'd been here in France. And about how Glynis was so much happier when Ken wasn't being in control and insisting on everything being perfect.

'I see,' said Dora. 'I believe they've been out for short spells several times since they bought the house here?'

'Yes, three – no, four times,' said Carol. 'But only for two or three weeks, and everything had seemed fine then.'

'But, as I understand it, this time it's not a temporary visit.'

'Well, no. This time they've actually moved here, not like just popping over for a holiday visit.'

'I think that's the key to the issue, dear,' said Dora. 'I think what we've got here is a case of OCPD.'

'What's that?'

'Obsessive Compulsive Personality Disorder.'

'Ouch,' said Carol. 'That sounds painful. Is it curable?'

'Not as such, no. Therapy can help, but it's what you might call inherent, you see.'

'No, Dora, I don't see.' Carol drained her wine glass and said, 'Oh shit.'

'Yes indeed,' said Dora. 'It would appear our men have taken the carafe and left us wineless.'

'Dora, sorry about the expletive, but what I meant was that Glynis has lived with this for twenty years or so. Mind you, I used to think she was just as bad.'

Nodding agreement at the wine bottle Liz was waving at them, Dora said, 'Yes, that often happens.'

'Dora, are you saying this OC whatsit thing is contagious or something?'

'No, no. But if someone lives with it, what usually happens is they avoid conflict by going along with the person who is afflicted.'

'What I fink,' said Liz, arriving at their table and pouring wine into their glasses, 'is that Glynis don't want ter do that anymore.'

'Sorry, dear?' said Dora.

'Yeah, well.' Liz put the bottle on the table and planted her hands on her hips. 'What you need ter know about me is I got amplifiers in my ears, innit.'

Laughing, Carol said, 'I can believe that. Not much escapes you, does it?'

'Not when it's somefin what matters, Carol.' Shrugging, she said, 'Most times, bar talk int important, an you can sort of tune out. Only she was a bit verbal like yesterday, an what she said was she was fed up wiv everyfin bein done the way what her husband says is right.'

At which point, ducking beneath the kitchen doorway, Gus announced that there was a pizza done and dusted. And he wanted to know if they was plannin on takin it wiv them, or was they goin ter eat it here?

Reluctant to abandon the discussion with Dora, Carol opted for them to eat it in situ. Which turned out to be a good move because, when Don and Lars rejoined them, and Don went through another half carafe, Carol and Lars learned a lot about Ken's problem.

According to Dora, he'd been able to put it on hold during the few occasions he and Glynis had temporarily spent time in France.

'But,' said Lars, 'he apparently reverts to form when they go back to England.'

'That's just the point,' said Dora. 'He won't be going back now they've moved here permanently, will he?'

'So what you're saying is…'

'What I'm saying, Lars, is that he can no longer escape back to the way things were.'

'So.' Lars scratched his beard, cast an anxious look in Carol's direction then looked back at Dora. 'What exactly does that mean?'

'I'm by no means an expert, you understand,' said Dora. 'But what it's suggesting to me is that, because he's no longer in a position to go back to the life he knows, he's transferred his normal self to his new environment.'

'His *normal* self.' Carol stared at Dora. 'What's normal about a man who dictates what his wife wears, and who paints their house when it doesn't even need painting?'

'Carol, dear.' Dora placed her hand on Carol's arm. 'To him, that *is* normal.'

'I think I'm getting this,' said Lars. 'He knows…he's seen that Glynis asserts herself when they're here. She doesn't want their new home to be a show house, so it's like he's needing to regain control or something?'

'Sort of,' said Dora. 'It's about not feeling secure, you see.'

Shaking his head, Don said, 'What beats me is how anyone could not feel safe here.'

'Don, dear, it's his marriage that doesn't seem safe here. D'you see?'

'What I see,' said Carol, 'is that if he doesn't get his flipping act together, he'll end up not having a flipping marriage.'

CHAPTER NINETEEN

Mike folded the letter he'd just read and put it back in its envelope.

'Well?' said Annie, stacking dirty plates. 'Do I get to hear what the story is?'

'The story, Annie, is that my two mothers conspired to get me to come and live in France, where they thought I belonged.'

'Okay.' She got up and went to the sink. 'Is that what the five years can't sell the house thing was about?'

'Yep. They figured I'd have to spend some time here, and their hope was that I'd decide to stay.'

'Crafty old biddies,' said Annie. 'They didn't get that wrong, did they?'

'That bit, no.' He picked up the envelope and told her to look at the postmark.

Peering over his shoulder, she said, 'What about it?'

'The date, woman, the date.'

'Oh, right. What's Aout?'

'August, but that's not important.' Passing the envelope to her, he said, 'Look at the year.'

'Okay, got that.' She passed the envelope back to him. 'Your mums weren't so old when they planned that, then. And you'd have been – what? Fourteen or so that year?'

'Fifteen, and those not-so-old biddies were already marrying me off.'

'Huh?'

'To a nice French girl, would you believe?'

'Who?' She sat back at the table and looked at him. 'What nice French girl?'

'I've no idea. It seems I was supposed to meet her in France, whisk her up onto my white charger and bring her to live in this house.'

'Yeah, well. I buggered things up on that one, didn't I?'

'You sure as hell did,' he said, hooking his arm round her neck and kissing her nose. 'Just think. I was supposed to get me a chic

French mademoiselle, and what I got landed with was some hick Norfolk gal.'

'Thart, bor,' she said, slipping onto his lap, 'is wot yew moight call a roight bugger.'

'Ah, but,' he said when Perdue jumped onto their laps, obviously deciding she wasn't going to be left out of the cuddling that was going on. 'I did end up with *this* little French madam, didn't I?'

'Talking of which,' said Annie. 'Shall we take a look at what else Madame Lanteine kept in her secret store?'

'Let's do that,' he said, pushing the shoe box aside and pulling something out of the large brown envelope.

'Hang on, Mike. Is there anything else in that shoe box? Other than letters, that is.'

'Don't know.' He lifted the letters and looked underneath. 'Oh, just some old photos by the looks of it.'

'May I see?'

'Sure. But it might be easier if...'

'Okay, okay.' Taking the cat with her, she got off his lap, sat back on a chair and started to sift through a small stack of photos. 'This must be you,' she said, holding up a picture of a little boy clutching a teddy bear. 'Oh, yes, it is you. It says "Michael trois ans" on the back. And this one is you at five-years-old, and here's one when you're...'

'Annie, let me see those.' He grabbed the photos, looked at them and said, 'There's something weird going on here.' Not bothering to answer when she asked what was weird, he spread out several hand-painted pictures on the table.

Picking up the phone, Annie heard Tina's voice saying, 'About that chest.'

'What about it?'

'Danny said you wouldn't let him pay you.'

'That's right, Tina. His bill came to less than what we got for the stuff he sold for us. Besides which, we owe you for putting me on to an income.'

'Well I want you to know I'm not happy about not paying for it.'

'Tough shit. Of course, you could always bring it back.'

'No way! I love that thing to bits. If you're really sure...'

'Tina, we're really, *really* sure. And that's carved in stone, okay?'

'Okay. Thanks a ton.'

'You're welcome.'

'The other thing I'm calling about is what was in it.'

'You know about that? We thought Lucie was the only one who knew about Monique's secrets.'

'What secrets?'

'All the things that were in the chest. Letters and a tooth and stuff.'

'Annie, I don't know anything about those, I'm talking about what was at the bottom of the chest. And I was wondering if you wanted it.'

'It's nice of you to ask, but why would we want a manky bit of wallpaper someone lined a chest with?'

'Not the wallpaper. I've already binned that, but I hung onto the packet thing that was under it in case it was important. Only Danny's coming over later to collect the last of the furniture for the Forteswhatsits, so I'll get him to bring it, shall I?'

'Yes, thanks, Tina. We'll see Danny later, then.'

'About half two I think he said. Um, Annie...'

'Yes?'

'You said something about secrets and...a tooth, was it? Sounds intriguing.'

'Er, Tina, if you've got your writing hat on, forget it. It's a no-go area.'

'Sorry, it's just I was getting story vibes here.'

'Okay, next time I see you I'll tell you the one about Goldilocks and three bears.'

Danny stared at the spread out paintings, scratched his head and said, 'But you told me you'd never been here before.'

'I haven't.'

'You never came as a kid and forgot like?'

'Nope.' Mike shook his head.

'So how come...' This time Danny pulled an ear lobe. 'I mean, there's no mistaking that's your back garden here, with the view and everything. And that one, that's got to be the front of this house.' Picking up another painting, he turned to the kitchen window and said, 'This one looks like the lane out the front, with Lucott's barns in the background.'

'It is,' said Annie.

'But the kid in all those pictures...you say he's got your face?'

'That's right,' said Mike, picking up the photos of him as a child and handing them to Danny.

Looking at each photo, then back at the paintings, Danny said, 'Yeah, it's the exact same face alright. Exact same expression and everything, but some of these photos are only head and shoulders, so whoever painted you into the pictures must've put the bodies on you.'

'That's true,' said Mike. 'And I sure as hell never remember wearing clothes like that.'

'Well weird, that is.' Danny did a bit more head scratching. 'Do you know who did the paintings?'

'My m – my aunt,' said Mike.

'Well, okay. We did hear as how she was a bit odd like. Did you know her at all?'

'No.' Mike shook his head. 'Never met her. In fact, I didn't even know she existed until she left me this house.'

'Well, one thing's for sure,' said Danny. 'She knew you existed, and it's like she pretended you were here or something.'

Mike cleared his throat and suggested he help Danny load the last pieces of furniture into his van. He was assured that, no, Danny didn't need any help to unload at the other end because the Fortescues were there and the missus would give him a hand. Oh, and by the way, they wanted to know if they could pop over and check out the candelabras. If Mike and Annie didn't want them, that was.

No, they didn't want them, but Mike had forgotten to include those when taking photos of everything else. But apparently Harriet had mentioned candelabras, and Felicity – or Flickers, as Harriet called her – had seemed keen.

'Right, I'll be off then,' said Danny, getting into his van. 'Ah, I nearly forgot this.' He took a small package off the van parcel shelf and handed it to Mike.

After breaking a disc of sealing wax and untying a narrow ribbon, Mike unwrapped a silver photo frame and said, 'Bugger. As if we haven't had enough shocks for one day.' Handing the frame to Annie, he asked her what she thought of that.

'What I think,' she said, 'is whoever that man is, he doesn't half look like you.' She turned the photo frame over, read an inscription on the back and said, 'Mike, I think we've just discovered that your father's name was Henri-Pierre.'

After saying that, yes, it might be fun, Carol put the phone down and went out onto the patio to ask Lars if he was up for an evening out.

'Who's asking?' he said, looking up from the novel on his lap.

'Glynis. She and Ken are just off to the Carry On for drinks and darts.'

'Really? Ken playing darts is shades of the Ken I thought I once knew.' Closing his book,

he asked, 'How did she sound?'

'Fine.'

'What, only one fine?'

'Stop it, Lars. You know she only does that triple thing when she's excited or agitated.'

'Right,' he said, getting to his feet. 'Only one fine is good, and the answer is yes. Can I have a pee first?'

She was waiting for him in the lane when Mike and Annie appeared from behind the walnut tree. 'Out for a stroll?' she asked as they got near.

'Carry On,' said Annie.

'I would,' said Carol, 'But I promised Lars I'd wait for him to have a pee.'

'Is that where you're going?' asked Mike.

'No, I've already had one. Do either of you play darts by any chance?'

'I'm glad you're here, Carol,' said Liz. 'I got somefin for yer what come in the post this mornin.'

'Ooh. Anything exciting?'

'I reckon,' said Liz, handing over a jiffy bag. 'You remember that Caribbean lad off that hotel boat, doncha?'

'Do I ever. The one with the amazing voice, you mean?'

'Thas him, yeah. Sent this for yer, innit. An one fer us an all.'

'Yay!' said Carol, taking a flat plastic box out of the bag. 'I told him I wanted a copy of his first album and, bloody hell, he's damn well done it.'

'Seems he's got into it big time,' said Liz. 'Says he's doin a

Europe tour this year.'

Her eyes misting slightly, Carol read the inscription on the inside of the CD case: *For Carol, with thanks for your support and encouragement. Love from Valentine.*

'Yeah, I got a bit choked an all,' said Liz. 'I won't ever ferget him an my Gus singin Bridge Over Troubled Water that night in here.'

'Me neither, Liz.' Carol's eyes became even more watery at the memory of the bad time Gus had been having, and how he'd sung that song with Valentine and announced he'd done it for Liz because she had been his bridge and seen him through.

But then, Carol had her own reason for remembering that night when Lars had come back into her life. He'd seen her through some troubled waters when she'd needed help, but when he'd sailed away to continue his cruising life, she hadn't expected to ever see him again.

Going to where the others were sorting out who should play darts against who, Carol said, 'Lars, you're going to have to buy me a CD player.'

With one match over, and another halfway done, Carol was up next. Thinking it was a good time to go and get another round of drinks, she went to the bar and said, 'You're looking a bit worried, Liz, is everything okay?'

'Nah, I int worried as such, Carol. It's just that old bloke over there.'

'What old bloke, where?'

'Him, over in the corner by the fireplace,' said Liz. 'He keeps starin at Mike, innit.'

'Does he?' Carol looked at an elderly man sitting on his own in the corner. 'Do you know who he is?'

'Nah. Never clapped eyes on him till recent weeks when he started comin in at odd times. An he don't say a lot when he is here.'

'Oh well, he looks harmless enough,' said Carol. 'And he looks vaguely familiar, so he's probably from one of the nearby villages.'

'Well he don't look familiar ter me, an I know most faces round here. But you reckon you seen him before?'

Casting another quick glance at the old man, Carol shrugged and said she thought she might have done, but she had no idea where. Hearing a cheer from the group by the darts board, she grinned at the sight of Glynis and Mike giving each other a high five.

Huh, so they'd won against Ken and Annie, then. Looking at Ken to see how he was taking that, Carol was pleased to see him drape an arm round Glynis and hold her hand up in a victory gesture. At which point, a couple of the local moped lads got up from a table and went towards the darts board.

'Oh good, that lets me off the hook,' said Carol, seeing one of the French lads shake Mike's hand after a brief exchange of words. 'Looks like game over for us.'

When she'd put the tray of drinks on the table the others had adjourned to, she was moving a chair to where she could see the strange man in the corner as Mike was asking if the lads' behaviour was normal.

'Of course,' said Lars. 'They've waited patiently for us to finish three games, and now it's their turn to use the board.'

'What I meant was,' said Mike, 'is it normal for French kids to be that polite?'

'Sure.' Lars shrugged. 'Do you find that unusual?'

'Where I come from it would be.' Mike shook his head. 'I can't say I've ever been in a pub where a couple of teenage lads would politely ask if they may use the darts board, let alone say thank you and shake your hand when you tell them to go ahead.'

'Ah,' said Ken. 'Such is the quality of life in Burgundy.'

'Which you seem to be enjoying,' said Carol. 'No regrets about leaving your Essex way of life, then?'

'I'm taking my test next month,' said Glynis. 'Ken's been taking me out for a practice drive most days, haven't you, Ken?'

For all the world as if that was the most natural thing for him to do, he said, 'Of course. Got to encourage my lady to be independent, haven't I?'

'I'd watch that if I were you,' said Mike, grinning at Annie. 'These women can get out of hand if you let them.'

'We've decided not to get a dishwasher, Carol,' said Glynis.

Seeing the slightly bemused look on Mike's face, Carol was wondering how she could discreetly warn him and Annie about the sensitive situation when the old man got up from his seat in the corner. As he passed their table, he paused momentarily and looked at Mike before going to the door and leaving the bar.

Okay, it was well known that Liz didn't miss much, and she

hadn't been wrong about this. The old man did seem to be interested in Mike, but that didn't signify anything, did it? Even so, Carol asked Mike if he knew anything about the man who'd just left.

'Sorry,' said Mike. 'I didn't notice him. Why, is it someone I should know?'

'No, no,' she said. 'I just wondered.'

It was when Carol glanced through the window and saw the old boy take his glasses off and polish them that she remembered where she'd seen him before.

'It's just that I think he was at your Aunt Monique's memorial service.'

'Which is more than I was,' said Mike. 'By the time I even heard of her, it was all too late.'

Declining Ken's offer to drive them all home, the other four strolled up the lane enjoying the warm night air and the sweet smell of freshly cut hay. It wasn't long before Rupert, Bovril and Sue Ellen trotted down the lane and joined them, Sue Ellen doing her usual vocal welcome with her tail swishing the air.

'Do they think they're dogs, or what?' said Annie. 'I don't think I've ever seen cats going for a walk with people.'

'Those cats think they *are* people,' said Lars.

'Rubbish,' said Carol. 'They know they're way above the people scale when it comes to intelligence.'

'I don't believe that,' was Mike's comment. 'I mean, our Perdue refused to go and live at the Lucotts' farm where she'd have been safe and looked after. Where was the intelligence in that?'

'She was waiting for you,' said Lars.

'Yeah, sure she was. We didn't even know we'd be coming here, and you want me to believe a flipping cat was waiting for us!'

'Was she wrong?' asked Lars.

'Well, no, as it turned out. But don't ask me to believe the cat knew that.'

'What you don't know,' said Carol, 'is that cats know many things. Take, for example, when I was scared and lonely and needed a living being to share my life, it was Sue Ellen's mum who decided which one of her kittens she thought I should have.'

'Really?' Annie stopped walking and looked at Carol. 'Does that apply to people as well?'

'Sorry, Annie. I don't quite see what that question means.'

'Nothing, really.' Annie shrugged. 'It's just...well, what I'm wondering is if some being or other somewhere decides who has which children.'

'Could be, I suppose,' said Carol. 'Why are you wondering that?'

'Oh, don't mind me.' Annie linked her arm through Carol's as they walked on to catch up with the men. 'I read somewhere that pregnant women can sometimes have strange ideas.'

'That's true,' said Carol. 'I remember when I was...hang on, are you telling me you're pregnant?'

'Didn't Dora tell you?'

'No. And what on earth makes you think she would?'

'I suppose,' said Annie, 'because it was her who told me.'

Chuckling, Carol said, 'That's our Dora for you. So how do you feel about it?'

'What, about her knowing before we did?'

'No, not that bit,' said Carol.

'We're only over the flaming moon,' said Annie.

By this time, they had reached Escargot Cottage, and the two couples exchanged goodnights, and, yes, it had been a fun evening which they should do again.

As Mike and Annie walked on to their house, he said that he'd found Ken good company this evening.

'He was, wasn't he?' said Annie. 'And when you catch her right, Glynis is fun anyway.'

'Grasshopper mind, or what?' he said. 'Where did her taking a driving test and them not buying a dishwasher suddenly come from?'

'Yes, well, she does that leaping from one subject to something completely unrelated thing. When we walked past the shower cabinets in Castorama, she asked if we were thinking of having one.'

'What, a shower cabinet?'

'No. She wondered if we were planning to have a conservatory. Oh look, Mike, Perdue's coming to meet us.'

'Yeah, right,' he said, squatting down and holding out a hand to greet Perdue. 'All that stuff about feline intelligence, and this stupid thing hasn't even worked out that I hate cats.'

Trotting a bit ahead, Perdue led the way home. But on reaching the house, the little cat went round to the side, stopped and looked back at them.

'Is that supposed to mean something?' asked Mike.

'I think what it means, Mike, is that we're supposed to follow her.'

'So we have to indulge a flipping cat now, do we?'

'Suit yourself,' she said when, after following Perdue, they found her sitting on the garden bench. 'Me, I'm going along with the idea it's too beautiful a night to go to bed yet.'

'Okay, I'll buy into that,' he said, looking up at a three-quarter moon and a positive blanket of stars.

After sitting for a while, enjoying the tranquil velvety atmosphere and commenting on how many stars were visible when there were no street lights, Annie said, 'You could phone your dad. It must be around early evening his time, and he just might know something about who Henri-Pierre is or was.'

'I don't think he'll know,' said Mike. 'He did tell me nobody knew anything about a man in Monique's life, or even that there was one until it became evident she was pregnant. Talking of which, you really have to phone your mum and tell her she's going to be a granny.'

'I already did.'

'When?'

'When you were showering before we went out.'

'And?'

'She was odd.'

'What sort of odd?'

'Hard to explain.' Annie shook her head. 'I thought she seemed pleased to hear from me.'

'Well it has been a few weeks, Annie.'

'I know, and I expected an instant tirade. I thought the first I'd hear would be an itemised catalogue of everything my dad has or hasn't done, but that didn't happen.'

'So what did happen? How did she react to your news?'

'She was...um...she did a lot of sniffing and said some things about feeling left out, and how she wasn't important and didn't matter sort of stuff.'

'Then what?'

'That was when I told her she *is* important. Like how could she even think my child's grandmother didn't matter.'

'So all was good then, was it?'

'No, Mike. That was when I got the tirade. About how I'd deserted her, and as if it wasn't enough that my father had deserted her.'

'Nice one,' said Mike. 'Is that all?'

'No. Would you believe she's had to leave the Women's Institute because her branch has allowed two Asian women to join?'

'Anything else?'

'I don't know, do I? It's a bit hard to hear when you've got the phone tucked in your armpit.'

CHAPTER TWENTY

Seeing an opulent-looking car stop outside, Annie told Mike it looked as if the Fortescues had arrived. Looking over her shoulder, he said, 'I thought Harriet said they were old.'

'Well one of them is,' she said, as a man who looked to be in his late seventies got out of the car. 'But she can't be much more than forty.'

'Are you talking stones or years?'

'Not funny, Mike. I agree she's a bit on the plump side, but who wouldn't kill for a face like that?'

'Fair enough,' he said when a large lady climbed out of the passenger seat, revealing quite a lot of thigh before adjusting a loose kaftan-like garment. 'Nice face, shame about the legs, as they say. I'll be in the lounge, call me if you need me. Only I need to get that design emailed out today.'

'Yeah, fine. They've only come to look at the candelabras, so I can deal with it,' she said, going to open the front door before the visitors had time to knock. Not that they seemed in a hurry to get to the door. The man seemed preoccupied with checking the car doors were locked, and the woman had stopped beside Tiggy. She was gazing at the campervan as if she'd never seen one before.

'That is so darling,' Annie heard her say. 'Truly amazing, don't you think, Toby?'

'Absolutely,' he said, walking past Tiggy without as much as a glance in the van's direction. After shaking hands with Annie and announcing that he was Toby Fortescue, and that was Felicity, he marched into the house.

'Do feel free to come in,' Annie muttered under her breath. She was uncertain whether to follow him or wait for his wife when the wife called, 'Do tell me, who painted it?'

'What, the van?'

'The hedgehog, darling, the hedgehog.'

'I've no idea,' said Annie. 'It was on there when we bought the van.'

'Such exquisite detail.' Felicity ran a finger along the hedgehog's spines. 'So vibrantly *alive*.'

Unable to come up with a response to that, Annie told her that Mr Fortescue was inside, and maybe she'd like to see the candelabras?

'Of course, cherub, of course.' And she marched into the house, leaving Annie to meekly follow in her wake in time to hear Toby say the candelabras would probably suit.

'How absolutely splendid,' said Felicity, completely ignoring the candelabra on the wall and going straight to one of Monique's paintings. With a rapt expression on her beautiful face, she tilted her head at several different angles, then moved on to another painting. Looking at Annie accusingly, she announced that they had not been informed of the pictures.

'That's because they aren't for sale,' said Annie.

'Oh but I simply *must* have them for my gallery. Shall we discuss commission?'

'I'm sorry, Mrs Fortescue, but they're Mike's, and there's no way he'll part with them.'

'But surely he can paint more like these?'

'Actually, he didn't...'

'Of course, they'd be worth more if they were signed. So if he could just do that?'

'No can do,' said Mike, coming into the hall. 'I didn't paint them, and as Annie said, they aren't going to leave this house.'

'I see.' Felicity looked from Annie to Mike, and for a moment there, it seemed she was going to march out as peremptorily as she'd marched in. Instead, she shrugged and said, 'It would appear my interest is unacceptable to you, Mark.'

'The name's Mike, Mrs Fortescue.'

'Felicity.' She held out a hand.

'So, Felicity,' said Mike, shaking the proffered hand. 'Can I interest you in a couple of candelabras?'

The deal was quickly done, and it was agreed that Danny would convey the items from their current position and install them in Chez Fortescue. The Fortescues were about to leave when Felicity asked if she may take another quick look at the paintings.

'Of course,' said Mike. 'Would you like to see the others?'

'You mean there are more?'

'Through here.' Mike led her into the lounge.

After staring at five more paintings, Felicity said, 'These are later than the one's in the hall. The charm of the others is their naiveté, whereas these display superb finesse. Who did paint them?'

'A relative.'

'Here, in France?'

'Yes, she never left France,' he said. 'In fact, as far as I know, she never left this area.'

'Oh, I believe she did, darling,' said Felicity. 'My guess is she spent time in Toulouse. You see, the style is distinctive.'

'How do mean?'

'The light, the shading on the trees. The nuances are there, do you see?'

'No.' Mike shook his head. 'Sorry, I'm not getting this.'

'Look at the grass in this one,' she said. 'See how each clump is different, and the way they merge to become what initially seems like any other meadow. But when one looks closely, it's obvious.'

'What is?'

'That your relative, whoever she is, was trained by one of the Debuet brothers. At the moment it escapes me which of them was landscapes.'

'Okay,' said Mike. 'Tell me something, will you?'

'Just ask, darling, just ask.'

'You've picked up on trees and grass and stuff, but what about people?'

'There are no people in these paintings,' she said. 'And so there would not be.'

'But what if someone trained by one of those Debuet guys wanted to paint faces?'

'Ah, that's a tricky one. You see...' But whatever she said next was drowned out by the strident blasting of a car horn.

'Yes, Toby. I'm coming,' she shrieked at a decibel level that came close to equalling the car horn.

Before getting into the car, she made that meaningless mwaa noise in the direction of each of Annie's cheeks and said, 'We must lunch sometime, cherub.'

'Yes, we must,' said Annie – mentally adding *not*.

'Next time you're in London, perhaps.'

'Oh, we don't do London, Felicity. The nearest we get to a metropolis is Dijon.'

As Felicity eased herself into the front of what must surely be a top-of-the-range Mercedes, Annie said, 'Thank you so much for buying our old furniture. It made all the difference to us being able to afford an indoor lavatory.'

With fixed smiles on their faces, they waved at the departing Fortescues, Mike squeezed Annie's bum and said, 'Naughty, naughty.'

'Sorry,' she said. 'That just sort of slipped out.'

'Nice one.' He grinned. 'Just wish I'd thought of it.'

Something about his current project was eluding Mike. He needed to get it to the client like yesterday, and he could have done without being distracted by the frigging Fortescues. Cursing when the phone on his desk rang, he snatched it up to hear a voice say, 'She's abso*lutely* miff.'

'Good afternoon, Harriet. What does miff mean, and who is whatever that is?'

'Miffed, and Flickers is.'

'Really? She seemed happy with the light fittings.'

'Mike, we're talking paintings here.'

'Ah. Yes, she wasn't what you might call happy about not getting her hands on those.'

'Actually, she's totally miz. What Flickers wants, Flickers does so expect to get.'

'Not this time, Harriet. Sorry, but those paintings are so not up for grabs.'

'No prob, your call. Apols if she pulled a harass on you.'

'It's okay. Um, Harriet, if that's all this is about...'

'Totally all. And well done you.'

Mike had only just put the phone down when it rang again. He was tempted to ignore it, thinking it might be bloody Flickers, but the persistent ringing wouldn't be ignored. Where the hell was Annie when she was needed? Making a mental note to not have his desk phone switched on when he was working, he gave in and picked up the intrusive instrument.

This time it was Carol, asking if he was busy.

'Not so as you'd notice,' he said.

'It's just that I'm worried about Lars. But if you're busy...'

'No, Carol, I'm not,' he lied. 'What's the problem?'

After listening to what Carol was worried about, Mike did wonder if she was overreacting. But, come on, she wasn't the type to be overly dramatic, was she? If Lars had gone out on his moped to take some books to Maiseronne, which was only going to take twenty minutes, thirty tops, and hadn't been seen for over an hour, then, yes, it was a bit worrying. Especially as Carol had phoned Glynis and got no reply. So they were obviously out, in which case, Lars was going to put the books in their porch and come straight back. But that hadn't happened. Carol had called his mobile but all she'd picked up was a message saying he was unavailable to take a call.

The fact that Lars had gone on his moped was down to the fact that Carol's Vauxhall had got a flattie. Which was why she couldn't go and look for him. So if Mike had a few minutes to help with putting the spare on?

'Sure, no worries,' he told her. 'I'll be with you in five.' After casting a lingering look at the design on his computer screen, he went through the open casement doors into the garden to where Annie was painting shutters and told her where he was going. Deciding it would be quicker to drive than to walk to Carol's house, he fired up Tiggy's engine and was with Carol in less than five minutes.

Twenty minutes later, they were still searching for the car jack. Tiggy's, dammit, was a different type and came nowhere near close to doing the job. Mike was trying to curb his frustration about the time he was losing. If he didn't get that design out today...'

But, having tried Glynis's phone and Lars's mobile again, Carol's anxiety level was rising fast. And what was more important here? A distressed neighbour or an irate client? Meanwhile, a paint-splattered Annie had walked down the lane to find out what was going on.

Her suggestion that they abandon the useless Vauxhall and take Tiggy made sense. So why didn't Mike go back to work, and she'd drive Carol to wherever? Okay, that seemed to make sense as well, but seeing the look on Carol's face made him wonder if she'd cope with the additional stress of Annie driving the campervan. Making an instant decision, he got into Tiggy and said he'd do it.

'Do you want me to come with you?' Annie asked Carol.

'Well, I...I am a bit scared, so...'

'Right, I'm coming with you,' said Annie.

Mike had taken the turning to Maiseronne when Annie remembered she hadn't locked the house.

'So?' said Mike. 'We live in Coulaize, not flipping Sheffield.

147

You'd hardly expect some vandal to break in, would you?'

'They wouldn't need to,' said Annie. 'Seeing as we've left the casement doors wide open.'

'We hardly ever lock our place,' said Carol. 'Except when we go off cruising, that is. In fact.' She turned to look at Annie in the back as Mike changed gear on approaching a sharp bend. 'We always leave the back door open at night when the weather's...'

'Oh Christ!' said Mike, slamming his foot on the brake pedal.

In front of them, blocking the road, was a breakdown truck with a hook attached to a car which was sideways on across the road. Imbedded in the car's radiator grill was the front wheel of a moped.

CHAPTER TWENTY-ONE

Typical of the Dutch, the car owners spoke English. Not that the shivering woman huddled in a blanket seemed capable of saying much in any language. Neither of them spoke French, and hadn't been able to understand what the paramedics had said. Yes, they knew the moped rider was alive, but they didn't know how badly he was injured, or where he'd been taken.

'But I am sure they will inform you,' said the man.

'Not when he didn't have any means of identification on him,' said a shaking Carol.

'Come on.' Mike put his arm round Carol's shoulders. 'All we can do is go home and make some phone calls.'

'Who to?'

'The police, for starters. They'll know something.'

'Yes,' said the Dutchman. 'They have been, and it was they who called for the breakdown service.'

As Annie led Carol to Tiggy, Mike said, 'What about you and the lady?'

'The policeman also have called for us a taxi.'

'Okay,' said Mike. 'As long as you're sorted.'

'Ja, we are good. Please to tell your lady we are much sorry.'

'I will,' Mike called over his shoulder, already getting into Tiggy, where Annie was squashed into the front passenger seat with her arms wrapped round Carol. Swearing about the narrowness of the road, Mike turned Tiggy with difficulty and silently thanked some god or other that he hadn't let Annie and Carol go on their own.

'It's okay.' Annie tried to comfort the shivering woman in her arms. 'They said he's alive.'

'How alive, though?' said Carol. 'That could mean anything.'

'Look, try not to worry. First we'll phone the police, and they'll be able to tell us which hospital he was taken to, then we can call them and find out.'

But there was no need to phone the police. As soon as they turned into the lane, they could see the police car at Carol's cottage.

'W-why are they here?' Carol's voice sounded in danger of cracking completely.

'We'll soon find out,' said Mike, pulling Tiggy to a stop as a policewoman approached the van. A rapid exchange in French went on through Tiggy's open window and, clutching Annie's arm, Carol said, 'What are they saying?'

'I don't know, Carol. It's too fast and I can't follow it.'

'The woman just said identité.' Carol's grip on Annie's arm increased. 'Oh god, they want me to identify his body.'

'Hang on,' said Annie. 'We don't know that's what they're saying.'

'And now that bloody policewoman is smiling,' said Carol. 'What the hell is that about?'

It wasn't until Mike had thanked the policewoman and hands were shaken that he was able to tell them. 'He's got a broken leg, a broken wrist, some bruises and he's been treated for shock, but otherwise okay. And right now he's in Dijon General being looked after.'

'You what!' said Carol. 'You mean I haven't got to identify a dead body?'

'No way.' Mike stared at her. 'Whatever made you go there?'

Releasing her grip on Annie's arm, Carol told him it was because she could have sworn something was said about identifying.

'Oh, that,' said Mike. 'That was about them identifying who he was through his moped number plates.'

'That's weird,' said Carol. 'He's got Dutch number plates on the moped and, as far as I know, no one would have this address.'

'Oh well,' said Mike. 'Let's just put it down to some inter-European tracking system or something. Um, are we going to sit in this van much longer?'

'No, Mike. I don't know how to begin thanking you both for...for being there when I needed you. But if Annie would just let me get out, I can cope now.'

'Are you sure?' said Annie. 'I'm happy to come in and stay with you for a while if...'

'Bless your bum, Annie, but you've done enough.'

'Okay.' Annie got out so Carol could be released from her position trapped between her and Mike. 'We're minutes away if you need us. Like, you'll be wanting to go to Dijon hospital, won't you? And don't forget you can't use your car.'

On their way back to their own home, Annie and Mike waved at Jean-Claude Lucott as he passed on his tractor. What they didn't see was him stop at Escargot Cottage, lift Carol's Vauxhall with the prongs on the front of the tractor, usually used for lifting hay bales, and change a wheel before lowering the car back to ground level.

Hey, who needs a car jack when they've got a neighbour like that? The taciturn farmer simply knocked on the cottage door and informed Carol her car was now a goer – or the French equivalent of those words, anyway – before climbing back onto his tractor and driving back to his farm.

As for how he even knew about a flat tyre, you'd have to ask Pascal la Poste about that.

'Bugger,' said Annie, when they turned under the walnut tree onto the track. 'What we don't need right now is visitors.'

'Well one thing's for sure,' said Mike. 'Burglars or vandals don't arrive in a Mercedes.'

'I'll leave you to it, if you don't mind,' she said. 'My head's cracking, and I'd like to go and lie down with a paracetemol.'

Mike found Felicity in the lounge, gazing at his computer screen. Given that the screen would have gone into sleep mode ages ago, the cheeky cow had obviously clicked on the mouse to get the design Mike had been working on to appear.

Seemingly completely at ease about being found uninvited in someone's home, not to mention poking her nose into someone's private computer, Felicity said, 'Wonderful. I didn't know you were an artist, darling.'

'What I am is a graphic designer,' said Mike. 'Um, is there something we can do for you?'

'Just one tiny detail,' she said, pointing at the computer. 'I'm not totally convinced about this section here.'

'Sorry?'

'Here, darling.' She picked up a pen from the desk and indicated the area Mike had been struggling with before being called out on a mercy mission.

'Er, right,' he said. 'To be honest, I'm not happy with that bit, but I can't seem to put my finger on why.'

'Colouring,' she said. 'Too much contrast, don't you think?'

Nodding, Mike said, 'You know, you could just have hit it.'

'Tone it down slightly, can you?'

Sitting at the desk, mouse in hand, he did a minor colour adjustment. 'How's that?'

'Excellent, darling, excellent. Do hope you'll forgive one for popping in sans appointment, but no one answered the telephone, you see.'

Realising that she'd cracked his problem, and he could get the design emailed out today after all, Mike thought he'd forgive her almost anything. Except – bugger it – had she come back to pile on more hassle about the paintings?

In a way, yes, she had. She had a proposition to put to him, but this time it wasn't about selling them in her gallery. What she would absolutely adore was a loan of one or two of Monique's landscapes.

'I promise to guard them with my life, darling. You see, I've been talking to Joselyn Tremain, my business partner, and he's terribly excited.'

'Is he?'

'Absolutely. He'll know instantly if they *are* influenced by Debuet, and if they are, we'll have scooped a coup.'

'Really?'

'Really, darling. No one in London has ever displayed a product of a Debuet protégé. You see, if that is what we have here, it would be sinful to not share a few.'

'Hang on.' Mike held up a hand. 'You said one or two.'

'Wonderful. So you'll agree to lending one or two. I am so delighted, thank you.'

Hearing Harriet's voice in his head saying, "What Flickers wants, Flickers expects to get", Mike realised he'd fallen right into it. And where was the harm? The paintings *were* exceptionally good. Did he have the right to be so selfishly possessive? It wasn't as if he wouldn't get them back, and if Felicity was promising to guard them with her life, he couldn't see anyone getting past that body.

A body that was now sitting at his desk looking at his computer screen. In answer to her question about if this was typical of what he did, he told her each design varied in accordance with his clients' requirements.

Clicking her fingers, she said, 'Business cards?'

'Yes,' he said, opening a desk drawer and handing her one of his own. 'I do those as well.'

'Need at least two dozen, darling. I know oodles of people in London.'

Feeling that having his business details passed around London could turn out to be a fair enough exchange for the loan of a couple of pictures, Mike fished out a box of cards.

'Excellent.' She got up and walked backwards and forwards in front of Monique's paintings. 'This one, I think.' Felicity tilted her head. 'Or maybe that one? So terribly hard to choose.'

In the end, she was torn between three. And in the end, Mike gave in and agreed to her taking three of his mother's paintings to be displayed and oohed and aahed over in a London art gallery.

It just so happened that good old Flickers had been confident enough to bring the appropriate packaging with her. 'In the Merc, darling,' she said. 'You'll find it on the back seat.'

Feeling like an errand boy, Mike went to fetch the specially lined cartons. He then asked when he would get his paintings back.

'No rush, darling. When we come back to France sometime.'

'Which will be when, exactly?'

'Not before Christmas at the earliest.'

'Okay,' said Mike, scribbling on a piece of paper as something Miss Pearls Pinkerton had taught him kicked in. 'If you could just sign and date this receipt.'

'No need, darling.' She flapped a hand. 'You know where the paintings are going to be.'

'Even so...' He pushed the paper towards her and handed her a pen. 'And we'll agree on a loan for four months max, shall we?'

With the precious cargo safely installed in the Merc, she squeezed her bulk behind the steering wheel and said, 'Oh, by the way. According to Joselyn, the Debuet brother who specialised in landscapes was the one called Henri-Pierre.'

After feeding Henri-Pierre Debuet into Google search, Mike found out that the man had indeed taught art students in Toulouse up until 1985, when ill health had brought about the closure of *l'Académie de Debuet de l'art*. He was also able to see samples of Henri-Pierre's work, and the fact that he was born in Paris in 1917. That would make him about sixteen years older than Monique, but no date was given for his death. So did that mean he was still alive?

And what if he was? Even if Mike had a clue how to trace him, what then? He could hardly drop in on the guy and say, Hi, I'm Monique Lanteine's son. I don't know if you remember her or not, but I believe you're probably my father.

Carol had phoned the hospital and been assured that, yes, Lars was definitely alive. In fact, he'd been giving the nurses a run-around according to an English-speaking nurse with what sounded like an Italian accent.

'Really? What's he been up to?' asked Carol.

In quite halting English, the nurse told her he'd insisted on having the hand part of the plaster cast for his broken wrist shaped round a beer can. The broken leg, however, was more serious. And, no, it was not possible for her to speak with the patient because he'd just had a pre-med prior to surgery.

Her stomach rebelling against the idea of anything to eat, Carol was opening a wine bottle when Liz rang.

'Carol, what the hell's goin on?'

'What's been going on, Liz, is that Lars somehow managed to plough his moped into a car.'

'Gawd! Is he alright?'

'I gather he will be when a few bones have got back in place, but whether or not the nurses will recover might be a different story.'

'It int too serious, then?'

After giving Liz a brief outline of Lars's injuries, Carol asked how Liz knew something had happened.

'We only had the coppers in here, innit. Askin about Lars, they was.'

'Asking what about him?'

'Where they could find some next of kin is what they wanted ter know. Put the fear a shit up me an Gus, that did.'

'But what made them think you'd know? It's not like they'd have known where to start looking.'

'It was on account of his moped insurance, they said.'

'But, Liz, I don't see what that has to do with you.'

'It was last summer, when he needed an address fer insurance, an he asked if he could use ours.'

'Ah. Gottit. Flipping heck, the police said they got his name through tracing the moped number plates, but I couldn't work out how the Dutch registration bods would know where he lives.'

'Yeah, well, my Gus reckons they got their ways ter do all sorts a stuff. I'll have ter go, Carol, we got a bunch a people comin in the bar. You'll call us if you need anyfin, woncha?'

What Carol needed right now was a hefty glass of wine. A situation that was endorsed by the fact that she had difficulty getting it all in a glass with a still shaking hand. She had taken a gulp of what had made it into the glass, and was mopping up the overspill when the phone rang again.

This time it was Tina. How did she know? Because she'd just called Annie about a teaching job. Then it was Harriet, who didn't say how she'd heard, but Carol must let her and Luc know what they could do to help, and they hoped poor Lars wasn't totally miz.

The next one to call was Dora Turner, who said she and Don had popped into the Carry On when Liz was in a tizz after the police had been in.

'Tell us what you need done,' said Dora.

'What I think, Dora, is that I need a recorded message on the phone. I'm beginning to sound like a parrot repeating broken leg and wrist.'

'It will take time, of course.'

'Dora, it would take forever. I haven't got a clue how to set up one of those answer message jobs.'

'Carol, dear, what I mean is you need to be prepared for quite a long recovery period. I believe Lars sustained severe bone breakage before?'

'Oh, right. More like smashed legs, you could say, when he crashed a helicopter. But that was years ago.'

'We'll talk about it when he's home, dear. But it might help to know I'm trained in rehabilitation physiotherapy.'

'Dora, is there anything you can't do, medically speaking?'

'Oh yes, Carol. I've never delivered a baby.'

155

CHAPTER TWENTY-TWO

To say Carol had a restless night would be as obvious as saying Sumo wrestlers are heavy buggers. In fact, she felt as if she'd been through a few bouts with at least one of those. Sure as hell, something had thumped her in the head, and her legs weren't functioning quite as they should when she hauled herself out of bed. And having three cats under her feet as she made her way downstairs was like trying to play hopscotch with elastic bands round her ankles.

Reaction, she supposed. Mind you, some food would help. Unable to face food last night, she hadn't eaten since yesterday lunchtime. Yes, right, food was a good idea, and she was standing in the kitchen wondering what would be easy to swallow when she heard a car draw away from the front of the cottage.

Funny, she was sure no one had knocked on the door. And who would be calling on her at this time of the morning anyway? After all, it could only be…

What? Looking at the kitchen clock, she couldn't believe it wasn't lying to her. The last time she'd looked at the time it had been on the bedside clock, and that had told her it was just after five. So she must have eventually fallen asleep after that because it was now twenty past nine, for heaven's sake!

And what the devil was going on outside? Flipping heck, it was like the M25, what with two cars turning in the lane within minutes of each other. Opening the door, she was in time to see Madame Purcell's taxi disappearing down the lane. She shrugged, and was about to close the door when Rupert decided to make an exit. Not an overdue one, considering the cat had been on the bed all night. As she looked down to make sure his tail was clear before closing the door, she noticed an assortment of items beside her doorstep.

Kneeling on the step, she read messages on a biscuit tin, a chocolate box and a bunch of flowers. Messages in French offering felicitations and hoping Lars would soon be well. Unable to control tears sliding down her face, Carol looked up to see Fabrice, Madame

Gruyot's son from the village shop, walking up the lane. He had come bearing a box of marshmallows, which he handed over saying his mother thought she'd have enough eggs.

And he wasn't wrong about that because, soon after, Jannine Lucott arrived with eggs and a lamb and vegetable pie. The eggs were for Carol because eggs are easy to eat when a person is not with a good appétit in times of trouble. The lamb pie was for Lars because, according to Jannine, hospital food wasn't particularly appetising. After assuring Jannine that, yes, she would be sure to let them know of anything they could do to help, Carol closed her door, picked up Sue Ellen and let a flow of emotion seep into the cat's fur.

A few minutes later, one of the village lads who often spent time with Lars on the barge arrived with a pot plant balanced on his moped handlebars.

So, Pascal la Poste had obviously been the supplier of verbal news along with the written ones in his post bag. When the man himself arrived, he didn't have any letters for Carol. But he stopped his little yellow van anyway to deliver a packet of freshly sliced ham courtesy of Marie-Clair the local butcher. Which he informed Carol was très important pour une personne à l'hôpital.

The tantalising aroma of succulent ham emanating from the waxed paper in Carol's hand kick-started her previously absent desire for food. Good grief, there was enough ham there to keep Lars in sandwiches for a week. Which led Carol to making an instant decision. A slice topped with one of Jannine's eggs could also be justifiably considered très important for a person who hadn't eaten a thing in the last twenty hours.

Having been told Lars had been in theatre for more than four hours of surgery, Carol was relieved to find him propped up on a bank of pillows, chatting in English to the other occupant of the two-bed room. What did alarm her, however, was the huge bulge under his covers.

'Carol, it's nothing to worry about,' he said, holding up his wrist. 'It's just the little Italian nurse I got plastered with over this bit reported that I was a naughty boy. So my punishment was to sleep in a tent.'

'Yes, Lars, very ho ho. What is that…that bulge thing about?'

'Just some scaffolding to keep the covers off my leg. You're allowed to kiss me if you like.'

'So what's the story on your leg?' she asked, after she'd grinned at the man in the other bed and told him it was now safe to stop looking at the ceiling.

The story wasn't the best she'd ever heard. Apparently, the metal plates and pins the Abu Dhabi hospital had put in place to hold the leg together after the copter crash had all been displaced.

'But...' She didn't want to ask, but knew she had to. 'You have still got the leg?'

'Yes.' He squeezed her hand. 'Although I have to admit, when I came to and saw the cage thing, that was exactly where my head was going.'

'Okay.' She breathed a sigh of relief. 'So what is the long-term situation?'

'If you'll pardon the pun,' he said. 'The docs are being a bit cagey about that. All I know right now is that I'll be in here for a week, maybe more. It depends.'

'On what?'

'On how the new nuts and bolts settle in. I gather it's to do with old scare tissue or something.'

'I see. I suppose that's what Dora meant when she said we have to be prepared for this not being a quick recovery job.'

'Dora? You mean she already knows what's happened?'

'Lars, the whole bloody village knows. Which reminds me, do you fancy a ham sandwich?'

'Yes please,' said the man in the other bed. 'If there's one going spare, that is. It's just they gave us pasta and meat balls for lunch, with no sauce or anything to help it down.'

After not much more than an hour, Lars was beginning to flag. Carol asked him if he wanted to sleep, and he said he wasn't sure he could keep his eyes open much longer, so if she didn't mind...

'No, it's fine,' she said, bending over to kiss him and run a hand over his thatch-like hair. 'You behave yourself, okay?'

'It's the anaesthetic,' said the other man. 'See, he's drifted off already. It does that to you for a day or so.'

Smiling at him, Carol said, 'When he wakes up, would you tell him I'll be back tomorrow afternoon?'

'Will do, lass. Be bringing any more of those sarnies, will you?'

'Maybe.' Carol grinned. 'Unless you fancy a lump of lamb and veggie pie, that is.'

'Ooer, that sounds right grand, that does. Got any gravy to go inside it, have you?'

'Don't you worry,' she said. 'It was made by a French farmer's wife, and she knows all about soaking lamb in well tasty sauce before wrapping it in pastry.'

'Me mouth's watering already. Name's Harry, by the way.'

Liking the look of his weathered face and twinkling eyes, Carol moved her chair to his bed. Well, she had driven twenty miles to do a hospital visit, and the man seemed keen to be friendly, so why not chat to the only awake person available?

During the next half hour, she found out he was sixty-six and lived on his own. No, he'd never been married. Came close once, but escaped in time and took up with Lucinda instead.

'Tiny little thing, she was,' he said. 'Did me for five years, but when her bottom started giving trouble, it was time to trade her in for a more modern one.'

'Funny,' said Carol. 'That's what happened to me.'

'You what?'

'I lasted twenty-nine years, though, before my husband traded me in for a newer model with less hefty bumpers.'

'Why'd he do that?' Harry cast an appreciative look at her slim, toned body.

'Probably something to do with her big knockers. But it didn't last long.'

'Well, me and Jemima have been together getting on for eleven years now, and she suits me grand. Bigger, see. Seventy foot long, so plenty of space for a bloke on his own.'

'Okay, right.' Carol's brain clicked into engaged mode. 'Are you telling me Jemima is a boat?'

'Narrowboat, lass. Right little beauty she is too.'

Glancing at Lars, who was well zonked out, Carol got to her feet and said, 'Sorry, Harry, I'm a bit out of sync at the moment. I'll see you tomorrow, okay?'

'He'll need books,' called Harry, as Carol went out into the hospital corridor. 'I've only got one with me, and he says he's read that.'

'No worries.' She popped her head back into the room. 'I'll bring enough for both of you.'

Feeling at least happy that Lars had been cheerful and had a nice roommate, Carol drove home thinking that what *she* needed was to be in bed having a good sleep. What she hadn't needed was the mention of bloody books, but Harry was right, Lars would need plenty of those. Presumably he'd actually delivered the books he'd been taking to Ken, and hopefully Ken had brought at least some with him when they moved here from England that she could take to the hospital.

And then it struck her befuddled brain. Several people had phoned, others had left gifts on her doorstep, but not a word from Glynis.

Curled up in a faded chintz-covered armchair the Fortescues had understandably not wanted, Annie was preparing a lesson plan. Or, rather, she was supposed to be doing that, but she kept being distracted by Perdue leaping around trying to catch a butterfly beyond the open doors to the garden.

But then, she supposed it was hard to concentrate after yesterday's traumatic event. They were anxious to know about Lars, but Carol had said she wouldn't have an update until she'd been to the hospital this afternoon.

Mike was presumably having concentration problems too, because he closed his laptop lid, went to sit in the other chair and said, 'Middle of October would be good.'

'Would it?' Annie turned a page of the lesson notes she was compiling.

'Do you reckon your mum could cope with the Eurolines bus?'

'About as well as she could cope with a leaking roof. Pass that book you're sitting on, will you?'

Passing an English grammar book to her, he said, 'She'd want to come, though, wouldn't she?'

'Come where?'

'Here.'

'Well.' Annie shrugged. 'I don't think we'll be planning to take a baby to England in a hurry, so if she wants to see her grandchild…'

'Actually, Annie, I was talking about the wedding.'

'What wedding? Mike, she doesn't know anyone here, so why would she want to come to France for anyone's wedding?'

'I'm not talking about anyone, am I?'

'Okay, so what has not anyone got to do with my mother and

Eurolines?'

Grinning, he said, 'I obviously don't talk in my sleep, then.'

'What's that supposed to mean?'

'Oh, just that I've had these nightmares about asking you to marry me.'

Annie stared at him for a full twenty seconds before saying, 'Mike, is that what you're trying to do here?'

'Annie, what do you think?'

'I...I don't know. What am I supposed to think?'

'Whether to say yes or no will do for starters.'

'Oh will it? You know what? If you want an answer to a yes or no question, you might want to consider actually asking the relevant question.'

'Okay,' he said. 'Do I have your full attention?'

'You do.'

'Wrong answer, Annie. I believe the correct term is I do.'

Trying to control what was threatening to erupt into a giggling bout, she said, 'Let's get this show on the road, shall we? Like, shouldn't you be on one knee or something?'

At which point, Mike got up, went to her chair, sank to his knees in front of her and said, 'Annestine Isabelle Lister, will you do me the honour of becoming my wife? To love, honour and obey and whatever?'

'Drop the obey bit and I might consider it,' she said.

'Okay, dropped. Now what? Only I'm getting cramp down here.'

'Um, let me think now. Oh yes, isn't there supposed to be something else involved in this scene?' Clicking her fingers, she said, 'Gottit. I believe it's called a ring or something like that.'

'Hang on,' he said, getting to his feet and pulling something out of his shorts pocket. 'Will this do for now?'

'Oh my god, Mike!' Annie gazed at a row of sapphires set in a heavy filigree gold band. 'That is some piece of kit.'

'Do you like it?'

'Like it? It's only to die for. Where the hell did you get it?'

'It's not new, Annie.' His voice had an anxious note to it. 'I sort of thought that it would do for now, then we could go to Dijon and buy whatever you choose.'

'Piss off, man. I want this and I want it now. Am I allowed to put it on please?'

'Hold on, woman. That bit of kit is dependent on an answer.'

'Okay, Michael Keith Flint. I do. I will. I want to, you idiot.'

Grabbing her, he said, 'I'll take that as a yes, shall I?'

Since getting back from the hospital, Carol had answered a stack of phone calls and tried Glynis's number at least three times. Coming to the conclusion that they were either out for the day or their phone was on the blink, she considered driving over to Maiseronne. But what was the point if they were out? Besides which, she was knackered. Added to that was the fact that they could surely have got in touch with her.

It wasn't as if she was lacking support, far from it. It was just that she and Glynis had been close friends for so long, and sometimes friends who've known you for most of your life mattered.

At least Carol had spoken to her two daughters, who she'd known all their lives, and she'd had to fend off their idea of coming over to be with her. As expected, Stephanie had done a fair amount of tearful sniffling. And Megan had been brusque and practical, which was her way of dealing with crises. Neither of which Carol felt she could cope with right now, so she'd made light of Lars's condition and assured the girls she would call for them if she needed to. And, yes, of course she'd keep them updated. But things would be fine when Lars was home, which shouldn't be too long.

She'd also called Orso, Lars's brother in Holland, and given him a similar story. Except he wasn't quite so easily convinced. But then, he wouldn't be, given that he knew better than anyone what Lars had been through ten years ago when he'd been told he had a fifty-fifty chance of ever walking again. Trying to allay the obvious anxiety in Orso's voice, Carol told him that, at least this time, Lars had fifty percent of two functioning legs.

'Yes, Carol,' said Orso. 'And this time he has you.'

Bugger, thought Carol, grabbing a box of tissues. How long was this grizzling thing going to go on whenever someone said or did something nice?

Mike's suggestion of them having a siesta was, of course, a bit crazy when the afternoon was nearly gone. But, as he'd said, it was a good idea to have a test run to make sure they were properly compatible before making the commitment of the *until death us do part* sort.

With her head on his chest, Annie said, 'Mike, why now?'

'Why what now?' he mumbled, his voice slightly blurred by post-coital drowsiness.

'What I mean is...' She propped herself up on one elbow and looked at his face. 'We've been living happily in sin for more than seven years, so what's wrong with carrying on as we were?'

'Because, Annie, we've had one bastard born in this house, and I don't want that to happen for our kid.'

'Oh, okay, I get that.' She subsided into the crook of his arm.

'Annie, I'm sorry, I didn't mean to be that blunt,' he said, turning onto his side and putting his other arm round her. 'There are other reasons.'

'Such as?'

'I love you. I want to spend the rest of my life with you. But...'

'But what?'

'I didn't dare ask you before because I was scared you'd say no.'

'Idiot.' She snuggled within his arms before, raising her head again, she said, 'Where *did* you get it?'

'What?'

'That ring.'

'It was in a Heinz baked beans box.'

'Sure it was,' she said. 'There just happened to be what is probably a valuable antique ring just sort of lying around in a Heinz beans box.'

'No, really, Annie. You remember clearing out that chiffonier thing before Danny took it away?'

'Yes, I chucked the stuff into one of the cardboard boxes we used to pack some things to bring here.'

'Which just happened to be a...'

'Okay. It was one of the cartons I picked up at Tescos. What else was in it?'

'Apart from the bag of jewellery, which I rummaged through and found the ring, there was what looked like a document case and...where are you going?'

Getting off the bed, Annie said, 'To look in that beans box. I want to see what other jewellery there is, and it wouldn't hurt for you to find out what's in that document thingy.'

Annie was sifting through what mostly consisted of brooches, bead necklaces and some chains with pendants on them when Mike said, 'Okay, here's one mystery solved.'

'What?' She looked up from the pile of jewellery. 'What've you found?'

'This,' he said, handing her a birth certificate. 'It says Delphine Labois.'

'But I don't get it,' said Annie.

'You will if you look at this,' he said, passing her a marriage certificate. 'Look at the date.'

'Oh. Charles Lanteine married Jeanette Labois in 1951. But wouldn't your Delphine mum have been born before that?'

'She was,' said Mike. 'Her birth certificate is dated 1947.'

'So that means...' Annie shook her head. 'Mike, what exactly does all this mean?'

'That Monique's father, my grandfather, married for a second time.'

'Uh-huh. So now we at least know why the name Labois, not Lanteine, is on your birth certificate.'

'My false birth certificate,' he reminded her. 'Oh shit!'

'What?'

'Annie, you've just agreed to marry Michael Flint. A man who doesn't legally exist.'

CHAPTER TWENTY-THREE

'Hello, Glynis. I'm glad you've phoned,' said Carol, her voice sounding clipped and cool even to her own ears. 'I was beginning to wonder if you were still alive.'

'Carol, I'm sorry I haven't been in touch, but...'

'Well, you know what? Plenty of other people have bothered to phone and stuff.'

'It's just that things have been difficult, and...'

'So tell me about it, Glynis. Would you believe I'm not doing exactly easy myself?'

'Oh...do you need any help or anything?'

'I do, actually. I need some books.'

'Do you? If you mean the ones you must have left in our porch, we haven't had a chance to look at them yet.'

'No, I don't mean those. I was hoping Ken would have some other ones I could take to the hospital.'

'Well, yes, he may have some he's finished with. But why do you want books for a hospital?'

'Because Lars is bored and would appreciate something to read.'

'Carol, what do you mean? You're not saying...you don't mean he's *in* hospital.'

'I gather you haven't heard, then.'

'Heard what? Carol, what's going on?'

'For heaven's sake, Glynis. Have you been out of the country since last Tuesday, or what?'

'Yes. But what's wrong with Lars?'

'You mean you *have* been...'

'Tell me what's wrong with Lars.'

'Glynis, he smashed himself up coming back from delivering books to your bloody porch.'

'Oh my god, my god, my god! What...how bad...what...Shut up, Ken, I'm trying to...'

The next thing Carol heard was Ken's voice asking what was wrong. After she'd given him a brief outline, he said, 'We're on our way, Carol. We'll be with you in ten minutes.' And the line went dead.

Within that ten minutes, Carol had demolished what was left in the tissue box. And a cold water face drench was more or less getting things under control when Sue Ellen jumped onto the draining board, head-butted Carol's arm and said, 'Mrrrup.'

'It's alright, pussy cat.' Carol buried her face in her beloved cat's fur. 'They *do* care.'

'Mrrrup, mrrrup, mrrrup,' said Sue Ellen.

'Bugger, bugger, bugger,' said Carol, grabbing the kitchen roll.

Confusing is about the best way to describe what went on next. What with two women talking over each other, and Ken trying and failing to gain some sort of control. After some tearful hugs – luckily Glynis had brought her own box of tissues – the disjointed conversation went vaguely on the lines of:

Where were you?...In England, how is he?...Why were you? I needed you here...We're here, we're here, we're here...I was so scared, but why did you go to England?...How bad, Carol?...You didn't tell me you were going...I know, I know, I know...He's being brave, but we don't know yet...I'm so so sorry, Carol...And I didn't know where you were, see...

Leaving them to it while he went into the kitchen seemed like the only thing for Ken to do for the time being. At least he knew how to control a coffee pot. By the time he went back to the lounge, having resisted the urge to run a bowl of hot soapy water and had simply rinsed out three mugs under the cold tap, things had calmed down.

Placing a tray on the coffee table, he said, 'Any chance of a coherent report on what Lars's situation is?'

The current situation, Carol told them, was that things had not gone as well as hoped, and he'd had a second session of surgery. She explained that the shin bone hadn't taken well to re-patching over the old injury and, as far as she could make out, a whole new metal plate had been required.

'And the other leg?' asked Ken.

'Okay, thank God. It was the left side that took the brunt.'

'Morale,' said Ken. 'How is that?'

'Good, good.' Carol nodded. 'At least in front of me, anyway. You know Lars, he'll joke his way through most things. And.' She grinned. 'He's got the nurses running around him and spoiling him rotten.'

166

'Can we visit him?' Glynis wanted to know.

'Yes, of course you can. He's had loads of people visiting, and...' Carol reached for Glynis's tissue box. 'I've had so much support.'

'Except from us.' It was Glynis's turn for the tissue box.

'Look,' said Carol. 'You're here now, and it wasn't your fault you...why were you in England, anyway?'

'We went because...' Glynis looked at Ken. 'Do you want to...'

'No.' He stood up. Going to the door, he said, 'I'll leave it to you. I think I'll take a stroll round the garden.'

'Glynis, what...is he okay?'

'Yes. At least, I think he will be. Carol, we went to England so he could have counselling.'

'Oh. That's good, isn't it?'

'It was Darren, really.'

'What was?'

'They had a row, see, and he threatened to walk out.'

'What!' Carol stared at her. 'Ken threatened to walk out?'

'No, Darren did.'

'Um, Glynis, who's Darren?'

'Ken's shop mananger,' she said, looking out at her husband weeding the rockery. 'From what I could make out, he said if he couldn't be trusted to run things, he might as well quit.'

'Ah. So Ken was still wanting to keep tabs on the business?'

'If you call phoning every day keeping tabs, I suppose you could say that. Not that that was what Clifford called it.'

'Clifford?'

'Carol, I told you Ken had counselling.'

'So you did. So I take it this Clifford is a counsellor. Have I got that right?'

'Are you okay with him doing that, Carol?'

'What? Who?'

Pointing to where Ken was now dead heading Carol's roses, Glynis said, 'Clifford did warn us it would take time.'

'That is *sooo* cool,' said Tina, practically drooling over Annie's antique engagement ring. 'And your story gets better and better.'

'Does it?' said Mike.

'Not half. Wow, we've got a baby, and now a wedding. And it's all happened in Burgundy.'

'Except they haven't actually happened yet,' Annie pointed out.

'As good as. My editor's gonna love it. Ta, Mike.' She took a coffee mug from him. 'Right, I'm on this one for next week's column. Unless you've got anything else to hit me with?'

'Flipping heck, what more do you want?' said Mike.

'Oooh, anything and everything. If you've got stuff you haven't let on yet, just spill now before I go into print.'

'On your bike, lady,' he said. 'Lots of stuff happens in Burgundy, but some of it's not for publication.'

'Er, right.' Tina looked at him. 'What you're saying is…'

'Nothing, I was joking.'

'Shame,' she said. 'I'll have to tell my antennae to back down, then.'

'What's that about, Tina?'

'Forget it.' She shrugged. 'Just a journalist vibe thing. Okay, so if I could just check I've got this right so far. The reason you never asked Annie to marry you before was because you were scared she'd say no.'

'Something like that, yes,' said Mike.

'Yeah, that happens. Danny and I lived together three years before the big Q came up. And then it was me doing the asking, but that's Danny for you.'

Tina had left, clutching her note pad and declaring her fingers were itching to get at that keyboard, when Mike asked Annie if Lillian was going to come over for their wedding.

'Well,' said Annie. 'My mother hasn't begun to work out how she'll possibly manage to get here, but she supposes she'll do it somehow.'

'But your dad and Maureen are definitely going to make it. Yes?'

'To quote my dad, they wouldn't miss it for anything. But there's something you need to know, Mike.'

'Which is?'

'Your future mother-in-law doesn't think it's worth the effort and expense just for a wedding that, in her opinion, is a bit late in the day.'

'Okay.' Mike shrugged. 'That's her problem.'

'No, Mike, it's our problem. She thinks it's only worthwhile if she comes for at least two weeks.'

'Annie, please tell me you're not serious!'

'I wish,' she said. 'Mike, we are talking mid October. What do you reckon the chances are of Eurolines being fully booked and not able to bring a single passenger to Dijon?'

'Zero. Zilch. Nada. Annie, how the hell are we going to cope with your mother for two bloody weeks?'

'I've no idea,' she said, getting up to go to the cupboard for a liquorice fix. 'Except Tina did say teaching work piles up in October, so I'll grab all I can and be out as much as possible.'

'Oh, thanks a bunch, Annie. Just leave me stuck here all day with your mother, why don't you.'

Grinning, she said, 'Well, if you had a proper job, you'd be out all day, wouldn't you?'

'Ah, so I'm not doing a proper job now, is that how it is?'

'Not according to my mother, you're not. I mean, what sort of man sits at home all day playing around with silly pictures instead of going out to work?'

'Is that it?'

'No. She simply can't imagine why I expect you to be able to support a wife and child.'

'Annie, how much money have we got left from the stuff Danny sold?'

'What's that got to do with anything?'

'Just that it might be enough to buy every Eurolines ticket going spare in October.'

'Carol, can you pop in before you go ter the hospital?'

'Yes, Liz. Is anything wrong?'

'Nah. It's just we got this whole stack a books fer Lars an that bloke what's in his room wiv him, innit.'

'Brilliant. I'm just leaving, so I'll be with you in a few minutes.'

When she walked into the Carry On, Carol gaped at what had to be at least a couple of dozen books piled up on the bar. 'Cripes, Liz,' she said. 'Where the devil did they all come from?'

'Harriet got these ones. She done what she calls puttin out a directive to everyone what's likely ter have English books, tellin em they got ter let her have em.'

'Bless her bum,' said Carol. 'Those will keep Lars and Harry going for a while.'

'Thas enough fer now then, you reckon?'

'I should think so, Liz. We're hoping he'll be home some time next week.'

'Okay,' said Liz, collecting books off the bar and putting them in a plastic bag. 'He'll still need em till he can get about more normal, won't he, so I'll keep the rest fer then.'

'You mean there's more?'

'Yeah, all them.' Liz pointed to the mantelpiece above the fireplace. 'Those ones are what people brought in on account of the notice.'

'What notice?'

'That one what Gus put on the bar. Int you seen it?'

No, Carol hadn't seen it. But then, she hadn't been in the bar for several days. She looked at the notice asking for books in English or Dutch for hospital patients, then at the row of books on the mantelpiece and said, 'Who brought them in?'

'Lotsa them come from the camp site, where there's mostly Cloggies. Then some from people round here,' Liz said. 'Some a them bin strangers what we int seen before, but they heard about it from people who do come in.'

'Liz,' said Carol, leaning over the bar to hug her. 'I don't know how to thank you.'

'Int no need,' said Gus, coming in from the kitchen. 'We got a few extra customers on account of those what dint know we was here till they was told where ter bring books.'

Tilting her head to look up at him, Carol said, 'Good. That's no more than you deserve.'

'Yeah, well,' he said. 'What I fink is, I done the notice, so don't I deserve one a them hugs an all?'

When Carol went into the hospital room, she found Harry sitting on the chair beside Lars's bed, and a different man occupying what had been Harry's bed.

'What's going on?' she asked.

'I've been evicted,' said Harry. 'But I was waiting to say cheerio to you before I got properly kicked out.'

'Oh, Harry. Does that mean our secret affair is over?'

'No chance.' Harry grinned. 'Got myself some good mates here, and I'm not about to let either of you go out of my life that easy.'

'Excuse me,' said Lars. 'Do I get to play a part in this scene?'

'Oh, sorry.' Carol bent down and kissed him. 'How are you?'

'Pissed off because Harry is deserting me, but relieved I don't have to put up with him anymore.'

Winking at the man who had played an important part in keeping Lars's spirits up since he'd been hospitalised, Carol said, 'Yes, I can get that relieved bit. Just think, I don't have to bring him sarnies and pies in future.'

'Did you bring any today?' asked Harry. 'Only I didn't get lunch on account of I wasn't supposed to be here since this morning.'

'Okay, sod it.' Carol unwrapped one of Jannine Lucott's pork pies. 'Halfsies do you?'

'Ta,' he said, taking half a large pork pie. 'That's all I was waiting for really. I'll get off now and leave you in peace.'

'Hang on,' said Carol. 'We will see you again, won't we?'

'Count on it, lass. Bonded we have, me and him. Both boaters, aren't we, mate?' He shook Lars's hand and said he'd see him soon.

'But where...how will we keep in touch?' Carol wanted to know.

'Knows all about that, he does,' said Harry. 'Right, I'll be off now.'

Sitting beside Lars's bed after Harry had left the room, Carol said, 'Do you want to fill me in on what's been going on since I was here yesterday?'

'Will do, Carol.' He caught hold of her hand. 'Do you want the good news first?'

'Yes.'

'They're pleased with the latest x-rays, and I'm outa here sometime next week.'

'Oh, Lars.' She wrapped her arms round him before fishing a tissue from her sleeve. 'And the not so good news?'

'I have to come in twice a week for checks.'

'We'll manage that, won't we? We'll cope with anything, whatever it takes just to have you home.'

'Carol, it's not going to be easy.'

'Bullshit. Bringing you to Dijon twice a week will be a piece of wee-wee compared to driving here every day to visit.'

'Getting me in and out of the car from and back to a wheelchair is not what I'd call wee-wee. Then there's the step up to the front door.'

'So we'll need a ramp and a hoist and tackle kit. So what?'

Inclining her head backwards to indicate the other bed, she said, 'Is he okay as a room mate?'

'Don't know, he hasn't spoken since they brought him in. But I'm going to miss that other bugger.'

'Me too. Does Harry live far away?'

'He's a boater, Carol. He lives wherever his boat is.'

'Which is where at the moment?'

'Somewhere down the canal near the River Saone, but he says as soon as he's properly fit he'll cruise up to Coulaize for a bit.'

'Ooh, I like it,' said Carol. 'I can carry on my secret affair with him. Did I ever tell you about this crazy Dutch bloke I fancied who lived on a boat?'

CHAPTER TWENTY-FOUR

Putting the phone down, Annie gritted her teeth, turned to Mike and said, 'Would you believe my mother thinks the Eurolines bus takes too long to get here?'

'Really?' His face lighting up, he said, 'Does that mean she's not coming?'

'Oh, she's coming. Just not by bus. After all, it's bound to be full of common people, and who knows what could happen to a woman travelling all that way on her own.'

'She wouldn't be on her own if she'd accepted Maureen's suggestion to come by car with them.'

'Come on, Mike. How could my mother possibly be expected to be trapped for hours in a car with *that woman.*'

'Yeah, right. That woman who was generous enough to offer to share a car with her.'

'Which my dad was never going to let happen,' said Annie, subsiding into a shabby but comfortable armchair. 'Why do you think he said he'd pay mum's travel expenses?'

Getting up from his desk, Mike said, 'I'll put the kettle on. What you need is a cup of tea.'

'No, Mike. What I need is a glass of wine.'

'But you're not supposed to be drinking wine, are you?'

'Who says?'

'Don't know.' He scratched his head. 'I just thought pregnant women weren't supposed to.'

'That's what I thought, but Doctor Devreua says different. He reckons a little white wine is fine. Mind you, he did say no more than two glasses a day.'

'One of which is coming right up,' said Mike, standing up with a grin on his face. 'Did he put a limit on the size of the glass?'

Returning with a couple of modestly-sized glasses of white wine, he handed one to Annie and said, 'Cheers. So what is the story on Lillian? You said she's not coming by bus.'

'Bugger, that tastes good,' said Annie after a few gentle sips. 'She's only flying over, isn't she?'

'Won't that be expensive?'

'Probably, but what's that to her? Her attitude is that *he's* paying, so why shouldn't she travel in style?'

'So we're back to square one, then.' Having drained his glass, Mike looked into it morosely.

'Not quite,' said Annie. 'We now have to drive all the way to Lyon airport to pick her up, instead of half an hour to Dijon station.'

'Annie, how long...'

'About two bloody hours.'

'No, I was going to ask how long since the doc said you could have some wine. It's just that I've been keeping off it because we thought you weren't allowed to drink.'

'Have this,' she said, passing her half empty glass. 'Dora told me bodies are good at saying what they need, and right now her theory is telling this body to give you what's left of this wine.'

'Cheers, Dora.' Mike raised the glass before emptying it. 'I knew I liked that lady the first time we met.'

'The thing is,' said Carol. 'Don's offered, Ken's offered, but it's going to be difficult getting Lars out of a low car and up into the wheelchair when we get home. So what I wondered was...'

'It's yours, Carol,' said Mike, putting a mug of coffee in front of her. 'Tiggy being that much higher, feeding him in and out again is the way to go.'

'Excuse me?' said Annie. 'Why are we talking about Lars as if he's a lump of meat?'

'Come on, Annie. That isn't what I meant, is it?'

'Oh, right.' She shrugged. 'It's just I was wondering if that's how you'll see me in a few months.'

Looking from Annie to Mike, Carol said, 'If I've interrupted a row or something...'

'No, you haven't,' said Annie. 'Well, not between Mike and me anyway. Sorry, I'm just a bit out of tune with someone else is all.'

'Anyone I know?'

'Not yet, but you'll meet her at the wedding. Carol, what the hell are we going to do with my mother for two frigging weeks?'

'That bad, hey?'

'Worse. Do you know how to spell pretentious snob in capital letters?'

'Annie, I'm not even sure I know how to spell pretentious.'

'Okay, let's settle for bigot.'

Shooting Mike a concerned look, Carol asked if there was a bit of hormonal overreaction going on here.

'If there is,' said Annie, opening a cupboard door and taking out a cellophane packet, 'I've been hormonal all my life.'

'Okay,' said Carol, watching Annie post liquorice ribbons into her mouth. 'Do you want to tell me about it?'

'I'll leave you to it,' said Mike, dropping a kiss on the top of Annie's head. 'Harriet's just arrived, and if this is going to be a girlie session it's no place for a bloke.'

'Froghet it,' said Annie through a mouthful of black gunge as Mike went to let Harriet in. 'Thish ishn't – shorry...' She swallowed a lump of masticated liquorice. 'This isn't a Harriet sort of thing.'

But how wrong could she be? After telling Carol she thought she might find her here, Harriet said she'd come to say Luc would pick Lars up in the Voyager.

'Thanks,' said Carol. 'That's good of him, but Mike's just agreed to do it.'

'No prob,' said Harriet. 'As long as you're sorted. So why so miz, sweetie?' She looked at Annie.

'Oh, nothing that wouldn't be solved if my mother wasn't such a bigoted snob.'

'Really?' Harriet sat at the kitchen table, picked up the coffee pot and poured some into Mike's used mug. 'Do tell. Bigoted snobs are *so* my thing. Shall we start with the bigot bit?'

'Sorry?'

'What, exactly, does your mater not tol?'

'Um...' Annie looked at her. 'I'm not sure I understand the question.'

'Tolerate, sweetie. Anything in partic?'

'Oh, right. Anything and anyone who doesn't particularly conform to her principles. And Mike doesn't, for starters.'

'Because?'

'Because artists aren't proper people who do proper jobs, are they? As for his mother being French, well...'

'Ouch, that's a bit heavy,' said Carol. 'Anything else she doesn't approve of? Except, sorry, maybe you don't want to talk about your mother like...you know, it's not really our business.'

Looking from her to Harriet, Annie thought, what the heck? They

175

were going to meet her mother anyway, and forewarned is forearmed, after all. Shrugging, she answered Carol's question with, 'You name it, she disapproves of it.' Ticking items off her fingers, she said, 'My dad, my dad's new wife, the Women's Institute, gays, ethnics, anyone who drinks alcohol. Need I go on?'

'No, sweetie.' The diamonds on Harriet's fingers sparkled in sunlight from the window as she waved a hand in the air. 'Do I take it you don't share the same preds?'

'If that means prejudices, like hell I do, Harriet. I don't give a toss about the Woman's Institute, but I used to bust a gut trying to teach English to ethnic kids. And two of the best male colleagues I worked with were what is known as an item.'

'Right,' said Harriet. 'Lesley and Claude will be down from Paris when your mater is here. You must all come for evening drinkies that Saturday at our cotts. Sorry, must dash, but we'll call that a date. Okay?' Turning to Carol, she said, 'Call us if you need bods.'

'Bods?'

'To lift darling Lars into the house tomorrow.' And on that passing shot, Harriet swept out.

'Yeah, well,' said Annie as Harriet's car roared off. 'I gather from Tina that their place is a bit sort of up-market. That should impress my mum.'

'Um, Annie...' Carol hesitated before saying, 'I'm not sure that's quite what Harriet has on her agenda.'

'What do you mean?'

'Well, let's just say she can be a bit naughty.'

'Carol, what the hell are you on about?'

'Never mind, you'll get it when you meet Lesley and Claude,' said Carol, getting to her feet. 'About half two would be great tomorrow if that's okay with you?'

'Sure.' Annie smiled. 'I think we'll all feel happier when we've got your bloke safely home.'

As it turned out, two hospital orderlies lifted Lars and made sure he was comfortable on Tiggy's passenger seat before folding a wheelchair and putting it in the back of the campervan. So no problem at that end.

At the other end, it was Jean-Claude Lucott who lifted Lars seemingly effortlessly in his arms and carried him into Escargot

Cottage. In response to Jean-Claude's question, 'Où vais-je le metre lui?' Carol, following with the wheelchair, said to put him in the garden room. Which, refusing to admit to having given in to a conservatory, is what she called the stone and glass extension beyond the sitting room.

Courtesy of a spare one from Annie and Mike's house, the sitting room itself was already equipped with a single bed beside the settee which opened up to become a double bed. It was going to be a while before Lars could climb the stairs to their bedroom, and no way was Carol prepared to let him sleep downstairs on his own. Sure, it would also be a while before any danger of her disturbing his leg while sharing a bed was going to stop being an issue, but at least they would be together at night.

Meanwhile, with Bovril purring on his lap, Lars sat in a wheelchair and gazed at the view from the garden room. God, it was good to be home. He didn't care that it was pouring with rain. The smell of wet earth through the open doors was heady stuff after the antiseptic atmosphere of an over-heated hospital room, with only a view of other buildings from the window.

Drinking in the cool, fresh air and feasting his eyes on the open vista, he felt this was nearly as good as sitting in Reiziger's wheelhouse listening to rain hammering on the roof. He'd always enjoyed the snug cosiness of that, and he would again. True, he had to accept it would be some time before he could drive his barge, probably not until next summer. But it would happen. Given time, he and Carol would again be able to just take off whenever the mood took them.

After assuring Carol that, yes, he was allowed to drink wine, they sat together and demolished a bottle between them. Thanks to Jannine, who hadn't quite yet gone off duty in the feeding hospital patients department, all Carol had to do was heat a lamb casserole for dinner.

With the aroma of juicy lamb, herbs and garlic wafting from the tray on his lap, Lars said, 'I'll do it, Carol.'

'What,' she said, passing him a spoon, 'you're going to eat all that?'

'No…yes, that too. But I will walk again.'

Putting her own tray on the floor, she knelt in front of him, caught hold of his good hand and said, 'I know you will. After the

177

wheelchair comes a walking frame, then crutches, and…'

'I've got five weeks,' he said.

'Lars, you've got as long as it takes.'

Shaking his head, he said, 'They get married in five weeks. Mike has asked me to be his best man, and he won't want me standing beside him propped up on a Zimmer frame, will he?'

'Okay, but he wouldn't expect you to push yourself beyond – damn!' Stepping over her tray of food, she went to answer the phone.

'Yes, Dora, he's home.'

'And how is he, dear?'

'Good. He seems fairly relaxed, except…Dora, he's got this idea that he's got to be walking in five weeks.'

'Ah. Would this be anything to do with a wedding?'

'You've got it. I'm just worried he'll force things and do more harm than good or something.'

'I see. Will it be all right if I pop in tomorrow for a chat?'

'I wish you would. It's just he's a stubborn sod, but he might listen to you.'

The first sign of morale not being as high as thus far displayed came in the morning because of the commode. Using his good arm and leg, Lars was able to transfer himself from the sofa bed to it, then into the wheelchair, but it was the next bit that threw him.

'I hate to see you doing that,' he said.

'What?'

'Having to empty that.' He pointed at the ceramic bowl she'd lifted out of the commode.

'Cut the crap, Lars,' she said. 'I don't have a problem with it, so why should you?'

'It's called pride, Carol.'

'So piss off with your pride thing, will you? I'd rather do this than drive to Dijon every bloody day to visit you.'

'You didn't have to do that.'

'No, sure I didn't. But if you'll excuse me, there is something I do have to do.' And she marched upstairs to empty a ceramic pot down the loo.

When she came back down, he grinned and said, 'I must admit I admire your choice of words when dealing with a shitty situation.'

CHAPTER TWENTY-FIVE

So many books had been collected at the Carry On that Gus had built shelves in the bar to accommodate them. It was Tina's idea that they run an exchange book system, and Mike designed and printed notices that were put up in shops and the supermarket in the nearest town. Consequently, Gus and Liz saw an increase in trade as Dutch and Brits came to Coulaize from further afield, and Glynis found herself called upon for assistance when things became hectic in the bar.

A situation which pleased her more than it did Ken. But, as she said to Carol, she'd passed her driving test, hadn't she? So why shouldn't she come and go as she pleased instead of relying on Ken? Then there was the fact that, for the first time since she'd got married, she had money she'd earned herself. Not that it was a lot, or that she actually needed it, but it was a nice feeling.

She was clearing dirty glasses from tables the first time Lars came in on crutches. 'Yay, you,' she squealed. 'What's made you suddenly mobile?'

'This,' he said, holding up his wrist. 'Got un-plastered today, so I can hang onto these things with both hands.'

'Thas good, innit,' said Liz. 'What I reckon is we should all get plastered ter celebrate.'

'Think I'll take a rain check on that one, Liz. I've only just got upright on one leg, and I don't think I'm ready to become legless just yet.'

Coming into the bar after parking the car, Carol nodded at a couple by the new bookshelves who had turned to look at her. She thought they looked vaguely familiar, but hearing them speak what sounded like Dutch or German, she assumed she'd probably just seen them in a supermarket or somewhere.

It was when she sat with Lars that they came to the table and the man asked in halting English if things were recovering well.

'Sorry?' She looked up at him.

'We are hope,' he said, looking at Lars. 'I and my wife are hope

179

you are not so much bad.'

Shaking his head, Lars said, 'Do you know me?'

'Excuse please,' said the man. 'My English is not well, but we are meeting the lady. And I think also you.'

Then it clicked with Carol, and she said, 'Lars, I think we can definitely say you've met.'

'Have we?'

'Yep. Head on, you could say. Or, more to the point, his car and your moped did a quick introduction job. And by the way, I believe what you have here is a fellow Dutchman.'

After that, Carol had no idea what any of them were saying. Leaving them to it, she went to sit at the bar and chat with Glynis and Liz, who were washing and stacking glasses after a busy lunchtime session.

'Do Lars know them?' asked Liz, nodding to where three people were now gabbling away in Dutch.

'He does now,' said Carol. 'I don't know who's apologising to who, but it was their car Lars met in a hurry.'

'Oh,' said Liz. 'We wondered, only we int never seen them before till they started comin fer the book exchange library thing.'

'Silver lining,' said Glynis.

'Sorry?' Carol frowned at her.

'There wouldn't even be a library if they hadn't smashed into him, would there?'

Trying to work out if there was some Glynis-type logic in there, Carol said, 'Sorry, Liz, what was that?'

'I was sayin, Carol, that old geezer was in again.'

'What old geezer?'

'You know, the one what was starin at Mike that night when you was all here playin darts.'

'Did you get anything out of him?' asked Carol. 'Like why he was interested in Mike.'

'Nah, Glynis served him, dincha, ducks?'

Shrugging, Glynis said she served a lot of people, so how would she remember? Picking up a tray, she said she'd go and clear the outside tables before going off duty.

Liz and Carol were talking about how Lars had come on in such a short time when Glynis came back and said, 'He asked about a young man who'd recently moved here.'

'Who did?' said Carol.

'Well, at least I think that's what he was saying,' she said, taking dirty glasses off the tray. 'But you know how bad my French is.'

'Glynis, would you like to give us a clue what you're talking about?'

'You asked about that old man, didn't you?'

'Er, yes, so I did. Did you tell him anything?'

'Carol, I've already said about my French. Mind you, I'm getting better with the local people round here, but he didn't sound like them.'

'Yeah, I fort that,' said Liz. 'More like how they speak in Bordeaux or somewhere down that way. He int from these parts anyway.'

Leaving them to finish clearing before closing the bar, Carol went to sit with Lars and the Dutch couple. With their incomprehensible conversation flowing over her head, her mind was wandering off on its own tack. Who was this old bloke, and why was he interested in Mike?

'Did I miss anything while I was out?' asked Annie, dumping her briefcase on the floor.

'What, apart from me?'

'Mike, I've only been gone three hours. But, yes.' She planted a kiss on his cheek. 'I did miss you. Anything else been going on?'

'Two phone calls. One from Felicity Flickers, and one from your mum.'

'Okay.' She pulled out a chair and sat at the table. 'You can tell me what Felicity had to say while you make a working woman a cuppa.'

'Don't you want to know…'

'Nope. Felicity first, and the other one when I've got a cup of tea in my hand.'

The news from Felicity was that her colleague, Joselyn, had been almost convinced about the Henri-Pierre Debuet influence. But, *just to be absolutely positive, darling*, he'd removed one of the water colours from its frame. What they'd found, which was *tremendously exciting*, was a scrawled inscription on the back of the painting.

'Really?' said Annie. 'What did this inscription thing say?'

'It said, Monique Lanteine, étudiant de excellance.'

'So? I think we already knew from the paintings that she must have been an excellent student.'

'Yes, but,' said Mike. 'It was signed by the man himself and – wait for it – it was dated March of the year I was born.'

'Heck! You were born in November, so...'

'So it would appear that Monique got herself pregnant in Toulouse.'

'Yeah, right,' said Annie. 'And I think we can safely say your mother's artistic ability wasn't the only thing her tutor admired.'

'True.' Mike put a mug on the table and said, 'Shall we move on to the other phone call?'

Shrugging, she asked what her mother had called to say.

'She phoned to give us her travel dates.'

'Oh.' Annie's mug had only made it halfway to her mouth before being placed back on the table. 'She's definitely coming, then.'

'Yep. Arrival the 15th, departure 30th.'

'You what! She's coming a week before the wedding and staying a week after?'

'Well, she was, until I told her we'd be away on honeymoon the week after.'

'You clever little liar.' Annie grinned. 'What did she say about that?'

'Oh, something on the lines of how could she be expected to stay in a country full of foreigners on her own. Sniff, sniff.'

'And?'

'And...' He poured boiling water over a couple of tea bags. 'I will accept cheques written on a postcard, bouquets of flowers if you like, or even a huge hug for being the genius I am.'

'Come on, man. What's the latest state of play?'

'The latest state of play, Annie, is that Lillian will now only consider coming for one week.'

'Wowee!' Annie leapt up and threw her arms round him. 'Did I ever remember to tell you I love you?'

It was several minutes later that Mike said, 'About that honeymoon thing...'

'Who needs it?' she said. 'Look outside, Mike. Look at what we've got here and ask yourself if there's anywhere better to be when you've just got married.'

'So you don't mind?'

'What am I supposed to mind?'

'Not having a proper honeymoon, I mean.'

'Mike, we don't need a honeymoon, proper or otherwise. For heaven's sake, we've lived together for years.'

'Funny, that's more or less what your mother thinks.'

'Sod that,' said Annie. 'What I think is I'm allowed a glass of wine on the strength of what's been happening while I was out.'

Picking up the phone, Carol heard Liz say, 'I'm glad you're in, only we got this feller in the bar askin where he can find you an Lars.'

'What sort of feller?'

'Tall, wiv curly grey hair. A bit of a looker fer his age.'

'Any other clues you could give me? Like, did you get his name, for example?'

'Oh yeah, I did fink ter do that.'

A few seconds later, Carol went outside and told Lars to get his bum up from the patio sun-lounger and put his best foot forward.

'Why? Are we going somewhere?'

'We are,' she said, handing him a pair of crutches. 'We're going to the Carry On to meet someone a bit special.'

Witnessing the reunion of two men who had bonded in a hospital room was a bit much for Carol. Leaving them sitting in the fresh air at an outside table after Harry had enveloped her in a huge hug, she went into the bar, hoisted her own bum onto a stool and asked Liz if she had a box of tissues handy.

'Here y'are, ducks,' said Liz, handing her some paper napkins. 'Glass a red, is it?'

'Thanks.' She took the filled glass. 'And a couple of beers for those two outside.'

'Okay, I'll take em out.'

'Told you, didn't I?'

'Sorry?' Carol blinked and looked at who was sitting on the barstool beside her. 'Oh, hello, Glynis. Sorry, I wasn't fully with it and I didn't see you.'

'I know. I did realise that, Carol.'

'Why are you sitting this side of the bar?' asked Carol. 'I mean, if you're not on bar duty…'

'Why am I even here is what you mean.'

'No, no. Why shouldn't you come here whenever you like?'

'He's lovely,' said Glynis, turning to look out of the window. 'We had a nice chat before you arrived, and I think him and Lars are good for each other.'

'Yes, I agree,' said Carol, following Glynis's gaze to where Harry and Lars were laughing with Liz about something.

'That's what I told you, see. About that silver lining.'

'Er...yes, I do remember you saying something about a silver lining a while ago, but I wasn't too sure what you meant at the time.'

'It's a sort of knock-on thing,' said Glynis, picking up her glass and taking a modest sip. 'Take your divorce, for instance.'

'Huh? What's that got to do with anything?'

'It's got to do with you and Lars being together, hasn't it? Carol, you know as well as I do that, if you and Barry hadn't split up, none of us would be here sitting in this bar in the middle of France, would we?'

'Okay, point taken,' said Carol. 'So why are you sitting in this bar on your own?'

'I'm not. Ken's over there playing darts with one of the Lucott farm workers. You wouldn't have imagined that when we lived next-door in Taggart Road, would you?'

And there was no denying that. Stiff, starchy Ken even playing darts wouldn't have happened until a year ago. Let alone doing so with a French farm labourer.

'So.' Carol looked at her ex next-door neighbour from Essex. 'How are things with you and Ken? It's just I've been a bit preoccupied with my own stuff lately.'

'We're okay most days,' said Glynis. 'More than we were before anyway, and time apart with me coming here to work helps. Did I tell you I'm going to spend it on clothes?'

'Um...no, I don't think I remember you mentioning that.'

'Well, it stands to reason, doesn't it?'

'Probably,' said Carol, wondering if this was going anywhere she might begin to understand.

'I mean, they pay it to me and, as Liz said, Ken's idea of clobber – that's what she calls it – isn't exactly right for a barmaid.'

'Glynis!' Carol swivelled on her bar stool and clutched Glynis's arm. 'Please tell me you aren't going back to how you dressed when you came here to see me on your own.'

'What, those short tight skirts and low-slung tops, you mean?'

'Well, I'm not talking about dungarees and brogues, am I?'

'Don't be silly, Carol. You know those tarty things were only what I wore when I came here to see you without Ken.'

'Oh good,' said Carol. 'So what we're talking here is just something a bit more casual than…what I mean is…'

'What I'm wearing now, you mean.' Glynis looked down at her sensible skirt and neat court shoes. 'What that Clifford therapy bloke said was it had to be compromise.'

'Uh-huh. Is that what this is about?'

'Well, it was me said we should come here for Ken to play darts, so I let him say what I wear if we did that.'

Carol looked at her friend and thought that, as long as you could follow the direction of her mind, she did often make some sort of sense.

'You and me could go together,' said Glynis.

'We could,' said Carol. 'Um…did you have somewhere in particular in mind?'

'I thought Kiabi, near where Casto Rambo is. That's where Liz gets her clobber, and she always looks the part, doesn't she?'

'It's right grand here,' said Harry, standing on the bridge looking around. 'Would Jemima and me be allowed to stay for a bit?'

'Put it this way,' said Lars. 'I was supposed to be just passing through last year, but I ended up staying all winter. And my boat won't be going anywhere for a while yet.'

'Get on board at all, can you?'

'I haven't tried yet, Harry. The gang plank's not wide enough to take me and a pair of crutches.'

'We could do it, you know.' Harry pointed to where Jemima was moored behind Reiziger. 'Put my plank alongside yours, see.'

Arriving back from a trip to the supermarket so they could offer Harry a meal, Carol's attention was caught by activity that made her say, 'What the hell!' Staring at what looked like two drunken sailors making their way unsteadily up a gang plank, she muttered, 'For Christ's sake, what are those idiots doing?'

By the time she'd parked her car and sprinted down the towpath, the two men had somehow made it into Reiziger's wheelhouse. Looking from one triumphant face to the other, she yelled, 'You bloody silly buggers! What if he'd fallen in the canal?'

'Then we'd probably have found out that plaster casts don't float,' said a grinning Lars.

'So not funny, Lars.' Flopping onto a wheelhouse seat, still panting from her sprint down the towpath, she said, 'Now what? Are you planning on taking me for a cruise with a parrot on your shoulder?'

'Fancy that, do you?' said Harry.

'No, Harry. I'm allergic to parrot feathers.'

'Okay, lass, I'll leave mine on Jemima. But how about the cruise bit?'

'Nice one,' she said. 'How about we prop Lars up, strap him to the wheel and see how he gets on with one leg and a wrist just out of plaster?'

'I can do it,' said Harry.

'Oh good, because I'm still out of breath, so I'll leave you to it, shall I?'

'No, lass. What I mean is I can drive this barge if you and him fancy a little trip for a few days.'

Lars's face lit up momentarily, then he said, 'Major problem. There's no way I can get below to go to bed or use the toilet. But if you're really up for driving this thing, I've just had an idea.'

'If it involves doing a regular balancing act on a gangplank at the risk of falling in the canal, forget it,' said Carol. 'Harry, you haven't really got a parrot, have you?'

'Carol, would I lie to you? Are you really allergic?'

'Pass on the first, and no on the second.' She grinned. 'I was lying about that bit.'

'In that case,' said Harry, 'I'll fess up about Ceremony.'

'Which means exactly what?' asked Lars.

'It means, mate, I got this parrot called Ceremony, haven't I?'

'Of course you have,' said Lars. 'Hasn't everyone?'

'No, straight up, mate. African Grey it is. Wicked little sod what swears like a trooper.'

'Now that bit I could believe,' said Lars. 'Who wouldn't, living with you?'

'Look, can we rewind a bit?' said Carol. 'Harry, if you're having us on, I'll...'

'Carol, would I lie to you?'

'Okay, skip that bit,' she said. 'We've already been there. So,

186

you've got this potty-mouthed parrot. Right?'

'Right. Told you that, didn't I?'

'So you did, Harry, so you did. And you're asking us to believe it's called Ceremony?'

'I am, lass, because that's its name, see.'

'Uh-huh.' Lars shook his head and said, 'I've a feeling I'm going to regret this, but would you like to tell us why it's called that?'

'Because the silly bugger walks around on the floor,' said Harry. 'So when folk come on board, I have to tell them not to stand on it.'

CHAPTER TWENTY-SIX

Mike was still fretting about filling in the requisite application forms to get married in France. Had they wanted to get married in Dijon or some sizeable town, it could have been more difficult. But local Mayors were easier to deal with, and had the authority to approve in a more lax way who was allowed to get married on their patch.

Proof that Mike and Annie were resident in the commune which included Coulaize was no problem. Mike's birth certificate, naming Delphine Flint née Labois as his French mother, had been accepted without question. Both passports were vetted and deemed in order, and the bans had been issued four weeks prior to the wedding date.

With no compunction whatsoever, Annestine Lister had signed her section of the forms. Michael Flint, however, had sat with pen poised and said he didn't know if he could. Why? Because he was worried about committing perjury or something on those lines.

'For heaven's sake, Mike,' said Annie. 'You're not in a law court under oath, are you?'

'No.' He ran a hand over his dishevelled hair. 'But I'm making a commitment to you, and I want it to be properly legally binding.'

'Look, Mike. We made a commitment to each other years ago. What more do you want? A piece of legal paper saying we can now sleep together?'

'Annie, what I want is for our child to be born into a legitimate marriage. Is that so much to ask?'

'No, Mike. But I can't help you with that. Why don't you go and run this whole issue by Lars?'

'Why him?'

'Because he's got his head screwed on, and Carol told me he has a way of dealing with angst stuff.'

'Yeah, right.' Mike went to stare out of the window. 'I just sit down with a man I've only known a few months and say oh, by the way, I'm not who you think I am.'

'You are who you are,' said Lars after listening without interruption. 'Did finding out about some paperwork change you into someone else?'

'No, but the paperwork, as you put it, is false.'

'So what will you do? Try to change all the documents?'

Sighing, Mike said, 'I have no idea how to do that. Besides, it would put my dad in a bad position, I suppose.'

'Exactly. Do you want to open a can of slugs?'

'Worms,' said Mike.

'Okay. You can change slugs to worms, but I think you cannot change the status quo. Would you pass me that fly swat please?'

With his face relaxing into a grin, Mike asked if he was going to swat the slugs or the worms.

'What I'm going to do,' said Lars, turning the fly swat upside down, 'is to push this inside my plaster and see if I can reach that damn itch.'

So it was that Mike returned from Escargot Cottage feeling a lot happier. Lars was right, none of anything was Mike's fault. He'd done nothing wrong or illegal, had he? And who needed to know what Delphine and Norman Flint had done? As Lars had pointed out, what they did was protect him and give him the love and care you would expect of natural parents. Compared to that, was it so wrong of them to register him as their child? And, of course, it was quite likely they didn't even consider the legality of what they did when they had no choice.

'As I see it,' Lars had said. 'They needed to ensure that they would be legally responsible for you. How else would they do that without the cooperation of your birth mother who was mentally sick at the time?'

So, yes, it did make sense. And after agreeing with Annie's *I told you so*, Mike said, 'You know that thing about lying to your mother about us going away for a honeymoon?'

'Yes.' She looked up from the apples she was peeling. 'What about it?'

'How do you fancy a mini canal cruise?'

'A bit like I fancy liquorice.'

'Okay.' He sat at the table and said, 'Here's the plan...'

Oh yes, she was definitely in favour of a couple of hours of cruising to a little village, where they would be left in peace on a barge called Reiziger. The plan being that Harry would take them to Flourenne, Carol would collect him and then take him back to drive the barge back to Coulaize a few days later.

'Brilliant,' said Annie, wiping her hands on a dish cloth.

'Where're you going?' asked Mike.

'To answer Maureen's email that came in when you were out.'

'What was it about?'

'About them saying they'd probably spend the rest of the week somewhere in Burgundy, and could we suggest somewhere nice and peaceful.'

Clicking on reply, Annie told Maureen that they did know somewhere nice and peaceful to spend a few days, and it wouldn't cost them a thing. It didn't take Maureen long to respond saying Walnut House sounded idyllic and, yes, of course they'd be happy to look after Perdue.

There was no doubt about it, Harry had fallen in love with Coulaize. It could also be true to say Coulaize had fallen in love with him, and it went beyond Lars and Carol, who he'd cruised to the village to catch up with for a bit. Other people he'd met when they'd visited Lars in hospital seemed happy to see him again, and that Dora Turner woman was a nice lady. Not to mention that her husband, Don, had turned out to be a stimulating opponent when it came to a game of chess.

Harry had also palled up with some of the locals who came to the canal to do a bit of fishing, which was another of his passions. Not that you'd eat your catch, what with the canal being a bit mucky like, but it was a grand feeling to sit on a bank with a rod and line and have a bit of a natter with Frenchies who didn't seem to mind how bad he was at speaking their language.

So, yes, all in all, Coulaize did seem like a good choice for a winter mooring. A bonus, of course, was the Carry On caff. Not just for company when he wanted it, but that big bloke didn't half turn out some decent grub at a decent price.

A bonus Harry hadn't anticipated was Dora's widowed sister coming to stay with the Turners. Him and the sister had clicked that first meeting, when Dora invited him for lunch. Josie played chess, and she enjoyed Scrabble, which was another one of Harry's favourites. Josie liked the same sort of books. Josie lived at Stoke Bruerne by the Grand Union Canal in England, and she loved to walk along the towpath and look at all the narrowboats. Just think, Harry's boat could have been one of the ones she'd seen. And to think he'd lived on Jemima at Braunston, only a few miles away, and here they were meeting in the middle of France.

One thing Josie had never done, but always wanted to, was actually go on a narrowboat. Well that could be easily rectified, couldn't it?

The very next day saw two people in their sixties cruising through a few locks. One of whom couldn't seem to contain her excitement at being allowed to open a lock gate. And the look on her face as she gazed around at the scenery they glided through – well, as far as Harry was concerned, seeing what looked like utter delight was, for him, a joy to behold.

As for when she'd looked inside the boat, anyone would think he was showing her a palace or something. But then, Jemima was his little palace, wasn't she? He'd always been proud of her, but today he felt like a king in his castle, and the canal and surrounding terrain was his domain.

By rights, he supposed he should have been irritated by Josie pointing out things: "Look at that outcrop of rock on that hillside" – "Oh, look at those lovely white cows" – "Aren't the trees beautiful with their autumn colours?"

After all, he'd seen it all before, hadn't he? Funny, though, how the lass made him realise he'd almost grown to sort of take the beauty and tranquillity for granted. But there was something a bit magic about seeing it afresh through someone else's eyes.

After finding a bit of canal wide enough to turn Jemima, they returned to the mooring at Coulaize. Just in time, as it happened, to partake of one of Gus's famous omelettes before Harry escorted Dora's sister back to Maison Lavande.

Walking back down the towpath, Harry tried to put his finger on what it was that made Josie seem special. Different, she was, from any of the other ladies he'd had relationships with over the years.

Ah well, hard to say what it was. But as he breathed in the October evening air with a bit of Autumn chill in it, he couldn't remember when he'd last enjoyed such a grand day.

CHAPTER TWENTY-SEVEN

It was only the third morning of Lillian's visit, and Annie was wondering why the hell she and Mike hadn't just done the deed and told her mother afterwards. It wasn't as if Lillian was particularly interested in her daughter's wedding, so why had she bothered to come all this way for the event?

Because – sniff – that was expected of a mother, wasn't it? Besides, if that Maureen woman was going to be involved, didn't Annie's own mother have a right to be here?

Replying on the lines of it might be nice if she was here for the right reason, Annie tore the top off a packet of liquorice. Only to be told that eating that stuff was an affectation, and all that talk about pregnant women having cravings was utter nonsense.

'Is it really?' said Annie. 'It's staggering to think how many people don't know that.'

'I didn't indulge in any stupid cravings when I was expecting you,' said Lillian.

Which was when Annie asked her if she even knew what it felt like to crave a baby.

'It's not all it's cracked up to be, Annestine,' was the reply she got. 'And neither is marriage for that matter, but I'll leave you to find that out for yourself.'

Tina, who had only popped in to ask if Annie could take over one of her lessons tomorrow, swung her head from one woman to the other. Flipping heck, it was like watching a tennis match and wondering how these two players had been allowed on the same court together.

'Sorry it's such short notice.' Tina took advantage of a pause and jumped in. 'But if you could manage it, I'd be truly grateful.'

'No problem,' said Annie. 'This afternoon, you say?'

'Well, actually, it's...yes, can you get away this afternoon?'

'Oh, I think I can manage that,' said Annie.

'Thanks.' Tina was already heading for the door. 'I've got the lesson plan in my car, so if you could...'

'Sure, Tina. I'll come out and get it.'

Standing beside her car in the lane, Tina said, 'Christ, and I thought you were exaggerating when you said your mum is a nightmare.'

'Come on, Tina, who'd need to exaggerate when the real thing is unbelievable?'

'Point taken. Is your name really Annestine?'

'Sad but true,' said Annie.

'That is so not you.'

'Yes, well.' Annie shrugged. 'The me my mum wanted me to be didn't exactly happen.'

'Alleluia to that. Um, you did get that the lesson is tomorrow morning, not this afternoon?'

'Is it really?' Annie managed a weak grin. 'Damn. Unless we want you to look like a liar, that means I'll have to go out this afternoon as well as tomorrow.'

'Cuppa at my place after lunch, then,' said Tina, getting into her car.

'Thanks, mate. You're a life-saver.'

'That's me all over. Hang in there, kiddo.' And she drove off, leaving Annie to go back indoors and demand to know why her mother had to be so rude as to not shake Tina's hand when she'd offered it.

The stuff about how such a common woman with all that ironmongery stuck in her ears was allowed to be a teacher is probably best left unsaid.

Tina was approaching the corner to pass through the village when Carol's car turned into the lane. Stopping her own car, Tina called through the window to ask if they needed help to get Lars out and into the cottage.

No, they could manage, she was told. Lars had just been liberated from plaster, and had progressed to being a walking stick job.

'Wicked!' Tina's face lit up. 'So we've got a crutch-less best man for Monday.'

'Absolutely,' said Carol. 'Have you just come from the prenuptial abode?'

'Yes. Have you met it?'

'We have.' Carol grimaced. 'Christ knows how Annie and Mike are coping.'

'Actually, I'm not sure she is coping,' said Tina. 'Still, only three

193

days to go before they get *their* liberation. Thanks to Lars's boat, I gather.'

'And let's not forget Harry,' said Lars, leaning forward in the passenger seat. 'The old bugger has come in a bit handy, seeing as I still won't be up to driving a barge for a while yet.'

'Yeah, let's not forget Harry,' said a grinning Tina. 'Rumour has it that Dora's sister won't be forgetting him in a hurry.'

'Really?' said Carol. 'What do you know that we don't?'

'Ah, well, Carol. If you don't keep up with the goss, who am I to spread rumours?' Adding that she'd see them at Harriet and Luc's on Saturday, she said, 'Maybe you'll catch up then. See ya.'

'Now what the hell was that about?' said Carol, as Tina's car disappeared round the corner.

'Could be about why we've not seen Harry for a few days,' said Lars. 'Is it okay if we go home now? It's just that I haven't seen our bedroom for some weeks, and I've got other things than Harry on my mind right now.'

'You think you can get up to the bedroom?' she said.

'So I was told at the hospital. Not to mention what else I'm now cleared to get up to.'

'You mean…'

'Yes.'

'For heaven's sake, Lars, why are we sitting here wasting time in a stationery car?'

'Funny you should ask,' he said. 'That's exactly what I'm wondering.'

And in case anyone else is wondering, the answer is, no, they didn't make it to the upstairs bedroom. After all, why waste time and effort climbing the stairs when there was a perfectly good settee that had been acting as a bed on the ground floor?

It was, of course, a well known fact that Harriet didn't do things by halves, and her little drinkies at the cotts gathering was no exception. As she'd put it to Luc, the more people to spread the load, the better to dilute the presh.

Lillian's delight as Mike pulled Tiggy into the forecourt was almost enough to compensate for having to arrive in a campervan. Not even trying to hide how impressed she was, she gazed at a building that screamed money and told Annie that this was more the standard she was comfortable with.

Fair enough, she did feel a bit out of her comfort zone when Harriet swooped on her and kissed both her cheeks, but once that was over, Lillian was free to look around and drink in the obvious opulence of Harriet and Luc's home. Oh yes, Lillian very much approved of *these* friends of Annie's.

Even the French people she was introduced to were well-dressed and quite charming, so maybe the French were not all peasants after all. At least these ones spoke English, so were apparently the educated sort. But as for that Tina woman and her rough-looking husband, why on earth had they been invited? The Lucotts were probably not so bad because they owned a sizeable farm, and weren't French farmers supposed to be quite wealthy? Not that you'd tell by the way they were dressed, of course. And what business did they and that Tina have bringing those children to an adult evening event?

Don and Dora Turner were acceptable, though. After all, wasn't he an accountant? The sister, however, wasn't quite as well-polished, and that man she seemed to be with was a bit rough round the edges, wasn't he?

Still, as Lillian settled on a velvet-covered chair and surveyed the scene in general, she decided this was going to be quite a fine do. Well, as long as those children behaved, she supposed. But was it really appropriate for the little farm girl to address that Carol woman by her Christian name?

Feeling a sense of relief that her mother seemed to be in her element, Annie decided it was safe to leave her and go and mix with some friends. Wandering over to where Carol and Lucie were chatting, the first thing Annie had to do was tell Lucie that, no, Perdue had not come home yet.

'Oh no,' said Carol. 'Has she been missing long?'

'A few days,' Annie replied. 'For some reason best known to a cat, she shot out of the house when my mum arrived and we haven't seen her since.'

'Ahah,' said Lars, joining them and handing a glass of citron juice to Lucie. 'Didn't I once tell you cats know many things?'

'Will she know when to be safe to return?' Lucie looked up at Lars.

'I believe she will,' he said, tweaking her lopsided ponytail.

195

'I am much hope for that,' said Lucie.

'Yes, Lucie.' Annie smiled at the anxious-looking little face. 'That's what I'm hoping for too.'

'Alfie and me can search. We are find her before, yes?'

'You did indeed,' said Annie. 'But I think Lars is right. Perdue will know...oh heck.'

'What is heck?'

'What? Oh, sorry, Lucie, I'll explain another time.'

'Uh-oh,' said Carol. 'I think Harriet's shock tactics have just entered the scene.'

'Yeah, right,' said Annie. 'And judging by the look on my mother's face, I think I need to go into damage control mode before she opens her mouth.'

Too late. Lillian, with her mouth resembling a cat's bum that's ingested a lemon, was already scuttling towards Annie. Pointing across the room to where a young woman had her arm draped across a stunningly attractive black girl's shoulders, Lillian said, 'Do they have to make it so obvious in decent company?'

'Oh, that's Harriet's sister and her partner,' said Carol. 'Lovely people.'

'If you say so.' Lillian sniffed. 'But where I come from – well – I mean...'

But she didn't get a chance to say what she meant because Lesley was approaching. Holding out a hand, she said, 'We haven't met, but I'm told you're Annie. Hi, I'm Les.'

'Yes, dear,' said Lillian. 'I think we can see that for ourselves.'

What should have been an *ouch* moment was allayed by Lesley hooting with laughter and saying, 'And you must be Annie's mother. It's okay, really it is. I do understand that it's not in order to shake your hand.'

Which was when Lillian turned to Annie and said, 'I'm ready to leave.'

'Are you?' said Annie. 'How about I find Mike and see if he's ready to leave?'

'Well.' Lillian sniffed. 'If me being insulted isn't enough. And, of course.' She glared at Carol, who seemed to be trying to hide her face behind her wine glass. 'All these people here are alcoholics, so if you don't mind...'

'No, Mother, I don't mind if you choose to leave.'

196

Now where the hell did that come from? Oh well, in for a penny...

'You'll find a sleeping bag in the back of the camper van, and Mike and I will take you to our home when we're ready.'

'Salute, sister,' said Lesley, raising her hand in a high five as, looking like a thunder storm about to erupt, Lillian stomped off. 'Is it safe to bring Claudette over to meet you?'

'Given that I'm marrying my feller on Monday, I'd say you're safe,' said Annie. 'By heck, though, she's a looker, isn't she?'

'Please,' said Lucie, tugging Annie's hand. 'May you explain me now what is heck?'

'Will we ever live it down?' said Annie when they were safely home and Lillian had huffed and sniffed her way up to bed.

Mike, who seemed to be finding it all rather amusing, said, 'Well now, it could take a year or two, but we'll probably be forgiven in time.'

'Not funny, Mike.'

'Come on, love. No one is holding your mother against you.'

'Huh – I'd like to hold her against a wall and hire a firing squad.'

'Can you wait till after Monday? I mean, we don't want to mess up the garden before the wedding party.'

'Which we've still got to get through. Shit, Mike, by the time she's left France, we'll have to go around apologising to what friends we've got left.'

The wedding ceremony itself was a brief, modest affair which took place Monday morning in the Marie, with Coulaize's Mayor officiating. The only other people present besides the bride and groom were Lars and Carol as witnesses, and Annie's mum and dad.

They left the Marie to be greeted by cheers and calls of good wishes from a group of local French people who had gathered outside. An old man they didn't recognise stepped away from the group to come and shake Annie and Mike's hands and offer his wishes for much happiness. Who he was they had no idea, but as he slipped away, he took his glasses off and polished them on a hanky.

The big event took place afterwards, in the form of a party in Mike and Annie's garden, which anyone and everyone they knew had been invited to attend. They didn't actually know the retired British Army padre who Ken had found in Maiseronne, but Major Williams was more than willing to carry out a more familiar ceremony after the official, and only legal, requirement.

Which was when Lars swapped his witness role for the standard British one of best man. And Graham did the father of the bride thing and gave Annie away to a man he trusted to take care of his beloved daughter. Mike's dad, who must have got up at the crack of sparrows in Chicago, phoned to say he and Mary-Lou were with them in their hearts.

The buffet spread put together by Gus was augmented by extra ingredients courtesy of Jannine Lucott, and it's fair to say a good time was had by all before Annie and Mike got into her father's car mid-afternoon. Instructed by Luc that it was the French thing to do, Graham hooted as he passed right through Coulaize and drove through a few outlying villages, followed by a posse of hooting and honking cars carrying wedding guests.

People came out of their houses and waved as the noisy stream of cars passed through sleepy villages, and Annie's face ached from smiling by the time they returned to Coulaize and the barge that was to take them for a honeymoon trip up the canal. A barge wearing a "Just Married" banner, bunches of balloons and even tin cans that trailed behind the rudder as Harry manoeuvred Reiziger into the lock above Coulaize.

All the guests were there, standing either side of the lock throwing rice and flowers. All the guests except one, that was. Annie looked for her mother to say goodbye, but there was no sign of her. Well sod her. Annie stared at the water pouring into the lock through the open sluices and felt as if it was washing away any last vestige of feelings of daughterly duty or whatever she'd thought she ought to have.

Once the barge had passed through the lock, the send-off party dispersed, and Dora and Don were home in time to join Josie at the bottom of Maison Lavandre's garden to wave as Reiziger passed.

'They did look happy,' said Josie, as she and Dora settled on the patio while Don went to open a bottle.

'And you, dear?' said Dora. 'I think we can say you're having a happy holiday, can't we?'

Sighing, Josie said, 'Dora, I can't thank you enough for having me here. I honestly can't think when I've had such an enjoyable time.'

'He's going to miss you, you know.'

'I think so, Dora. And it's not going to be easy for me to leave at the end of the week.'

'So don't, dear. It's not too late to change your travel arrangements, and you know you're welcome to stay longer.'

'No, no.' Josie gazed down the garden to where the canal could be seen beyond the gate. 'I really need to get back home.'

'Do you? Yes, I daresay you have things to do.'

'Well, you know how it is,' said Josie. 'I mean, there's the beetle drive at the village hall, a Tupperware party on Monday, then the Women's Institute jumble sale a week on Saturday.'

'Oh yes, dear, I can quite see how pressing those engagements are.' Dora reached over to rearrange a mauve cushion on a wicker chair before saying, 'Do you want to talk about the real reason?'

'Dora, I think...' Josie twisted her wedding ring round her finger. 'I think it's best to put some distance between us.'

'I take it you mean between you and Harry.'

'Well.' Josie actually blushed. 'You know what they say about...you know...'

'Know what, dear?'

'What they say about when you meet someone on holiday. Like when you *think* you know how you feel, but...'

'Ah,' said Dora. 'So you think things may be a bit more than just friendly companionship, do you?'

'That's just the point. I don't know what it is, do I?' Josie shook her head. 'I need to get back to my normal life so I can sort things out in my head.'

'What I think,' said Don, placing a bottle and glasses on the table, 'is that Josie should consider coming here for Christmas.'

'But, Don,' said Dora. 'We've promised to go to England to spend Christmas with the children.'

'Oh yes, so we have.' He winked at Josie as he put a crystal glass of chilled Chablis in front of her. 'But you'd be fine here on your own, you know. Let's face it, there are enough people around to look after you, so you wouldn't be lonely, would you?'

Reporting in to collect Harry a couple of hours later, Carol also reported that Annie's dad was on his way delivering Annie's mum to Lyon airport.

'And Maureen?' asked Annie.

'No, she's not on her way to Lyon. We've moved their gear from the Carry On, and she's currently making herself comfortable in your house. Oh, and by the way, when I left she was making a huge fuss of Perdue.'

'Brilliant! The little sod's come home, then.' Annie leaned back in a deck chair, smiled up at Mike and said, 'Phew, we can really relax now.'

Saying that, no, she wouldn't stop for a drink, Carol said to Harry, 'Come on, you old rogue. I gather I've got to get you back in time for a dinner engagement.'

'Have you, lass?'

'According to Dora Turner I have. When I came past their house, she informed me they were hoping you'd join them to partake of an evening meal.'

'Best get my act together then,' he said, his eyes twinkling as a grin split his face. 'Don't want to keep our Dora waiting, do I?'

Feeling the last dregs of tension seep out, Annie turned from waving at the back end of Carol's car and said, 'Bliss, or what?'

'Being married to me, you mean?' said Mike. 'A bit soon to arrive at that, isn't it?'

'To be honest, Mike, I'm not sure I've fully taken that on board yet. I'm still trying to believe we somehow got through last week.'

'Forget last week, Annie. We've got a few days here to unwind, so come here, Mrs Flint, and tell me we've done a good job today.'

Some time later, when they emerged from a cosy session in a cosy cabin, Mike said, 'I don't know if it's appropriate or not, but is it okay if I say I'm hungry?'

'No worries,' said Annie. 'Lars's barge comes fully equipped with a meal we only need to pop into his oven.'

'What sort of meal?'

'Well now...' She lifted a lid off a casserole dish. 'Judging by the delicious aroma hitting my nostrils, I'd guess it's bouef bourguignon.'

'Correct me if I'm wrong,' he said. 'But wasn't that what Lars brought us the first night we properly moved in to Walnut House?'

'Yes, I seem to remember he did.'

'Bugger, Annie. The last time we ate one of Lars's bouef bourguignons he made us pregnant.'

CHAPTER TWENTY-EIGHT

Lovely as the little village of Flourenne was, the October weather, which had been kind enough to hold good for a wedding, was now not that great. Anyway, by the end of the third day, Annie was becoming keen to go home.

'Me too,' said Mike. 'I'm a bit anxious to see if we've still got a cat, and it would be good to spend a bit of time with Graham and Maureen before they go back.'

'I know,' said Annie. 'They came all this way and I hardly caught more than a glimpse of them.'

'Right.' Mike stood up. 'All we have to do is let Harry know when to come and take us back to Coulaize.'

'How do we do that?'

'We phone him.' Mike picked up his mobile. 'Have you got his phone number?'

'No, I haven't.' Annie shook her head. 'You'll have to ring Carol and Lars and ask them for it.'

'And their number is?'

'I have no idea.'

'Okay, right,' said Mike. 'What we'll have to do is phone home and get your dad to take a message to Carol, so she can get a message to Harry, so he can…Annie, what's our number?'

'Don't ask me. Come on, Mike, when have I ever needed to dial my own number?'

'Fair comment,' he said. 'But don't you keep a list of people's numbers we call?'

'Yes, I keep it beside our phone at home.'

With a frown etching his forehead, he looked at her and said, 'So what now?'

'I'd say that, right now, we're a bit sort of stuffed, wouldn't you?'

Scratching his head, he said, 'This is stupid. No one will come and get us until we let them know.'

'Oh, great,' said Annie. 'And here was me looking forward to spending Christmas at home.'

'Look, there's no need to panic, Annie.'

'Really? So why are you pacing around this wheelhouse like a caged animal?'

'Because I'm panicking about how far it is to walk back to Coulaize!'

It was some minutes and a liquorice ribbon later when Annie asked him if he'd brought his wallet.

'Well of course I did. I mean, I was compos mentis enough to realise we'd need money while we're here.'

'Yeah, right,' she said. 'Are you compos mentis enough to know if you've still got that Café Carillion card in your wallet?'

'Nice one, wife. Thank god I married a woman with brains.'

Fine, so it took a phone call to Liz, to make a phone call to Lars, who didn't know Harry's number either.

'Doncha worry, Lars,' said Liz. 'Gus'll nip down an tell Harry ter call yer. But it won't be till tomorrer, on account of it'll be a bit late by the time we close up ternight, innit. Sorry, ducks, I gotta go, it's bleedin bedlam here.'

'No problem, Liz. I'll get Carol to drive down and speak to Harry now.'

When he put the phone down, Carol asked him what she had to speak to Harry about.

Looking at her blankly, he said, 'I don't know, but it's got something to do with Mike phoning the Carry On because it's the only number they've got with them.'

'So call Mike's mobile, Lars. Maybe something's gone wrong with your barge.'

'Shit, that didn't occur to me. What's his number?'

Which was Carol's turn to look blank.

'Right,' said Lars, with a hint of panic in his voice. 'We'll have to drive to Flourenne and find out what's up.'

They were approaching the bend towards Maison Lavande when, who happened to appear walking arm-in-arm but Harry and Josie. Yes, Harry had written down Mike's mobile number before leaving them on Reiziger. No, he didn't have it on him, but if they could just nip him to Jemima…

In the end, four relaxed people went to bed that night with a feeling of relief. The feelings of the other two weren't of relief, but more of sadness. Even so, one of them, with the ever-present tang of canal water in the air, and one with the scent of purple viburnum wafting through a bedroom window, did have something to look forward to.

Oh yes, it would be right grand to bring Reiziger back to Coulaize with a special lady on board, wouldn't it?

And as far as Josie was concerned, she couldn't think of a better way to spend the last morning of her holiday.

'We're having a really lovely holiday,' said Maureen, releasing Annie from a warm hug. 'It'll be even better now you're home and we can see you a bit.'

Annie, who supposed she was feeling a bit tearful on account of being happy to be home and relief that Perdue had come running to meet them, fished a tissue from her sleeve.

'And,' said Maureen. 'If we move back to that lovely café where you fixed us up for bed and breakfast...'

'Don't you dare,' said Annie. 'We've only got two days, and I want you and my dad here so we can spend all the time we can together.'

'If you're sure that's what you want,' said Graham.

'I do.' Annie turned to her dad. 'I want...I need...' And her voice gave way.

Coming into the kitchen after checking his emails, Mike found his wife sobbing against her father's chest. As he went towards them, Maureen caught hold of his arm and said that it might be best to leave them alone for a bit. Albeit protesting, Mike acknowledged the nod from the man who was now his father-in-law and allowed himself to be led out of the room.

Assuring Mike it was probably just hormones, Maureen looked out at the back garden and the view beyond and told him he and Annie had got themselves a little bit of heaven here.

In the kitchen, Annie slumped down onto a chair and said, 'It was hell, Dad. Why does she have to be like that?'

'I don't know, love,' he said, sitting across the table and reaching for her hand. 'I'm just sorry you had to go through that.'

'Yeah, well.' Annie dabbed her face with a screwed up, soggy tissue. 'You went through it for...how long were you married before you moved out?'

'Sixteen years.'

'But you left when I was sixteen, so you must've been married for...when did you get married, Dad?'

'Five months before you were born.'

'Oh! I didn't know that.'

'And you weren't supposed to,' he said, taking a hanky from his pocket and handing it to her.

'Dad, did you ever love her?'

'I was responsible for her, Annie. But she's a hard person to love.'

'Yeah, right, so tell me about it.' Annie blew her nose. 'God, I'm sorry, I never realised you got trapped because of me.'

'Like I said, you weren't supposed to.'

'But…' She hesitated, not quite sure how to cope with what was hammering into her head. But it was there, so best to bring it out and face it. 'Dad, was it because of having me she turned out like that?'

'No, love. According to your Auntie Eileen, she was…um, to put it in Eileen's words, she was a pain in the arse even when they were children.'

'So how come you…I mean, why did you…you know.'

'I think they call it rebound or something.' Graham got up, filled the kettle and put it on the gas hob.

Annie waited until he sat down again before saying, 'Go on. I might as well get the lot while we're at it.' And she sat and listened while he told her how he'd just been dumped by his girlfriend at university, he was home in Norfolk for the Christmas holiday, and he went to a party and got sloshed.

'That's all I needed,' said Annie. 'I exist because my dad got pissed and jumped the nearest woman at a frigging party!'

Graham looked at her for several seconds before saying, 'That wasn't exactly how it was.'

'So how was it then, Dad? Come on, I was the end product, so I think I'd like to know how I came to have a mother who doesn't give a shit about me.'

'Okay.' Graham flexed his fingers, pulled two and cracked a couple of knuckles, drew a deep breath and said, 'I was a suitable target. A sort of trophy, if you like. I was a university student, and I was going to become someone. Someone, she told her sister, Eileen, who was better than that common plumber she had married.'

'Go on.'

'I'm not saying I was blameless, Annie. I didn't exactly put up any resistance when…when…' He shrugged.

'When what, Dad?'

'When Lillian led me upstairs.'

'Huh? You're telling me *she* seduced *you*?'

'Like I said, I wasn't blameless, Annie. All I can say in mitigation is that I was hurting and vulnerable. But that doesn't exonerate me from doing what I did.'

'Whew,' said Annie. 'And to think, I never knew any of this.'

'Ah, well,' said Graham, the hint of a grin twitching the corners of his mouth. 'You're a married woman now, so it's okay for you to hear about the facts of life.'

'Dad, I'm glad you've told me. I've been feeling so guilty about not being able to love...bugger that, I can't even tolerate her.' Getting up and putting her arms round Graham, she said, 'Thanks, Dad. I think you've just cut an unwanted umbilical cord and liberated a married woman.'

'I don't know what that's about,' said Mike, coming into the kitchen. 'But I think someone should liberate that flipping kettle. It's been whistling fit to bust for the last five minutes.'

After refilling the dry kettle, Mike made tea and took it into the lounge. As the sound of children's voices could be heard, Maureen said, 'I hope you don't mind, but I told that little French girl it would be okay for them to collect some of the windfalls from your orchard.'

'Good move,' said Annie. 'I'm sick of making apple pies, and they'll just lie there and rot.'

'But I thought you put those hundred and one pies in the freezer,' said Mike.

'Idiot. I mean the surplus apples will rot.'

'Now that would be a shame,' said Graham. 'The little lad says they int got any apple trees in his garden, which is a bummer cos his mum int half good at knocking together real quality apple crumbles.'

The little lad in question was now banging on the casement door and yelling, 'You gotter come and see.'

'What's up?' asked Mike, opening the door.

'Mrs Tiggy Winkle's in your orchard,' announced Alfie.

'What!' Turning to Annie, Mike said, 'You must have left the handbrake off.'

'Nah, not your van,' said Alfie. 'I mean a proper one.' And he sped off back to the orchard, leaving the bemused adults to follow in time to see a hedgehog emerge and slowly wander across the lawn.

'Oh look, Mike,' Annie squealed. 'I've never seen a live one before.'

'I don't think I have either,' he said. 'Seen a few dead ones on roads, though.'

'Thank you, Mike,' said Annie as Lucie joined them. 'I don't think the kids need to know about those.'

Shrugging, Lucie said, 'It is normal. They are much slow, and for cars it is easy to make their guts to graters.'

'Luce,' said Alfie, with more than a hint of scorn in his voice. 'I keep telling you it's guts for garters.'

'Okay.' She glared at him. 'But this will not happen for Mrs Tiggy Winkle. Here she is safe.'

'Oh,' said Graham. 'You know Mrs Tiggy Winkle, do you?'

'Yes.' She looked up at him. 'I am…I have read the book of Annie. But I do not know what is goff…goff red.'

With a snort, Alfie told her she meant goffered. 'That's when she does that ironing thing, see.'

'So,' said Graham, looking at Alfie. 'You know the Beatrix Potter books too?'

'Yeah.' He shrugged. 'I had them when I was little because me mum reckons they're quality books, but I like ones about dragons and stuff best.'

Lucie telling Alfie off for saying *me* mum instead of *my* mum, led to him telling her she was a stupid girl what's afraid of dragons, so what did she know?

Leaving them to it, the others went back to their tea and Maureen asked what that guts and garters thing was about.

'You don't want to know,' said Mike. 'If I remember rightly, it's got something to do with a cat's balls.'

Josie phoned the Turners to say she'd arrived home safely. Oh, and could they let Harry know?

'Couldn't you call him yourself, dear?' said Dora. 'I'm sure he'd like to speak to you.'

'No, we've agreed to leave some space between us, so if you don't mind…'

'No problem. But, Josie, you do have his mobile number I take it?'

'Um, probably, somewhere. And thanks, Dora, I had a wonderful holiday with you.'

'You were very welcome, and we'll see you again soon I hope.'

'It depends. I just need to get my feet back on the ground and try to sort out what's going on in my head.'

'I do understand that, dear. But don't overlook what's going on in your heart, will you?'

'It's been a long time, Dora. Coming up to eleven years since I lost Phil, and you sort of get used to being on your own.'

'Yes, I can quite see that. But is that what you want?'

'I don't know anymore. I suppose it's just what I'd become resigned to and…well, I have only known Harry for just over two weeks, so…'

'Josie, dear, there's no need to make any decisions yet. Just take your time, and I'll be sure to let Harry know you're safely home.'

'You've got his mobile number?'

'You know, I'm not sure I have. But never mind, I'll just pop down to his boat.'

She found Harry, huddled in an anorak, sitting on the canal bank with a fishing rod. Not that he was doing anything with the rod because it was lying sideways across his knees.

'Shouldn't there be a line and hook involved in this exercise?' said Dora, after standing beside him for several seconds.

'Oh, hello, lass.' He looked up at her. 'Miles away, I was, and didn't realise you were there.'

Not failing to notice that the usual twinkle in his eyes was absent, she said, 'I thought you'd like to know Josie called to say she's arrived at home safe and sound.'

'That's good.' He nodded.

'Is it?'

'Is it what?'

'Good that she's safely back in England.'

Looking at her face, so like her sister's, he said, 'To be honest, lass, I'd be a damn sight happier if she was still safely here where we could look after her.'

'Give her a bit of time, Harry.' Dora laid a hand on his shoulder. 'Don't quote me on this, but I have a hunch she'll come round to realising that for herself.'

CHAPTER TWENTY-NINE

Feeling rough, and not wanting to take her late-summer cold into a hospital, Carol accepted Dora's offer to drive Lars to Dijon for physiotherapy. Which turned out to be a good move because Dora just happened to slip her qualifications paperwork into her handbag.

The Bachelor of Science degree, acquired through Open University when she took a break from nursing while her children were small, plus later hands-on experience did the job. Firstly, this gained her entry to the physio session to witness Lars's treatment. Secondly, after being interviewed by some high-ranking medical officer, it was agreed that she could participate in the patient's rehabilitation in his own home.

Accurate designs were found on the Internet, and Danny had no problem constructing the parallel bars bit of kit. 'Nah, no charge,' he said. 'Had the timber and stuff going spare, didn't I?'

So it was that, bullied by Dora at home in addition to weekly sessions at the hospital, Lars was literally striding ahead, as he put it. Consequently, in early November, they were able to go for Harry's offer to take them cruising. Looking forward to a brief trip before the canal closed its gates for the winter months, Lars and Carol, plus three cats and a walking stick, boarded Reiziger.

Stepping onto the side deck, Carol heard Harry's voice say, 'Good morning, lass. It's a grand day.'

'Hiya, Harry,' called Carol, turning to help Lars get off the gangplank before going back to the car to fetch their bags.

'Morning, mate,' said Lars, going into the wheelhouse and finding it empty. 'Where the hell are you?'

'Engine room,' came a muffled reply. 'Be with you in a mo.'

Leaving the cats to do their normal thing of scrambling on deck, Carol went into the wheelhouse to be greeted by what sounded for all the world like Josie's voice saying, 'Hiya, Harry.'

'Huh?' Carol looked at Lars sitting on a wheelhouse seat, then down to where he was staring at the floor. At which point, Bovril strolled into the wheelhouse and a parrot said, 'Oh shit.'

Seemingly unabashed by such a greeting in what Bovril considered to be *his* wheelhouse, he approached the alien creature and hissed at it. Showing no indication of backing off, the parrot, in a male voice with a distinctly Welsh accent, said, 'Sit! Sit, sit, sit, you silly bugger.'

'Sorry about that,' said Harry, emerging from the engine room. 'He picked that up when my mate, Owen, used to bring his Doberman on Jemima back in England.'

As Carol scooped Bovril up off the floor, Harry said, 'It's alright, lass, he won't hurt the cat.'

'Maybe not,' she said. 'But this one's a bit of a sod about catching birds.'

'Silly sod, silly sod, silly sod,' said Ceremony, climbing up Lars's trouser leg to perch on his knee. Tilting its head to one side, the bird looked up at Lars and said, 'Biscuit, biscuit, biscuit.'

'Flipping heck,' said Carol. 'Have we got to spend the next few days with Glynis's triple verbosity thingy?'

'Silly old fart,' said the parrot, and vocally emitted a raucous imitation of flatulence.

On the issue of flatulence, Annie had come to the conclusion that overdosing on liquorice justified Mike's complaint about her lifting the bed covers on a regular basis. Realising this nightly occurrence wasn't conducive to marital harmony, she eschewed the black stuff in favour of sherbet lemons. And it was true to say that flushing away the end product of a high consumption of liquorice was something Annie felt she could do without. So, yes, she was pleased about that problem disappearing round the bend.

A problem she hadn't quite managed to come to terms with was what to do about her mother. Should she put her head in the sand and wait and see what, if anything, came via a phone call from Norfolk? But after three weeks, Annie was becoming stressed out with the tension, so she dialled her mother's number.

'I did wonder if you would deign to call sometime,' said Lillian.

'I'm calling now. So how are you, Mum?'

Sniff.

'I see. Well, in case you're interested, I'm fine. And, apparently, so is the baby.'

'No doubt you've informed your father about that.'

'Yes, I have, actually. Which may have something to do with the fact that he's phoned a couple of times to ask.'

'Yes, well, I still don't understand why you even asked that woman to attend your bizarre wedding affair.'

'And I still don't understand why you came, not to mention why you left France without even saying goodbye.'

'Annestine, you knew very well I had to get to the airport.'

'Which you couldn't do until my dad had seen Mike and me off on a barge, so where's the reasoning in that?'

'Ask yourself, Annestine, why I didn't come to that stupid boat to see you off.'

'You know what? I don't think I want to ask. I think I've got all the answers I need. Oh, and by the way, I answer to Annie.'

'That is so typical of your lack of appreciation. And to think, I gave you a name that would make you stand out from the common herds.'

'Which I won't inflict on my baby. It's due towards the end of March, and if you're interested, my dad will be kept informed. Goodbye, Mother.'

Before reaching out to take his shaking wife in his arms, Mike paused long enough to grab a couple of sheets of kitchen roll. Dabbing at Annie's face, he said, 'It had to be done sometime.'

'I know.' She sniffed and blew her nose. 'I have to let it go, it's not doing George any good.'

'Who's George?'

'That little man in my stomach. He's kicking like he thinks he's George Best trying to score a winning goal or something.'

In bed that night, Mike propped himself up on one elbow, looked down at Annie's face and felt a sense of relief that she was looking more relaxed than she had done recently. Breathing in the tang of sherbet lemons mixed with the underlying smell of toothpaste, he laid a hand on the mound Annie's stomach had become. Without opening her eyes, she laid her hand on top of his and murmured, 'Game over, and all is calm in the locker room.'

While peace reigned in Walnut House, all hell was breaking loose on Reiziger. Or, more to the point, the barge was breaking loose from its mooring as a freak gale hit it side on around six in the morning, resulting in it being swept across the canal as the mooring stakes failed to hold.

Harry was the first one to shoot up into the wheelhouse, followed closely by Carol after they were woken by the thump as the barge hit the bank on the other side of the canal. It took Lars a bit longer to join them, and together they looked out at the devastation as trees toppled and fell across the canal. Powerless to do anything, all three instinctively ducked when the large tree that was now swaying and threatening to crash across Reiziger's bow finally uprooted and landed in the canal with its top branches mere inches from the front of the boat.

'Hell, that was close,' said Harry, mopping his sweating brow.

'Hell, hell, hell,' said Ceremony from his cage on the wheelhouse seat. The next thing the parrot was shrieking was the sound of a siren as it rent the air.

'Pompier call-out,' said Carol. 'They're on it already, so this must be serious.'

'Too right it's serious,' said Lars. 'We're deep in the shit. I'm supposed to be in control of this ship, and there's sod all I can do about it.'

'Cool it, mate,' said Harry. 'Now that tree's down, there aren't any others close enough to do us any harm.'

'Sure,' said Lars. 'We're only on a boat that's not moored to anything. And it's not safe for any of us to go out there and do anything about that.'

'Look, mate. We're only plastered against a bank with a sodding great tree in front of us, so we're not going anywhere, are we?'

Leaving Harry to deal with Lars, Carol went below to make tea. By the time the kettle had boiled, the wind had abated as abruptly as it had whipped up, and she carried a tray up to the wheelhouse to be greeted by laughter. No, it wasn't the parrot laughing. Obviously deciding the fun was over, he muttered, 'Silly buggers.' Then tucked his head under a wing and was apparently ready to go back to sleep.

So what were the silly buggers laughing about? Oh, right, they were reminiscing about that nurse in the hospital who'd had a crush on Lars and kept popping into their room to ask if he needed a bedpan or anything.

'Big old gal, she was,' Harry told Carol. 'Given half a chance, she'd have got into bed with him. Then you'd have been well crushed, wouldn't you, mate?'

'Tell me more,' said Carol, handing Harry a mug of tea. 'Looks like we'll be stuck here for a while, so entertain me, why don't you.'

It was nearly two hours and not yet full daylight when a truck arrived and two men and a girl, all toting chain saws, began the work of liberating a trapped barge. The girl shook her head at the offer of tea and asked if they had any beer on board.

With the movement of the top tree branches being dragged out of the water, Reiziger was also on the move and drifting away from the bank. Luckily, the girl, who was apparently in charge of operations, was as adept at catching mooring ropes as she was at catching beer cans.

Aided by Reiziger's bow, with Harry expertly manoeuvring the vessel, the remaining bulk of the tree trunk was nudged against the far bank, and they were free to go. With just five locks between them and Coulaize, everyone on board was anxious to get home and see the extent of damage wreaked in their own village.

What they saw on the way did nothing to alleviate their anxiety. A team of pompiers was dealing with the next lock cottage, that seemed to have had its roof almost sliced in two by a fallen tree. The lock gates were open in their favour, and as Harry entered, Carol went onto the side deck and called out to ask about the people who occupied the cottage.

The news was that both the lock keeper and her son had not survived. This was shocking to hear, but it hit Harry particularly hard because the lock keeper's son was one of his fishing pals. Looking at Harry's ashen face, Lars grabbed hold of the ship's wheel and said, 'Shift yourself, mate. I'm taking over.'

At Harry's protest, it was Carol who surprisingly said, 'Let him do it, Harry.'

'But, lass, he…'

Trust him,' she said. 'He wouldn't do it if there was any chance of putting us in danger. And if you and I don't operate this lock ourselves, we're not going anywhere.'

Between them, Harry and Carol dealt with the sluices and the gates, and as Lars steered his boat out of the lock and into the open canal, he said, 'It wasn't my fault. I did everything I could.'

'Well of course it wasn't your fault,' said Carol. 'You were hardly in control of the wind, were you?'

After muttering in Dutch for a few seconds, he said, 'I was

supposed to be in control, but it was the Shamal.'

'Shamal? Lars, if that's a Dutch word, we don't know what it means.'

'Dessert wind,' he said. 'Came out of nowhere and there we were in this sand storm.'

'Ah. Are you talking about the helicopter crash?'

As if he hadn't heard her, he said, 'I did my best to get us out, but once sand gets into the works…by the time they got to us, he was already dead.'

'Who was?'

'Co-pilot. Young man in his twenties.'

Alarmed to see him beginning to shake, Carol caught hold of his arm and said, 'You taught me how to drive this thing, so let me…'

'No! I was responsible for that copter. I lost control. I'm not about to let that happen with my ship.'

He got them into the next lock before Carol asked him how his leg was holding up.

'It's beginning to hurt,' he said.

'Right.' Harry stood up. 'Like we boaters always say, there's only ever one skipper, and I believe that's supposed to be me on this trip.'

'Fair point,' said Lars. 'You're a good mate, Harry.'

'Yeah, and I'm a good skipper too. So you shift your bum onto that seat and let me get us and your barge safely home.'

As they left the last lock which took them into Coulaize, it was hard to believe the gale had happened at all. Only a few miles from their night mooring, the village sat serene and intact.

Once Reiziger was safely moored, and Carol and Lars and three cats were on their way to Escargot Cottage in their car, Harry realised how shaken he was by what had happened in the last few hours. Not so much what had happened to them because, well, they'd come through it unscathed, hadn't they?

No, it was more what that freak gale had done to a woman and her son in a lock house. Then there was what Lars had said about a young man who died because of a desert sand storm. Pondering on the vagaries of weather, which no man, however clever, has any control over, he checked that Reziger's mooring ropes were good and secure.

Back on Jemima, he picked up his mobile, called the Turners and demanded to be given Josie's phone number.

213

'How are you?' he asked, when Josie answered her phone.

'Not bad, Harry. How are you?'

'Not good right now. I wish you were here.'

'Oh, Harry. Are you ill?'

'Not as such, no. But the thing is, lass, none of us know what's lying in wait for us round the next corner. And you and me are wasting time when we could be together.'

CHAPTER THIRTY

'I want it. Full details, the lot,' said Tina, after listening to Carol's brief account of what was already being labelled "Night of Terror in Burgundy" in Tina's head.

'Sure, you can have it,' said Carol. 'We've done with it, so it's all yours.'

After writing copious notes, Tina tapped a pencil on her spiral-bound note pad and said, 'And the rest?'

'The rest of what?'

'Come on, if the rumour has any legs, you'd know, wouldn't you?'

'Rumour? What rumour would that be?'

'Yeah, like you don't know about a summer romance maybe coming back to life.'

'Tina,' said Carol, shifting Rupert off her lap to go and make more coffee. 'I don't do riddles, so you'll have to fill me in on that one.'

'Well, now.' Tina grinned. 'Am I right in thinking your scary experience has anything to do with Dora's sister coming back on Wednesday?'

'Search me, Tina. You'd have to ask Harry about that.'

'Great,' said Tina, scribbling a note in her pad. 'I'm right on base there, then.'

'You, you sod, should come with a label round your neck saying: Beware, I'm on your case.'

'Uh-huh. So it is true, then. No thanks.' Tina held up a hand when Carol asked if she was ready for a coffee refill. 'I'm a woman on a mission, and I've got people to see and interrogate.'

'Well you go easy on Harry,' said Carol. 'Any word of you bullying my favourite toy-boy and I'll be on *your* case.'

'Nah, don't do bullying, me. Besides, I'm not ready for him yet.' Shoving her notebook in her bag and heading for the door, she said, 'That'll have to wait till I know if Josie is up for agreeing to have anything written about them.'

'Good,' said Carol. 'Dare I ask which victim you're heading for now?'

'Oh, just popping up to see Annie and Mike.'

'Um, Tina, you're not doing a piece about Annie's mum, are you?'

'Come off it, Carol. Far too personal, and I don't mess with mates. Not that I'd waste column inches on that cow anyway. See ya.'

Smiling as Tina gunned her little car's engine and took off like a bat out of hell, Carol couldn't help wondering what interesting snippet about Annie and Mike had caught the girl's attention this time.

'So how did you know about it?' asked Mike.

'I didn't. Well, not till I read the newspapers on line and spotted this.' Tina pulled a printout from her bag and handed it to him. 'It is your Monique Lanteine, isn't it?'

Staring at a Times article with yesterday's date on it, Mike nodded. So, Felicity hadn't been wrong. His mother's paintings with the Henri-Pierre Debuet connection had attracted a lot of attention in London.

After reading the first paragraph, Mike said, 'The big boys have already got the story covered, so what's in it for you?'

'About a hundred quid initially,' she said. 'Unless you're prepared to pose for me, that is. They pay more for piccies, see? And if you could let me have a photo of your relative who painted them...'

'No.' Mike interrupted her.

'What, no you won't pose, or...'

'I've never even seen a photo of her.'

'Look, Mike.' Tina looked at his face which was showing signs of agitation. 'We don't have to do this if it's going to bother you.' With bated breath, she waited and watched his face, which seemed to be reflecting a series of emotions. Reluctant as she was to push for it, this was a biggie for Tina. According to the Times article, the art gallery owner hosting the paintings had refused to reveal the source from which she had attained the loan of them. So if Tina could be the one to...

'I'm not going to be a poser, even for you,' he said.

'Actually, I was kidding about that. To be honest, Mike, it would probably be best if you were kept out of the whole issue. In fact, we don't even need to mention Coulaize. It could just be a little unnamed village anywhere in Burgundy where I just happen to know those paintings were discovered.'

'Okay, I'll go for that,' said Mike, getting up to fill the kettle. 'If that's a cert, you can take photos of the other paintings.'

'What other paintings?' Tina's neck cracked as she swung her head to where he was standing at the sink. 'There's only supposed to be three of the buggers.'

'Oh, right. So you wouldn't be interested in the other seven then?'

'What! Mike, are you serious?'

'Only as serious as those buggers hanging on the wall in the hall.'

'Brilliant or what!' Tina didn't even try to contain her excitement as she jumped up and threw her arms round Mike. 'This is so going to put me on the map.'

Clutching a tin of paint and a dripping brush, Annie walked into the kitchen, grinned and said, 'Would you like to put my husband down and tell me what this map thing is about?'

With her animated face looking ready for take-off to another planet, Tina grabbed hold of Annie's arm and said, 'I tell you, mate, you made a good move when you married this guy.'

'And I'll tell you, mate,' said Annie. 'Grabbing at a woman with a loaded paint brush was a well duff move.'

'No worries.' Tina looked down at her legs. 'I believe jeans with sunshine yellow streaks are all the rage these days.'

'That's good news, then,' said Annie. 'But apart from that kettle Mike's got in his hand, would someone please tell me what the hell's going on here?'

'What I don't get,' said Annie, 'is why Flicky Flickers is refusing to reveal where she got the paintings.'

'Because,' said Tina, 'she'd hardly want anyone hot-footing it over here and finding the others, would she? Besides, it makes their gallery look even more important if they're the only one's in the know about how or where the goodies came to light.'

'But they're not, are they?'

'No, Annie. They know they're not, but they don't know about me, do they? They wouldn't know who I am, what I do or what I know.'

'Tina, would you like to de-encrypt that for me?'

'Look,' said Tina. 'They have no idea you just happen to have a shit-hot journalist mate who's panting to reveal the true story. I mean, come on. You'd hardly expect to find one of those in a sleepy little village tucked away in the middle of rural Burgundy, would you?'

Mike, who had been reading the Times article more thoroughly, snorted and said, 'The bloody woman is lying through her arse.'

'What about?' asked Annie.

'Well, he said,' passing her Tina's print out. 'If you don't count the fact that the current owners didn't have a clue what valuable treasures were collecting dust in their attic...'

'Attic! What attic?'

Pointing at a paragraph,' he said, 'Never mind that, read this bit here.'

'I will when you've moved your finger off it.' As she read, Annie's eyes widened and her jaw was well on its way to hitting her chest. Looking at Tina, she said, 'How can she get away with saying she has no idea if those are the only three paintings that exist, but her gallery is on a trail of enquiry in the hope of acquiring more. Christ, she bloody well knows there are seven more right here in this house.'

'Ah-ha,' said Tina. 'She's *not* going to get away with it, is she?' Turning to Mike, she said, 'You need to be sure about what I'm itching to do, because I need your hundred per cent go-ahead on this.'

Looking alarmed, he said, 'Precisely what are you planning to do, Tina?'

'Only blow her lying arse out of the water. Who knows, it may even dump her gallery in the nasty brown stuff, so this could turn out to be well serious.'

'Okay...but...' Annie looked from one face to the other. 'Will that dump us in trouble?'

'No way,' said Tina. 'You own the things, and I don't even have to mention your name or anything about you.'

'But it'll be obvious you know us.'

'Not if I was given a tip-off and decided to follow up.'

'But hang on,' said Mike. 'The woman knows Danny, she knows he's been here, so she could cause grief for him.'

'What? All she knows about my Danny is that he's a building labourer who thinks painting is what you do to walls and door frames. She wouldn't expect him to recognise a serious landscape painting if it bit his bum.'

'But he's got the same surname as you,' Annie pointed out.

'Not my writing name, he hasn't. I've been writing as Tanya

Willis since before I even married Danny. Mike, what are you grinning about?'

'Oh, nothing much. Except she more or less bullied me into letting her borrow those three paintings for her own glory, and it sounds as if she's planning to harass me for more. What I'm thinking here is something on the lines of poetic justice.'

'I like it,' said Annie. 'And you're forgetting she walked off with a stack of your business cards, which haven't actually yielded any business, have they?'

'Well she'd hardly go round her London art cronies handing out those cards, would she?' said Tina. 'Not when she wants Mike's whereabouts and name kept under wraps.'

'I suppose not,' said Annie. 'Tina, is your name really Tanya?'

'Annestine,' said Tina. 'Is your name really Annie?'

'Fair enough.' Looking at the kettle still clutched in Mike's hand, Annie said, 'Are you going to boil that thing, or what?'

Not only did Tina's provincial newspaper editor grab the story and run it, he'd got the art editor of a national paper snapping at his heels. Playing his cards close to his chest, Tina's guy pointed out that the story had been given to him on an exclusive basis. He did, however, indicate that he would consider letting them have permission to print it. Provided the freelance journalist who owned the copyright agreed, that was. Oh yes, he did think she could be persuaded to be amenable – at a realistic price, of course.

No, he wasn't at liberty to reveal the source of the information, but he had it on good authority that it was a hundred per cent reliable. As he said, he wouldn't have gone to print on it himself if he wasn't sure the facts were bona fide, would he?

Alfie didn't understand what any of that meant. All he knew was that his mum had leapt around the room like a maniac and said they were going to have a bumper Christmas. As for Lucie, she was excited about the pictures of Madame being famous in an important English newspaper. The fact that it seemed to have something to do with Alfie's mama made it even more special. So much so that Lucie refrained from nagging Alfie about his English for nearly three days.

But then, when the first snow fell in early December, the kids had more important things to think about. Like, should their snowman have a bulgy nose made from a potato, or a pointy carrot one?

'Nah, you're right,' said Alfie. 'Them carrot ones are boring. Everyone's snowman has one a those.' Having let Lucie have her way on that one, Alfie reckoned it was only fair she help him build a snow dragon, wasn't it? Which turned out to be easier said than done, and when they stood back and surveyed their efforts, both of them admitted it wasn't exactly what you'd call a quality dragon.

The snow didn't last long enough for Coulaize to have a white Christmas, but at the beginning of the third week of December, it was still showing its face for a white wedding. Not that it was the conventional type of white wedding with a bride wearing a frothy meringue dress. No, this was more a case of the bride, looking serene and lovely in a pearl grey outfit, with her groom wearing slacks and a borrowed blazer, emerging from the Marie into a flurry of snowflakes.

Like natural confetti falling from the sky, the snow gently drifted down onto their heads and shoulders as Josie and Harry walked the short distance from the Marie to the village church to have their marriage blessed.

Harry did appreciate Dora's offer to hold a reception at Maison Lavande, really he did, but he had thanked the Turners and insisted he'd be more comfortable with a casual gathering at the Carry On café. Like that, he explained, anyone who wanted to would feel free to drop in. The people he had in mind were his French fishing mates and a couple or so lock keepers he'd palled up with. None of whom would have attended a formal do in someone's posh house.

Albeit briefly, those people did come to the Café Carillon. They came together as a group and raised their glasses to toast the bride and groom's happiness. On a more sombre note, instigated by Harry, their glasses were raised again in salute of absent friends.

Sharing the memory of the gale, and moved by the significance of Harry's gesture, Carol joined in with that salute to the lock keeper and her son who had perished. She was hugging Harry, and he was saying how, if it hadn't been for that gale, he might never have plucked up the courage to persuade his Josie to come back when Glynis tugged at Carol's arm.

Fishing a tissue from her sleeve, Carol turned to Glynis and said, 'Don't you dare talk about silver linings.'

'I wasn't going to, Carol. I was going to say that man is here.'

'Man? What man, where?'

'He's out there, reading that notice about the bar being closed for a private party.'

After looking through the glass door as a man polished his glasses before moving to the window and peering in, Carol looked round the bar and, spotting Mike, went to him and asked if he knew the man who was outside.

'I don't,' said Mike. 'But I've seen him before. He came up to Annie and me and wished us happiness when we left the Marie after our wedding thing.'

'Well he seems to know you,' said Carol. 'Or, at least, he seems interested in you.'

'Okay,' said Mike. 'If he's the one Liz was telling me about, I think I'll just go and have a quick word with him.'

By the time he'd got through the throng and out of the door, the strange man was already walking away. Sprinting through falling snow, Mike caught up with him on the bridge and, addressing him in French, asked if he was someone he should know.

'Non.' The old man shook his head and started to walk on. After a few steps, he turned, held out a hand and said, 'Mon nom est Debuet. Henri-Pierre Debuet.'

Taking a deep breath, Mike clutched the old man's hand and told him he thought they had things to talk about. Agreeing that standing out in the snow was not a good place to talk, Henri-Pierre pointed to his car that was parked the other side of the bridge.

CHAPTER THIRTY-ONE

Narrowly missing Mike as, deep in thought, he didn't even notice the car, Tina swung into a space in front of the Carry On. Leaping out of her car without stopping to switch off the engine, she yelled, 'Mike, hang on. We need to talk.'

'Not now, Tina,' he said, holding up a hand. 'I have to find Annie.'

'But, Mike...' She ran and caught hold of his arm. 'This is serious.'

'Sorry,' he said. 'Whatever it is will have to wait. I need to talk to Annie now.'

'So you've seen it, then?'

'What?'

'Today's paper.'

'No, I haven't,' he said. 'Look, I'm sorry, love, right now I've got other things on my mind.'

'Mike, are you okay?'

'Yes, I think so.' And he went into the bar to be greeted by Annie asking where the hell he'd been. 'You shot out without a word,' she said. 'And when I went out to look for you...Mike, is something wrong?'

'No...yes. What I mean is, we had something wrong, but I now know the truth.'

'The truth about what?'

'Annie, can we just go home? There're things I want to tell you.'

'So this Henri-Pierre guy in that photo who's a dead-ringer for you isn't your father after all then?' said Annie. 'So why the photo of him in the bottom of that chest?'

'Yes, well,' said Mike. 'He told me he did give Monique the photo.'

'Why?'

'Because he was in love with her.'

'And yet...' Annie paused, trying to get her head round what Mike had just told her. 'It seems she wasn't in love with him.'

'That's right. Apparently, Henri-Pierre only later realised she rejected him because it was his brother, Gerard, she wanted. And, as it turned out, she got him. Or should I say he got her.'

'Got her pregnant, you mean?'

'Yes. Which was why Monique suddenly left Toulouse and came home.'

'Okay, but why would she do that? I mean, if she and Gerard were in love, and...'

'Because, Annie, that was when she discovered Gerard was married.'

'Shit!' Annie got up, went to the glass casement doors and stared out at the wonderful world Monique had bequeathed to Mike. 'The poor woman. No wonder she cracked up.'

'Yes.' Abruptly standing up and going towards the kitchen, he said he was going to make some tea. When he came back with a teapot and two mugs, he said, 'Okay, do you want to hear the rest?'

Curled up beside him with her feet up on the shabby but comfy settee, Annie listened to what else Henri-Pierre had told Mike. About how, when he'd got the story from a distraught Monique, he had tried to persuade her to marry him so he could take care of her and her child. But all she wanted was to get away from anything to do with the Debuet family.

'So,' said Annie. 'You've found an uncle. But what about your father?'

'He's dead.'

'Oh.'

'Remember I looked them up on the Internet and found out the Debuet Academy in Toulouse had closed because of ill health? It was Gerard who was ill.'

'I see.' Annie looked at Mike and said, 'This is all a bit much to take on board, isn't it? How do you feel?'

'Weird. I mean, I found out a lot this morning, but...'

'Go on.'

'Well, I've discovered an uncle, I've found out who my father is...was...and, Annie, what if my mother had married Henri-Pierre?'

'Then you would have been brought up in France, and I wouldn't be here now.'

'I know.' He gripped her hand. 'And that's scary.'

'But we are here together, Mike. And we've got this lovely home for our child to grow up in.' Shaking her head, she said, 'Life is strange, but the thing is, we get what we get, and a lot of what happens is pretty much out of our control.'

'That's more or less what Henri-Pierre said. Sort of on the lines of, if Monique had agreed to marry him, he wouldn't have the marriage he does have, or his beautiful daughters.'

'Hmm,' said Annie. 'So you've got some beautiful female cousins into the bargain.'

'Apparently so.' Mike's face relaxed into a grin. 'Just think, the poor sod could have been lumbered with me instead.'

'Now that's what you'd call a lucky escape,' she said. 'Where do he and his family live?'

'Paris.'

'So what's he doing hanging around in Coulaize?'

'We didn't really cover that,' said Mike, gazing into his empty tea mug. 'All I know is he comes to Dijon occasionally to do art workshops or something.'

'So will you see him again?'

'I don't know.' He shrugged. 'That wasn't mentioned, but he gave me his card, so I suppose it's been sort of left up to me.'

'A bit like that,' said Annie, swinging her legs off the settee and reaching for the teapot. 'Left up to you, a woman could die of thirst here.'

'Well, if you're going to be mum,' he said, passing his mug to her.

Without saying a word, she filled the mug from the teapot and handed it to him. 'Um,' he said, peering at the content of the mug. 'What do you call this?'

'Good question, Mike. One you can answer, maybe?'

'Pass.' He put the mug on the table. 'Annie, how do you fancy going back to the wedding party?'

'Lead me to it,' she said. 'It beats sitting here drinking lukewarm water coloured with a dash of milk.'

At the Carry On, Glynis had shed the jacket of the trouser suit Ken had wanted her to wear, rolled up the sleeves of the blouse she'd chosen, and was in her element behind the bar. Not that there was any serving of drinks going on when Annie and Mike arrived back. In fact, not even the chinking of glasses or hum of chatter disturbed the atmosphere.

The only sound was a rendering of *I am Sailing* as a rich baritone voice filled the room and fell like velvet onto the ears of a rapt audience.

Holding up his hands to still the applause, a young black man said, 'Thanks y'all. That was for the bride and groom, to wish them a happy life on board their boat.' Shaking his head at the calls for encore, Valentine Corrella went to Liz and said, 'I wish I could stay longer, but I have to get to Paris for a gig tonight.'

'I can't believe you just turnin up like that,' said Liz. 'You shoulda warned us.'

'To be honest,' said Valentine, 'it wasn't exactly planned. We were driving up from Lyon after last night's concert, I saw the sign to Coulaize and couldn't resist calling in.'

Watching the gorgeous singer exchanging affectionate farewells with several people, Tina was practically wetting herself. For heaven's sake, the man had become famous after being discovered when he'd been working as crew on a hotel barge on this very canal. And here he was in sleepy little Coulaize, humble as you like, hugging people Tina actually knew.

Was this a cool story, or was this a cool story!

But then, catching sight of Mike standing by the door, Tina's euphoria evaporated as what she needed to talk to him about kicked back in. As the temporary respite afforded by Valentine Corrella's charismatic appearance faded, Tina was back to grinding her teeth and clenching her fists.

'Not now and not here, sweetie,' said Harriet, laying a hand on Tina's shoulder.

'What? Oh, sorry, Harriet, I didn't see you there.'

'I think what you need to do is think it through, then I suggest a sesh with all involved.'

'Um, Harriet, what are you talking about?'

'I would imagine whatever it is you're seething about,' said Harriet.

'And how would you know what that is?'

'Sweetie, Luc has a positive pash for reading the Brit newspapers on line.'

'Ah...okay...so you know about that cow's response to what I wrote?'

'Absolutely,' said Harriet. 'And you do know, of course, that Luc just happens to be a legal bod.'

225

'Yes, well.' Tina shrugged. 'But this stuff is happening in England, so a French lawyer is going to help exactly how?'

'Search me,' said Harriet, her gold bracelets colliding with each other as she raised her hands. 'I leave all that biz to Luc.'

After a quick glance at the clock over the bar, Tina said, 'It'll have to wait anyway. I've just about got time to say cheerio to Josie and Harry, then I'll have to shoot off.'

Returning her hug, Harry said, 'Thanks for coming, lass. It's been right grand having all these lovely people around us.'

As Tina called out a general goodbye to whoever was still in the bar, Mike caught hold of her arm and asked what she needed to talk to him about.

'Sorry, Mike, no time to explain. Alfie's due home from school any minute. Check your email when you get home, I'll send you a link.'

Annie was preparing a meal when, saying he was going to check his emails, Mike went to the lounge and switched on his computer. A few minutes elapsed before he called Annie to come and see. In response to her asking from the kitchen if it could wait, only she was up to her wrists in flour, he told her that, no, she really needed to see this. Like now.

Muttering something on the lines of did he want steak pie for dinner or what, she came into the lounge wiping pastry-encrusted hands on a damp dish cloth and said, 'This had better be important.'

'You tell me,' he said, pointing to a newspaper article on the screen.

'Oh heck,' she said, after reading the first paragraph. 'Looks like Tina could be in trouble.'

'Or not,' said Mike. 'Read the whole thing, Annie.'

'Okay, okay, I'm reading it.'

Interspersed with gasps and a few *what the hell* type of mutterings, Annie read:

Some doubt has been cast on the authenticity of an article written by a Ms Tanya Willis. This little-known journalist has thus far written only cosy stories about ex-patriot life in Burgundy, but recently reached beyond that brief with a controversial article about possibly important pieces of art.

The significance of the art lies in the fact that, in London, the Felice Gallery is currently hosting three landscape paintings thought to be influenced by the prestigious Henri-Pierre Debuet. It was in response to news issued about these paintings that Ms Willis published an article disputing the gallery owner's claim that only those three paintings by Debuet pupil, Monique Lanteine, have as yet been discovered. According to Ms Willis, the gallery owner, Felicity Fortescue, does, in fact, know the whereabouts of further paintings by Monique Lanteine. Ms Willis goes as far as to support that statement with photographic evidence of other paintings which she claims Ms Fortescue has seen.

When interviewed, Ms Felicity Fortescue made this comment: "It is correct that a few other landscape paintings, supposedly from the same stable, were shown to my representative. But his instinct and trained eye led him to select just the three we have on display in the gallery."

When asked if she could throw any light on the photographic evidence of the other paintings supporting Ms Willis's article, Ms Fortescue told us that she happened to know that the owner of the genuine ones currently in her possession is, himself, a talented artist. She could only suggest that, being aware of the potential value, he could possibly have emulated Monique Lanteine's style and painted more pictures with hopes of financial gain. Ms Fortescue added: "I view Tanya Willis's maligning statements as a blatant attempt to discredit my integrity. Furthermore, how this person would be expected to know about anything relating to a subject beyond her normal mundane realm is something of a mystery."

And the mystery continues. Is there an attempt to subject the art world to a possible scam? Will Ms Tanya Willis be able to authenticate her words? Will Ms Fortescue's claim that no other paintings by Monique Lanteine have yet been discovered turn out to be a valid claim? At this point, it is open to speculation, and only investigation into the provenance of the supposedly further paintings is likely to supply the answers. Meanwhile, Ms Fortescue has said that the three paintings entrusted to her will stay in her possession until the matter is resolved.

'Flaming arseholes,' said Annie, looking up at Mike. 'I wish to hell that woman had never set foot in our house.'

'I know, me too. More to the point, I wish to hell I hadn't let her get her grasping paws on those paintings.'

'Mike, does Tina know about this?'

'Yep, she sent me the link to it. And according to her email, Luc's on it.'

'What's it got to do with Luc?'

'I'm not sure.' Mike scratched his head. 'Well, except that he's a lawyer.'

'So are we talking libel here or something?'

'I don't know, Annie. But apparently he's worried about Tina bursting into print without knowing the full implications of what she's dealing with.'

'I suppose that makes sense,' said Annie. 'And it's nice that he cares.'

'Well, Tina reckons Luc's a good bloke to have in your corner, and she's asking if we can go to his place for a meet this evening.'

'Okay.' Leaving sticky pastry where her fingers had been clutching the edge of the desk, Annie got up and said, 'Forget steak pie for dinner. Can I interest you in a hastily defrosted lasagne?'

Tina was looking somewhat strained, Luc was looking completely relaxed and Harriet, handing out canapés and drinks, was looking…what? Could that be glee written on her face?

Shuffling her chair a bit further away from a roaring log fire, Annie popped a sherbet lemon in her mouth and waited to hear what this was going to be about.

Going through the article paragraph by paragraph, Luc pointed out there were only suggestions, and none were solid enough to be called libel – which he pronounced as *leebelle*. When he said that Tina knowing the truth was an advantage, the word sounded like *advantarge*. There was something soporific about Luc's calm, mellifluous voice speaking English with a cute French inflexion, and Annie's concentration on the subject in hand was drifting after what had turned out to be an eventful day.

And to think, less than six months ago, Annie wouldn't have even imagined meeting people like Luc and Harriet, let alone being made welcome in their fabulous home. In fact, it was beginning to be difficult to associate their lives in Sheffield with the life she and Mike had discovered here in Burgundy. Letting her mind wander, Annie was wondering if she and Mike were even the same people, and her eyes were giving up the struggle to stay open at the point where Harriet suggested Tina write a counter article, and Tina said that would only lead to another counter one from Felicity, and so it would go on forever.

But all eyes swung to Mike when he said, 'Not if we squash all this crap once and for all.'

'We wish,' said Tina. 'Got any bright ideas how we do that?'

'By quoting the woman's lies and blowing them out,' he said.

'Non.' Shaking his head, Luc said that the better tactic would be to not refer to the article, but to simply write an independent one stating the true facts without mentioning Felicity's name. 'This would suffice to show she is not representing the truth,' he said. 'And it would also serve to show Tina knows how to be professional.'

'Got that,' said Tina. 'The cow has slagged me off, but I don't need to resort to doing the same to her.'

'So,' said Annie. 'Does that mean she gets away with those disparaging remarks about Tina not being expected to know stuff beyond the mundane?'

'Not important,' said Tina. 'It's not about what she thinks of me.'

'This is correct.' Luc smiled at her. 'And by not responding to the taunt, Tina would maintain dignity greater than hers.'

Grinning, Tina said, 'Excuse me, Harriet, but I think I just fell in love with your husband.'

'This is permitted,' said Luc with an answering grin. 'Now we make a list of things factual.'

'Okay.' Mike nodded. 'Let's do that, shall we? Starting with a receipt signed by her, so we can wipe out that suggestion of her male representative finding the goods.'

'Nice one,' said Tina. 'Am I allowed to mention the receipt, Luc?'

With a Gallic shrug, he said, 'There is a better way. If you make words to show it was Felicity who discovered the important art, that will do two things. It will negate her words, and will show you are giving her the credit. Then what has she to have against you?'

'Nice one.' Tina scribbled in her notebook. 'Anything else?' With pen poised, she looked at Mike.

'Just that she's stuffed herself by saying the paintings will stay in her possession until things are resolved.'

'You think this is also not valid?' asked Luc.

'Yes. If an agreement that she returns the paintings within four months counts for anything.'

'Okay,' said Annie. 'But what about her saying Mike could have recently painted the others?'

'Empty words,' said Luc. 'They are words of a woman clutching at...at...paille?' He looked at Harriet.

'Straw, darling,' she said.

'Quite so.' He shrugged. 'She knows that was a thing stupid to say, and the way to show contempt is to not acknowledge that she said it.'

'Fair enough.' Tina did more notebook scribbling. 'But it's sooo tempting to say that a supposed art expert would be expected to know that petty suggestion hasn't got legs.'

Luc shrugged again, but it wasn't clear if he was agreeing or if he didn't get the bit about legs. Turning to Mike he told him he should write to Felicity and ask that she honours the agreement to return the paintings by the agreed date. 'It must be in formal terms,' he said. 'With a minimum of three weeks notice. I will write for you the words to use.'

'Thanks,' said Mike. 'But what if she doesn't comply?'

'Then we threaten legal action. But I think that will not become necessary.'

Skipping on from that, Tina referred to the final paragraph in the article and asked how important the provenance thing was.

'If that could be established,' said Luc, holding up the article print-out, 'the legs of this newspaper report are crippled.'

Which was when Mike said that, he couldn't make any promises, but it should be possible to prove that Monique Lanteine was the original artist of all ten paintings. When he got to the bit about contacting Henri-Pierre and asking him to verify provenance, Tina looked in danger of hyperventilating.

'Wh-what...how...' She stared at Mike. 'Come on, you're not telling us you know the man!'

'Well, I've only met him the once,' said Mike. 'But he gave me his contact details and, trust me on this, he knows a lot about Monique Lanteine.'

'Bugger,' said Tina. 'That's twice I've fallen in love with someone else's feller in one evening.'

Harriet didn't use the same F word other people did, but everyone knew what she meant when she said, 'I think we can safely say we've got Flickers fornicated.'

CHAPTER THIRTY-TWO

Carol picked up the phone with one hand and used the other to grab Rupert, who had a thing about chewing phone cables. Tucking the cat under her arm, she said, 'Sorry, Glynis, what was that you were saying?'

'I brought puddings from England.'

'Did you? What sort of puddings?'

'Christmas ones, Carol. You know you can't get them here.'

'Well, yes, I had realised that. Is that what you've phoned to tell me?'

'No, I'm checking you're okay to come to us for Chrissie dinner.'

'To be honest, Glynis, I'd sort of assumed you and Ken would be okay with coming here. It's just that we thought we'd invite Harry and Josie.'

'Won't they go to Dora and Don?'

'No, the Turners are going to England for a family Christmas.'

'Oh, right. Annie and Mike haven't got any, though.'

'What, Christmas puddings?'

'Carol, they haven't got any family here, have they?'

'No, but neither have Tina and Danny, so maybe they're going to get together.'

'Well I think it would be fun.'

'What would?'

'If we could all get together. I used to hate having to spend Christmas with Ken's parents, but none of us have to do that duty thing anymore, do we?'

Carol couldn't argue with that. How many times had she heard people moaning about having to spend Christmas with their own parents or the in-laws alternate years? In a lot of cases it was about obligations, which had nothing to do with the joy or fun of Christmas itself.

Putting the phone down, Carol asked Lars what he thought the chances were of hiring a marquee for next week.

'What for?' he said.

'So we can collect everyone together and celebrate liberation.'

'Oh, and here was me thinking it might be something to do with Christmas.'

'What I fink is,' Liz said to Glynis, 'we got the space an all the plates an stuff, so why not do it here?'

'Liz, that would be great, but Christmas day is one of the few times a year you close and have a day off.'

'Yeah,' said Gus. 'But we're closed Monday nights, innit. So you could do like the French an have yer Christmas dinner on Christmas Eve.'

'An we won't want ter make a profit, will we, darlin?' said Liz. 'Not so's our friends can get togevver fer Christmas.'

'Which means you two as well,' said Glynis. 'You'd have to sit and eat with us, so we could all pitch in with the work.'

'Suits me.' Gus grinned. 'How about I order what grub yer want wiv me trade discount, hand over me kitchen an let you lot wait on me?'

Calling in at Escargot Cottage before driving back home, a beaming Glynis affected a Cockney accent and said, 'I got it sorted, innit.'

What began as a plan to get just a few friends together sort of escalated. The first couple of phone calls Glynis made began with a tentative, 'I don't know if you'd be interested or not...' But gaining confidence from the responses, her tone changed to more on the lines of: 'We'll count you in, then. And I'll put you down for preparing sprouts, shall I?'

In answer to Harriet phoning her, Glynis said that of course they could join in. And by all means Lesley and Claudie would be welcome. Not feeling comfortable about asking Harriet's delicate hands to peel several kilos of potatoes, Glynis accepted the suggestion of a few trays of canapés, even though those weren't actually on her list. But imagining foie gras and caviar, she said, 'Go easy on expense, though. The plan is to split all costs between whoever attends.'

'No prob,' said Harriet. 'Call it a contribution gratuit. And I'll get Claudie to do a bucket of her fantas truffle sauce.'

Adding four more people to the guest list, and canapés and truffle sauce to the who-was-doing-what list, Glynis was beginning to think of herself as a bit of an ace party planner. Quite an elating thought, really, for someone who'd been conditioned to believe she wasn't capable of organising a dish washer.

But no – Glynis shook her head. Better not to go there. To be fair, Ken did seem to be trying not to be so bossy and assertive. He'd obviously taken on board what that therapist guy, Clifford, had said, and that was good, wasn't it?

Even so, when Ken came in just then, it was a bit odd to see him looking worried. Even odder when he said he might not have done the right thing.

'Why, what have you done?' she asked.

'Well,' he said, putting a baguette on the draining board. 'I ran into that retired Army chap in the boulangerie.'

'You mean the padre one who did the thingy at Mike and Annie's wedding?'

'That's him.' Ken nodded. 'It was a bit awkward because he asked us round to have drinks with him and his wife Christmas Eve.'

'That's nice of them,' said Glynis. 'But I assume you told him what was going on?'

'I did, yes. But the thing is, he wanted to know if it was open to anyone, so I told him I'd have to ask you.'

'Why did you do that, Ken?'

'Because it's your show, and I didn't want to interfere.'

'Ken.' Glynis went to him and put her hands on his shoulders. 'Have I shut you out on this?'

'Sort of,' he said, putting his arms round her. 'But that's okay. It's important for you to do your own thing.'

'Well,' she said. 'Why can't it be *our* thing? I mean, we used to do everything together, didn't we?'

Tightening his arms and holding her close, Ken said, 'Too much so, I suppose. But now it's almost like we lead separate lives.'

'I know.' She nodded her head against his chest. 'Ken, are we trying too hard?'

'I don't know, Glynis. It's just that I'm scared of saying or doing the wrong thing.'

'Eggshells,' she said.

'What?'

'I'm doing it too, Ken. Trying not to stand on them.'

'Oh, I see. You mean it's like we're walking warily round each other all the time?'

'Ken, I can't breathe.'

'But I'm trying not to...I mean, I'm trying to give you your own space to breathe in.'

'No, Ken.' She wriggled in his arms. 'I mean you're holding me too tight.'

'Sorry.' He released his grip, caught hold of her hands and said, 'Maybe we should talk to that Clifford man again. Just to...I don't know...to find out if we're going in the right direction.'

'Okay, if that's what you want,' said Glynis. 'Or we could try and find our own.'

'Our own?'

'Middle of the road, Ken. You know, so we can walk down it together.'

'Do you think we can?'

'Maybe.' She shrugged. 'If we sod the eggshells. Anyway, I think you should phone him.'

'Who? Clifford?'

'Major Williams, Ken. Tell him they're welcome to join the party. Oh, and find out if his wife is up to peeling several kilos of spuds.'

Emerging from the bathroom after carrying out his daily motions Lars announced, 'It's gone all floppy.'

'Has it?' said Carol, looking up from where she was kneeling in front of the Aga. 'Bugger, I don't know if Viagra's available in France.'

'Carol, I'm talking about the toilet roll.'

'Oh, right. You can blame Tina for that, and you'll find the kitchen roll is floppy as well.'

'Uh-huh.' Lars scratched his beard. 'Is there something going on I need to know about?'

'Crackers, Lars.'

'Would you like to enlarge on that?'

'It's quite simple, really. They don't sell Christmas crackers in France, so Alfie's making them.'

'Of course,' said Lars. 'I can't think why I didn't realise that as soon as I picked up the spineless toilet roll. Am I allowed to ask why you're measuring the oven?'

'Because Gus has ordered what he calls an effin great turkey, and I've volunteered you to cook it.'

'Good timing, Lucie.' Tina smiled at the girl and led the way into the kitchen. 'I reckon Alfie could do with some help.'

'What is it he does?' asked Lucie.

Looking up from a paper hat he was cutting out of wrapping paper, Alfie said, 'Hi, Luce. I'm making these, then I gotter make more crackers to put em in.'

'Please, what is crackers?'

'Them,' he said, pointing to a pile of already completed ones. 'It's what we have at Christmas in England.'

'You make many,' she said.

'Yeah, we need lots for the party. And we're having jelly, what you French kids don't know about neither.'

Taking a tray of mince pies out of the oven, Tina asked Alfie where he got the idea from that there would be jelly.

'That Harry bloke told me,' he replied. 'He said his wife is doing trifle with jelly what she got in England. Only he reckons that'll have booze in it, so he said he'd get her to make some jelly on its own.'

'Good old Josie,' said Tina, tipping the little pies onto a cooling tray. 'We wouldn't be having these if she hadn't brought out jars of mincemeat.'

As the aroma of freshly baked mince pies permeated the kitchen, Lucie sniffed appreciatively and said, 'I think your party for English people will be much good.'

'It int our party, and it int just for the English,' said Alfie. 'Is it, Mum?'

'What you mean, Alfie, is it *isn't*,' said Tina, glaring at him. 'But yes, Lucie, it's for anyone who wants to come.'

Her little face looking anxious, Lucie asked if her family would be permitted.

'A course,' said Alfie. 'It's for all us friends.'

'And this can mean French friends also?' Lucie was still obviously not sure where she and her parents stood on this.

'Luce,' said Alfie. 'I said all us friends, didn't I? If we only had English ones, you wouldn't be me best mate.' He ran a glue stick down the edge of a paper hat before adding, 'And all them other kids

236

at school wouldn't be me mates neither, would they?'

'Yes, well, Alfie,' said Tina. 'I don't think you can invite *all* of them to the party.'

'Mum, that's not what I meant, is it?'

'I know, lovie.' She ruffled his hair. 'I was only teasing.'

Her little face lighting up with a mischievous grin, Lucie said, 'I know what is teasing.'

'Bet you don't,' said Alfie. 'That int an English word I learned you yet.'

For once refraining from correcting her son's speech, Tina mentally applauded his cosmopolitan attitude. And to think, Danny had fretted about how the kid would cope in a French school. But then, moving the family to France hadn't been an easy decision. No, not easy at all when it meant taking a six-year-old out of the only environment he'd known and expecting him to adapt to a completely different way of life, not to mention a new language. In fact, she and Danny had had several rows about it before taking the plunge. The clincher, if they'd needed one, came when Alfie had done a bunk when he'd heard them talking about going back to England.

Okay, so he'd got it wrong because he'd thought they meant permanently, whereas the partially overheard discussion had been about going back to put their house in Kent on the market. The memory of how frantic they'd been when their kid had gone missing for hours was still enough to give Tina the shudders. But overriding that was the thought of how all those people in the village, moped lads included, had turned out en-mass and formed a search party.

That had all happened over a year ago, but inspired by Alfie's words to Lucie just now, Tina was thinking in terms of an up-date article about how things had turned out for this family. She'd already sold the story about how they'd bought the run-down stone house for very little cash, with the intention of using Danny's building skills to turn it into an investment as a gite to rent. And about how, seeing her family enjoying the relaxation and freedom they found whenever they spent short visits in Burgundy, she'd pushed for them making the little house into their home instead.

Right now, though, her main concern was about her poor old computer playing up. It was frustrating enough having to wait till January before that Henri-Pierre guy came to check out Monique's paintings, without worrying about whether or not she'd still have a functioning computer to write that all important article.

Meanwhile, leaving Lucie to educate Alfie on the subject of cows on heat teasing bulls, Tina took her mobile phone outside and called Glynis to check if the Lucotts were on the party guest list. Apparently Glynis hadn't thought to include them. But not to worry, she'd be on it right away.

'Oh, and Tina,' said Glynis, 'I don't suppose you or Danny play anything, do you?'

'Well, we do play Yatze sometimes. And Cluedo or Monopoly with Alfie.'

'Actually, I mean anything musical. It's just that Major Williams's wife plays the saxophone.'

'Oh, does she? Um, Glynis, is that relevant to anything?'

'Well she asked if she should bring it, and I said yes. I mean, I could hardly say no, could I?'

'Uh-huh. Glynis, is there a reason you're telling me this?'

'It's just that I think it would be best if she wasn't the only one.'

'Look, I'm sorry, but I'm going to have to ask. Could you explain what this is actually about?'

'I'm talking about entertainment, Tina. At the party.'

'Oh, right. I didn't know there was going to be any.'

'No, neither did I until I heard about Liesel Williams's saxophone.'

'Okay, Glynis, I think I'm getting the picture here. Entertainment has somehow got onto the agenda, and now you're looking for people to perform. Have I got that right?'

'That's what I've been saying, Tina. So I can count on you to do something, can I?'

'Er…Glynis, that wasn't exactly where I was heading. But, yeah, I can probably come up with a humorous poem or a monologue or something.'

Feeling guilty after Maureen's phone call asking how things were, Annie had given in and sent her mother a Christmas card. Although why she'd succumbed to emotional pressure from her step-mother was a bit hard to grasp. Maureen had said they hadn't heard from Lillian since the wedding, and asked if she'd contacted them recently. When Annie said they hadn't heard from her either, the concern in Maureen's voice was difficult to ignore.

'She seems to have cut herself off,' Maureen had said. 'I hope she's okay.'

'Well,' Annie replied. 'She knows how to get hold of us if she isn't. Let's face it, she's never hesitated to dump on any of us before, has she?'

'I know. But maybe Graham should pop round and check on her.'

The next thing Annie heard was that her dad had visited her mum, only to be kept standing in the rain on the doorstep. Still, Graham had been able to report that Lillian wasn't ill or anything. Well, physically, anyway.

When it came to Christmas Eve, Annie was glad she had sent that card wishing her mum a happy Christmas. After all, it was the least she could do at this time of year, wasn't it?

Late morning, when Pascal la Poste squeezed his bulky body through the door of his little yellow van, Annie was still hoping her mother had reciprocated. But what the rotund postie delivered was a brown envelope containing cards Kylie had forwarded from the Sheffield address. And she'd slipped in one from her and Gaz with a note.

'Oh, right,' said Annie, reading the note. 'Their baby is now three months old, and what with us being so good with the furniture and stuff, they named it after us.'

'Which one of us?' Mike asked. 'Is it a girl or a boy?'

'She doesn't say, but they've called it Flint.'

Pascal, however, hadn't delivered anything with a Norfolk postmark.

'Don't let it get to you,' said Mike.

'No, Mike, I won't. I'm buggered if I'm going to let her upset me anymore.'

'Bloody mothers,' he said. 'You and I didn't do great in that department, did we?'

'You can say that again.' Annie shrugged. 'I guess whoever doles them out was having a laugh when we were allocated ours.'

'Yeah, well.' He grinned and kissed her nose. 'But they made up for it when they were dishing out wives.'

'That's true,' she said. 'You well lucked in with whoever was in that department.'

'And can I assume you're happy with what you got?'

'Mike, I love you to bits, this is our first Christmas in this lovely place, and we're going to a party as Mr and Mrs Preggers. What's not to be happy about?'

Glynis was well happy. She'd been anxious, of course she had, but her party, as Gus insisted on calling it, was turning out brilliantly. Between them, they'd put all the small bar tables together and, yes, Ken had been right about that. Having everyone sitting together round one big table had been the way to go, and Glynis was pleased with the way that was working.

Mind you, she would have been happier wearing the bright red blouse she'd bought, what with it being a cheery Christmas colour, but Ken had chosen the pale blue one. Which was fair enough really because she'd decided on the paisley skirt, and she *had* asked his advice about what to wear with it. Okay, she did feel a bit dowdy compared to some of the other women, but at least Ken was happy to have been partly involved in what she wore.

Not that anyone could have matched Liz anyway, with her fluorescent orange top and a pair of reindeer antlers that flashed intermittently when she operated the switch lodged in her cleavage. As if that wasn't festive enough, she had a glittery gift label pinned to her left boob with the words "A Gift to Mankind" on it.

Feeling a bit bemused, Josie looked around at the happy faces in the Carry On and tried to grasp the fact that she was actually taking part in this event.

It was all a bit bizarre, really. Well, it was to a woman who was used to spending time with people her age or older. Not that there was anything wrong with that, it's just that Josie hadn't envisioned a situation where she'd be surrounded by such a mix of lively people who didn't seem to have a problem with her being a wrinkly. In fact, there was young Danny – what would he be? No more than thirty, Josie reckoned – but he was nattering away to that retired army officer like there was no such thing as an age difference.

'You alright with this, lass?' Harry placed a warm hand on Josie's knee.

'I am, Harry, I am,' she said, squeezing his hand.

'That's okay then. It's just you seem a bit quiet, and I was wondering if you might be missing Christmas in England or something.'

'What's to miss?' said Carol from the chair beside Josie. 'Well, unless you count things like crowded shops full of harassed mums yelling at screaming kids, that is.'

Nodding, Josie said, 'You mean those mums with trolleys loaded as if food was going to be rationed for weeks?'

With me standing in a queue waiting to pay for my pathetic little basket of food for one was going through Josie's head as she turned to her new husband and said, 'Harry, do you want to know what I was doing this time last year?'

'Go on.'

'I was sitting on my own in my house and wishing it wasn't Christmas Eve.'

'That's sad, that is.' Harry ran a finger down the side of her face before tucking a loose strand of grey hair behind her ear. 'But I suppose…I mean, what with your son and his family being the other side of the world and all.'

'You know what?' Josie looked at his concerned face and tried to think how to explain to someone who'd never had any children. 'I do miss Keith, of course I do. And I miss not seeing the grandkids, but most of the time I don't dwell on it. It's enough to know they're happy with their life in Australia, but the thing is, there's something about this time of year that puts some sort of emotional pressure on people.'

'Ain't that the truth,' said Carol. 'It's like things you can handle the rest of the year sort of get more difficult to deal with just because it's flipping Christmas.'

'Sorry,' said Josie, turning to Carol. 'I hope what I said didn't hit a nerve or something.'

'Nah, all history now.' Carol grinned. 'I was just looking back and remembering what a total mess I was my first Christmas here.'

'Really?'

'Yep, really. You can trust me on that. But then, I'd been doing a loony act most of that year anyway.'

'I find that hard to believe,' said Josie, looking at the other woman's contented face. 'Maybe you were just missing England?'

'No, it's more like I was hung up about my husband waiting for the previous Christmas to get neatly out of the way before dumping me.'

'Oh dear,' said Josie. 'I'm sorry to hear that.'

'Don't be.' Carol patted Josie's arm. 'He'd actually done me a favour, it's just that it took me a while to realise that.'

'I see.' Thinking about what it was like for her the year her Phil died, Josie said, 'Of course, it doesn't help to have the television ramming Christmas down your throat.'

'True.' Carol nodded. 'Just as well I didn't have a telly here because I'd probably have thrown something at the screen.'

'Argh, don't I know that feeling,' Tina chimed in. 'Only it's a computer screen I've been wanting to smash all week.'

'Bugger,' said Carol. 'Your kit still playing up, is it?'

'And how. But it's great, this party.' Tina grinned. 'It means instead of cooking Christmas dinner tomorrow, I can play with that new laptop Danny thinks he's got hidden in the wardrobe.'

'Aw, bless,' said Carol.

'Yep, he has his moments. And there was me thinking he hadn't taken any notice of me swearing at my old one, but that's Danny for you.' Tina nodded to where her husband was arm wrestling with Major Williams's German wife and said, 'You wouldn't believe my Danny was an Army squaddie when I met him, would you?'

Just then, a group of people further down the table erupted into laughter, and Liz shrieked, 'Gawd, Harriet, you int half a bleedin card.'

'And you, wench,' said Harriet's plummy voice, 'Are a frightful brat.'

Smiling at Harry, Josie said, 'Oh yes, Harry, I think I can safely say I *am* alright with this.'

If Gus hadn't ordered such an effin great turkey, and if the Lucotts hadn't added roast saddle of lamb to the proceedings, and if Frau Williams hadn't gone over the top with roast potatoes, and if Lars's chestnut stuffing hadn't been quite so delicious...

But before this sounds even more like a Rudyard Kipling poem, suffice it to say it was hardly surprising people were begging for mercy before facing trifle, mince pies and Christmas pudding. Which seemed a good time to belt out some Christmas carols, although it has to be said that carols accompanied by a saxophone wasn't exactly a traditional way of doing it.

In the meantime, the Lucotts left to have a second meal with Jannine's parents and siblings. And a sleepy Alfie, with promises that some jelly would be saved for him, gave in to Gus carrying him upstairs to a guest room. But not before he'd been assured that, yes, they'd be sure to save some for Lucie as well. 'Only she int never had jelly before,' he told Gus. 'Not raspberry or lemon or any of them sorts what that Josie lady made.'

With the children off the scene, Harriet's sister changed the tone of the entertainment with a hilarious monologue about how to get away with breaking wind in church. Looking a bit embarrassed, Luc glanced at the man sitting across the table and said, 'Sorry, Padre, I hope that didn't offend you.'

'Not at all,' said Major Williams. 'I found it highly amusing, and I stand guilty as charged.'

'Come on,' said Danny. 'You're not saying you've ever done it in church?'

'Who hasn't?' The major chortled. 'But believe me, when it gets trapped inside a pulpit, that can be seriously dire. Now, is this delightful congregation going to offer any more entertainment?'

Strictly speaking, a somewhat sloshed Glynis using a hairbrush as a microphone and singing *I just called to say I love you* should have been total cringe. But there was something endearing about the way she was sitting on Ken's lap and gazing into his face.

At first, it looked as if Gus was going to deny the yells for him to sing. But he eventually caved in when Liz said, 'Do Bridge for me, darlin.'

So once again, Gus's wonderful baritone voice soared to the Café Carillion's ceiling with a rendition of *Bridge Over Troubled Waters*. Some of the hushed audience remembered the last time he'd sung it, when he'd said it was for his Liz because she was his bridge. But even those who didn't even know about his troubled time of the previous year were moved by the performance. However, no amount of calls for more were able to persuade him to sing again.

Sure, that was a hard act to follow. But picking up on what seemed to be an anti-climatic slump, Glynis banged a hairbrush on the table and called, 'Next.' When nobody answered the call, she said, 'Right then, you'll all have to be force-fed Chrissie pud, trifle and mince pies.'

'Okay, okay.' Fishing the ever present spiral-bound notepad from her bag, Tina said, 'If you can bear to bear with me, I'll read you a sonnet Danny once wrote for me.' Ignoring Danny's *I did what!* she delivered:

My life's in commotion with all my devotion.
The heat in my heart is as warm as a fart,
And I knew from the start that I could just part
The waves on the ocean with that hot emotion.
Your lips when in motion are full of love potion,
Your wonderful eyes are like blueberry pies.
And the size of your thighs
Gets sighs from the guys
And makes them all mellow like strawberry jello.
You made something glow when you whispered hello,
Then I felt something rise and point to the skies,
And I knew right away I was one lucky fellow.

Once the groans and applause had abated, Carol said, 'Oh well, if we're going all poetic and intellectual, here's one for you…

A bright young dude called Freddie Toad
went boinkity boink along the road.
And there he met a cute frogess
all togged out in a wedding dress.
'I'm glad you're here,' the frogess said.
'I kinda need someone to wed.'
'Okay,' said Fred. 'I'm cool with that.
I've got a jacket and a hat.
But I'll need cash to buy a ring.
So how about we say next spring?'
'Oh no,' she said. 'We can't delay.
I'm already in the tadpole way.'

The grand finale had been Liz shaking her booty while doing a lap dance act to a vaguely recognizable Glen Miller medley played on a saxophone, with a few bum notes thrown in. By shortly after midnight, at least some of the desserts had been demolished before the party began to break up.

Outside, Danny curtailed an argument with Tina about which of them was in a fit state to drive home. Saying he'd had very little to drink, he asserted his authority by getting into the driver's seat and starting the van. A couple of kilometres up the road, she said it was a good thing, but why hadn't he had much to drink?

'Because,' he said, 'one of us had to stay responsible for...Oh shit!'

'What the hell are you doing?' she yelled, when he screeched to a halt and started to turn the van.

'Going back to get our Alfie,' he said.

As Josie and Harry disappeared down the towpath, Carol waved from the canal bridge and yelled, 'Sherry Chismash.'

'And you, lash,' came the reply.

With arms linked, Carol, Lars, Annie and Mike spanned the narrow lane as they made their way home. And it wasn't clear who was supporting who. Except that, as Annie was the only sober one among them, it could easily have been perceived that the others were relying on a pregnant women to keep them upright.

Announcing that she was verra verra squiffed, Frau Williams commanded her husband to drive her home.

'No can do, sugar plum,' he said. 'I can't actually remember where I left the car.'

Although Ken was able to locate his Volvo, it was agreed that none of them were up to driving the seven kilometres to Maiseronne. Which was when Luc stepped in and saved the day – or rather the night – by saying he had a taxi on the way. No, it wasn't going in the same direction, but he would tell the driver to return and collect them after delivering his lot home.

So it was that, instead of luxuriating in a rare sleep-in next morning, Liz and Gus were disturbed by the comings and goings of cars being collected outside their bedroom window.

'Bummer,' said Liz. 'But seein as how we're awake, darlin, how do you fancy...'

Which was as far as she got before Gus demonstrated exactly what he fancied for Christmas.

CHAPTER THIRTY-THREE

New Year's Eve at the Café Carillion had been a popular event ever since Gus and Liz had acquired the place eleven years ago. It was something most people looked back on with memories – albeit often hazy – of a great night out. Although some people had been known to cringe a bit when heads cleared and memories best forgotten began to surface. Take Carol, for example, who never did find out whose wellies and bobble hat she'd come home in at about three in the morning her first New Year in Coulaize.

Standing in her garden room, looking at the blanket of snow enveloping everything in sight, including three cats, Carol said, 'I can't see us doing the conga down the towpath tonight.'

'I can't even see us getting through this lot to get to the Carry On,' said Lars.

And he hadn't been wrong about that. Less than an hour after Jean-Claude and his trusty tractor had cleared the lane, a further heavy snow fall had obliterated his effort. Answering Glynis's phone call to say they weren't going to risk trying to make it to the do at the café, Lars told her they were planning to give it a miss as well.

'Well at least you wouldn't have to dig your car out to get there,' said Glynis. 'And you could manage on foot with your frame thing, couldn't you?'

'Possibly, if I could find the barn door.'

'What? You mean you've lost it?'

'Not lost it, exactly. It's just sort of temporarily mislaid behind a snowdrift.'

'Lars, are you talking about a door or a climbing frame?'

'Glynis, I'm talking about a walking frame, which is behind a barn door, which is behind a snowdrift. Now, if only I had got a climbing frame, my problems would all be over.'

'If you say so, Lars. Um, could you put Carol on please?'

'Yes, that could work. Except she's rubbish at climbing.'

At which point, Carol snatched the phone. After assuring Glynis that, no, Lars wasn't sloshed at three in the afternoon, she put the phone down and asked Lars what the hell he was playing at.

'Just practising Glynis speak,' he said as the phone rang again. 'Shall I get that?'

'No.' Carol grabbed the receiver. 'Probably safer if I do.'

This time it was Jannine Lucott, saying her family had telephoned to say they would not be coming to see the new year in with them. 'We have much food prepare,' she said. 'We think it will be good if you help with the eating.'

'We'd love to,' Carol said. 'But getting to you could be a problem.'

'Jean-Claude is make the arrange avec Annie and Mike. It can be also for you.'

Putting the phone down, Carol informed Lars they were going out after all.

'Where?' he asked.

'Chez Lucott,' she said.

'One small issue occurs to me. How the hell do we get there through a mountain of snow?'

'By tractor of course. Is there any other way?'

'You are kidding, aren't you?'

'Nope. Didn't I ever tell you about the time I went to the farm for a birthday meal on JC's John Deere?'

'No, and I still think you're kidding.'

'Trust me, Lars, it's a stylish way to go to a dinner party. Mind you, I was the only passenger that time. Not sure how it's going to happen with four of us.'

As anyone who's ever experienced it will know, once you've managed to get into a hay cart, it can be quite comfortable being perched on straw bales. It helps, though, to do it with deep snow beneath the two wheels, compensating for the cart's lack of suspension.

Even the pregnant woman had no complaints. But then, when two lovely men gently lift you on board, and a third one solicitously wraps a blanket round you, what's to complain about?

The snow continued to fall for several days, but the following week, the residents of Coulaize were able to move out of the village without worrying about whether they'd be able to get back in again. But, not happy with his sat nav's instruction to turn into a lane that still looked a bit dodgy, a DHL courier van driver bottled it and delivered a carton to the village shop. 'Pas de problème,' Madame Gruyot assured him, happily signing for the large package without having a clue about the controversy surrounding what it contained.

It was late January, with sunshine glistening on what was left of the snow on hedgerows and grass verges when Henri-Pierre Debuet eventually made his way to Walnut House.

He greeted Annie courteously, but obviously had little interest in talking to her beyond asking where her child would be born. When she told him she would have the baby in Autun hospital, he nodded and left it at that. Which was probably just as well because Annie had struggled a bit with the man's accent, and was happy to leave Mike to do whatever communicating was called for.

Not that there was a lot of that going on unless you could count nods of apparent approval. Without saying a word, Henri-Pierre slowly moved from one hung picture to the next. After repeating the exercise even more slowly, he took off his glasses, polished them on an old-fashioned hankie and expressed disappointment that one particular painting he'd hoped to see was missing.

'Ah,' said Mike, going to his desk and pointing to three as yet to be re-hung paintings that had arrived on the handlebars of Madame Gruyot's son's moped.

'Oui,' said Debuet. Moving one of them to one side, he ran a hand over the frame, took his glasses off and wiped his eyes while muttering in rapidly delivered French. Some of which escaped Mike, but what didn't escape him was the old man's emotional reaction. Taking a guess that this was the painting Debuet had inscribed, Mike picked it up, handed it to him and said that he thought his mother would like him to have it.

Refusing Annie's offer of lunch, Henri-Pierre informed them that, before his afternoon art class, he would have a meal with his neveu in Dijon. It was only after the man had left that Annie asked Mike how many Debuet brothers there were.

'Don't know,' he said. 'Why?'

'I just wondered.' She shrugged. 'Because this nephew of his could be your cousin, couldn't he? Unless…'

'Unless what?'

'Unless…' Annie paused and picked up a half empty packet of sherbet lemons. 'Unless he's the son of the only other brother we know about. Did you find out anything about Gerard's family? Like if you've got any half-siblings or anything?'

'Ah, well, he was a bit cagey about that.'

'What sort of cagey?'

'The sort where you pick up on vibes when you hit a subject someone doesn't want to talk about. Annie, I wish you'd stop eating those, you'll rot your teeth.'

'I know. That's what Dora said when she caught me stocking up on them yesterday.'

'Well maybe you should listen to her.'

'Mike, the last time I listened to Dora in the village shop I ended up buying a pregnancy test kit.'

'Yes, and she gave you the name of a good doctor. So let's hope she knows a good dentist.'

'No worries, I did listen to her,' said Annie, dumping the half empty packet in the pedal bin and taking a box of aniseed balls out of her pocket. 'I put the sherbet jobs back on the shelf and bought these instead.'

'Annie, don't even think it.'

'I know, I know, these probably aren't much better. But apparently they're made by monks, so they can't be all bad.'

'That's not the point, Annie.'

'So what is the point?'

'Have you forgotten the smell of aniseed makes me throw up?'

'Oh.'

'Yes, oh. If you as much as open that box, you'll be a divorced woman long before your teeth fall out.'

Unable to bear the suspense any longer, Tina phoned when Mike and Annie were having lunch. Skipping the *Hello Mike, Tina here* bit, she said, 'Well, did the man himself turn up this morning?'

'Yes, he did,' said Mike. 'And yes to the next question.'

'Yay! So all the paintings are real?'

'If by that you mean they were all painted by Monique Lanteine when she was his student, yes, it's as real as it gets. And I've got his signature on that.'

'Wow, so we've got the provenance thing and I'm good to go, am I?'

'Looks like it. When do you plan on submitting your article?'

'As soon as I've run it past Luc. He wants to check I don't say anything that could come back and bite me.'

'Okay, so the proverbial will be aiming for a fan soon then?'

'You could say that. But, Mike, I want to check you're still okay with being named as the owner.'

'Like I said, I don't have a problem with that.'

'Okay, as long as you're sure. My editor guy is waiting for the article, and apparently so is the art editor of the national paper that ran the last one. Oh, and Mike, I want to know where you were born.'

'Er…Tina, I don't…is that relevant to anything?'

'Well, it's just that I want to pitch to a couple of provincial papers with the local person interest angle.'

'Which means what, exactly?'

'Basically, it means I should be able to sell a story about how you and Annie got hold of some previously undiscovered works of art. And then there's the thing about you knowing this famous Henri guy. I know Annie comes from Norfolk, but I need to know where you hail from so I know which local paper to approach.'

'Oh, I see. Um, I doubt if it matters where I was born because I grew up in Sheffield. Will that do you?'

'Perfect. Thanks, Mike, I owe you for all this stuff.'

'So you do. Are you any good at baby sitting?'

'You've got it, pal. It's yours any time you need it.'

'Could we have that in writing?'

'Piss off, Mike. I don't do writing.'

Annie's mother had given up reading her local paper. Well, it was full of things about common people, some of whom had no right to be called local if the colour of their faces was anything to go by. And how on earth could someone called Burundi claim to have been born and brought up in Norfolk? Even worse, he'd not only been allowed to enter his vegetables in some village show, but he'd walked off with a first prize after his stupid marrow had beaten ones grown by real Norfolk people.

Oh well, at least the local bridge club had escaped dubious membership so far. Mind you, it was probably only a matter of time before it went the way of the Women's Institute. Meanwhile, Lillian considered it safe to go and play bridge with people who were reasonably intellectual. If you didn't count that Mrs Haggerty, that is.

As it happened, it was Mrs Haggerty who was holding things up at the bridge gathering the last week in February. Two groups had already started playing while Lillian's group was waiting for the woman to turn up. And when she did arrive – all of seven minutes late, if you please – she didn't seem in the least concerned about the inconvenience she'd caused. Instead of simply apologising and taking the fourth chair at the waiting table, the silly woman started waving a local paper and gabbling in that thick Irish accent that was enough to make any decent person cringe.

Trying not to visibly shudder, Lillian merely sniffed and picked up the cards that were waiting to be dealt, and made a big thing of shuffling them. Which was when she realised everyone else was getting up to look at the newspaper in Mrs Haggerty's hand. How anyone could understand what the woman was gabbling about was beyond Lillian, but Barbara Pullman's decently modulated vowels did manage to penetrate Lillian's disdain.

Few people have been known to ignore that lady, and Lillian was no exception. After all, Barbara Pullman was the doctor's wife, but that wasn't all. Her extremely loud voice would have made her hard to ignore whoever she was.

'Surely that's your daughter,' she boomed, taking charge of the newspaper and brandishing it at Lillian.

'Pardon?' Lillian gaped at her.

'Yes, it *is* your daughter. I'm sure it is,' said Barbara. 'You naughty thing, you never told us she was married to an important artist.'

With the open paper now spread out on the table on top of the cards, Lillian stared at a photograph of Annestine and that man she'd married. Once her numb brain had taken in the headline at the top of a full page spread, she said, 'Well, you know how it is. One doesn't like to boast, does one?'

But with the benefit of having read the whole page, Mrs Haggerty said, in a voice all too clearly understood, that it wasn't himself who was important. All he'd done was inherit some French woman's paintings.

'Along with her house in France,' said Lillian. 'Rather a grand house, actually.'

'Really?' said Mrs Haggerty. 'What's so grand about it, then?'

'Oh, you wouldn't believe what it's like. It's a large property.

With its own orchard.' Looking around at the attentive audience, Lillian went into overdrive and added, 'In fact, it's completely surrounded by acres of land.'

'So how come they inherited all that from this French woman?' Mrs Haggerty wanted to know. Turning to the others, she said, 'It's her who's the important painter, see.'

'Well, actually,' said Lillian. 'The important French painter was related to my son-in-law. And, as you would expect...' She paused to smile smugly. 'He inherited her talent as well as her estate.'

'For sure,' Mrs Haggerty admitted grudgingly. 'It does say something in the paper about him being artistic and designing graphs or something.'

'Oh, I think that means he's a graphic designer,' said Molly Frinton, Lillian's timid bridge partner. 'That takes skill, that does. My son spent a lot of time at college learning how to do it.'

'Quite so,' said Lillian, not having a clue what a graphic designer is. 'It just so happens that my daughter's husband makes a lot of money out of his skill. Which means, of course...' She shot Mrs Haggerty a withering look. 'It means that my Annestine lives very comfortably, thank you very much.'

Lillian would have liked to tell Bridget Haggerty to put that in her pipe and smoke it. But, as she said when she phoned Annestine that evening, that would have made her sound as common as the woman herself, wouldn't it?

What Annie said, in answer to Mike's question about why on earth Lillian had suddenly remembered her daughter existed, was that he ought to be sitting down to hear this.

'Okay,' he said, pulling out a chair and sitting at the kitchen table. 'So what's the story? Is she ill or something?'

'I think or something would cover it,' said Annie. 'Hang onto your hat, Mike, this is going to be tricky to handle.'

'I'm ready, so hit me with whatever it is.'

'Well, it's like this...are you sure you're...'

'Annie!'

'Okay, okay.' She sat opposite him at the table, took a deep breath and said, 'Would you believe your mother-in-law thinks the sun shines out of your bum?'

'Oh, very ho ho. Would you like to try again with something I might believe?'

'No, really, Mike. You are so the bee's knees. And, as she told the bridge club today, she always knew her daughter would make a good marriage.'

'That's it, then,' said Mike, running a hand through his hair. 'We thought she was having mental issues, and now she's finally flipped.'

'Seems that way.' Annie shrugged and got up to finish peeling potatoes.

'What about you?'

'Me? No, I don't think I'm about to flip just yet.'

'What I mean, Annie, is what did she say about you and the baby?'

'Baby? Oh bugger – I forgot to remind her I was having one of those.' Putting the last potato on the draining board, Annie asked if he wanted chips or mashed.

'Tut, tut, Annestine,' he said. 'Aren't chips what common people eat?'

'So I'm told. I'll slice, you put the chip pan on.'

CHAPTER THIRTY-FOUR

March came in like the proverbial lamb. Meadows around Coulaize abounded with the real things doing a Zebedee act, people threw open windows and doors and breathed the soft air and scents of spring, and in his cage on the roof of a narrowboat, Harry's parrot was giving it one with an imitation of the sheep. Oh yes, he'd got the full vocal range, had Ceremony. From the plaintive wails of new born lambs, sounding for all the world like human babies, to the deep-throated baas of adult mums.

Much as Josie had enjoyed winter snuggled in the cosy narrowboat, it was lovely to take a chair and a book onto the canal bank beside Jemima's mooring. Not that she did a lot of reading on account of people strolling by and stopping to chat. Admittedly she only understood scraps of what the French people said, but they seemed to be satisfied that she smiled and nodded a lot. Most of them seemed keen to point out the chateau up there on the hillside, and Josie had no problem smiling and nodding about that rather splendid view.

Joining her on the bank and leaning his head back to allow the warmth of the sun to bathe his face, Harry asked, 'You okay, lass?'

'Harry,' she said, putting her book on the ground and reaching for his hand. 'I wish you'd stop asking me that.'

'Well, I worry a bit.'

'Yes, I can tell that by the number of times you've asked if I'm okay.' Waving a hand to encompass the beautiful scenery she still found it hard to believe was now part of her life, she said, 'Why wouldn't I be okay with all this?'

'Yes, but…' He paused and ran a hand over what was left of his grey hair. 'It can't have been easy for you this winter. I mean, as homes go, Jemima isn't exactly spacious for the two of us, is she?'

'Well, I suppose not. But I knew that when I came here to live with you, didn't I?'

'True enough.' He nodded. 'It's just that I worry you might be missing your house.'

'Harry, it's only a house. When it comes down to it, it's only four walls and a roof.' Getting to her feet, she said, 'In fact, it's high time I thought about selling it. Bread and cheese do you for lunch?'

'Champion,' he said. 'Go down a treat, that would. And I could fancy some of those pickled onions your Dora brought from England.'

Sitting in the sunshine, with plates balanced on their knees, they were munching their way through lumps of Camembert and baguette when Harry said, 'I don't think you should do anything hasty.'

'Don't you?' said Josie. 'In general, or anything in particular?'

'I'm talking about selling your house. The thing is, lass, I'm not a young man.'

'Really?' Josie grinned at him. 'I'm glad you told me that. Have I got time to save up for a bath chair?'

'No, seriously, lass. I worry about if...when I...you know.'

'Pop your clogs, you mean?' Turning to look at his concerned face, Josie laid a hand on his shoulder and said, 'Harry, we're both only in our sixties. I'd say we don't have to fret about that just yet.'

'True enough. But the thing is, I'd sort of assumed you'd have your house to go back to if needs be.'

'I see.' Josie looked up at a clear blue sky and tried to ignore an encroaching cloud that was threatening to mar her peace of mind. 'So,' she said, 'you think I should keep it in case I might need it for some reason?'

'All I'm saying, lass, is not to rush into anything.'

Coming from the man she had impulse married, Josie thought that was a bit rich. And she said as much, hoping to put the twinkle back in his eyes. But that didn't happen. Instead, he treated his hair to another swipe and said, 'I'm just worried you might regret doing something else in a hurry.'

Now what was that supposed to mean? Had she been in too much of a hurry to move in with a man who wasn't used to sharing his home, never mind his life? Before she came back, Harry had ripped out the single bunk in his cabin and installed a double bed, which didn't leave much space to move around. Was she, Josie, taking up too much space in the life of a man used to moving around as and when he pleased?

After all, when it came down to it, what did she really know about him? And it wasn't as if there was anyone around here who knew much about him either, was there? As far as she knew, he'd simply happened to turn up in Coulaize because of a chance meeting in a hospital room.

Almost as if he'd tuned in to her thoughts, Harry said, 'Funny thing, fate.'

'Is it?' said Josie. 'I'm not sure I believe in fate.'

'You're not serious!' He stared at her. 'What d'you think brought us here so we could meet?'

'Well, it was a Euro Star train that brought me. And you came on your boat, didn't you?'

'I'm not denying that,' he said. 'But what I'm saying is, it was fate that made those two things happen to coincide.'

'Actually, Harry, it was Dora persuading me to come here for a holiday, and you coming here to catch up with Lars that made it happen.'

'Precisely.' He nodded. 'Which I reckon was all part of fate's plan. Someone or something brought it about because it was meant to be.'

'I see.' Josie put her elbows on her knees, cupped her chin in her hands and let the words *it was meant to be* float around in her head. This wasn't sounding like a man who was regretting his loss of space and freedom, was it? Shaking her head, she dared to let her mind chase away that ominous cloud that had been threatening to move in on her.

'So,' she said, getting up and collecting their lunch plates. 'If you're asking me to believe all that, do you reckon I'd be tempting fate if I sold my house in England?'

'I don't know, lass.' He squinted up at her. 'All I'm saying is, think on.'

'I am thinking, Harry. I'm thinking about you phoning after I went back to England and saying none of us know what's round the next corner.'

'I did say that, yes.' He nodded. 'And I said we were wasting time when we should be together.'

'Well, that got me back here, didn't it?' She bent down and planted a kiss on his leathery face. 'And what I'm thinking now is, we should be enjoying the moment and this lovely spring weather.'

Whether spring really had sprung, and how long the sun would continue to shine, was debateable. But the current weather was

256

conducive to al fresco meals, and the pungent aroma of smoke and barbecued meat hung in the still air.

Having given up on last year's folding barbecue, which was doing more folding than staying upright, Ken spent a day building a proper one. Standing back to admire his finished product, he suggested Carol and Lars should come over for an inaugural lunch.

'We'd love to,' Carol responded to Glynis's phoned invitation.

'Is Friday okay with you?' said Glynis. 'Ken's keen to show off his erection, but he thinks it needs a couple of days to settle before it's really firm.'

'Um, right. We'll see you on Friday, then. Is it a glass or plastic affair?'

'Carol, Ken built it out of bricks.'

'Glynis, I'm asking if we should bring proper wine in a glass bottle, or if the stuff in plastic will do.'

'Oh, definitely the plastic. It is only a casual barbecue you know.'

So casual in fact that Ken was dressed in shorts and an open-neck shirt that could almost be called scruffy – well, by Ken standards that is. But there was nothing casual or scruffy about his impressive brick-built edifice. Judging by the standard of perfection there, a spirit level and a plumb-line had been involved.

After dutifully admiring it from every angle, Carol said that every garden should have one.

'Does that include ours?' Lars wanted to know.

'Why not?' she said. 'I doubt if our rickety old metal job will last much longer.'

Going for an informal rustic look, and for what happened to be conveniently available, Lars cobbled together a load of stones left over from the building of the garden room. Forming a chimney out of irregular-shaped stones turned out to be a bit tricky, so he settled for an old terracotta one he found in the barn.

It would probably have been okay if Sue Ellen hadn't head-butted the chimney before the cement dried, but then Glynis wouldn't have been in a position to ask Lars why his leaned to one side.

'Does it?' he said. 'I can't say I've ever noticed myself. You'd have to ask Carol about that.'

'Oh, it's not important,' said Glynis. 'It's just that Ken's is flared at the bottom, and it tapers to a narrow bit at the top.'

'Whatever floats your boat,' said Lars. 'I'm happy to say I've never had any complaints.'

Burgundy basked under clear blue skies and ever increasing warmth for over a week. Then the lion – who wasn't strictly due until it was time for him to see March out – roared in prematurely bringing torrential rain. Reservoirs above Coulaize filled to capacity and beyond, and the little River Ouche, that normally flowed gently on its way to Dijon, rose above its banks and flooded surrounding fields.

The first dry, sunny day saw washing lines merrily waving their wares in a gentle breeze, then flapping frantically as it became apparent the lion hadn't quite finished having fun. He'd got a grand finale to unleash as yet, and it arrived in the middle of the night.

Annie had been awake for a while, listening to rumbling thunder and wondering if the spasmodic rumbling in her belly had anything to do with the paella they'd had for supper. But as the thunder came closer, a sharp pain coincided with a flash of lightning and had her sitting bolt upright in bed.

'Wassup?' mumbled Mike. 'Has it started?'

'No, stop fussing, will you?' said Annie, getting out of bed. 'He's not due for at least ten days.'

'Where're you going?'

'To the loo.'

'Make sure you put the landing light on,' he muttered. 'And call if you need me.'

'Mike, I think I can cope with having a pee on my own. Just go back to sleep.'

He was on the point of doing that when several things happened. Starting with an ear-splitting crash of thunder and a flash of lightning directly overhead, immediately followed by Annie's scream as the light went out. As another flash illuminated the landing, Mike sprinted to where Annie was kneeling on the floor and squatted down beside her.

'Are you coming or going?' he said.

'What?'

'Annie, did you make it to the loo, or do you want me to help you get there?'

'Mike, where I want you to help me get to is the hospital.'

'But I thought you said…'

'Never mind what I said. I think our little man is saying different.'

'Oh. Right. Okay.' His voice sounding more than a little shaky, he said, 'Where is it?'

'In Autun – remember?'

'Annie, I know where the hospital is. Where's what you were planning to wear to go there?'

'I don't know. I hadn't actually decided on an appropriate outfit.'

'Look, just give us a clue here.'

'Does it matter?'

'Unless you think naked is an appropriate outfit, I need to find something to put on you, don't I?'

'Anything easy to slip on will do. I think my ba…ba…Argh!'

When the contraction abated, she said, 'Where were we?'

'I'm not sure. We only got as far as ba ba argh before you perforated my arm with your finger nails.'

'Bathrobe. Blue towelling one.'

'Which is where?'

'In the garden. On the washing line.'

'Okay, forget that.'

'Why?'

'Because, Annie, it's bucketing down out there.'

'Sod that, then. I'm going back to bed until it stops.'

'But I thought you said…'

'Mike, stop telling me what you thought I said. The hospital said I don't need to go in until contractions get to ten minutes apart. So if you'd just help me get up off the f-f-f – Aaargh!'

The easiest thing to grab in a hurry was the bed quilt, and Mike draped it round her before man-handling her downstairs in the dark. Telling her not to move until he'd got Tiggy to the front door, he belted outside and fired up the engine.

'Right, here we go,' he said, helping her into the passenger seat. 'We'll be there in about thirty minutes. Just hang on.'

'I'm doing that,' said Annie, gripping the seat belt she hadn't been able to get round her for a while. But at least it was coming in handy now to hang on to as Tiggy slid and bounced between waterlogged ruts.

'Good girl. We'll be fine once we get off this track and – Oh shit!'

Whether it was brought on by the onset of a contraction, or

259

whether the contraction was brought on by what Tiggy's headlights were showing them is hard to say. But suffice it to say Annie's expletive was somewhat stronger than "Oh shit".

As farmers do in adverse weather conditions, Jean-Claude Lucott had been up and about checking on livestock. Having satisfied himself all was good on the farm, he hoped the same could be said of his human neighbours. From the top of the lane, all he could see was darkness, so presumably everyone's electricity had been taken out by the storm.

Either that or they were all safely tucked up in bed. Which was what he was heading for when lights that had nothing to do with the storm caught his attention. There was no mistaking that these were vehicle headlights, and they could only be coming from one place. So, that must mean a baby had chosen a stormy night to make an appearance.

Smiling at the thought of the little additional neighbour their Lucie was so excited about, Jean-Claude expected to see a camper van turn into the lane. But why didn't it do that? Why had it stopped before even reaching the end of the track? When it still hadn't moved after a few minutes, there was only one thing Jean-Claude could do. And it wasn't the planned going back to bed thing.

He hadn't taken more than a few strides before his powerful flashlight homed in on a walnut tree which was looking distinctly odd. A few more strides and the torch revealed a tree that, obviously struck by lightning, had split from top to bottom. And one half was now across the track entrance.

Right, this was a job for a tractor. Fifteen minutes and a couple of contractions later, half a walnut tree had been dragged out of the way of a campervan on an urgent mission. Now all Mike had to do was get this show on the road.

'Stay calm,' he told Annie.'

'Yes, calm would be good,' she said when he stalled Tiggy's engine the second time. 'Maybe you should try that?'

'Annie, I am totally calm.'

'Oh, so why are you trying to start the engine with second gear engaged?'

'Actually,' said Mike, moving the gear lever from fourth to neutral. 'It wasn't in second gear.'

'Whatever. Can we go now?'

'Right.' After double checking the gear lever was set to neutral, Mike turned the ignition key, and cursed unprettily when the engine emitted a few hesitant coughs before dying with a feeble croak. A performance that became weaker with each turn of the key until the final attempt evoked nothing more than a dull click, followed by several more *Oh Shits* and other similarly appropriate comments.

'What's wrong with her?' wailed Annie.

'I don't know,' said Mike. 'Could be water in the carburettor.'

'The what?'

'Carburettor.'

'What does that mean?'

'It means we're stuffed.'

'Not if you grab Jean-Claude before he – damn. Too late!'

'Bummer,' said Mike, as the tractor reversed towards the farm. 'Now what?'

His scrambled brain was fluctuating between sprinting up the lane to grab Jean-Claude, or down the lane to bang on Carol's door, when headlights illuminated the scene. This time heralding the arrival of the Lucott's Cheroke Jeep. Two men were attempting to extricate a woman in advanced labour from a campervan when a shriek seemed to suggest it may well be too late to make the thirty minute drive to Autun. A further clue came in the form of Annie clutching a belly that seemed to have taken on the characteristics of a minor earthquake.

'Merde,' said Jean-Claude, getting back into the Jeep. 'Attendez ici.' And he shot off down the lane, leaving Mike muttering, 'Yes, mate, we'll wait here, shall we? Like we've got a choice or something?'

It was a little over ten minutes later when, wearing a purple dressing gown and coordinating mauve slippers, Dora Turner climbed out of a Cheroke Jeep. She took one look at Annie and said, 'Right, dear. No time to waste, so let's get you into the back of this thing.' Turning to Mike, she said, 'I assume there is a bed of sorts?'

'Er...yes...right. I just need to unfold it.'

'Well make it quick, dear. I've a feeling this baby is going to arrive before the ambulance.'

'Actually, Dora, I didn't get round to calling for one,' said Mike.

'In hand,' she said. 'Don was on the phone as I left.'

With the bunk bed folded down across the width of the van, there was just about enough room for Dora to kneel at the bottom and attend to the business end. Mike, meanwhile, was restricted to kneeling on the front seat. Not a big deal because he was none too keen to see what was going on further down the line anyway, and at least he was able to reach his arms over the back of the seat and stroke Annie's head. Then there was the fact that her pulling his arms out of their sockets seemed to be an important part of this giving birth affair.

'We have a head,' announced Dora. 'Now, dear, one jolly good push and...yes...that's splendid...good girl.'

It was only after a full baby emerged that Dora sat back on her heels and shakily asked Mike if he had any brandy in his house.

'Wh-what! The baby needs brandy?'

'No, dear. I do. You see, I've never delivered a baby before.'

It's fair to say that quite a few people in Coulaize had experienced a disturbed night. However, with the storm rumbling into the distance, those not otherwise occupied had drifted back to sleep.

The occupants of Escargot Cottage were no exception until, alerted by the sound of something seemingly hell bent on removing the chimney, if not the entire roof, Carol shot out of bed.

'It's only a helicopter,' muttered Lars.

Looking out of the window, Carol said, 'Oh God, it could be Annie!'

'No, it's definitely a chopper,' said Lars. 'Or maybe aliens are popping in.'

'That'll be it,' said Carol, grabbing the nearest piece of clothing. 'It's a spaceship with flashing lights and SAMU written on it.'

Which was enough to make Lars sit up and say, 'It sounds like it's landing. Can you see where it's coming down?'

'Yes, yes, it's in the meadow up the lane and...oh hell, I think it is to do with Annie.'

If she hadn't been trying to put Lars's shirt on while belting down stairs in the dark, and if Bovril had been a white cat instead of a black one asleep on the third step from the bottom, maybe Carol wouldn't have lost so much time. As it was, by the time she'd managed to limp halfway up the lane, a helicopter was already taking off, and advancing headlights made it necessary to leap to the grass verge.

Bringing his car to a halt, Don Turner leaned out of the window and asked if she was alright.

'Yes, I'm fine,' Carol lied, getting to her feet and adjusting her weight to the good ankle. 'What on earth are you doing here at this time of night?'

'Collecting my good lady,' he said. 'Who I'm sure is just bursting to tell you what's been happening.'

'Not as much as I'm bursting to hear,' said Carol.

Meanwhile, out of deference to his still sometimes troublesome leg, Lars had gingerly made his way downstairs in darkness. He was groping in a drawer for candles when Carol came in and switched the light on.

'Well done you,' he said. 'It hadn't occurred to me that the power was back on.'

'Um, Lars,' said Carol. 'I gather it didn't occur to you to put some clothes on?'

'Don't mind me, dear, I've seen it all before,' said a voice from behind Carol. 'I don't suppose you'd have a drop of brandy, would you?'

Apparently it had something to do with flash flooding making road travel from Autun a bit dodgy. But what the heck, it had been something of a traumatic night anyway. Okay, so being air lifted to Dijon maternity hospital instead hadn't been part of the plan, but it has to be said that the paramedics had been on the ball. A cord had been cut and clamped, and a twenty-minute-old baby and his mother were now safely installed in a hospital bed.

Gazing at the red puckered face of his son, and the matted hair sticking out like a loo brush from his wife's head, Mike said, 'I hope you two know it's illegal to look that beautiful without a licence.'

'Bloody hell, Mike,' said Annie, peering at him through heavy-lidded eyes. 'You look a total wreck.'

'Well, you know how it is,' he said. 'I have had a bit of a rough night, but I won't bore you with the details.'

'For heaven's sake, you look like a man who could do with a coffee infusion.'

'Okay, I'm not about to argue with that. I'm a bit overdue for some bladder relief as well.'

'Mike, go and do what a man has to do.'

'Are you sure you're all right?'

'Yes, Mike. Well, apart from being light-headed and desperate for some sleep, that is.'

When a nurse had taken the baby off to be checked over, Annie was drifting nicely towards that much-needed sleep when another nurse came in and started fitting a blood pressure cuff in place. Albeit feeling somewhat disorientated, Annie obligingly opened her mouth to accommodate a thermometer. And apparently all was well, if the nurse's nod of approval was anything to go by.

It was the arrival of a doctor, and Annie's reaction to him, when things went haywire. Which wasn't supposed to happen because this particular doctor had been chosen as the right man for the job on account of he was the one who spoke English.

It began with Annie giggling when he addressed her as Meesus Fleent and said he would examine her. This was followed by her asking him whose white coat he'd nicked.

Apart from a slight frown, the doctor was apparently unfazed as he slipped a mask over his lower face, donned a pair of latex gloves and pulled back the bed cover. When Annie told him to stop messing about the doctor said, 'Relax. I weel not hurt.' And he began to gently probe the area between her belly button and the bit that would have been shaved if there had been time to attend to that detail.

'Just gerroff, will you?' said his patient, slapping his hand. 'It was you messing about down there that got me into this in the first place.'

'Please to calm yourself,' said the doctor, reaching for her pulse.

'Okay, enough,' she said. 'This is so not funny.'

'What ees it you find ees not so funny, Madame Fleent?'

'That silly accent, for starters. Just stop arsing around, will you.'

Which was when the doctor and the nurse exchanged glances and started talking about reaction and sedation. In fact, a needle was approaching Annie's arm when Mike came in clutching a polystyrene coffee cup and demanding to know what was going on.

'We theenk,' said the doctor, placing a restraining hand on Annie's shoulder, 'that the maman ees having the delusion.'

'You can say that again!' said Annie. Pushing the doctor's hand from her shoulder, she sat up and stared at Mike a split second before the doctor turned and stared at Mike.

'Incroyable!' said the doctor.

'What's incredible?' said Mike, shooting an alarmed look in Annie's direction. 'Why on earth is he…Bloody hell!'

The lowering of the doctor's face mask and a polystyrene coffee cup hitting the floor happened simultaneously. Seemingly unaware of hot coffee splattering his legs, Mike stared at a face that looked for all the world like the one he saw in his shaving mirror every day.

To be fair to the doctor, he seemed to recover quite quickly. Well, after all, he was a professional man who was here to carry out his professional duty. Which he did with impressive efficiency before bending down to retrieve a loaded syringe from the floor. Only then did he remove his mask again and turn his attention back to his patient's husband.

'Would you like to tell me who you are?' said Mike. Getting no response beyond an apparently mesmerised stare, he tried, 'Qui es-vous?'

No, that didn't activate the man's vocal chords either, and it was the nurse who said, 'Il est Docteur Debuet.'

'Uh-huh.' Mike looked at a face that, on closer inspection, had a wider chin than the one he shaved regularly. And a slightly different-shaped nose compared to the one he was used to seeing in his mirror. Even so, there was still a question begging to be asked.

'I don't suppose your father's name was Gerard, by any chance?'

'Mais oui,' said Doctor Debuet. 'That ees the name of my father.'

At which point, the nurse who had removed the baby carried him back into the room. Presumably deciding he'd been left out of the proceedings long enough, Baby Flint emitted a squawk that would have done justice to a constipated parrot.

'Okay,' said Mike, pointing to the syringe in the other man's hand. 'If you'd be good enough to put that thing down, I'll introduce you to my son. The latest episode in this bizarre family saga.'

CHAPTER THIRTY-FIVE

'I want the details, and I want them now,' said Tina, with her pen poised over her notebook.

Yes, well, Carol had heard these words before. But that was after a traumatic experience when Reiziger had been hit by a freak gale. The difference being that this time it wasn't Carol's story, it was Annie and Mike's story. That is if you don't count the fact that it involved Dora and Jean-Claude, or the fact that Carol's subsequent sprained ankle had later been treated by a retired nurse on a high having just delivered a baby in the back of a campervan.

Not that Tina was even interested in a bandaged ankle. No, what Coulaize's resident journalist wanted here was facts about a helicopter landing near Escargot Cottage while Tina – dammit – had been fast asleep.

'Sorry, mate,' said Carol. 'I can't give you the actual factual facts, as in the sort of eye witness stuff you need.'

'Come on, Carol. You must have seen and heard something.'

'Yes, I saw a helicopter land, and then I saw a helicopter take off. And I heard it had taken Annie and the baby to hospital.'

'And?'

'That's it. Honestly, Tina, I'm not the right one to give you any accurate details. How did you hear about it anyway?'

Shrugging, Tina said, 'Pascal la Poste. Who else would have delivered the news before anyone else even knew it had happened?'

'There you are, then.' Carol grinned. 'You could always interrogate him.'

'Sure, like you'd trust the accuracy of what *he* tells you.'

'Oh, don't underestimate Pascal, Tina. He *is* able to tell me who my letters are from before I've even had a chance to open the envelopes.'

'Yeah, me too. Are you going to give me the gen on this story or not?'

'Not.'

'Why not?'

'Because, my little ferret, I'm not the one who knows the full story.'

'Okay,' said Tina, putting the cap on her pen. 'Where's Lars?'

'Down at the canal, checking on his barge after the storm. Why?'

'Well, you know.' She tucked her notebook into her capacious bag and stood up. 'I'm just wondering if he saw anything more.'

'Tina, Dora saw more of him than he saw of anything.'

'Dora? What's any of this got to do with her?'

'More than it has to do with me, and she can tell you far more than I can. Get the phone for me, will you? Whoever it is will have rung off by the time I hobble there.'

'It'll be Liz,' said Tina, grabbing the phone. 'Oh, hi Liz...Yes, she's here, but you won't get any sense out of her...Dunno really. Let's just say she's doing an *I know nahtheeng* sort of act. But she did let on that Annie's had the baby...Yes, they're fine as far as we know...Sure, I'll ask Carol to give you a bell when she knows more.'

'Okay,' said Carol, when Tina put the phone down. 'How the hell did you know it would be Liz on the phone?'

'No-brainer,' said Tina, opening the cottage door. 'I saw Pascal heading towards the Carry On when I came past.'

It was late morning when a taxi dropped Mike at Escargot Cottage. He was keen to get home, but he'd promised Annie he would let Carol know about the baby.

Oh, right, they already knew he'd arrived in the night. Yes, Mike told Lars, mother and baby were in good shape. No, no, he wouldn't come in, he had some phone calls to make and some sleeping to do.

'Give our love to Annie, and we'll catch up with you later,' said Lars. 'I hope you are able to sleep through the noise.'

'Lars, mate,' said Mike. 'I reckon it'll take more than that to keep me awake.' But he wasn't so sure about that as he walked up the lane and the sound of a heavy industrial chain saw grew louder.

Stopping to ask Jean-Claude's cowman how long it would take to clear the fallen tree, he was assured it would be no more than thirty minutes or so. Pointing to an already loaded trailer, the cowman said he would take it to the farm and cut it into logs before delivering it to the Lanteine house.

So, as far as the locals were concerned, Walnut House was still Monique Lanteine's place. Obviously history died hard in these parts, which brought Mike's mind back to the unexpected encounter with a man who'd turned out to be part of his personal history. Doctor Debuet had been called to attend to another patient, but before Mike left Annie's bedside, the doctor had returned and said, 'I am now feenished my night of work. May we please to talk?'

After making a pot of coffee, and realising he was far too hyped up to contemplate sleep just yet, Mike carried a mug through to the lounge, opened the casement doors and walked out into the garden. The beautiful garden, with the wonderful view of undulating meadows dotted with sheep and bouncing lambs. Fluffy clouds and hazy sun lighting the hills in the distance, seemingly denying that a vicious storm had even happened just a few hours ago, had a calming effect on Mike's over-active mind as it relived the events of the night.

As he had just told Annie's dad in Norwich and his own dad in Chicago, both Annie and the baby were fine. And the panic and – let's face it – moments of sheer terror, were already fading and being replaced by the image of the joy on the face of the woman he loved as she held their son to her breast.

Yes, he should of course have made another phone call to Norfolk, but he'd shelved that on the basis that he wasn't yet ready for Lillian to burst his euphoric bubble. Cowardly maybe, but he'd readily accepted Graham's offer to pass the news on.

Then there was the issue he was only now feeling able to let in. In addition to being presented with a beautiful healthy son, Mike had found a half brother. A man Mike had warmed to as they'd chatted in the hospital restaurant, and one he hoped would become part of his life.

Whilst obviously surprised to discover Mike's existence, Jaques Debuet hadn't seemed particularly shocked. It appeared that French people were fairly open-minded about extra-marital affairs, and even at the age of ten, Jaques had been aware that his father had been less than monogamous. But he and his sister had nevertheless enjoyed a happy family childhood, and Jaques was now happily married himself and living in a village north of Dijon with his wife and two children.

The two men had shaken hands then exchanged cards with their contact details. It was agreed that, once Annie and the baby had settled back home, the Debuet family would visit and introduce Baby Flint to his uncle, aunt and cousins. And to think, none of that would have happened if Tiggy hadn't thrown a sulk when she was supposed to have taken Annie to Autun hospital.

Hearing a vehicle stop near the house, Mike walked round to the front to see Lars getting out of Tiggy. 'She's a goer,' said Lars. 'Just needed a bit of drying out under the bonnet.'

'Thanks, mate, you're a hero. I was wondering how I was going to get back to Dijon.'

'Plenty of folk around who would have stepped in,' said Lars. 'By the way, Carol wants to know the baby's name.'

'Good question, but one I'm not yet qualified to answer. I suppose we should acknowledge the person who was responsible for him being safely born, but I'm not sure I could live with a boy called Dora. Then again, if it hadn't been for Jean-Claude...'

'Justin,' said Lars.

'Sorry?'

'You could tell them both he is named in their honour for being on the scene just in time.'

Anxious to be sure about the date his son was born, Mike checked his computer. Yes, that magic bit of kit confirmed it was the sixteenth of March. Which yanked Mike's mind back to the last time he'd written that date. It was when a solicitor called Miss Pinkerton had asked him to sign and date a receipt for a yellow folder.

As Mike stretched out on the settee and drifted towards sleep, he was joined by someone who had waited for them to realise that Miss Pinkerton's yellow folder had contained a new life. A life they couldn't have even dreamed of a year ago. Possibly due to brain overload, or maybe it was to do with paws pounding his chest and the sound of loud purring, but Mike was dreaming now.

And it was only a dream, wasn't it? Of course it was. For starters, cats don't have boobs on their chest, do they? And there was no way the string of pearls hanging from Perdue's neck was really hooked over her left mammary gland.

52357587R00152

Made in the USA
Lexington, KY
26 May 2016